made for MAYHEM

MAYHEM HOCKEY CLUB BOOK 2

AIMEE VANCE

Revel Books
Paperback ISBN: 978-1-963848-16-8

Edited by Brittany Corley & Sarah Brennan

Cover art and Illustrations
Copyright © 2026 Chelsea Kemp

Cover and Interior Formatting
Copyright © 2026 Aimee Vance

www.aimeevancebooks.com

*To the ones who smile bigger when everything hurts,
and the friends who see right through it*

*And to Josh
We'll miss you forever*

This story deals with the loss of a sibling/parent and the complicated grief that follows. While I wrote it rooted in love, healing, and found family, I wanted to share this upfront so you can take care of your heart as you read.

1

TY

Three Years Ago

Pain is temporary, glory is forever, or so the saying went. At thirty-four, I called bullshit.

I pulled on my black hoodie, rotating my shoulder a few times to loosen it back up after tonight's hockey game. The joint protested, the pain sharp, stubborn, and far too familiar. Nothing seemed to touch it these days. Not the ice baths, not the therapy the team insisted on, not even a summer off.

Around me, the locker room thinned out in waves, guys packing slower than usual. This was the last time this group of guys would be together, and we all knew it.

"Ready for the off-season?" Matt O'Connell asked, grabbing his wallet and keys off the shelf above his stall. "Big plans?"

"Not sure yet," I said. Fuck, I had no idea what came next. "You?"

"I promised the wifey a beach vacation. We're leaving

tomorrow—Turks and Caicos. Rented a bungalow for two weeks. Hoping I can forget how shitty this season was."

I nodded, rolling my shoulder again even though I knew it wouldn't help.

Some people might call the Chicago Storm's season a growth year. Developmental. Transitional, even. A polite way of saying we'd spent months figuring out what didn't work.

Really, we sucked.

"You headed to the bar?" Matt asked, slinging his duffel over his shoulder. "One last night with the boys?"

I dropped my gaze to my phone, pretending to scroll when I couldn't look away from the group text that had come in sometime during the second period.

MOM

Good luck tonight, Ty! Sorry we couldn't make it.

EMMY

WHAT? Why didn't you tell me before now?! I would have flown in.

MOM

Something came up last minute with the store, and Dad couldn't step away.

EMMY

Really? Even when you knew it might be his last game in the NHL?

We talked about this—you were going because Jace has a tournament this weekend, and I can't go.

MOM

Sorry, honey. We'll come to the next one.

EMMY

> That's the point, Mom. There is no NEXT
> ONE. He's retiring. He's done.

"You good?" Matt asked.

I lifted my head and nodded, the motion automatic. "Yeah, buddy."

I slid my phone into my back pocket, ignoring the string of new messages from Emmy outside the group chat—probably already tearing into our parents or making plans to fix something that wasn't hers to fix.

My parents' absence shouldn't have surprised me. It shouldn't have hurt. Birthdays, milestones, games I'd circled on the calendar months in advance—there was always a reason, always something more important somewhere else.

I loved them, but I'd also learned the hard way not to expect much from them. Expectation was where disappointment lived.

Maybe that's why my sister and I hung on so tight to each other, why I always went out of my way to show her how much I loved her with my actions, my presence, even if I sucked at saying it.

But this one... Shit.

This one hurt.

Every time the locker room door opened, I could see all the family members milling about, waiting for their husbands, boyfriends, brothers, sons... whatever these boys were to them. The people who loved them were just outside, waiting with open arms.

But I was alone.

I was always fucking alone.

With a sigh, I clapped Matt on the shoulder, then gave it a squeeze. "I'm great. Have a good off-season. Enjoy the beach."

He grinned and flicked my overgrown beard. "At least you can get rid of this now. You're starting to look a little lumber-jack-y."

I huffed a quiet laugh and dragged a hand through the dark scruff covering my jaw. I'd grown my beard out hoping we'd claw our way into a wild-card spot, maybe buy ourselves a little more time. Give my parents more opportunities to not show up for me.

Luck hadn't been on my side.

"I don't know," I said. "I'm kind of attached to it now."

I took one last look at the empty stall, the *Ty "Huddy" Hudson – 55* label above it there for the last time, then shouldered my bag and walked away. Matt and I walked out together, him chattering on about his off-season plans and me offering polite platitudes until the heavy door swung shut behind us.

The parking garage was bright and cavernous, concrete reflecting the glare of overhead lights. Sound carried here—footsteps, laughter, the distant chirp of a car alarm—everything bouncing back a second too late as my teammates moved on with their lives.

Matt stopped at his SUV and popped the hatch. "Last chance," he said, nodding toward the exit. "It's gonna be packed with everybody having family in town."

"I'm good," I told him, not needing the reminder that it was just me here tonight. No wife and kids. No parents. No friends. Not even Emmy. "Have a great trip."

He grinned, shut the door, and rolled out, headlights sweeping across the wall before disappearing down the ramp.

I crossed to my truck, opened the tailgate, and dropped my

bag in. The thud it made sounded final, like punctuation. I stood there longer than necessary, hands braced on the edge of the tailgate, staring at nothing in particular.

Engines turned over one by one. The garage emptied in stages until the noise thinned and the surrounding space grew too big, too open. My ears rang in the sudden quiet, each breath coming out a little more jagged than the last.

I rubbed a hand across my chest, feeling like something was squeezing all the air out of the space where my lungs were supposed to expand. My heart kicked harder as tomorrow loomed all at once, uninvited.

No morning skate.

No rehab schedule.

No reason to be anywhere at a certain time.

No one needed me.

Just an empty condo thirty floors up with floor-to-ceiling windows and a view of the water—beautiful, quiet, and oh so wrong.

My grip tightened on the tailgate, the metal digging into my palm enough to break me out of my spiral. Reaching into my bag, I grabbed my black Chicago Storm hat and tugged it down over my hair. My phone vibrated in my pocket as I shut the tailgate a little too hard, but I ignored it.

With each uneven breath, my hands started to buzz with leftover adrenaline that had nowhere to go. I flexed them, then pulled my hood up over my hat, the fabric narrowing my vision and muting the world enough to make it bearable.

The truck was right there.

Home was minutes away and the bar only a small detour.

But the idea of being alone, whether at home or in a crowd, made everything worse.

I stepped back, turned away from the truck, and started

walking instead. Past the painted lines. Past the exit sign glowing red against the concrete.

No plan. No destination.

Just movement.

Cold spring air hit my face the second I stepped outside, sharp enough to make me inhale. The noise followed—crowds spilling onto the sidewalk, voices layered over each other, the city loud and alive.

A knot of people stood at the corner waiting for the light, most decked out in jerseys. I slowed, keeping my hat low over my brows, trying to stay unnoticed.

The walk sign flashed, and the crowd surged forward, filling the crosswalk in one noisy wave, there and gone like a receding tide.

I waited for the sidewalk to clear, but it didn't. Not entirely.

My steps faltered, eyes catching on the woman in front of me—bright and unmoved, like the city had left her behind just for me.

Long wavy blonde hair hung loose around her shoulders, lifted by the wind in a chaotic halo. She tugged at the edges of a thin long-sleeved pink shirt, underdressed for the bite in the April night air. Ripped jeans hugged her hips in the perfect silhouette as she ran the toe of one patterned sneaker over the top of the other, staring at her phone.

That tightness in my chest eased the longer I looked at her. The noise dulled. The spiral I'd been stuck in all evening loosened its grip just enough to breathe.

"Huddy!"

The sound yanked me back to the sidewalk. A kid stood to my right, tugging hard on his dad's sleeve, eyes lit up with excitement.

"That's him," the kid said, loud and certain. "That's Huddy."

The dad followed his gaze and smiled, a little apologetic. "Sorry—he's a huge fan."

Of course he was.

The familiar reflex slid into place, smooth as muscle memory. I bent at the knees, softening my voice and face. The version of me everyone expected.

"Hey, buddy," I said. "What's your name?"

The kid told me, and I listened like it mattered—because, to him, it did—and grinned at the right moments, acting like I wasn't holding on to my emotions by a fucking thread.

"Any chance we could grab a picture?" the dad asked, already pulling out his phone.

I stood and slung an arm around the kid's shoulders. The smile came automatically, practiced and convincing.

The phone clicked. Once. Twice.

"Thanks, man," the dad said, genuine. "You have no idea how cool this is."

"No problem," I replied, giving the kid a quick fist bump before they moved off toward the curb as the light changed.

The second they were gone, the smile slid right back off my face, too hard to hold in place.

I turned back to the street and she was watching me. Our eyes met, and the corner of her mouth tipped up.

The light changed again. Someone bumped into me from behind, shoving me forward, my chest brushing her shoulder. Instinct kicked in—I put a hand out, shielding her from the press of bodies, resting it lightly on her back.

She sucked in a breath, blue eyes snapping up to mine, and I immediately pulled my hand back, lifting it where she could see.

"Sorry," I said.

"No." She shook her head. "You're good."

The crowd thinned until it was just us again on the corner, my feet refusing to move. When the silence stretched, I tipped my chin toward her phone, the map glaringly obvious on the screen.

"You're not from here," I said.

She huffed a laugh. "What gave it away? Me staring at my map like it personally betrayed me?"

"Dead giveaway."

"I got off at the wrong stop," she said. "Possibly the wrong line. Honestly, I have no idea where I am or how to get back to the apartment I moved into today."

I scrubbed a hand along my jaw, the reflex to help battling the voice in my head telling me not to get involved.

"Maybe I'll—"

I stopped her with a light touch to the arm, careful this time. "Hang on." I nodded toward her phone. "Where are you trying to go?"

She turned the screen so I could see the red pin. "Uptown. I think. Unless this map is lying to me, which feels possible at this point."

I scanned the busy street—the traffic still snarled, the trains not back to normal yet after the post-game surge. "We can walk a bit. Get you somewhere easier to navigate until things calm down."

Her brows lifted, those blue eyes sparkling in the streetlights. "*We*? If you're thinking about robbing me, I should warn you, it's a bad idea. I'm very nice, and you'll feel extra bad when you realize I have literally nothing to my name."

A real laugh—surprising and unguarded—broke through. "Good to know," I said. "I'll cross you off the list."

She smiled, quick and bright, then went back to her phone.

"Come on." I tipped my head east. "Worst case, you end up with a great story about narrowly avoiding a mugging."

She slipped her phone into her pocket and fell into step beside me. "I feel very reassured."

"Good," I said. "I'd hate to ruin your first night in the city."

Her eyes flicked to me, studying my face mostly hidden in shadows between my hood and hat. "Huddy, right? Is that your name?"

I stared down at her, waiting for the realization of who I was to click, but it never did. So instead of giving her anymore, I just nodded.

"Huddy," she repeated, one brow lifted. "What kind of name is that? Sounds like a nickname."

I shoved my hands in my pockets, avoiding looking up at the Chicago Storm banners hanging from the streetlights brandishing my name and face. "It is."

She waited for more, eyes bright with curiosity, but I didn't offer an explanation.

"Just Huddy?" she pressed, a hint of a smile tugging at her lips.

"Just Huddy."

She narrowed her eyes in suspicion. "So, if that's the nickname, what's the real one? Hudson? Humphrey? Horatio? Oh, wait!" She pointed at me. "Herbert. You look like a Herbert."

I bit the inside of my cheek to keep the grin from slipping. "Not even close."

"Okay, Huckleberry," she tried, leaning toward me like she was deadly serious about solving this mystery. "Harold? Sir Wallace T. Hudsington the Third?"

A laugh broke free before I could stop it—low and rough, the kind I hadn't heard from myself in far too long.

Her face lit up as if she'd won something, and her shoulder bumped into my arm. "There it is. I knew you could smile."

"Don't get used to it," I muttered, but my lips still twitched.

"I'm Daisy," she said, then glanced up at me with mischief written all over her face. "Since you so kindly asked."

I shook my head, barely holding back another laugh. "Nice to meet you, Daisy. Welcome to Chicago."

She grinned, the look so natural on her face I couldn't help but stare. "Thank you. I always dreamed of moving here, but I am very afraid to admit I already regret it."

This time it was my turn to arch a brow as we stopped at another crosswalk. A gust off the lake cut down the street, rattling the banners overhead and carrying the smell of exhaust and chili dogs from a cart farther down the block.

"Already?" I asked, glancing at her. "That didn't take long."

She laughed, but it came out a little breathless. "I know. It's dramatic. I've been here for maybe six hours."

"Dangerous amount of time. Long enough to panic. Not long enough to know anything."

"Exactly. I haven't even met my Craigslist roommate yet."

I stared down at her, disbelief obvious on my face.

She held a hand up, then started walking again when the light turned. "I know, I know. Dumb decision. It was impulsive, and the pictures looked nice, and I didn't do *no* research like Vi assumed." She turned around, walking backward one step in front of me once we'd crossed the street. "That's my older sister. Much more responsible than me. Worthy of robbing, probably."

Again I grinned, unable to remember the last time I'd smiled this much in a single day. "Noted."

"I did research, kind of, and a friend of a friend of a friend vouched for this new roomie, so I don't think I'm moving in with a serial killer? But it wasn't until I got here and put my bags in the closet of a room that I realized what I was doing. So I ran."

I nodded, understanding that feeling all too well. "And got on the wrong train."

"And got on the wrong train." She waved an arm in front of us, gesturing at the steam rising from the manholes, a rat scurrying along a brick wall, and the garbage overflowing out of the trash can. "Taking in the beautiful sights Chicago has in store for me. We're not in Kansas anymore, Toto."

I brushed at my beard to hide my smile. "Okay, yeah. Maybe this part's not selling it."

She glanced over, hopeful. "But there's a better part. Right?"

"There is," I said without hesitation. "I promise."

That earned me her full attention.

"Once you're past the chaos, it's nice," I said. "Uptown is a little eclectic. You can see the historic bones of the city there, but it's a mashup of old theaters, late-night diners, music spilling out of bars, and lake access that's more low-key."

Her steps slowed a little as she listened. "Okay, that doesn't sound so bad."

"The city grows on you."

We stopped near a train entrance, the familiar rumble echoing up from below. I nodded toward the stairs, already dreading the idea of letting her go. "Blue Line will get you downtown. Then you can catch the Red north from there."

"Thank you." She pulled her sleeves down over her hands,

looking from the stairwell and back to me. "For not robbing me. And for walking me this far."

"Anytime."

She didn't know that this little walk had been exactly what I needed to pull myself out of a negative spiral. How badly I'd needed the quiet, anonymous companionship.

Daisy didn't move right away. Neither did I.

The train rumbled somewhere below us, the sound rising through the grate like a reminder, but we stood there a beat too long, caught in the space between going and staying.

She took two steps toward the entrance, then stopped and turned back toward me. "Truth or dare?"

I blinked, not at all expecting that. "What?"

She grimaced, her nose scrunching up in a way that was decidedly cute, then looked away. "Sorry. I'm panicking about going home again. And that sounded a lot smoother in my head."

I followed her gaze to the stairwell, the Blue Line sign glowing above us, ready to take her out of my night. Back to whatever waited for her beyond this corner. This was where it ended, where I went back to my own spiral, with my own uncertain future yawning before me.

"I shouldn't have said anything. I'll just—"

"Dare."

She looked back at me in surprise, a slow smile spreading over her face. "I should have known you'd be a dare guy."

"So." I pushed my hood back and lifting my hat to readjust it over my hair. "What is it?"

Her shoulders angled toward me, turning her back to the train whistling down below us. "I dare you to spend the night with me."

My eyebrows hit my hairline, and her hands quickly covered her face.

"Not—" She waved a hand between us, cheeks flushing. "Not like that. I don't mean sleep together or anything. I—" She stopped, exhaled. "I'm very bad at this."

I tucked my chin, trying to hide my amusement, but also more than a little intrigued by whatever she was offering.

She peeked up at me, clearly mortified. "I mean. You're very hot. Objectively. But this is not me hitting on you."

A smile slipped out before I could stop it.

"Objectively," I repeated.

"Yes." She waved a hand over my body. "Tall, dark and handsome really does it for a lady. Everybody's type. Not *my* type, but you know, other people's. I'm not making this better, am I?"

"No." I was glad my beard hid how big my grin had spread, not wanting to further her embarrassment past this gentle tease. "I can't decide whether I'm flattered or insulted."

Daisy made a little mock frown, nodding her head back and forth. "On second thought, a Craigslist roommate and my inevitable murder sounds pretty good. So I should—"

She jerked a thumb over her shoulder toward the train station, and I reached out to grab her arm, letting my big hand circle her dainty little wrist.

"I would love to spend the night with you, Daisy."

Her big blue eyes tipped up toward me, glancing back and forth between my own, looking for a hint of sarcasm. I slid my hand down her forearm until her small hand was in mine, then traced a thumb over the back of her hand. Even this small touch with the sleeve of her shirt between us was enough to make my heart race. Not like before when panic was on the horizon, but like the beginning of a hockey game, where I knew this was about to be the night of my life.

"Now I believe it's my turn," I said, my voice a little rougher. "Truth or dare?"

"Truth," she whispered, not breaking eye contact.

"Do you like cheeseburgers?"

Instantly, her face split into a wide grin, eyes alight with so much life it felt a little bit like staring at the sun. "Why, yes, Huddy. Yes, I do."

2

Daisy

I was a liar. A big ol' lying liar, waiting for my pants to spontaneously combust the moment I said the man in front of me was not my type. Because *wow*.

Huddy still held my hand, tugging me further down the street and away from the train that would take me to my apartment. It was a little odd, holding hands with a virtual stranger, but he gripped it like maybe he needed the connection. And I couldn't seem to pull away.

I'd always been impulsive and a little too trusting, but the stern set of his jaw and his eyes scanning the streets felt protective in a good way, not in a I-might-still-rob-you way. Heat radiated off him, a steady comfort I had no business craving so much.

"Where to?" I asked belatedly, my brain scrambled by the expanse of Huddy's broad shoulders. He was a foot taller than me and his long strides showed it. I hustled to keep up, not quite ready to drop his hand either.

Huddy tipped his head down to look at me. "You good with a hole in the wall?"

His hazel eyes were rimmed in gold under the streetlights, showing a mix of kindness and humor that had me weak in the knees. Most of his face was covered in a dark beard that seemed a little unkempt, but it did nothing to detract from the city-cowboy thing he had going for him. Dark hoodie, dark hat, dark jeans that were plastered to muscular thighs, leading down to worn-in cowboy boots that seemed more than a little out of place for Chicago.

He was a conundrum, and I was somehow incapable of looking away.

"Sure," I said, a beat too late. Despite the bitter wind I should have seen coming—this was the Windy City after all—my cheeks warmed with a blush that probably spread all the way down my neck. "I'm easy."

With his hand in mine, I felt the rumble of his laugh, even though he didn't make a sound, just enough to realize what I'd said.

"Oh, my God. I cannot win."

I tugged my hand from his grip, ready to run back in the other direction and away from this man who had my mouth uttering words with a dirty undertone at every turn. He loosened his grip, enough to give me the choice to leave, but not enough to let me go easily.

And somehow, that seemed to encapsulate everything about this night.

Maybe I wasn't the only one running from whatever came next in my life.

"Truth or Dare?" I asked again when the silence dragged on between us.

"Well, since I'm such a *dare* guy, truth."

"Where were you going before this little side quest?"

His steps faltered for a moment, then he regained his long

strides, walking with purpose once more. He didn't answer right away, but I could see the indecision warring on his face. Brow creased, eyes looking anywhere but me.

"No where."

"That's cheating." I nudged him with my elbow. "You have to answer honestly."

He shrugged those big shoulders, his fingers tightening in mine. "It's the truth. I quit my job today, and I'm moving tomorrow. I didn't want to go home, or out with my friends. So, I just started walking."

"Why don't you want to go home?"

He looked down at me when we stopped at the next block, hazel eyes looking amused. "But now it's my turn. Truth or dare?"

I tapped my chin with my free hand. "Dare. Please don't make me regret this."

The light turned, and I stepped off the curb, still smiling, still riding the easy rhythm of the night. I liked cities like this—noise, motion, a hundred places to look at once. It was easier to stay on the surface when everything around you was moving too.

Unfortunately, that also meant I didn't see the car until it was already coming fast.

Headlights cut through the dark. An engine roared. Tires screamed as the car blew through the red light, and the sound hit something deep in my chest, sharp and immediate.

For one suspended heartbeat, time slowed, and the weight of everything I held at bay came crashing down—the panic, the grief, the loss, the things I didn't think about if I wanted to keep breathing.

Huddy moved before I could.

One second he was beside me, the next he was in front of

me, his arm wrapping around my waist, pulling me back as the car skidded to a stop. He planted himself between me and the danger without hesitation, like his body had already decided the outcome.

By the time we reached the other side of the street, my heart was pounding—from fear, yes, but also from the negative thoughts and doubts and regrets swirling beneath the surface of my mind.

See? This is a sign. I shouldn't have come here.

I'm not good enough to cut it on my own.

Violet wanted me gone because it's easier when she doesn't have to take care of me, too.

"You good?" Huddy asked. His hands were warm on my shoulders, his attention steady, grounding me in the here and now.

I nodded woodenly, shoving aside my creeping thoughts. I chose joy the way I chose air—without stopping to think about it. Not because the sadness and fear weren't real, but because if I let myself linger there, it would pull me under.

He ducked his head to meet my eyes, that hazel gaze careful and concerned.

I smiled, feeling myself balance out once more. "Yeah," I said lightly. "Still waiting on my dare."

Live music drifted out of a bar across the street, drunk patrons milling about after midnight as *(I've Had) The Time of My Life* began playing. Huddy followed my gaze to the crowd dancing and singing, then looked back at me.

"I dare you to dance from here 'til the next corner."

A laugh stuttered out of me, sudden and breathless, like the sound itself shook the last of my fears loose. I dropped his hand and spun to face him.

Instantly, I launched into the Patrick Swayze dance-walk—

knees bent, shuffle step, fingers snapping to the beat. "You're going to regret this."

"*I'm* going to regret this?"

"Oh yes." I pointed at him, already swaying. "I'm about to embarrass us both."

The music pulsed through me, loud enough to drown out everything else, and I leaned into it—shimmying, circling my arms, letting my body take over in what I hoped was some semblance of rhythm, but who knew at this point. I danced in place as he walked closer, waiting until I could wrap an arm around his waist and circle him, my other arm flung wide like I was claiming the sidewalk as my stage.

Without thinking, I started to sing along, hips moving freely now, every ounce of hesitation burned off by the rhythm. This—this—was where I lived best. In motion. In moments too bright and loud to leave room for doubt.

The song grew quieter the farther we moved from the bar, but I belted out the lyrics anyway, meaning every word as it rolled into the chorus.

"Please don't do the leap," Huddy said when I started to dance backward again.

I waggled my brows, dropping lower, shaking my ass harder to the beat. "But how else will I know if this could be love, Huddy?"

He stopped moving, feet planted, shoulders squared, looking unsure what I was about to do—but bracing for it anyway. Hands loose at his sides, knees bent just enough, ready for whatever chaos I threw his way.

The fact that he didn't tell me to stop—that he didn't laugh it off or try to rein me in—hit me so hard in the chest I almost missed a step. This man, who'd known me for all of a few city blocks, wasn't trying to control the moment.

He was meeting me in it.

Before I could think too long about how bad of an idea this was, I took off running.

I laughed at the dawning horror on Huddy's face as he realized I actually meant it. Right here. On a dark city street. No practice. No plan. Just trust.

He bent his knees, hands out, just as willing as I was to see how this played out.

At the last second, I slowed, throwing my arms around his neck instead of attempting a suicidal leap, feeling his hands land solidly on my waist as we collided.

"Jesus Christ," he breathed, like I'd knocked the wind out of him.

His hands tightened as he spun me in a circle, my laughter spilling free, bright and unstoppable. My arms cinched around his neck, my whole body buzzing with the sheer, reckless joy of it.

When he finally stopped, I slid down his chest, skin tingling where we were still pressed together. "You really thought I was going to try to leap into your arms over your head?"

His hands stayed on my waist as he shook his head, chin tipped down toward me. "I had no fucking idea what you were about to do."

"Would you have tried to lift me?" I asked, still grinning when I loosened my hold to rest my hands on his shoulders.

"I mean," he said honestly, "I wasn't going to drop you."

The words landed heavier than they should have. His hands. His certainty. The way he said it like it was a given.

Even with how little I knew about Huddy, I believed him. That if it came down to it, he'd do whatever he could to keep me safe.

And shit—that was hard to wrap my head around.

Safety, especially with men, had always felt theoretical to me. Something other people grew up with, but I'd never experienced. My mom was gone before I learned what it meant to lean on someone, and my dad had taken the first exit he could find. Since then, I'd learned to move fast, stay light, keep my feet under me. It was just me and Violet against the world.

"You're not exactly convincing me I'm out of the danger zone," Huddy said, glancing down at where my hands still rested on his shoulders.

I looked up at him, breath shallow now, joy still humming under my skin. "I think you could use a little more time in the danger zone," I whispered. "That's where the real joy is. Where you feel it."

"Oh yeah?" His hands tightened on my waist.

When his gaze dropped to my mouth, it stole what little air I had left. I wet my lower lip without thinking, and his eyes tracked the movement, focused and intent.

My smile faded—not from fear, but from the sudden weight of how big this felt. How much this moment mattered. As cliché as the song was, I knew one thing for sure.

I'd never felt like this before.

Seconds ticked by, the world narrowing until it felt like we were standing inside a fragile bubble, stretched thin and shimmering. Waiting for him to kiss me. Or step away. To do *something*.

Whatever happened next, I was sure it would change everything.

A siren ripped through the night as it passed us, loud and sudden, and I jumped.

Huddy's hands tightened on my waist, pulling me into his chest on instinct alone. My heart slammed hard, reacting before my thoughts could catch up—his heat solid and grounding through our clothes, soft and comforting and lighting me on fire all at once.

"Sorry," Huddy said abruptly, releasing me like he'd crossed an invisible line. The loss of his hands was immediate and disorienting.

I cleared my throat and dropped my gaze to the cracked sidewalk between us, the scuffed high-tops I'd doodled all over suddenly fascinating. Safer than looking at the man I'd been certain was about to kiss me.

Get it together, Daisy.

"Burgers," Huddy said, waving a hand forward like nothing else had happened between that decision and now.

He didn't reach for my hand again, and the absence felt bigger than it should have.

I followed when he started walking, silence settling between us this time. Usually, I hated silence, filling every available second with words, jokes, songs—anything to keep things light and moving. But now my mind flickered anyway—headlights, screeching brakes, the way his hands had locked around my waist like he'd already claimed me as his to protect.

Two more blocks down, we stopped in front of McDermott's Pub. The windows were a little greasy, the sign chipped with age, and neon lights flickered inside. This place was the definition of a hole in the wall, and Huddy stood there, holding the door open with an air of confidence that said this was not his first time here.

I stepped past him, shivering at the shift from wind to warmth as the heavy door swung shut behind us, sealing in fryer grease and stale beer.

The bartender looked up, rag frozen mid-swipe. His gaze

bounced between me and Huddy, eyebrows climbing higher with every pass.

"Well, I'll be damned." His lips twitched. "Huddy, I'd have thought you'd take a pretty girl like this somewhere a little nicer than my pub."

I blinked, then waved both hands in front of us. "Oh—oh no, no, we're not—this isn't—" My words tripped over each other, heat crawling up my neck. "You know what? Nevermind."

Huddy adjusted his hat and looked down at his boots, and I filed that away. The motion was subtle, but I'd already noticed how he ducked his head when he was trying to hide something. This time, the corner of his mouth twitched like he was fighting a smile.

The bartender chuckled and went back to wiping the counter, though I could still feel his curiosity following us as Huddy steered us toward a booth near the back.

We slid into cracked vinyl seats, the silence settling in again—this time too loud to ignore.

"Truth or dare?" I asked.

"Truth." Huddy grabbed a menu from the wall, handed it over, then folded his hands on the table like he was bracing for impact.

"Oh, I see." I took the menu but didn't open it yet. "Now you're just trying to throw me off with all these truths."

"Or I'm afraid you'll dare me to do the Dirty Dancing lift in a grungy bar with slippery floors," he said. "Risking both our lives."

I laughed. "Nah. I need to keep that one in my back pocket. It requires the element of surprise."

Before I could say more, the bartender appeared with a basket of fries, setting it down between us.

"Get a head start," he said, nodding at Huddy. "This guy eats fast."

Huddy leaned back, arms crossing over his chest. "Come on, Gus. Don't do me like that."

"Well, if you're not gonna get my boys to playoffs this season," Gus shot back, "I figure I don't owe you shit."

The words were light and familiar, spoken in a sarcastic tone I knew meant they were friends.

But Huddy's reaction didn't mirror Gus's tone. His gaze dropped again, jaw tightening just a little—enough that I noticed. Enough that I knew this wasn't just a joke that landed wrong.

"Playoffs?" I asked.

Gus glanced at me, then Huddy, then back at me. Whatever answer lived there stayed put.

"What can I get you?" he said finally.

I didn't look at Huddy. Didn't press. Instead, I turned my attention to Gus.

"What's your favorite thing here?"

"This guy always gets the bacon cheeseburger," Gus said. "Grilled onions, ketchup and mustard. Never tomato. And don't even think about mayo."

My brows lifted as I peeked at Huddy over the edge of the menu. "Oh. So you're a *regular* regular."

"Something like that," Gus said, clearly enjoying himself.

"Okay," I decided. "I'll do the cheeseburger too. And a Daisy Cutter."

Huddy raised a brow. "You pick that just because it's got your name on it?"

I grinned. "It feels like a good omen, right?"

Gus wandered off, leaving us alone again. The bar was

mostly empty—just a couple people playing pool in the corner —like the rest of the world had forgotten this place existed.

"Good omen, huh?" Huddy asked.

"Mmhmm." I popped a fry into my mouth. "You didn't rob me, and these fries are excellent. Seems promising."

He huffed out a laugh, smoothing a hand over his beard. This time, it reached his eyes.

"Do you always put that much stock in luck?"

"I wouldn't say I'm superstitious," I said. "But I am a *little* stitious."

This time he grinned, and knowing I was the one to make him smile felt like taking a shot of the sweetest liquor—pure joy, straight into my bloodstream.

"My sister and I have a whole theory that things come in threes. In our experience, it's usually bad things. But then it's like the universe apologizes for being so shitty and gives you one really good thing to make up for it. A reminder that everything can change in the blink of an eye, even when it doesn't feel like it. To keep looking for the good."

He raised a dark brow. "Sounds like a convenient way to justify a bad week."

I laughed and grabbed another fry. "It's not a justification, it's science. Well. Maybe not *science*. Emotional science? Is that a thing?" My hand waved as the words picked up speed. "Okay, example. My sister's car died—smoke-billowing-on-the-side-of-the-road dead. Then the roof in our apartment caved in during a rainstorm. And then we got a phone call that my aunt passed away."

His expression softened, and I blinked away my emotions lingering just beneath the surface.

"She was my mom's sister. We lived with her during the

summers after my mom died when I was young. So that one really sucked."

"I'm sorry."

"But then came the good thing." I pushed forward before the sadness could settle. "Maggie left everything to us, including her old farmhouse. Cute little town, gorgeous views. Middle-of-nowhere perfect."

"Sounds like my kind of place." He leaned in slightly. "But you didn't want to move there?"

"We did. My sister and niece moved in, and I stayed for a few weeks. But the whole time she kept telling me this was my chance to move to Chicago like I'd always wanted. To take my half of the inheritance and chase big dreams. To not keep living the same small-town life we'd always had."

"And so you're here."

I waved a hand around us. "And so I'm here."

"Still full of regrets?"

"I believe it was my turn to ask a question."

Our hands brushed as we both reached for a fry, that same spark zipping between us.

"Hit me."

"This one's kind of a first date question, but how would your best friend describe you?"

"That's deeper than I expected." He adjusted his hat, fingers dragging through his hair as his gaze slid to the window. I'd call this one Avoidance.

"I feel like I just gave you a freebie." I tossed a fry at him, bouncing it off his thick beard. "So let's hear it. Aside from tall, dark, and handsome."

A grin tugged at his mouth when his eyes finally came back to mine. "I doubt Beckett would call me tall, dark, and handsome, but maybe I'm wrong. It's been a while since we've talked."

"Okay, so Beckett." I stole another fry, lifting it to throw again if he avoided the question. "How would he describe you?"

He stared out the window again, jaw working. "He'd probably say I'm reliable."

"That's it? Just reliable?"

He shrugged. "I show up. When people need something, I'm your guy."

A slight frown crossed his face that didn't track with what most people would say was a compliment, so I waited for him to continue.

"I guess he'd say I don't ask for much. Don't complain. Don't make things harder than they need to be." A pause. "And that I'm a grumpy motherfucker."

I laughed. "I think you just *look* grumpy. Hidden beneath all that facial hair."

The corner of his mouth tipped up. "I'm plenty grumpy."

"Sure."

That earned me a real smile—slow and a little crooked.

"What about you?" His gaze held mine. "How would your best friend describe you?"

"Oh, easy. Impulsive. Optimistic to a fault. A little reckless. Classic avoidance patterns when life gets hard."

"That tracks."

I kicked his boot under the table, grinning. "*Hey.*"

"Reckless can be good."

I paused, fry halfway to my mouth. "I did move across the country to live with a roommate I found on Craigslist and asked a stranger to spend the night with me."

"Okay. Not *all* good."

"Thank you. Credit where credit is due."

He shook his head, eyes alight with amusement, and I was giddy with delight over making this self-proclaimed grumpy motherfucker smile. "So Beckett relies on you."

Huddy let out a shallow breath, then gave me a quick nod. "People usually do."

The way he said it—like a fact, not a boast—settled deep in my chest.

"Well." I broke the moment with a smile. "That explains why you're so good at not letting strangers get run over by cars."

"Occupational hazard." He said it easily, like it was something he'd never questioned. "Take the hit so someone else doesn't."

I wasn't sure what Huddy's occupation was, but with every word, I was starting to understand him anyway.

The bar hummed around us—neon buzzing, classic rock low on the speakers, the TV flickering overhead. Somewhere between the L station and here, I realized I wasn't thinking about how badly I already missed my sister. Or how terrified I was that I'd fail here, just like everyone always seemed to think I would.

I was just here, present, with him.

And I couldn't decide if that was wonderful or terrifying.

3

TY

When Daisy said I could probably use more time in the danger zone, I didn't think this was what she meant.

Sitting across from a beautiful woman in my favorite bar wasn't dangerous in the obvious ways. But the ease of it—the way she drew things out of me I usually kept locked down—was another story.

Reliable.

And I was, wasn't I?

The first to drop my gloves for a teammate. The first to step in when my sister's husband crossed a line. The first to smooth things over, fix what was broken, explain away my parents' emotional blind spots.

I took hits, one after the next, and I stayed standing.

For the most part, I didn't even mind it. I liked being needed. Liked knowing I mattered because I was useful.

What I didn't like—and what sat heavy in my chest tonight—was realizing how rarely anyone stepped up for me in return. How empty the stands had felt at my last game. How quiet the end of it all had been.

Tonight, reliable felt invisible. And that didn't feel good at all.

And then there was Daisy, throwing fries at my face when I tried to pull back in on myself.

She was everything I wasn't—life instead of duty, laughter instead of silence. Sitting across from her, I didn't feel like the guy who'd just kissed his only dream goodbye. I was still me— still a little solemn, still a little grumpy—but smiling more than I had in years.

"You're something else, you know that?"

She grinned, taking it for the compliment it was. "I've been told that before."

Gus reappeared a minute later, balancing two baskets in his hands. He slid two burgers in front of us, the smell of grilled beef and caramelized onions filling the booth.

"Here you go," he said. "One Huddy Special. And one sacrilegious order with mayo on the side."

Daisy clapped her hands together. "Perfect. Thank you."

I rolled my eyes at the mayo, not convinced she wasn't doing this to irritate me. Somehow, that felt very on brand.

She picked up her burger, inspecting it like a jeweler examining a diamond, then took an unapologetically massive bite. A soft, unfiltered sound slipped from her as she chewed, eyes fluttering closed like she'd forgotten I was sitting right there.

And just like that, my attention snagged on her mouth. The quick swipe of her tongue catching a smear of sauce at the corner of her lips. The satisfied curve of her smile when she swallowed, unconcerned with how she looked doing any of it.

Fuck, she was stunning—not in the shiny, curated way of the women who used to trail the team from city to city, all polished edges and practiced interest. Daisy was real.

Unguarded. Like she hadn't shown up tonight planning to be noticed at all.

Her long, wavy blonde hair was still a little wind-tossed and messy. The soft pink T-shirt and ripped jeans looked chosen for comfort, not effect, and when she shifted under the table, I caught a glimpse of scuffed high-top sneakers with hand-drawn flowers all over them.

She was curvy too—full hips, soft thighs, a body that looked warm and real and too easy to notice. The attraction hit fast, settling low before I reined it in.

I cleared my throat and forced my eyes elsewhere. "How old are you?"

The question came out more abrupt than I meant it to, but I didn't take it back.

She blinked, surprised, then smiled like she was trying to decide if she should be offended. "Twenty-four."

I nodded, then grabbed my burger.

Daisy chuckled. "Relax, Grandpa. You're not robbing the cradle, and this is just for tonight, right? We're friends of convenience."

My brow raised, then I chewed and swallowed my first bite of burger. "*Grandpa*? I'm 34."

"Well, Daddy felt a little forward, don't you think?"

I choked on air, coughing hard enough that Gus glanced over from the bar.

Daisy threw her head back and laughed at my reaction, muttering *Daddy* under her breath before she picked up her burger again.

"Damn," she said when she swallowed. "This is criminally good."

"It's decent."

"*Decent*?" She shot me a look of mock outrage, then

reached for the tiny dish Gus had set beside her plate. With exaggerated care, she dipped the corner of her burger into the mayo, moving in slow motion. "You know what would make it better?"

"Don't say it."

"Maaaaayo," she sang, taking another dramatic bite and groaning again, just to prove her point.

I leaned back, fighting a grin and failing. "Maybe you're a child after all."

"And you're the burger equivalent of an old man yelling 'Get off my lawn'." She licked a dot of mayo from her thumb before slipping it between her lips to get the last of it. A soft little pop sounded as she pulled it free. Just like that, I was shifting in my seat, trying to discreetly rearrange myself beneath the table. "Burgers and mayo is an elite combination."

She took a sip of her Daisy Cutter, unaware that she'd just knocked the air clean out of me.

"Okay, these questions have gotten a little first date-y, and that's not what we're doing here."

"What *are* we doing?" I asked, having lost the plot with each passing moment.

"Passing time on a night neither of us wanted to be alone." She shrugged, like it was just that simple. "Having fun with a new friend. Or, at least, *I* am."

"We can't be friends." The words came out harsher than I'd planned, and Daisy's broad smile dipped a little. "At least, for more than tonight. I'm moving tomorrow, and you just got here."

She shrugged, then grabbed her burger again. "Okay. So just for tonight. Now I gotta get serious with these questions."

"We're already playing truth or dare."

"Sure," she said. "But I'm changing the rules."

"That's not a thing," I said flatly. "There are very clear-cut rules in truth or dare."

"Well, it is now." She took another bite. "Questions while we eat. When we're done, dares can be back on the table."

I set down my burger, studying her. "Okay, so what are these new rules?"

"Questions you'd never ask on a first date, but secretly want to," she said. "Answer the first thing that comes to mind. No clarifying. No follow-up questions. You ask, I answer. I ask, you answer."

I nodded once. "Okay. I can do that."

She leaned forward, eyes squinting. "Worst habit?"

"Leaving wet towels on the floor."

Daisy wrinkled her nose, and I chuckled before asking, "Biggest pet peeve?"

"Whining."

Follow-up questions were on the tip of my tongue, but that was against her new rules.

"One thing you wish you could stop doing?" Daisy asked.

My answer was like a gut punch, it came so fast. "Saying things are okay when they're not."

She rubbed a hand over her heart, then gave a little nod. "Boy, I get that one."

"Why'd you leave your sister if you didn't want to move here?"

Daisy grimaced, then put her hands over eyes. "I hate being a burden."

"I doubt she sees it that way," I said, breaking the rules when her shoulders sagged under the weight of the admission. "She loves you, yeah?"

She waggled a finger at me, then said, "One thing you'd never tell a first date?"

I leaned forward, waiting until she did the same, her smile coming back as we had our heads almost together. "After a long day, nothing takes the edge off quite like ice-cold chocolate milk, straight from the carton."

Daisy gasped, pulling back enough to put her hand over her mouth. "You *rebel.*"

I sat back, arms crossed over my chest. "I know. You'll never look at me the same again."

She cackled, and I couldn't help but laugh along with her. "Lights on or off?"

Just as abruptly as she'd started laughing, she stopped. Amusement still danced across her features, but now there was a level of heat to it I hadn't seen from her yet. I hadn't meant the question to sound so dirty, but now I couldn't help but imagine soft light spilling across every inch of Daisy's skin, sprawled out beneath me. That's exactly what I'd want, given the opportunity to take this further than just one night. But that wasn't what this was.

"On," she said, her voice a little rough. "What's something that could make you walk away, even if you didn't want to?"

I didn't hesitate. "Not being chosen back."

Daisy's smile faltered for just a second, so fast I might've missed it if I wasn't looking for it. Then she nodded, like she understood more than she let on.

She picked up her burger, and I followed her lead, the moment settling quietly between us.

When she finished, I tapped my fingers on the table. "Okay. Last question. Who's your hall pass?"

"Easy." She threw her napkin down and grinned. "Tom Selleck."

I reared back, not at all expecting that answer. "Really?"

"Oh, hell yeah," she said. "Give me the *Magnum P.I.*

version, though. Have you seen his mustache? Honestly, that might be peak facial hair right there."

Without meaning to, I scratched at my playoff beard. "Should I be insulted?"

"Oh, I like a beard." Her eyes flicked over me in a way that made my chest tighten. "But a mustache? That's a statement. That says, 'I have power tools and own multiple flannel shirts.'"

Her eyes took on a mischievous, untrustworthy gleam as she slid her empty basket aside and folded her hands on the table. "Truth or dare?"

After everything we'd just admitted, there was only one answer. "Dare."

Her smile widened. She leaned forward, lowering her voice like she was about to share a secret. "I dare you to shave your beard into a mustache."

I blinked once. Twice.

"Into a—" I stopped and shook my head. "You're kidding."

Daisy watched me, lips twitching. "Nope."

"Right now?"

She shrugged. "Do you have other plans tonight?"

I opened my mouth, then closed it again. I thought about the empty apartment waiting for me. About packing boxes. About the absolute nothingness waiting for me tomorrow.

"No," I said finally.

Her eyes sparkled. "Then what's the problem?"

I looked down at the table, then back at her. "You realize this is my face."

"And?" she said. "Beards grow back. I'm not pressuring you—you can say no. But that's the dare."

I huffed out a laugh and reached for my wallet, pulling out cash and dropping it on the table. "You're unbelievable."

She hopped out of the booth, practically bouncing from foot to foot. "So, are we doing it?"

"I can't believe I'm doing this," I muttered, sliding out after her.

She grabbed my arm and tugged me toward the door. The night air hit us like a reset button—cool, sharp, and buzzing with city noise. Daisy bounced ahead of me on the sidewalk, hands shoved into her jean pockets, almost vibrating with excitement.

"I just want you to know," she said over her shoulder, "this is already my favorite dare I've ever given."

"You say that like this is a regular occurrence."

She grinned. "You'd be surprised."

We stopped at a corner drugstore, fluorescent lights humming overhead. I held the door for her, and she shot me a pleased look on her way in.

Inside, I headed straight for the grooming aisle, grabbing a beard trimmer, a pack of disposable razors, and shaving cream like I'd done this a hundred times before—which I had, just never for this reason.

Daisy leaned against the shelf, arms crossed, watching me like this was the most entertaining thing she'd seen all week.

"You sure?" I asked, holding up the trimmer one last time.

She nodded, those blue eyes alight with joy. "Oh, hell yeah."

I snorted and headed for the register, paying without thinking too hard about it. It was just hair, and I'd already decided I was going to shave tonight. It wasn't like I couldn't shave the mustache off the moment I got home.

The men's restroom was empty, thankfully. I locked the door behind me and stared at my reflection, trimmer heavy in my hand.

What the hell are you doing?

I pictured Daisy's grin, how she'd dared me without hesitation. She looked at me like this spontaneous, fun version of myself already existed. And dammit if I didn't like that.

I turned the trimmer on.

The first pass sent dark hair tumbling into the sink. I paused, breath catching, and watched it slide toward the drain like evidence. Years of habit. Of sameness. Of being exactly who everyone expected me to be.

I kept going.

The beard fell away in uneven clumps, exposing skin that hadn't seen the light in a long time. With every pass, something loosened in my chest. Like I was carving away more than hair, shedding weight I hadn't realized I'd been carrying.

When I shut the trimmer off, the sink was a mess and my reflection looked...different.

Lighter.

I cleaned up the edges with a razor, careful and precise, until all that remained was the mustache. Bold. Unapologetic. A statement, just like Daisy had said.

The guy in the mirror looked like someone who said what he meant. Someone who took chances. Someone who didn't always play it safe.

Someone Daisy would laugh with.

I cleaned up the sink, splashed water on my face, and took one last look before heading out.

The door opened, and Daisy's head snapped up, already smiling.

But then her mouth fell open. "Oh," she breathed. "Oh wow."

I lifted a brow. "That bad?"

She crossed the space between us in three quick steps, eyes

raking over my face. "No," she said. "That... That is dangerous."

Something warm settled low in my stomach, liking the way her eyes couldn't leave my face, memorizing every line.

Maybe I *was* reliable, unwilling to say no to something asked of me, even in a playful game with no stakes. But I didn't feel careful or stuck or any of the other things I so often did when I did things solely for other people's benefit.

I felt like someone new.

Someone who might just be brave enough to keep feeling this way, even after tonight.

4

Daisy

Under *no* circumstances was I prepared for that mustache. Sure, it had been my idea, but absolutely nothing prepared me for the reality standing in front of me now.

With his beard gone, Huddy's jaw was sharp in a way that felt almost unfair—clean lines, strong and deliberate, hiding beneath that rough exterior this whole time. The mustache only emphasized the planes of his face, bold and unapologetic, turning him from quietly handsome into *are you kidding me right now.*

Now, I could see the curl to his dark hair, swooping up at the nape of his neck beneath his hat. Even his shoulders looked broader, nothing about him hidden beneath the scraggly facial hair.

When I finally made it up to his bright hazel eyes, they were focused on me, watching me watch him.

"Dangerous?" he said, one brow lifting like he was amused despite himself.

I swallowed, my mouth having gone dry. This was the same Huddy as a few minutes before. Reliable, rule-following

Huddy who drank chocolate milk straight from the carton and thought mayo on burgers was a crime. Except now he looked like he could ruin lives with a single look, but might apologize for it afterward.

"Yes," I said. "You look like you either fix motorcycles or solve crimes on the beach at sunset. Maybe both."

He huffed a quiet laugh, heat flickering in his eyes, and my stomach dipped in response. I couldn't ignore how close we were standing, or how easy it would be to reach out and test whether that mustache felt as soft as it looked.

I didn't. Barely.

Instead, I turned toward a rack of sweatshirts nearby, flipping through them with exaggerated interest. Generic sizing was great in theory. In practice, it usually meant *will fit my shoulders* or *will fit my chest*, but rarely both. Being soft and curvy had its perks, but buying anything off a rack without trying it on was always a gamble—especially when my boobs arrived in a room a full second before the rest of me.

"Tourist chic," I muttered, holding up a navy crewneck that read CHICAGO in block letters.

Huddy hummed. "Bold."

"I like to blend in," I said. "Nothing says local like screaming it across your chest."

I was still flipping through sizes when he reached over me, stopping my hand. I looked over my shoulder, savoring his warmth at my back.

"Here," he said.

I turned in time to watch him pull his hoodie over his head. The hem lifted, just enough to expose a strip of skin and the hard lines of his stomach, and my brain blue-screened. Yes, I could see the width of his shoulders beneath his hoodie, and I'd guessed he was toned everywhere, but seeing was believing, and boy, was I believer in the abs I'd just seen. His chest was covered in a light dusting of hair, dark against his skin, and I had to bite my cheeks to keep my tongue from rolling out like a carpet. By the time my brain rebooted, he was holding the hoodie out to me.

"You don't have to—" I started.

"I know," he said, calm and steady. "But you've been shivering for hours."

That did something to me. The quiet kind of care I only accepted from my sister—and even then, reluctantly.

I took it, fingers brushing his for half a second longer than necessary, and pulled it over my head. It swallowed me in the best way—soft, warm, oversized in all the right places. It smelled like him—clean soap and cold air, with a faint trace of pine that felt out of place in the city.

"Better," he said with a quick nod.

I tugged the sleeves down over my hands. "Won't you be cold now?"

He shook his head. "No. Cold was kind of a constant growing up. I'm used to it."

"Well, thank you," I said as we stepped back outside. The wind still had teeth, but it didn't cut as badly bundled in his hoodie. I glanced up, noticing the sky had shifted from black to charcoal, the edges of night softening like it was preparing to give way.

Huddy checked his watch, then looked back at me. "We should probably head home."

The word *should* lingered between us, heavy and reluctant.

"Yeah," I said. "I guess time caught up with us."

He ordered a car without ceremony, phone already in hand.

"Where to?" he asked, passing it to me.

I typed in my new address, a knot forming in my chest as soon as I hit confirm. Finality had a way of sneaking up on me like that.

The car pulled up soon after, not giving me any time to reconsider this.

Inside, the city blurred past the windows, streetlights streaking gold across the glass. The quiet between us felt heavier than any of our confessions all night. Not awkward, but weighted like we were both holding something fragile, unsure where to set it down.

I tugged his hoodie tighter around me, all too aware that this was slipping toward an ending I hadn't agreed to yet.

I shouldn't feel like this, I told myself.

I'd known him for hours. Not days. Not weeks. *Hours.*

He hadn't promised anything. Hadn't even tried to push past the edges of tonight. And that was what I'd asked for, right?

Just companionship on a lonely night. Innocent and uncomplicated.

So why did my chest ache like I was about to lose something important?

I glanced over at him. Huddy stared out the window, jaw set, mustache catching the glow of passing lights. Still solid. Still calm. Still not reaching for me.

And maybe that was the problem.

If he'd flirted harder, I could've dismissed this as chemistry. If he'd tried to kiss me again, I could've chalked it up to attraction. But he hadn't. Instead, Huddy stayed exactly where he was—present, steady, respectful.

Dangerous in a different way.

I swallowed, my instinct screaming at me to be the one who left first. To step out clean before this turned into something that hurt far worse than I was prepared for. Leaving was easier than being left.

The car slowed, and I frowned, peering out the window.

This wasn't my street.

Instead, we rolled to a stop beside dark sand and an endless stretch of water, the lake barely visible in the thin, pre-dawn light. The horizon was just beginning to soften, night loosening its grip.

I turned to Huddy, confused. "Uh—this isn't—"

"I know," he said. Then, after a beat, "Truth or dare, Daisy?"

My breath caught, the meaning behind his words landing all at once. Not a joke. Not a throwaway line.

A reach.

"Dare," I said, echoing our very first conversation—back when I'd been the one asking him to stay.

"Watch the sunrise with me," he said, one hand braced on the doorframe, like he was steadying himself.

I didn't answer right away.

The silence stretched, my heart pounding so loud I was sure he could hear it. Inside, every alarm bell I had was ringing, trying to get my attention—not because of him, but because of how much I already cared. How easily he'd slipped past my defenses.

He shifted, jaw tightening. "You know what—never mind," he said, backing off just as quickly as I had. "I'll take you home. Driver?"

His retreat was careful, protecting me even now, but I hated the sadness on his face more than I hated the idea of how much this would hurt tomorrow.

I grabbed his hand before he could pull away, lacing our fingers together. "I'm not about to lose now."

His hazel eyes snapped back to mine, surprise flickering across his face. Uncertainty, too. *Good.* If I was going to be standing on unsteady ground, he could join me.

I scooted closer and reached past him to open the door myself. "Come on."

He got out first, then turned to help me out, his grip firm but questioning, like he was still waiting for me to change my mind.

But I couldn't now.

The cold lake air hit my face as my shoes sank into the sand, the sky just beginning to bloom with pale color. I tightened my fingers around his, anchoring myself to the moment. The beach was quieter than I expected, the sound of the waves softly lapping against the shore. The lake stretched in front of us, dark and glassy, the horizon brushed with pale pinks and blues that looked almost unreal. I knew Lake Michigan was big, but standing here, it felt like an ocean.

I slipped my arm through his, tucking myself closer for warmth. He was only in a short-sleeve shirt now, hands shoved deep into his pockets, but his shoulders were still relaxed like the cold didn't bother him in the slightest.

"What the heck," I said, tipping my head back to look at him. "Why aren't you freezing?"

He chuckled, the sound vibrating through his chest. Before I could say anything else, he pulled me in. One arm wrapped around me, solid and sure, holding me against him like it was the most natural thing in the world.

When he rested his chin on the top of my head, I melted. There was no other word for it.

"I played hockey for a very long time."

"That explains the thighs," I said, and his chest rumbled with another laugh.

When the wind picked up again, I looped my arms around his waist, fitting against him like I'd always belonged there, my cheek pressed to his chest. He hugged me back, and I tried and failed to remember a time when a hug had felt this grounding. This safe.

We stood like that as the sun broke free of the horizon, light spilling across the water, turning the lake molten gold. A new day, quietly demanding we take notice.

It was both a beginning and an ending, symbolic in a way I didn't want to acknowledge.

Eventually, we walked back toward my place in silence, fingers laced, shoulders brushing. The lobby was warm and bright compared to the outside, the elevator humming as we waited.

He pulled me in for one last hug, slow and deliberate. When we pulled apart, he brushed a loose strand of hair away from my face, studying me like he was committing me to memory.

"I'm proud of you," he said. "For being brave. For starting over, even when it's scary. You're going to do so many wonderful things, Daisy. I know it."

My throat tightened, his words soothing every fear I hadn't even spoken aloud.

"And you, Huddy," I said, the words tumbling out before I could overthink them. "You are such a good man. It is so easy to care about you." I swallowed, my eyes burning with tears I refused to let fall. "Just—make sure whatever comes next is what *you* want. Not just what everyone else needs."

Something shifted in his expression, like I'd hit a truth he didn't hear often enough.

He nodded once. Then he stepped back.

The elevator opened, and I got on before I could change

my mind. He lifted a hand to wave goodbye, and as quick as the night began, it was over. The doors slid shut, and I began to rise.

With every inch I moved away from him, my breaths came quicker, pulse hammering in my veins.

My hands shook as I pulled my phone out for the first time all night and pulled up my text chain with my sister.

DAISY

Do you believe in soul mates? Because I think I just met mine.

The elevator chimed as I passed the second floor, and I looked at the number 5, glowing on the side panel. I slid the phone back into the pocket of my hoodie, only now realizing it was Huddy's hoodie, not mine.

"Shit," I mumbled, then slapped the button for the floor above. My legs bounced as the elevator came to a stop, then the doors opened at a speed fit for a turtle.

The moment they were wide enough to let me through, I sprinted down the hallway, racing to the stairs. I took them two at a time, imagining him waiting in the lobby for me, just as devastated as I was to say goodbye.

By the time I burst back into the lobby, breathless and wild with hope, it was empty.

He was gone.

5

Present

Some days the universe didn't just kick you when you were down—it spit in your coffee, too.

I stared at the weird blob floating on top of my latte, tilting the mug slowly as if that might help me diagnose the problem. Spoiled milk? Or had my roommate actually spit in it this morning?

Both felt equally possible.

Living with Lauren for the last three years had been a slow, grinding lesson in endurance. I wasn't sure what I'd expected from a roommate who listed her spare bedroom—closet, really —on Craigslist, but an eternal party girl with no respect for personal space or common decency hadn't been it.

Lauren didn't have a job. She had a dad with a credit card and a vague "budget" she liked to complain about when it tightened. In those months, my increased rent conveniently covered the gap. After years of the same game, I did my best to avoid her—late nights, early mornings, headphones always in

—because everything in Chicago was expensive, and misery was cheaper than moving.

As if summoned by my thoughts, my phone buzzed in my hand with a text message.

LAUREN

Hey, so heads up. I rented out your room.
You need to be out by Friday.

I stared at the screen, rereading it as if the words might rearrange themselves into something less insane.

DAISY

What do you mean, out by Friday? That's tomorrow. You can't do that.

LAUREN

Dad checked the lease. We never signed a new one after the first year.

My stomach dropped as I thought back over the last few years, trying to remember if that was true.

LAUREN

He says you've been month to month for, like, two years. And you're paying below market price.

I scrolled through my email, heart pounding, trying to look for any digital footprint that what she said wasn't true. Anything about the apartment usually came from her dad's attorney, and there it was—two years ago. A renewal notice I meant to print and sign, but never had.

DAISY

Why didn't you ever say anything?

LAUREN

You never asked.

Tomorrow morning, btw.

I'm throwing a party and don't have time to
have you messing up the place.

My grip tightened around my phone, my thumbs flying over the screen as I typed and deleted every rage-filled thought that flitted through my mind.

DAISY

So I just have to leave?

LAUREN

Yes. ASAP.

Anger flared hot and fast, immediately followed by something that felt a lot like relief. The thought sat there, ugly and undeniable, that I might have stayed forever if Lauren hadn't kicked me out. Sure, I knew I avoided conflict at just about any cost, but I was ashamed I'd let my unhappiness go this long.

And there's one.

I shoved the phone into my bag and headed into the office. My apparent lack of housing would have to wait until later.

Parker Collective was typically bright and busy—phones ringing, calendars packed with donor luncheons and community fundraisers, the low hum of people who believed in the events we planned and the money we brought in for the charitable organizations we worked with.

Today, it was quiet. Too quiet.

That should have been my first clue.

"Daisy, hey." My boss, Jerry, motioned me into his office before I'd even set my bag down. "Can we chat for a minute?"

I plastered on my best fake smile, dropped my things in my

tiny cubicle, then followed him into his corner office. "Did you hear from the Fairview team? They seemed pretty happy with the gala on Friday night."

He blinked, looking surprised. "The—oh. Yeah. Yes." He nodded. "They were thrilled. You did a great job. Really great."

Relief flickered through me. "Good. I thought the rain plan might've—"

"No, no," he cut in. He shifted, then finally sat down, folding his hands together. "You're great with contingency plans, always ready to pivot at a moment's notice. Everything went really well."

"Thanks," I said, his praise not explaining the bead of sweat trickling down Jerry's brow. "So, what did you want to chat about?"

The breath he took was more like a gale-force wind.

"We're downsizing." Jerry slowly looked up from his desk to meet my eyes. "Unfortunately, your position has been cut. I'm sorry, Daisy."

I blinked several times, trying to make sure I had heard him correctly. "I'm sorry, can you say that one more time?"

"This is never an easy conversation to have, especially because you're such a hard worker."

I nodded on autopilot while my right leg did the *Cha-Cha Slide* under his desk, unable to sit still. My brain started sprinting a hundred miles a minute through everything this meant for my life.

"Who else is being let go?" I asked, clinging to the question as if it made a lick of difference.

Jerry stacked and re-stacked the papers. "Right now, we're starting with just your position."

My spine stiffened, heat creeping up the back of my neck. "So, am I being laid off or fired?"

He attempted a sympathetic smile that only made me want to launch my coffee at his face. "A little of both. Fundraising and event planning is a small network, and everything is connected to our donors. Unfortunately, they have a lot of sway the more they spend. But I thought at least this way, you can file for unemployment, which I felt better about, considering your circumstances."

My head jerked back. "My circumstances? What circumstances?"

Jerry's gaze darted to the window as if an escape hatch would open there. "Well, you and Lauren…"

I gripped the chair's armrest hard enough that the faux leather squeaked. "Me and Lauren, what?"

His Adam's apple bobbed, a bead of sweat trickling off his forehead and down his temple. "You don't know yet."

"Oh, I know plenty about Lauren." My voice was sharp and fast; my patience dangling by a thread. "I'm trying to connect the dots as to how *you* know my lint-licker of a roommate evicted me not even 10 minutes ago, insisting I be out by the end of the day."

Jerry winced, dabbing a tissue along his brow. "Why did Donor Relations tell us since you two had a spat and you were moving out, it would be easier if we let you go too?"

"They WHAT?" My voice cracked up about three octaves, outrage detonating inside me like a firework.

"I'm so sorry," Jerry whispered. "They said you can't have run-ins with the Kingsleys, and you know how they're connected to everything in Chicago. This is terrible, and I feel horrible."

My mouth fell open. Words refused to form at first. Then they tumbled out in sharp little bursts. "So she's kicking me out of my home"—*one*—"and asked Daddy to use that donor money to have me fired"—*two*—"So what's number three?"

Jerry was turning green, looking like he might throw up on his desk. "I don't follow."

"Come on, Jer-Bear, complete the set. I collect catastrophes in trios."

"You want more bad news?"

A laugh burst out that sounded more like a bark. "Don't go soft on me now, Jerry. What's next? Did my car get towed? Is the USDA banning cherry flavoring? Come on, rip off that Band-Aid for me, buddy."

His face crumpled. "I really am sorry, Daisy. I'll write you a shining letter of recommendation. We can use every connection I have to find you something else."

I blew out a sharp breath, forcing myself not to flip his desk like a bad game of Monopoly. I knew where the blame belonged. Jerry was just the messenger. The knife in my back had Lauren's fingerprints all over it.

I managed to keep it together long enough to shove my things into the cardboard box Jerry dug out of a supply closet. Walking down the hallway was a lesson in humility, balancing what had to be the most deranged assortment of belongings anyone had ever been fired with.

Front and center was a half-dead snake plant, slumped over like it, too, had given up on me. Wedged beside it, a stack of notebooks full of ideas that had never seen the light of day. Most embarrassing was a single black stiletto I'd been missing for over a year, discovered under the back of my desk like a crime scene clue to the inner workings of my neurodivergent brain. Too bad I'd already donated the other one.

A gallon-sized bag sat on top, full of envelopes addressed to

Dizzy. Each one contained cute little stickers my niece loved to send me, knowing I, too, couldn't resist the siren call of a good holographic cow wearing roller skates. Each one was too precious to me to use. Instead, they'd been sitting in my drawer for years because what if I came up with somewhere better to put it later?

This little chaos box was a perfect representation of my time here: a shiny, messy graveyard of dreams that didn't fit anymore. Maybe they never had.

My coworkers' heads popped up like meerkats when I walked by, pity painted all over their faces. I lifted my chin higher, praying no one would ask if I was okay—the answer was a resounding no, and I refused to cry in front of them.

As I reached the elevator, my phone buzzed in my pocket. The box wobbled as I tried to reach for it, and the heel nearly made a break for it down the hall, so I let the call go to voicemail.

By the time I got to the parking garage across the street I'd paid to store my car in, the weight of it all pressed down—not just being fired, but the years I'd wasted here.

I'd come to Chicago chasing a new adventure, thinking that living the big-city life was the change I needed. That it would be full of fun experiences and new friends and opportunities I couldn't even imagine. That I'd be fine living on my own, not relying on my sister to fix all my many problems I usually created for myself.

Instead, the last three years were spent in a beige cubicle and hiding from a narcissistic roommate.

I blamed Huddy, my mystery man, for setting the bar too high. Every day after that first one here had been a little more of a letdown until I'd arrived at rock bottom with a box of junk I didn't even care about.

I sniffed back the tears, refusing to let them fall, and crossed the parking lot to my old red Volkswagen Beetle.

My phone rang again as I pried open the trunk and wedged the box inside, shoving it against the usual chaos: a half-full trash bag of items to donate I'd been carting around for months, a pair of golf clubs from my three-week attempt at being sporty, and—of course—the other black stiletto.

"If this is my reward for such a shitty day, I. Will. Riot."

The phone shrilled for the third time. I finally tugged it free, ready to give whoever kept calling a piece of my mind, but the screen displayed an unknown number from Colorado.

My chest tightened, heart racing at who would call me. Spam didn't call three times in a row, and the only people I knew in Colorado were my sister and niece.

It continued to ring as I slammed the trunk. This time I answered. "Hello?"

"Is this Daisy Winslow?"

"Yes. Who's calling?"

"This is Dr. Montgomery with Mountainside General Hospital in Glenwood Springs. Are you Violet Winslow's sister?"

"Yes," I managed, though my voice came out thin and shaky. "What's going on? Is she okay?"

There was a pause, and that momentary silence said everything before the words even landed.

My knees buckled as the doctor kept talking, the world narrowing until all I could hear was the rush of blood in my ears. I gripped the edge of the Beetle's roof, but my fingers slipped and I slid down the side of the car until I sat down hard on the garage floor.

His words broke through in shards, jagged and senseless.

Headaches.

Tests.

Brain cancer.

Too late.

She's gone.

Each one cracked against my ribs like a stone, and my brain refused to string them together, refused to let them mean what they meant.

I pressed the phone tighter to my ear, eyes burning, the parking lot spinning around me as if I'd been shoved underwater. Somewhere, a car door slammed, a train went by, and someone laughed. The world kept moving, but mine came to a screeching halt.

Three.

The biggest, baddest three there ever was.

And then, like a second wave I wasn't ready for, one word rose above the rest. "...Juniper."

My mouth moved before my brain could catch up, and I leapt to my feet. "Junie—oh, God. She's just a kid. She—she's afraid of the dark, or at least she used to be. I don't know anymore. And she won't eat carrots unless they're the crinkle-cut kind. She—" My voice cracked, the words tumbling out in fragments, useless and desperate. "Where is she? Who's with her? She's not alone, is she? Please tell me she's not alone."

Dr. Montgomery's voice softened, but I kept pacing. "She's not alone, Ms. Winslow. She's perfectly safe. They've placed her with a temporary foster, someone who lived next door to your sister. Has Juniper mentioned the Hudsons before?"

The name tugged at something in my memory from one of our many weekly phone calls. I could hear Junie's voice rattling off stories about the neighbor's animals: the dog that always ran the fence line, the chickens with ridiculous names she loved.

"She's in excellent hands," Dr. Montgomery assured me.

I nodded, even though he couldn't see me.

There was a pause, then gently, "Ms. Winslow, are you okay? Do you need help? Is there someone we can call for you?"

A high-pitched laugh burst out of me, sharp and too loud in the quiet parking lot. It wasn't funny, not even close, but my body didn't know what else to do. Help? Someone to call? I had no one.

No home.

No job.

No Violet.

Nothing left but a box of junk and an eight-year-old niece who needed me in Colorado.

The sound cracked off into silence, leaving me gasping, my phone hot against my ear. "No," I whispered. "There's no one. But I'm okay."

I wiped my face on the sleeve of my shirt, shoved the phone into my pocket, and forced myself to move, already thinking through the logistics of getting out of here as fast as possible.

Pack a suitcase.

Fill the Bug with gas.

Get on the highway.

I chanted my to-do list in my head, trying to stay focused.

Sure, my world was unraveling at an alarming rate, but the Winslow girls were good at rising from the ashes. And this was not the time to fall apart.

6

TY

Yesterday felt like a hundred years crammed into one day.

Junie napped in my lap outside her mom's hospital room while the doctors and social workers spoke in whispers and passed me clipboard after clipboard to sign. By the time they let me take her home, Violet was gone and Junie was placed in my care.

Watching my favorite little girl cry herself to sleep on my couch at Copper Ridge nearly broke me. Sure, I'd been preparing for this exact scenario for months, but jumping through hoops to get foster certified didn't do shit to prepare me for the fact that Junie had just lost her mom.

I carried her to bed and stood in the doorway longer than I should have, memorizing the rise and fall of her breathing, promising myself I could hold her world together.

This morning, that felt like a daunting task.

Tom Petty drifted from the ceiling speakers while I worked the griddle. Junie sat at the island in a one-piece blue pajama set covered in rainbow-colored kittens. She had her chin perched on her fist, glasses a little crooked, and her blonde hair sticking up in a dozen different directions. Rowdy lay under her feet, tail thumping in time with her breathing.

"Behold," I said, sliding a plate in front of her. "Your favorite Mickey pancakes."

She pushed it back toward me, not bothering to sit up straight. "They smell weird."

I pressed a hand to my chest. "That's the smell of culinary greatness. Disney sent me an offer letter already this morning, asking me to come work for them."

A twitch pulled at the corner of her mouth. Not a smile yet, but the start of one.

"You gotta eat something, Junebug," I said. "Last I checked, cowgirls loved pancakes."

She poked one with her finger, eyes dull and tired in a way no eight-year-old's should ever be.

"Tell you what." I pushed the plate back toward her again. "If you help me feed Uno after breakfast, I'll let you give him the good hay."

Her head lifted a fraction. "The green hay?"

"The very one. Premium llama dining."

She pushed her glasses up her nose, sitting upright. "I think he likes me better than you."

"That's because you have two eyes," I said. "He respects that in a person."

That earned a small snort.

"Okay." She grabbed the pink fork I'd set out for her. "But you also have two eyes."

"Mm, yes, but they're not pretty blue like yours, are they? Mine are more like Uno's poop brown than the brightest Colorado sky."

She giggled for real this time, the sound small but enough

to crack something loose in my chest. "Maybe like the wood chips in the chicken coop."

"Hey, that's an upgrade from poop. I'll take it."

She took a bite of the pancake, and I finally let my shoulders drop.

The next few days would be full of court hearings, caseworkers, and a dozen things I couldn't control, but right now, in this minute, she was eating. Breathing. Looking a little like the little girl who'd stolen my whole heart.

"Attagirl," I said. "Uno's waiting."

She shoveled another bite into her mouth, then hopped off the stool, Rowdy close behind. The fact that my dog had decided it was time to never leave her side gave me hope that *somebody* in this house knew what they were doing. It just wasn't me.

I rinsed her plate, letting the warm water run longer than necessary, listening to her little footsteps thump down the hall. "Put your rain boots on and let's go," I called.

"Okay!" she shouted back, voice lighter already.

I'd spent the past few weeks reading everything I could find about children and grief—stacked books on my nightstand, dog-eared pages about honesty, stability, and routine. I'd even called my therapist for a last-minute session, wanting to make sure I was ready for this.

Ready.

What a joke.

Playing hockey was all about the pressure to perform, to defend my teammates. My family life wasn't that different— eldest child to two parents who weren't that interested in being parents meant I'd spent my whole life trying to be good enough to make them notice me, then making sure my sister never felt the same way I did. At least I knew what I *didn't* want to be as a dad, so that had given me a false sense of security.

Turned out being a parent—even a temporary foster parent—was fucking hard.

I wiped my hands on a dish towel and followed her.

"All set?" I asked as I turned the corner into the foyer. The old hand-scraped floorboards creaked under my feet, worn smooth by decades of boots and dogs.

Junie zipped her pajamas to her chin and tugged on her boots, hood with little cat ears half-swallowing her hair. "Ready."

I opened the door, and the crisp air swept in, smelling of dew and pine. "Then let's go see the boss."

She took off the second I stepped aside, Rowdy bounding after her, the screen door banging shut behind them. The yard was still slick with morning dew, each blade of grass catching the early light like glass. The chickens erupted in a flurry of feathers and indignant clucks as Junie ran through them, arms flung wide, laughter spilling into the cool air.

Cooper Ridge had been in my family for generations, leaving the Hudson legacy on the little town of Linwood. These lands used to be a fully operational cattle farm with land stretching up into the Gore Range, but that went by the wayside when my grandfather opened the hardware store in town. My parents had spent their years here growing the business in every way they could, letting the barn and all its glory days disappear.

I hadn't intended to bring this all back to life after I retired, but then Rowdy was dropped in my lap, a rescue puppy in need of a home. Then came the misfit crew of animals that occupied the barn now, one after the next, almost always at the begging and pleading of the little girl running through the yard.

The sun was just cresting the ridge as I stood on the front porch, the scent of damp earth mixing with wildflowers and cut hay. The fields beyond the barn shimmered green, still heavy with shadow, and my newest rescue, Uno, grazed lazily by the fence line.

Junie crouched low in the grass, whispering to my newest hen. "Come here, Chickira. Don't let that big bad rooster push you around."

"Oh, it's Chickira now?" I asked, biting back a smile.

"I know you said we should name her Henrietta, but that's very unoriginal," Junie said matter-of-factly. "Did you know it's the most common chicken name in America?"

"I did not know that."

"There are fifty-two thousand chickens named Henrietta," she added with the deadpan expression to tell me exactly how she felt about this. "Google says so. So I went looking for other pop culture names for her that fit the theme you have going here."

I brushed a hand across my mustache, hiding my grin. "I like it. Chickira it is."

She shrugged, not looking away from the hen now eating corn from her open palm. "I think we should start keeping a list of names for new animals we could get, now that I'm living with you."

The unspoken reasoning behind her words hit like a stick to the ribs, my heart hurting for her. Did I want more animals to take care of? Fuck no. But I would do anything to make this little girl smile, no matter how long she got to live with me. "That sounds like a great idea."

Rowdy barked once, agreeing with me.

Junie slipped her hand into mine as we started down the dirt path toward the barn, her fingers small and warm against my calloused palm. "So," I said, "what's on the agenda today? Chickens? Uno? Hockey replays?"

"Uno first."

"Good idea. He's got a busy schedule. My people had to call his people just to set up this breakfast meeting."

The barn waited in the soft sunlight, red paint peeling at the edges, the smell of hay and dust curling out from the half-open doors. Junie helped me tug a bale toward the fence line where Uno stood, one ear flicked forward as if he'd been expecting her.

"Hi, Uno," she whispered to my one-eyed llama, reaching up with a fistful of hay.

He leaned forward and licked her cheek. Junie giggled, bright and unguarded, too full of life for a girl who'd lost so much. The sound cracked something open in my chest.

She wiped her cheek on her sleeve, still petting Uno's coarse white wool. "When's Dizzy coming?"

Dizzy. Even the silly nickname for this mysterious aunt filled me with dread. I'd only ever heard of her in stories, and I didn't like the idea of Violet's sister never once coming to see them in the three years they'd been my neighbors. I grew up with parents who sometimes forgot I existed, and that was the last thing I wanted for Junie.

"I don't know, kiddo," I tossed another flake of hay over the fence. "As soon as she can."

Junie's mouth curved, just a little. "She drives fast, so I bet it'll be soon. Did I tell you about how she used to sneak me candy when Mom said no? She'd come in to tell me the best bedtime stories about the moon that ate donuts and burped stars, and we'd eat our sour cherries under the covers."

I smiled, though something heavy settled low in my chest. That all sounded great through the eyes of a kid, but where the hell had this woman been the past few months? Not at the hospital. Not when Violet got sick. Not when things got bad. "She sounds great."

Junie nodded. "She's the best. You'll see."

I hoped she was right.

The early sun climbed higher while we did the rest of our morning chores, and Rowdy flopped into the shade of the fence, one ear twitching at a fly. I tried to take comfort in the familiar quiet, but the faint rattle of an engine pulled my attention toward the two-lane highway.

A little red Volkswagen zipped past, going way too fast for a road that could chew through suspension like nothing. I watched it disappear behind the trees, then turned back to Junie as she patted the weirdest llama I'd ever met.

"Did you know llamas have three stomach compartments?" Junie said, still focused on Uno. "One's called the rumen, and it makes gas."

"Is that right?" I said, folding my arms on the top rail of the fence. The car passed again, this time heading back toward town.

She nodded while playing with Uno's ears. "Llamas hum when they're happy. Or nervous. Or lonely. Or mad."

"Is Beckett a llama then?"

Junie grinned at the mention of my best friend. "He hums a lot, but I don't think so."

She hopped off the fence, tugging my hand as we headed toward the side of the barn where the barn cat had stashed herself and her kittens. Junie crouched down, whispering something only cats and eight-year-olds understood, lifting a tiny gray kitten to her chest.

The car passed a third time, slower now, and I turned my attention to it. I was far enough outside town, cars didn't just show up. They belonged, or they didn't.

When the little red Bug turned into the shared gravel drive between my house and Violet's, Junie looked up too.

"Who's that?" Junie asked, clutching the kitten closer to her chest.

The unease that had been simmering since breakfast climbed higher when the car parked. "No idea."

The driver's door opened, and a blonde woman stepped out, shielding her eyes against the sun with one hand as she looked around. She squinted at Violet's house, turning a slow circle like she was trying to figure out where the hell she'd landed.

Junie gasped. "Dizzy!"

The kitten hit the ground as she tore off down the driveway, rain boots kicking up tiny stones.

I rushed after her. "Junie—hey, slow down!"

"*Dizzy!*" Junie belted.

The woman dropped to her knees on the gravel driveway, arms out. Junie collided with her at full-speed, arms wrapped tight around her aunt's neck.

She stayed on her knees, arms wrapped around Junie, her face hidden against the top of the girl's head as they clung to each other. All I could see was sunlight catching in her blonde hair and the tremor in her shoulders as she held Junie close.

I slowed as I neared them, my heart pounding in my chest. Something in me pulled toward her, sharp and instinctive, forcing me to take notice.

When she finally looked up, the world stopped.

Blue eyes. That same impossible blue that had once looked at me over a basket of fries in a dim Chicago bar.

Blonde hair. Those same messy waves that had whipped around her face on the windy beach at sunrise.

Full lips. They looked different, not tugged into a mischievous smile, but the same ones I'd almost kissed years ago.

Suddenly, I wasn't standing in my gravel driveway in Colorado. I was back on a cracked city sidewalk, watching a woman choose joy like oxygen.

Three years fell away in a heartbeat. The noise, the grief, the distance—gone. All that was left was the shock and the rush of memory, the sting of every *what-if* I'd buried and the one night I'd never been able to forget.

Dizzy wasn't just some aunt who'd be stopping by.

She was Daisy. *My* Daisy.

My pulse stuttered once, hard. The same pull I'd fought that night slammed back into place, unwanted and unstoppable. And under it, the slow realization that this time, I couldn't walk away.

7

Daisy

By the time I turned onto the gravel drive leading to Aunt Maggie's place—after passing it once, then somehow doing it *again*—my eyes burned from being awake too long. The sun hung low at my back, spilling soft golden light across the mountains ahead of me.

I'd spent half my childhood here. Summers that smelled like wildflowers and mountain air, Violet always a step ahead of me, daring me to jump higher, climb faster, be braver. Everywhere I looked held memories of happy days with the people I had loved and lost.

I cut the engine and stepped out, gravel crunching beneath my boots, then turned slowly, taking it all in. The property hadn't changed much—two houses, just like always. The big one sat farther back, solid and quiet, its windows catching the light. An older couple had lived there when I was younger, their kids grown and gone, but I didn't know if that was still the case.

But it was the smaller house near the road that stopped me in my tracks.

Aunt Maggie's house. *Violet's* house.

Everything was downtrodden, beaten down by years and snow. I couldn't remember if it was this bad before, but the paint peeled off the siding in chunks now. The porch leaned a little, looking as tired as I felt. A ceramic frog with a chipped foot sat on the top step—the same one I'd given Aunt Maggie one year for her birthday. Off to the side, a bright blue bike leaned against the railing.

I couldn't stop staring at the flowerpots lining the steps, every shade of the rainbow imaginable. Bright and mismatched in that messy, joyful way my sister loved.

My chest squeezed tight.

While I was in Chicago trying to prove I wasn't a helpless mess, Violet had been here. Living in the house Aunt Maggie left us. Raising her daughter. Turning childhood summers into something permanent. Something real.

I'd stayed away because coming back meant facing her. Over the many bad days we'd shared in our early lives, she and I had developed an ability to see straight through each other. I'd stayed in Chicago because I couldn't bear the thought of her looking at me and knowing exactly how miserable I was. How badly I'd failed.

And apparently, she'd stayed here, unable to tell me that she was sick.

She'd lived here without me.

She'd *died* here without me.

"Dizzy!"

The sound cracked through the morning air, familiar enough to splinter something inside me.

I jerked my head up just as a blur of blue fleece came flying down the driveway—Junie, all wild hair and flushed cheeks, rain boots slapping against the gravel.

She was bigger than I remembered. Older.

The last of my strength seeped out of me, and I fell to my knees, arms open. Before I could even brace myself, she slammed into me at full tilt. Junie threw her arms around my neck like she was the one here to hold *me* together.

For a heartbeat, everything else disappeared. Chicago. My job. The endless highway. The house. The emails full of paperwork about cremation waiting for me to read. All of it fell away under the weight of a little girl clinging to me as if she never wanted to let go.

I buried my face in Junie's wild, poofy hair, breathing her in. She smelled like maple syrup and cold mountain air. "Hi, sweet girl."

I pulled back just enough to cup Junie's face in my hands, tears streaking her cheeks, a gap-toothed smile splitting through them.

"I told him you'd get here fast," she said with a grin.

I pressed my forehead to hers, hearing just enough of Violet in her voice to splinter something in my chest. "Yeah, well," I whispered. "I was so excited to see you, I had to get here as fast as I could."

A low throat-clear sounded from behind us—deep, deliberate.

I looked up.

Boots first. Scuffed leather planted wide in the gravel, toes dusted pale from the drive. Denim stretched over thighs that looked unfairly solid. My gaze dragged upward, slow and unwilling, taking in broad shoulders filling out a well-worn T-shirt, strong forearms browned by the sun.

His face was still hidden, tucked into shadow beneath the brim of a black baseball cap. The sun sat at my back, outlining him in light but giving me nothing where it mattered. Dark hair curled at the nape of his neck.

Even without seeing his eyes, he looked like he could chop wood, fix fences, and ruin lives before breakfast.

Junie twisted beside me, grinning wide.

"Ty, this is Dizzy!" she announced. "Dizzy, Ty."

He shifted his weight, one hand hooking into his pocket. "Yeah, kid. I figured that out."

The sound of his voice, low and rough, hit like a cold plunge, sharp and breath-stealing.

Recognition didn't creep in.

It *slammed*.

I knew that voice.

I let Junie go and stood, brushing dust off my leggings with both hands before sticking one out toward him. "Daisy," I said. "Violet's sister."

He looked down at my hand, the brim of his hat still shadowing his face. My pulse stumbled, hoping I hadn't misread that night three years ago. Surely he remembered me, right?

I sure hadn't forgotten *him*. I'd never looked at a cheeseburger the same.

Time ticked by slowly as I waited for him to move, but he stepped forward and put his hand in mine. Warm. Rough. Familiar in a way that made my stomach flip.

"Ty," he said. A pause. "Or Huddy, I guess."

As he lifted his head, the light finally caught him—caught the crooked curve of his mouth first. I looked up, excited to see the man I'd been hunting down for years. But the sight of his dark mustache made my brain stutter, skidding sideways into the past.

Three years ago, he'd only shaved it on a dare. Only because

I told him I had a weakness for them—big, stupid Tom Selleck mustaches that had no business working on anyone.

And Huddy, incapable of losing even a silly game of Truth or Dare, had done it.

Of all the times I'd imagined finding him again someday, nothing, and I mean *nothing,* had prepared me for the fact that he still had it.

A flicker of amusement lit his eyes, quick and sharp.

That wasn't a stranger introducing himself.

That was a man who remembered exactly where we'd met, what we'd said, and how it had felt.

A laugh slipped out before I could stop it—half nerves, half *you have got to be kidding me.*

"Ty Hudson."

Those hazel eyes I'd never been able to get out of my head lit with amusement. "So, you figured it out, then?"

"Not nearly as cool as Sir Wallace T. Hudsington the Third, but yes," I said. "Hard to ignore your face on Chicago Storm banners around the city once I paid attention."

Three years ago, I hadn't known his real name. He'd just been Huddy—the hot guy with the beard and the crooked grin who'd spent one unforgettable night with me doing nothing and everything. For months, I'd tried to find him. Not in a stalkery way, but a *please tell me that night happened* kind of way. But he'd retired and disappeared before I ever got the chance. No interviews. No charity appearances. Nothing. It was like he'd fallen off the face of the earth.

It was dizzying to stand this close to a man I'd spent the last three years dreaming of. A man I'd half convinced myself I'd imagined. Told myself those few hours had been small to him —something he forgot before the elevator doors even closed.

But now he stood here, wearing my weakness on his face like a weapon.

That didn't feel like he forgot me. Not at all.

For a moment, neither of us said a word. We just kept shaking hands far longer than appropriate. His mustache twitched—almost a smile, almost not. My mouth hovered somewhere between a laugh and something dangerous.

Three seconds of eye contact, three years of unspoken history.

"Do you want to see the kittens?" Junie piped up, tugging on the hem of my shirt.

I dropped his hand as if it had burned me, feeling my cheeks flush with heat.

Once I started walking with her, June skipped a few steps ahead of us, boots crunching against the gravel. "Okay, so first let's meet Dolly Pawton—she's the barn cat, and she had kittens. Five of them. They're perfect. Then there's Cluck Norris. He's the rooster. He's very mean. Oh, and Uno—he's the llama with only one eye. He's new. We got him at the auction. He likes me more than Ty because his eyes are the color of woodchips. Did you know llamas are related to camels?"

She delivered the list like she was introducing the world's weirdest royal court, and I grinned down at her.

"I did not," I said, then glanced at Ty. "Dolly Pawton, huh?"

He didn't even blink. "Lotta mice."

A laugh burst out of me, bright and startled, out of place with the reason for this visit. "She's working nine to five, just trying to make a living?"

The corner of his mouth twitched beneath that unfairly

perfect mustache—barely there, but heaven help me, I saw it. A subtle nod.

It hit me again how hot it was that he had a sense of humor tucked beneath all that broody cowboy quiet.

Ty hung a few steps back, hands shoved into the pockets of his worn jeans. At his side, a sleek black dog with three legs hopped along in perfect rhythm, his own personal shadow.

I crouched, holding out a hand. "And who's this handsome guy?"

"Rowdy," Junie said with a smile. "He got hit by a truck when he was a puppy, but Ty saved him. Now he's the boss here at Copper Ridge."

I looked up at Ty, squinting against the morning light. "You save puppies and grow mustaches? Dangerous combination, Huddy."

His mouth twitched again—closer to a smile this time— and it did ridiculous things to my insides.

"Don't encourage him," Junie muttered, sounding far older than her eight years. "That's what Emmy says."

I faltered for half a step. *Emmy.*

The name hit like a spark on dry kindling. My gaze flicked down—zero chill—to his left hand resting against his thick thigh. No ring. But my imagination didn't need evidence. Oh no. It could run a full-length feature film on two little syllables.

In my head, Emmy was perfect.

She wore soft cardigans and smelled like sugar cookies and emotional stability. She probably made perfect cinnamon rolls at sunrise, fostered one-eyed llamas and orphans on weekends, and rescued misunderstood roosters just for fun. She and Ty hosted neighborhood bonfires, slow-danced in the kitchen, and had the postcard-perfect small-town life. Emmy laughed softly, never raised her voice, and always had a hair tie when you needed one. And every night, she got to run her hands through his thick, dark hair and kiss that unfairly gorgeous mustached face like it deserved to be kissed.

Meanwhile, my own life resembled a burning dumpster rolling down a hill with a feral raccoon hanging on the side. If it weren't for Diet Coke, cherry candy, and denial, my emotional infrastructure would collapse faster than a house of cards.

Of course, Ty was perfect. Of course, Emmy existed. And, of course, I felt a sharp, stupid twist of disappointment.

I didn't deserve to feel that way. Not even a little.

Three years had gone by since that night together, where nothing had even happened between us. Just because I couldn't move on didn't mean he hadn't.

Squeezing my eyes shut, I took a deep breath, remembering why I was here. No matter what had—or hadn't—happened between Ty and me, Junie was what mattered. Even from this short little introduction, it was clear Ty was a huge fixture in her life, and right now, she needed everyone to rally around her.

No matter that I wanted to run back to my little beat-up VW and speed away, I couldn't. At least, not yet. Not until the hearing tomorrow.

Junie continued to ramble as we reached the open stretch of the yard, pointing out the mountains and the flowers and every single animal in sight. The big farmhouse sat at the back of the property, all wraparound porch and rugged good bones. A gleaming blue vintage truck sat out front, in much better shape than my little beater. The barn was neat and well-kept, and the air smelled of hay, earth, and whatever dangerous pheromone Ty Hudson radiated.

I caught myself sneaking another glance at him—at the

strong line of his jaw, the way his T-shirt revealed tan, corded forearms that had no business being that distracting.

But now I wasn't just looking because he was gorgeous. I was looking for the Emmy in his world. The one who made sense next to all this steadiness. Who *wouldn't* want him?

Junie spun around, walking backward now, hands flapping as she talked. "Be careful with Cluck Norris," she warned. "He's the boss of the whole flock, and he remembers faces. If he decides he doesn't like you, he'll chase you forever. He even went after the mailman once, but Rowdy tackled him before he made it to the road."

"He sounds nice," I said, forcing my voice to stay light.

"She's not wrong," Ty added, voice low and rough. "Stay away from him if you can."

I side-eyed him, trying to find my footing again. "Do you let all your animals rebel or just Walker, Texas Rooster?"

A quiet huff of laughter slipped out of him, low and warm, and my heart had the nerve to trip over itself.

Junie kept chattering on about each of the animals, her voice bubbly as if the world hadn't fallen apart around her. And for a few precious minutes, I believed it. Like I wasn't the woman who'd lost her home, her job, and her sister in a single night.

I was just Daisy—fun aunt, slightly feral city transplant, walking up a gravel drive next to a man who looked far too good in denim.

The porch steps creaked beneath our feet as we reached the top. Junie was still in full tour guide mode, bouncing from Cluck Norris to Uno to Rowdy like she owned the entire damn farm. I was about to ask her how many animals lived here when a horn honked down the gravel drive.

All three of us turned.

A sleek Range Rover rolled toward us, sunlight glinting off the windshield as it passed my sad little VW parked down by Violet's house.

Junie's face lit up, already bouncing on her toes. "That's Emmy!"

Of course it was.

Of course, Emmy drove a Range Rover.

Of course, she had her life together enough to own a car that cost more than my entire net worth.

The SUV crunched up the gravel, rolling to a stop near the farmhouse steps. My chest felt like someone had turned up the pressure valve, every stupid little imagined scenario I'd spent years building ready to pop.

The driver's door opened, but the woman who stepped out wasn't the cardigan-clad domestic goddess I'd pictured. Her short brown hair was piled into a messy little bun, and she wore an oversized Denver Yetis hoodie, black leggings, socks, and Birkenstock slides.

No cinnamon rolls.

No apron.

But the bright, easy smile on her face as she crossed the yard toward us? And the huge diamond on her hand?

Yeah. That fit the picture perfectly.

Junie tore off the porch, fleece pajamas flapping behind her like a flag, and launched herself at the woman with all the force of a small, enthusiastic tornado, just as she'd hugged me moments ago.

Emmy grinned, then kissed the top of her head. "Hey cowgirl. How did you know I needed a hug?"

Then her gaze lifted to me, and she crossed the remaining few feet with that same open smile.

"You must be Dizzy." Her hands opened as if the only

logical next step was to hug me too. "Junie hasn't stopped talking about you. I'm so, so glad you're here."

I hesitated for half a heartbeat, then stepped forward, not wanting to be rude to the people Junie loved. Her arms closed around me without a moment's hesitation, warm and solid and real. When her hand smoothed over my back in a motherly embrace, the weight of it all hit.

Every mile I'd driven.

Every hour I'd spent convincing myself this wasn't real.

The job I didn't care about, the eviction I probably should've seen coming, the call that cracked my world in half.

All of it stacked up, heavy and undeniable.

My sister wasn't going to be the next car to pull into the drive, the next one to hug her daughter.

Not now.

I sank into Emmy's hug, letting myself feel it—the first embrace from anyone other than Junie since the world tilted sideways.

For a second, it was too much.

Too warm.

Too kind.

"I'm so sorry about Violet," she said, her voice soft but sure.

"Me too," I managed, my voice rough. I stepped back, blinking fast, trying to patch myself together into something that didn't look like their next pitiful rescue animal unraveling on the porch.

Emmy Hudson wasn't the image I'd built in my head. She was *better*. Genuinely nice and impossible to hate. And that fucking sucked.

Over her shoulder, Ty stood on the porch, hands still shoved in his pockets, watching me. His expression didn't soften, but something flickered there when he saw my smile falter.

"C'mon," Emmy said, brushing a hand over Junie's head. "Did my brother make you pancakes? After that last Pilates class, I'm starving."

Brother.

My gaze snapped back to her, then to Ty, whose jaw flexed just enough to confirm it. All that imagined perfection—the slow-dancing, llama-fostering, apron-wearing wife? It cracked down the middle, leaving me feeling off balance.

Emmy wasn't his wife.

She was his *sister*.

And somehow, that might have been worse.

8

TY

My sister led Daisy into my house, the two women chatting as if they'd known each other far longer than the three minutes we'd been standing on my porch. Meanwhile, I stood there trying to reconcile the last thirty minutes of my life, because *what the fuck*.

Junie slipped her hand into mine and looked up with a grin I'd wanted to see so damn bad only an hour ago. It loosened something tight in my chest, even as everything else threatened to strangle me.

Once we stepped inside, I pointed to the bathroom off the entryway. "Go wash your hands for me."

She nodded, then skipped down the hall. Her little footsteps echoed against the walls as I walked toward the kitchen.

Daisy and Emmy were already sitting at the table side by side. Emmy had her hand over Daisy's, leaning in, her voice warm and easy as Daisy told her about driving through the night to get here. My sister had that effect on people—she made them feel at home before their shoes were even off.

"Where's your stuff?" I asked, and both women turned toward me.

From the way Emmy's mouth pressed into a flat line, I could tell I'd bulldozed straight past tact. But tact wasn't in my wheelhouse right now. *Sorry your sister died. I've thought about you for three years, never regretting anything more than walking away. Please don't take my kid away from me,* didn't fit into any conversation starter I knew.

Daisy tucked a piece of pale hair behind her ear. "Oh. Just one bag. I can unload it at Violet's house later when I take Junie home."

A low grunt rumbled out of my chest. "She's staying here."

"Ty." Emmy's voice was all warning, carrying a whole world of meaning behind just my name. Like that was all she needed to put me back in line. Normally, it would have worked. But this was Junie we were talking about, and her warning barely made a dent.

Sure, Daisy and I had shared our deepest, darkest secrets with each other three years ago. From those few hours together, I probably understood her better than most people. But I didn't *know* her.

Even more so, this was Junie we were talking about, and fear of the unknown had a chokehold on me. Gut-wrenching terror that tomorrow, a judge would say that little girl didn't belong with me, and they'd both disappear forever, just like Daisy had when she'd gotten on that elevator.

I leaned my hands against the counter, grounding myself on the cool marble. "The caseworker said she's staying here with me until the hearing," I said, quieter now but still firm.

Daisy opened her mouth to argue, and I held up a hand.

"I'm not kicking you out," I said. "But the court granted me temporary custody. She's *my* responsibility. If you want us to go down to Violet's house, fine. But I'm staying with her until I'm told otherwise."

Daisy's brows lifted, sharp against the mess of pale hair framing her face. She leaned back in her chair, arms crossed over her chest. "Is this how it's going to be? You're going to fight me on this in court tomorrow?"

"I'm going to do what's best for Junie," I said, mirroring her posture and crossing my arms. "And right now, I still think that's me."

For a moment, something flared between us, her exhaustion meeting my fear right in the middle of the kitchen. Then Daisy let out a disbelieving laugh and looked out the big picture window behind her.

Junie's feet slapped against the floor a second later, breaking the tension.

"I'm clean," she announced, holding up her hands as evidence. "Are there more pancakes?"

I ruffled her wild blonde hair as I walked to the oven. "Of course, there are."

I'd made extra on purpose—even on good days, Junie's eating was hit or miss. Berries? Yes. Anything green? Hard no. Only one brand of chicken nuggets was allowed in the house, and pancakes were her current obsession. I'd learned that over months of scraped plates, early mornings, and sitting at this same kitchen counter convincing her to take one more bite.

I knew these things not because a caseworker told me, but because I'd been here. I'd been her safe place for months of headaches and hospital stays. I'd been the one waiting with open arms to hug her after she said her last goodbye.

Daisy didn't know those things. Not yet.

I slid a pancake onto Junie's favorite purple plate and set it in front of her at the counter. She climbed onto her stool, ripped off a corner, and dipped it into the little syrup cup. The world might implode if any sauce touched her food before she deemed it worthy.

The weight of Daisy and Emmy's eyes prickled against the back of my neck, and I knew they were noticing everything.

How relaxed Junie was with me.

How she'd made this house hers months ago.

How none of this was temporary for me.

"She spends a lot of time here," Daisy said quietly.

Junie nodded around a mouthful of pancake. "I like Ty's house. I have my own room, and the bathtub is huge."

I finally turned to face Daisy. She wasn't looking at me anymore, but at the space around her—the big farmhouse kitchen I'd redone two years ago, trying to erase the bad memories of my childhood that clung to the old wallpaper. Wide windows facing the mountains. Warm wooden cabinets I'd installed myself. The hand-scraped floorboards that told a story of decades of Hudsons before me. Ones I had hoped to share with Junie for the next ten years.

Standing here now, anxiety crawled up my spine; every plan I'd made seemed too fragile to examine.

Tomorrow, it could all disappear.

Tomorrow, I might lose her.

Once Junie finished her pancakes and walked her plate over to the sink, the energy seemed to fade out of her. She grabbed her stuffed rabbit, then curled up on the couch. Rowdy followed her as if he too could feel the moment the weight of everything came crashing back down on my girl.

I stood at the kitchen sink, washing the last of the dishes until Emmy came and hip-checked me out of the way. "Go," she said in a low whisper meant only for me. "I'll do that, and you deal with"—she waved a hand at my whole body—"whatever this is."

"You just pointed at all of me."

"Yes, well, I'm currently deciding if I need to turn you into Body Snatchers, because what the fuck, Ty?"

I frowned down at my sister, trying to rein in my reaction. Because *what the fuck,* indeed.

Daisy left the table and went to my couch, sitting next to where June rested her head. With a gentle tap on her shoulder, she urged Junie onto her lap, then began brushing her fingers through her tangled mess of hair. "Should I tell you a story?" she asked.

Junie's little head bobbed, and she curled up tighter into a ball. "Yeah."

I leaned back against the counter, letting my sister take over the dishes, but didn't seem capable of moving. Daisy began a story about a family of bunnies that all had superpowers, each one more outrageous than the next. June didn't laugh when she was supposed to, but she did offer tidbits to the story when prompted, showing she was listening.

Watching them together made me catalog every similarity between them. Daisy's hair was a shade lighter than Junie's, but the waves were the same, soft and wild around their faces. They both had those same freckles dusting their noses, like the sun had marked them as its favorites. The same blue eyes, too—Daisy's older, Junie's softer—but capable of wrecking me in the same way.

While Junie felt mine in every way that mattered, it was obvious Daisy claimed a piece of her too.

Fuck.

The water shut off as Emmy finished rinsing the last of the dishes, then bumped the dishwasher closed with her hip. She wiped her hands on a towel and gave me that look—one part sister smug, one part *don't test me*. When she jerked her head toward the hallway, I followed her to the front door like an obedient idiot.

"Behave," she said, voice soft but deadly, like I was her unruly fifteen-year-old son instead of her thirty-seven-year-old brother. "Or else."

My brows shot up. "Or else, what?"

She crossed her arms, her mouth curving in a way that meant she was about to hit me where it hurt. She nodded toward the living room.

I followed her gaze.

Daisy and Junie were curled up together on my couch, both sound asleep. Daisy's head had fallen back against the cushion, mouth parted just slightly, one hand resting on Junie's back like it had always belonged there. Junie's limbs were thrown over Daisy's lap, socked toes dangling off the edge of the couch.

The sight slammed into me like a clean hit to the boards.

"You'll lose that, Ty," Emmy whispered. "You'll lose both of them."

The air left my lungs in one long, uneven exhale.

Emmy rose on tiptoe, kissed my cheek, and smacked the underside of my hat as she pulled away. The damn thing flew off my head and landed a few feet away on the entry rug. "Bye, jerk."

I huffed out something that might've been a laugh if my chest didn't feel so fucking tight. "Bye, pest."

When the door shut behind her, the house fell into the kind of quiet I'd always loved out here—soft, steady, mountain-quiet. Only this time, it wasn't comforting.

It was heavy.

Rowdy lifted his head from where he lay tangled between Junie's legs, ears twitching, then laid it back down, satisfied nothing required his attention.

I stepped farther into the living room, hat dangling from my hand, eyes locked on the couch.

Even asleep, Junie had one hand fisted in Daisy's sweatshirt, like she wasn't letting go. And Daisy... she looked like she wouldn't let her, either.

It shouldn't gut me the way it did. But it did.

Because she wasn't just Violet's sister.

She was the one Junie was supposed to grow up with; the only blood family she had left. And if the courts decided that's what was best for her—if Daisy wanted it—she'd be gone. Junie would leave this house. This life. *Me.*

The fear that had been simmering all day surged through my chest.

Junie fit with me like a puzzle piece I'd never realized was missing, and Daisy... shit, once upon a time, I thought maybe she did too.

Those few hours spent with her three years ago had lived rent-free in my mind since, always wondering if I'd made a mistake not chasing her up the elevator. But now, here she was, once again delivered to me, as if fate was screaming at me for messing up the first time.

I reached down and took off Junie's glasses, then dropped onto the armchair across from the couch, elbows on my knees, hat dangling from my fingers.

I should've been figuring out what to say to the judge tomorrow.

How to make sure Junie stayed here.

How to make them see I was her family, too.

Instead, I sat there like an idiot, watching two Winslow

girls sleep on my couch, and realized just how badly I didn't want to lose them.

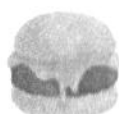

The girls dozed for several hours, Daisy slowly falling to the side and Junie inching up until she lay as the little spoon in front of her aunt. I threw a blanket over their legs and closed the blinds, trying to give them both the rest they needed.

I, however, couldn't rest. My mind raced in a thousand different directions, trying to think of ways I could beg everyone to see how much Junie and I loved each other. How desperate I was to be a part of that little girl's life.

My phone buzzed in my pocket, dragging me away from Junie and Daisy curled on the couch as if they had always belonged there. I backed down the hallway toward my room before pulling it out.

BECKETT

Checking on you. How's your favorite blondie?

TY

Which one?

BECKETT

Wow, that was easy to get you to admit.
Emmy says the aunt is a 10.

She also says you were rude and weird.
Story time, bro.

I pinched the bridge of my nose, cursing the fact that my sister was now engaged to and living with my best friend.

TY

Not a story.

BECKETT

Uh-huh. And I'm great at Pilates.

You don't get weird for no reason. Spill it.

I hesitated, staring down the hallway toward the living room. I'd never told anyone about Daisy, not even sure what I'd say.

TY

I met her once.

BECKETT

...

What the hell does "met her once" mean?

Oh shit, did you sleep with her?

TY

Jesus Christ, no. She's 10 years younger than me.

BECKETT

Mm, you're both adults now though. Age is just a number, buddy.

So if you didn't sleep with her, why the weird vibe?

TY

It was the night I retired.

We just walked around the city and talked. It didn't matter.

BECKETT

...Yeah, I can tell.

You've been sitting on this for three years?
Jesus, Huddy.

TY

Wasn't anything.

BECKETT

I love the smell of your bullshit.

TY

I didn't think I'd ever see her again.

BECKETT

Ohhh. So this is like soulmate shit. This is
so much better than I expected.

TY

Stop

BECKETT

Zero chance. This is prime-time level
drama. I need to tell the boys.

Mystery girl reappears, gorgeous, living
next door, practically family…

Pass me the fucking popcorn.

TY

I'm blocking you.

BECKETT

No you're not.

The wooden floorboards creaked beneath someone's feet coming down the hall, and I slid my phone back into my pocket, standing up. Daisy stood in the doorway to my bedroom, sleep-rumpled, soft, and unfairly beautiful. Her shirt hung off one shoulder, her hair a mess, and for one traitorous second, all I could think was how she looked like she belonged here.

"Sorry," she said, resting a hand on the doorframe. "I didn't mean to fall asleep."

I shook my head, trying to get my brain to focus. "You needed it. No need to apologize."

I stepped toward the hallway, but she lifted a hand, stopping me in my tracks.

"Wait."

She glanced over her shoulder at Junie sprawled in a tangle of blankets on the couch, then stepped inside and closed the door behind her. The soft click of the latch felt louder than it should have.

"We need to chat," she said.

I shoved my hands into my back pockets and forced a steady nod. "All right."

She exhaled as if she was steadying herself. "Tomorrow we have the custody hearing for Junie. But I need to know what the plan is for tonight."

"I already told you," I said. "You're welcome to stay here, or I'll come with you to Violet's house. But I'm not leaving Junie. Not tonight."

Something flickered across her face—surprise, maybe. Sadness, definitely. "Ty, I... I appreciate what you've done. I know this has been a lot. But just so we're on the same page, I intend to get custody of Junie tomorrow. She's my niece. I came here for her."

I clenched my jaw. "And I'll do whatever it takes to stay in her life, for as long as she wants me in it."

Her brows knit. "I don't get it. I mean... you're not family."

My breath punched out rough, the words sharper than a blade. "I've been here." The words came out too harsh, edged with everything I'd kept inside. "For *months*. How many nights do you think she's slept in that room down the hall while Violet was in the hospital? How many mornings have I made her breakfast? How many days have I driven her to school or brought her to practice with me or stayed up when she couldn't sleep because she was worried her mom was dying?"

Her lips parted, but nothing came out.

"It's been *me*," I bit out, hating how emotional I sounded. "I've been fighting for her before there was even a fight."

The silence that followed was heavy with grief. Daisy's eyes shimmered, like she was holding it all in by the skin of her teeth. And why wouldn't she be? We wouldn't even be having this conversation if her sister weren't gone.

I hadn't meant for it to sound like an attack, but fear had a way of sharpening everything. Of turning the truth into something that could wound.

"Daisy—" I started, her name rough in my throat.

She shook her head, swallowing hard. "I just... I need a second," she whispered, and looked away.

The air between us buzzed with everything neither of us knew how to fix.

She was grieving for her sister.

I was terrified of losing Junie.

And this—whatever this undeniable *thing* was between us —had nowhere to land.

"Daisy," I tried again. "I didn't mean for it to come out like that. None of this is simple. Losing Violet..." I dragged a hand over my jaw, trying to find the right words and failing. "It's heavy. For all of us."

She let out a sharp, disbelieving laugh that caught at the edges. "You think I don't know that?"

Her voice cracked open, raw and loud in the stillness of my room. "Violet was my sister, Ty. *My sister.* And now I'm supposed to figure out how to be a parent while I can barely wrap my head around the fact that she's not here. Junie is literally it. She's all I have left. And yeah, I wasn't here before, but I am now. And I'm *not* leaving her alone."

Her words hit like body blows. Not because they were unfair, but because they were true.

There was no bad guy in this. Just two people standing in the wreckage of someone else's life, trying to grab hold of what was left.

"Fine," I said, because I didn't know what else to say.

"Fine," she echoed, chin lifting stubbornly.

The air between us burned, hot and brittle, both of us too strung out to soften.

I blew out a breath. "I'll show you to the guest room."

"Fine."

"*Fine.*"

When she didn't move, I stared at her, jaw tight. "Might be easier to open the door if you got out of the way."

Her eyes narrowed, but she stepped aside without a word, crossing her arms as I opened the door and walked out into the hallway. I led her to the guest room—the one right next to my master suite.

She stepped inside, scanning the space. It wasn't much, just a clean, simple room. A big bed. A dresser. Warm light spilled in from the windows overlooking the mountains.

"I can grab your bag," I offered. "And move your car up."

Her spine straightened, shoulders squaring like I'd insulted her without even trying. "I can handle it."

"Wasn't saying you couldn't."

"Good."

"Great."

She brushed past me, the scent of her fruity shampoo still

clinging to the air she left behind, and stalked down the hallway toward the front door. I stood there a second longer than I should have, staring at the empty doorway.

The night had grown quiet outside, giving way to dusk. In the stretch of silence only filled by the wind in the trees just outside the window, realization hit me square in the chest.

This wasn't just a custody hearing tomorrow. This was a battle nobody wanted, but both of us refused to lose.

And I had no idea who would still be standing at the end of it.

9

Daisy

My leg bounced, my sneaker squeaking against the floor of the county courthouse with every jittery tap.

"Daisy."

Ty's voice was low enough that it vibrated through me. His hand landed on my thigh—firm, warm, and far too distracting—and pressed down just enough to still me.

"Sorry," I muttered, shoving his hand away before he noticed how fast my pulse was racing.

The courthouse smelled of lemon polish, the walls lined with wood paneling from another era. Sunlight streamed through tall, narrow windows, catching floating specks of dust in the air.

Last night had been tense. I could tell Ty was nervous about today, and I sure as hell was. Until this moment, I'd somehow managed not to think too hard about the legal side of Violet's death and becoming Junie's guardian. In my head, it was simple: Violet left a Will, my name was on it, and we'd sign a few papers before heading off to whatever new life came next.

Except—what *was* next?

No job. No apartment in Chicago. Just a car that smelled like fast food and desperation. I hadn't even packed—just left a sticky note with my address on the bedroom door. After everything Lauren had put me through, she could handle the rest.

And I definitely didn't have anywhere for Junie as stable as Ty's beautiful farmhouse. My mom died when I was Junie's age, and I hardly remembered the logistics of everything that came after. We'd scraped by on Dad's single salary until he'd decided we weren't his responsibility anymore. Then, it was just me and Violet.

Life had made me scrappy, good at getting by in a pinch. But would the courts see that as a positive? Or would it just look like I was far too unpredictable to be a guardian?

My leg started bouncing again, the squeaking resuming like a countdown clock.

I stared down at my high-tops with little daisies painted on the sides, dirty from years of wear. "Why didn't I pack anything else?"

"Hmm?" Ty said. He sat next to me in a bespoke suit, looking like he'd just come off a GQ magazine shoot for *Man of the Year.*

"Nothing," I mumbled. It wasn't like I was about to confess that his stupid mustache and steady presence were making me spiral in too many directions.

After I figured out who the mysterious Huddy was, I'd scoured the internet for any trace of him. There were plenty of press photos in suits back when he was in the NHL, but real life was different. The fabric framed him just right, accentuating how broad his shoulders were. He looked clean and composed under the slant of sunlight from those courthouse windows. And he had definitely combed his mustache.

In comparison, I looked like a *before* photo from those

pitiful makeover shows from the early 2000s. Jeans with a coffee stain from last week. A wrinkled Foreigner T-shirt. Hair that had chosen violence after drying without all of my expensive products I'd left behind in Chicago. Everything about me screamed *unemployed and unprepared.*

If I'd been the one on the judge's stand, looking down at us, I knew who I'd pick. After all, this wasn't just some procedural box to check.

This was *real.*

I was about to walk through those doors and convince strangers I was fit to raise a child. To parent an eight-year-old.

I wasn't ready for that.

I wasn't even ready to think about *why* all of this was happening.

My hands shook, only in part from the energy drinks I'd pounded this morning. "Holy shit," I whispered.

Ty turned his head toward me. "What?"

"I'm going to be her guardian," I said, the words slipping out. "I don't even have on matching socks."

He didn't laugh. He didn't try to fix it with some big speech. He just said, quiet and steady, "She loves you."

And shit, how did he know the right thing to say? Just like three years ago when he'd stood on the beach, fingers tangled in my hair, telling me to be brave exactly when I needed to hear it.

But today, I didn't feel brave.

No, today I was terrified and sad and lonely and a hundred other emotions I didn't want to inspect. Instead, I let out a shaky breath. "Love isn't a parenting qualification."

"It's a good start. You'll figure it out."

His voice was so calm it almost made me angry. Because I didn't feel like I would *figure it out.* When there was a kid depending on me, time was a luxury I didn't have.

"Breathe," he said, somehow sensing I'd forgotten that was important.

I let out a big exhale, gaze fixed on the double doors ahead. "I'm just preparing for them to hand you full custody and send me packing."

His head tilted my way. I didn't have to look to feel his steady, infuriatingly patient gaze. "You don't know that."

"No," I said. "I don't. But what if my good luck was that my car didn't die coming over Vail Pass? We both know there was *a lot* of luck involved in that. So then, is this the part where everything else comes crashing down? One: my tragic wardrobe. Two: my tragic *everything else*. Three: some horrific, unforeseen circumstance I don't even have the brainpower to conjure right now. Are plagues still a thing?"

"You look fine," Ty said, looking straight ahead.

I huffed out a laugh. "I look like I'm here for a restraining order instead of a custody hearing."

His jaw flexed, hands shoved into his pockets. "You're family. From everything I've read, that will go a long way."

That made me pause. From everything he'd read?

How much time had Ty spent researching family court? Obviously, he'd gone through the steps to be foster certified, and it was clear he loved my niece, but I still didn't understand the full story between them.

How she looked at him. Why his house already felt like hers.

I opened my mouth to ask, but the doors creaked open and a bailiff stepped into the hall.

"Daisy Winslow and Tyler Hudson. The judge will see you now."

I stood so fast that the room spun. Sensing my distress, Ty

grabbed my elbow, and together we walked through the double doors.

Inside, the courtroom felt too small for the magnitude of the moment. I took a seat at a table meant for attorneys I'd only ever seen on TV, surrounded by papers, files, and words like *placement* and *temporary custody* hanging in the air.

Ty sat beside me, calm as a granite statue. I tried to channel that energy, but the closest I could get was a tornado about to touch down.

"Ms. Winslow," the judge said, looking at me over his reading glasses. "I understand you arrived from Chicago yesterday?"

I nodded, hands clasped in my lap. "Yes."

The caseworker flipped through a file. "She's listed as next of kin and guardian nominee in Violet Winslow's Will."

There it was—my name attached to something heavy. I should've felt anchored by it. Instead, it felt like I was going to pass out, because *oh shit, my sister had a Will because she—*

"Ms. Winslow," the judge continued, "we have a few questions regarding custody of your niece, Juniper Winslow. I'll hand it over to Sandra Diaz, your appointed caseworker."

I nodded, the motion feeling a little violent I was breathing so hard. As if sensing my distress, Ty's hand found mine under the table and slid into mine. Our fingers laced together, just like they had three years ago when that car had almost hit me. It shouldn't have steadied me as much as it did, but something about him always seemed to make my racing mind slow down.

The caseworker tapped her papers on the table, then smiled at me. "Thank you for getting here so fast. It's important to us that we do whatever we can to keep families together. I'm sure Juniper was glad to see you."

That sounded nice, but I didn't dare let the tension out of my shoulders, waiting for the other shoe to drop.

"Can you tell us about your current housing arrangements?"

Well, that didn't take long. "I—uh—don't have... arrangements."

Her brow lifted, then she jotted something down on the paper in front of her.

I kept going before she could. "Chicago was home until about 48 hours ago, when my roommate ended my lease right before I got the news of"—my mouth went dry, unable to say the words *my sister's death* aloud—"the news. I grabbed what I could reach and left."

"I see," Sandra said, which sounded a lot like *Strike One*. "And employment?"

One word made me want to sink through the floor, but instead I plastered on the fakest smile I'd ever worn. "I'm between jobs."

That was the polite way of saying unemployed with a savings account as healthy as a six-day-old banana.

She nodded, then jotted some more, likely checking off boxes on a *Reasons Daisy is a Disaster* list.

"What about my sister's house?" I looked at the judge, pleading with him not to dismiss me so fast. "My Aunt Maggie left it to us, so my name should be on the deed. Does that count as housing?"

He looked at Sandra, who put her pen down. As bad as her pen scratching across the paper was, this felt *worse*. "You're correct, yes. Our office visited the property this weekend to collect some of Juniper's belongings for Mr. Hudson. Unfortunately, the house is under extensive renovation. In its current state, by Colorado law, it is unsafe for a child. The kitchen needs to be gutted due to water damage. There is only one livable bedroom. But the real problem is the exposed wiring in just about every room."

I blinked. "Wait. What?"

"Apologies. I assumed you'd already seen it."

"No, not the inside yet. I stayed with Ty"—I winced at the judge—"Mr. Hudson."

The judge's expression stayed neutral, and that didn't feel great either.

Sandra looked up at the judge, a sad smile on her face. "Given the current state of the home and the lack of other established housing, we're classifying Ms. Winslow as unsafe for placement today."

The breath whooshed out of me.

Just like that, I wasn't enough.

Wasn't qualified for this.

I'd failed my sister in ways I never had before.

I'd failed *Junie.*

"Please," I begged, hardly recognizing my voice when it came out so weak. "She's all I have left."

My eyes burned with unshed tears, but I refused to let them fall. "My mom. My aunt. My apartment. My job. My sis —my..."

The word got stuck in my throat, unable to keep going. A tear tracked down my cheek anyway, and I brushed it away, furious it had the audacity to expose how fragile I felt in this moment.

"I can't lose Junie. I love her more than anyone on this earth, and—" My breath hitched. "I'll figure it out. I promise."

I glanced sideways at Ty, expecting him to gloat after his hard stance last night. Instead, his brow furrowed, his hand tightening in mine. He didn't look surprised—but he did look worried.

"The timing of all of this feels unfortunate," the judge said. "It's almost always in the best interest to keep families together. Despite your circumstances, I don't see a reason to keep her from you, Ms. Winslow."

I breathed a sigh of relief, wiping at my cheeks again, giving him a gentle nod.

"But I also can't dismiss the situation," the judge continued, offering me a sad smile. I was getting sick of those. "The court will continue Juniper's temporary placement with Mr. Hudson."

The words hit harder than I expected.

"However," he added, and my heart snagged on the word, "per Violet Winslow's last Will and Testament, she formally nominated both you and Mr. Hudson as co-guardians of Juniper."

The words seemed to echo in the too-small courtroom.

"The court gives considerable weight to a parent's expressed wishes," the judge continued. "While a will does not automatically transfer legal custody, it is clear Ms. Winslow intended for both of you to play active roles in her daughter's life. Given Mr. Hudson's established relationship with Juniper and Ms. Winslow's status as next of kin, the court finds a shared temporary guardianship arrangement appropriate at this time."

I frowned, staring over at Ty, trying to process the fact that my sister had named him alongside me. Sure, he'd gotten foster certified—maybe even preparing for something like this—but for Violet to have formally nominated him?

That meant she hadn't been guessing.

She'd been planning.

Ty looked just as stunned as I felt, but the judge continued.

"As such, the court will grant temporary co-guardianship to both of you, effective immediately. Juniper's primary physical placement will remain with Mr. Hudson for the time being, due to the stability of his housing and employment."

The words still stung.

"Ms. Winslow," he said, turning to me, "you will remain in Linwood for the next six weeks while background checks, home evaluations, and the primary caregiver assessment are completed."

That caught my attention. "Six weeks?"

The caseworker nodded. "That is the standard review period. You'll need to be available for home visits and to participate consistently in Juniper's daily life. The goal is continuity for Juniper during this time of grief and to determine whether a transition to your primary custody is appropriate."

"She'll be living with me?" I asked before I could stop myself.

"Given your current housing situation, Juniper will remain placed with Mr. Hudson," the judge clarified, "but your involvement will be active and ongoing. Regular visitation, shared decision-making, and cooperative planning between the two of you. If your housing and employment stabilize, the court will revisit permanent placement at the six-week review hearing."

Beside me, Ty's posture shifted—shoulders straightening, chin lifting. While I sat there trying not to hyperventilate, he looked steady. Not smug. Not triumphant.

Just ready.

"Bi-weekly check-ins," the caseworker added. "No overnight removal from Eagle County without prior authorization. The two of you will be expected to work together to create a plan that serves Juniper's best interest. She is a grieving child who has lost her mother. Keeping her in a familiar environment, with the people she already trusts, is critical right now. And Ms. Winslow—this is your opportunity to demonstrate stability."

My jaw clenched. *Demonstrate stability.* I wanted to tell her stable didn't mean happy. Last week I had a roof over my head and a job that paid me okay, but I'd never been more miserable.

Well, *now* I couldn't say that, because it turned out I could, in fact, be more miserable. But none of that mattered right now.

The judge looked between us. "Questions?"

I shook my head because nothing else I said would make a difference.

We signed papers until my signature looked like a toddler's scribble.

Outside, the sun was too bright. The air too cheerful. I stopped on the courthouse steps, gripping the railing as if the ground might give out beneath me.

Ty paused a step below me, sunlight slanting across his face. Something about the way he looked at me made my chest tighten. It wasn't pity or smugness. Just that quiet steadiness and concern that both grounded me and made me want to throw something at him.

"Are you okay?" he asked.

I laughed, sharp and too loud. "Oh, sure. Everything's great. I have no house, no job, a sister that"—I swallowed down the word I couldn't say—"and I just found out I'm co-parenting with you."

His mouth twitched as if he was trying not to smile. "So I'm number four then? Lucky number?"

I rolled my eyes and took a breath that didn't do a damn

thing to calm me down. "Did you know my sister's house was *uninhabitable*?"

"I've been inside your sister's house less than a handful of times."

I frowned, even more confused why my sister had named him in her Will. "So how does this even work? I live next door in the construction zone? See Junie every other weekend? On the third Thursday of the month?"

Ty sighed, then brushed a hand across his mustache. "You live with me."

My head jerked back. "What?"

His gaze stayed fixed on the mountains, like it was easier to look at the horizon than at me. "You stay in the guest room, and we just... figure it out. That's what Junie will want."

"I'm not living with you," I argued, because my brain was already flashing red warning lights. "I can't do that."

"Why not?" he asked, finally looking at me.

I made a helpless noise somewhere between a laugh and a groan. "Because it's—you're"—I gestured at him—"*you.*"

He raised a brow. "Me."

"Yes, *you.* The guy with the house and the savings account and the whole good-citizen thing. You look like you're an advertisement for responsible adults, while I look like I crawled out of a Goodwill bin."

Ty said nothing. He just stood there, steady as ever. Which, frankly, annoyed me.

I threw up my hands. "What happened to doing things for yourself, Huddy? That was the plan, right? But now you have a savior complex, rescuing injured puppies, one-eyed llamas, and jobless, homeless, pathetic aunts."

He came up one step, then another, closing the distance

until my breath caught in my throat. I had to tip my chin up to meet his eyes, the world shrinking around us.

The sun was at his back, warm light catching in his hair, framing him like some kind of maddening, golden-hour cowboy fantasy. He was close enough that I could smell the faint trace of soap on his skin, the clean heat of him curling around the edges of my nerves.

"You're not pathetic, Daisy." His voice dropped low, quiet enough that the words landed like a hand against my sternum. "I just spent an hour in a courthouse discovering how resilient you are with every piece of your story that unfolded. And yet, you haven't let even one aspect of your struggles dim your light. Who better to teach Junie how to dance in the rain?"

My breath hitched.

Everything around me faded in the distance until all I could feel was him. His height, his warmth, his stupid, quiet steadiness pressing in on me.

Too close. Too much. And yet I didn't step back.

This was the problem. Three years ago, our connection was instant. Undeniable chemistry that went beyond physical attraction. Every time I remembered him, it wasn't how hot he was, although that didn't hurt either. But it was everything *else* I couldn't forget.

Maybe it was because that silly game of Truth or Dare had us laying our insecurities out to dry, baring the parts we'd shown no one else. Or maybe it was something else entirely.

No matter what it was, time hadn't done a damn thing to lessen it.

I was too drawn to him, and this living arrangement would be six weeks of *complicated* I wasn't prepared for.

"You're awfully poetic for a guy who wears cowboy boots to court."

He smirked, slow and infuriating, then leaned forward to whisper in my ear, "Don't tell anyone."

I let out a snort I didn't mean to. And just like that, the weight pressing down on my chest lightened.

He turned toward the parking lot. "Come on. Emmy's waiting. Junie'll be ready to go."

Junie. The world snapped back into focus, reminding me why I was standing here trying so hard not to unravel.

I followed him down the courthouse steps and to his truck, my heart still hammering against my ribs.

Six weeks of this.

Six weeks of trying not to stare.

Six weeks of pretending that spark didn't exist.

Shit.

10

TY

The highway stretched ahead of us, cutting through the Vail Valley in long ribbons as it curved alongside the Eagle River. I cracked the windows of my old truck, letting the early summer wind and the sharp scent of pine rush in. A radio station out of Glenwood Springs hummed low, classic rock filling the cab as background noise meant to break up the quiet tension.

Daisy angled toward the window, golden hair whipping loose around her face. She closed her eyes, lashes resting against her cheeks, pulling whatever peace she could from the air. And after everything she'd just revealed about her life in that court-room, I couldn't blame her.

So much loss.

So much hurt.

So much pain I didn't think she showed anyone.

When her hair whipped forward again, I reached behind me, grabbed my Mayhem hat from the back seat, and dropped it onto her head. "Here."

Her eyes flew open—blue and startled beneath the bill. I

felt her gaze settle on me, heavy and searching, clocking the way I'd stepped in again without being asked.

Unfortunately, because of how our story began, she already knew this about me. I acted first. Helped first. Gave first. Then hated myself for expecting anything back.

What she didn't know was that I couldn't stop myself—especially not with her—even if I tried.

A careful smile tugged at her mouth, small and restrained. She pulled her hair through the snapback and twisted it into a loose ponytail. "Thanks."

I kept my eyes locked on the road, not trusting myself to say more after the morning we'd just survived. And hell—she looked good like this. Jeans. A T-shirt. Wind-tousled hair. My hat.

Too good.

No matter how inconvenient, Daisy Winslow had burrowed under my skin the second she challenged me to Truth or Dare three years ago.

Back then, energy spilled out of her, reckless and bright—laughing too loud, dancing in the street, singing as if she dared life to keep up.

This Daisy carried herself differently. Quieter. Dimmed. Life hadn't just worn her down; it had taken pieces and never given them back.

She turned back to the window, arms crossing over her chest, shutting me out again.

I was used to silence—I chose it often enough myself—but this one twisted something restless in my chest, the urge to do something, *be* something, that might pull her back from wherever she'd gone.

I tightened my grip on the steering wheel.

Six weeks of living together was going to be a problem.

A blonde-haired, blue-eyed, impossible to ignore problem.

The radio crackled with static, then slid into Blondie's *Call Me.*

From the corner of my eye, I watched Daisy's fingers start tapping against her leg. A moment later, she sang along under her breath. Her voice sounded more cautious than I remembered, but it filled the cab anyway. When the chorus hit, she sang louder, clinging to the rhythm as if it could hold her up.

I glanced at her again, hoping for a glimpse of the girl who'd spun circles around me, dancing in the street.

She caught me. "What?"

"Nothing," I said. "Didn't take you for a Blondie fan."

Her mouth tilted, that almost-smile again. "The Foreigner shirt didn't give me away? I love your Grandpa rock."

My lip twitched, barely holding back a smile at that familiar bite. "Oh, we're back to this then?"

"You're still old, right, Daddy?"

"Jesus Christ," I muttered. "Don't say that."

This time she chuckled, and it was the most genuine sound I'd heard from her all day. "I love classic rock, though. Blondie. Stevie Nicks. ZZ Top. Genesis. And *Magnum P.I.*–era Tom Selleck, obviously."

I huffed out a laugh, shaking my head. "I wondered when this would come up."

Her grin flashed quick and sharp, dimples cutting into her cheeks. "Have you kept the mustache all this time? Or did I time my arrival just right to witness it again?"

The back of my neck warmed. Damn her for remembering. "I don't know what you're talking about."

"Oh, shit." She turned toward me, one leg folding up onto the bench seat between us, eyebrows lifting beneath my hat. "You *kept* it, didn't you?"

This time I looked out the window, avoiding her. "Turns out you were right. A duster is a good look for me."

"I can't believe I've missed out on three years of this." She waved a hand at my face, then let out a slow sigh and turned back toward the window.

I flicked a glance at her, then back at the road. If she only knew how often I'd replayed our goodbye—how many times I'd wondered what might've happened if I hadn't walked away.

We drove the rest of the way back to Linwood in an easy silence. Daisy knew every song on the radio and sang along, soft at first, then louder when she forgot to be self-conscious. The music seemed to smooth the sharp edges, unwinding the tight coil in her shoulders, until she resembled the woman I'd met years ago.

If I didn't know better, I never would've guessed her life had just been upended.

The *Welcome to Linwood* sign came into view when I exited the highway, painted in cheerful blues and greens. We rolled down River Street, mountains wrapping close on every side. The storefronts lined up in mismatched colors, looking a mix of modern amenities and the remnants of a Western mining town. We didn't have much—a grocery store, a coffee shop, a bar, a restaurant, an outfitter, and Emmy's Pilates studio—but it was just enough.

Hudson Hardware sat at the center of it all—barn red with crisp white lettering, the double doors thrown open to the summer air. Hanging planters spilled ivy and bright yellow pansies out front, just like my dad had always done.

Linwood in summer meant the mountains turned green, the air smelled like pine and river water, and the rink stayed just cold enough to keep the heartbeat of the town going. Even nestled in the Vail Valley, we weren't a ski town—not really. We were a *hockey* town.

Beckett and I had taken over coaching the Mayhem last fall, two former players trying to give these kids the same sense of home we'd found on the ice. After bringing back the town's first state championship in over a decade, I finally felt like I belonged here. Like this was my home.

Daisy's gaze flicked from storefront to storefront as we drove through. For a second, I wondered if she saw it the way I did—not just a town, but a sanctuary.

She leaned back against the headrest, finally looking at ease, and I couldn't bring myself to look away.

By the time we turned onto my sister's street, the afternoon light stretched across the neighborhood, soft and golden.

Emmy's house sat at the end of the block—a little two-story place with light-blue siding and white trim, the porch just big enough for a rocking chair and a hanging basket. The matching detached garage sat at the end of the driveway, a basketball hoop bolted to its side. Before we even turned into the drive, the sounds of my crew carried through the open windows.

Beckett had Junie perched on his shoulders, the two of them standing at the top of the driveway.

Jace, Emmy's son, stood next to them with a basketball in his hands.

Silas "Smash" Delgado, one of the Mayhem's defensemen, stood under the hoop with a sly smirk on his face.

Miles "Pickles" Claussen, our goalie, was off to the side with his hands cupped around his mouth, heckling non-stop.

Molly Morreau, our star center, sat in a lawn chair like a queen, calling out shots into a red megaphone. "Okay, your turn, Juice. These two idiots are done, so we're down to you and Junie-Girl. Spin around three times, under the leg, off the garage, into the hoop."

Jace groaned, but bounced the ball twice. "Why did we say you could call the shots? That's not possible."

Junie grinned wide, then leaned down and whispered in Beckett's ear. My best friend held a hand above his head, and she slapped her little palm into it, the two of them already scheming.

"I swear, you're evil," Jace said to Molly, then attempted her instructions. He spun, bounced, and threw the ball, aiming right for the garage siding. Unfortunately for him, it bounced off in the wrong direction, not making the hoop.

"That was embarrassing for all of us," Molly called through the megaphone. "I award you no points."

Jace shook his head, then passed the ball to Beckett.

"Think we can do it?" Beckett said, looking up at Junie above him. He was six-foot-four, so she sat high in the sky, her little face as serious as I'd ever seen it. She gave him a brief nod, and Beckett grinned.

He bent at the knees, then bounced the ball twice, focusing on the hoop. Without waiting, he wrapped one hand around Junie's leg draped over his shoulder, then spun. She squealed in delight, hanging onto his shaggy hair as he bounced the ball between his legs, then passed the ball up to her. Junie held it just right, as if they'd been practicing this, and tossed the ball over his head. It sailed through the air, bounced once off the garage siding, once on the rim, and miraculously dropped in.

"HORSE!" Pickles whooped. "They've got two points on you. You're outta here!"

Delgado threw his hands in the air. "You can't use the kid as an extension of your own height. That's cheating!"

"Maybe if you'd grown in the last six years, you could be a little HOR too," Miles shot back.

That earned him a glare, and about two seconds' warning before Delgado launched himself at him. The two of them went down into the grass, wrestling with shouts about "goalie interference" and "unsportsmanlike conduct."

Molly didn't even flinch, lifting the megaphone again. "Two minutes for excessive whining."

The second I stepped out of the truck, the noise from the driveway shifted fast.

"Holy crap," Delgado said, pointing at me as if I'd grown another head. "He's wearing real clothes."

Miles picked his head up from where he lay pinned underneath Delgado, grass sticking to his wild hair. "Where's your hat? I need you to tip your head down—we have a bet going on whether you're bald under there."

Jace squinted down at my feet. "Are those the same boots, though?"

"You look like a finance bro at a parent-teacher conference," Molly added with a smirk.

"Oh dang, he *does,*" Delgado said.

Beckett shoved his hands into his gym shorts pockets. "You just lost so much aura, bro. Watch and learn how to have rizz all nonchalant."

The kids all groaned, throwing anything they could find at Beckett as he laughed.

"Never again," Molly called through her megaphone. "You've lost speaking privileges for a week, Coach."

I dragged a hand over my neatly trimmed mustache. "You're all hilarious."

Junie slid off Beckett's shoulders and sprinted over,

throwing her arms around my waist. I ruffled her hair, my chest loosening the way it always did around this crew.

"Hey, bug," I said. "You take Smash down?"

She tilted her chin up, those too-big front teeth showing in her wide grin. "Yeah, I did."

"I swear, she's got better aim than half the team," Beckett said. "We need to get you on the ice, Rookie. Wanna come to the rink with us tomorrow and try it out?"

Junie shook her head, then looked back at Beckett. "No skating, but I want to go."

I was glad I still had my head tipped down so only she saw my smile. This kid was something else. The way she advocated for what she was and wasn't comfortable with? Fuck, I loved that. "Rookie, huh?"

She looked back up at me with that big, toothy grin. "They said I need a nickname if I want to be on the team someday."

I nodded, then looked at Jace. "Is your mom inside?"

My nephew glanced at the back door into Emmy's kitchen. "Yeah."

"Rook!" Miles shouted from the grass, still pinned under Delgado. "Come tickle him!"

Junie sprinted across the lawn, and Delgado let out a high-pitched squeal the second her little fingers hit his ribs.

"Go for the neck," Molly drawled from her chair, sounding bored.

Miles wriggled free, flipping positions and holding Delgado down by the shoulders while Junie kept tickling the poor kid like a pint-sized agent of chaos. Smash laughed so hard he started snorting, and it set Junie off too.

Damn, I loved this.

After I retired, there'd been a hole in my life I couldn't seem to fill. I'd come home expecting to work alongside my dad at the hardware store, fixing what had frayed between us by meeting him where he'd always been happiest.

Instead, Dad had a heart attack and left the store to me, packed up his life, and moved to Arizona with Mom. Just like that, I went from son to caretaker—of the business, of the legacy—without ever getting the chance to be either alongside him.

I should have known they didn't need me. Didn't *want* me.

But then Beckett came home last fall and signed us both up to coach the Mayhem. These loud, chaotic kids stormed in and gave me more purpose, more joy, than I could ever repay.

Coaching them, watching them grow, being a part of something again—this was my home. My family. My legacy.

When Daisy didn't come forward, I glanced back at the truck. She stood by the passenger door, my hat still perched on her head, watching the whole circus with wide eyes.

I raised a brow. "Last time I checked, daisies weren't wallflowers."

Every head in the driveway snapped toward her like I'd just dropped a puck. Delgado propped himself up on his elbows, grass in his hair and a grin spreading across his tan face.

"Oh, shit," he said. "Coach brought a little Ten to practice."

In unison, Beckett and I said, "Language."

Daisy's eyebrows shot up at "Ten," but the corners of her mouth twitched. She shoved her hands into her back pockets and gave me a look that was equal parts unimpressed and amused.

Junie sprinted toward Daisy to wrap her in the same rib-crushing hug she'd given me. "This is Dizzy!"

Miles fixed his glasses with the back of his hand, leaving a streak of bright green grass smeared across the bridge. He wiped his palms on his jeans, then lifted a hand in a sheepish wave.

"Hey," he said with a crooked grin. "I'm Miles Claussen, but they call me Pickles. Cuz of my last name. Claussen Pickles? Everyone has nicknames. Jace is Juice, and Delgado is Smash, and Molly is uh… Molly."

Molly groaned, shaking her head at his awkward introduction, and I fought to keep a straight face as Pickles' ears turned bright red.

Before Daisy could react, Delgado popped to his feet, brushed grass off his shorts, and spread his arms wide. "C'mere, Ten. I'm a hugger."

I stepped in and shoved him in the chest before he got too close. "Dial it back, Fabio."

"Coach," Delgado laughed, stumbling a step but not losing the grin.

From her lawn chair, Molly didn't even look up. "You're all idiots."

"Beckett," my best friend said, hand out to shake. She took it, and Beckett's grin widened, staring at me over her shoulder before looking back at her. "You must be Daisy. Welcome to Linwood."

The moment he released her, Junie grabbed Daisy by the hand, tugging her toward the group.

Jace, however, didn't join the chaos.

My nephew hung back near me, arms crossed, his gaze flicking between me, Daisy, and Junie. That look on his face wasn't just teenage attitude—it was the quiet wariness you learn when people leave. His dad was a piece of shit, and Jace had learned early not to count on anyone sticking around. Beckett had been working to repair that over the last six months, but I knew Jace loved Junie like she was his sister. I could see it written all over his face: the fear she might get pulled away.

Damn, I felt it too.

I squeezed his shoulder, leaning in to murmur, "Be nice."

He said nothing, but he didn't shrug me off either.

"Alright, Rookie's aunt," Molly said, sitting forward just enough to be heard. "Your turn."

Daisy blinked. "My turn?"

"Yeah." Molly pointed toward the hoop. "Spin around three times, between the legs, bank it off the garage, nothing but net. Winner takes all."

Delgado whooped, then passed her the ball. "Ten's up!"

Daisy reached for it and immediately fumbled the damn thing. It slipped through her hands, bounced off her knee, and she scrambled to catch it before it hit the ground. She finally snatched it out of the air, cheeks flushed, but smiling.

She bent toward Junie. "Okay, *Rookie*. No promises. But you did it, so maybe I can too."

Junie clapped her hands as if this was the most exciting moment of her life.

Beckett stared right at me, a smug look on his face.

Oblivious to it all, Daisy took a deep breath, spun around twice, and attempted to bounce the ball between her legs. Instead of bouncing back toward her hands, the ball launched forward like a cannon shot—not at the garage, not at the hoop —but at Delgado's chest.

It nailed him with a solid *thump*, knocking the air out of him.

He stumbled back, gasping, "I'm—fine!"

Molly grinned. "Honestly, that's a better outcome than I ever hoped for."

The kids howled with laughter. When Daisy was sure

Delgado was okay, she laughed too, hands on her hips, chin on her chest. The late afternoon sun hit her hair just right, turning the loose strands around her face into gold. She was flushed, a little windblown, completely unpolished, and the most beautiful woman I'd ever seen.

The back door creaked open, and Emmy stepped out, looking unsurprised by the chaos. She grinned at Daisy and said, "I see you've met the world's worst welcoming committee. Sandwiches are ready inside."

In a damn near Pavlovian response, the boys stampeded toward the door. Queen Molly strolled in among her jesters, knowing they'd give her whatever she asked for.

Junie tugged Daisy's hand as they followed. She glanced back at me, cheeks still pink from laughing, a spark in her eyes that cut straight through whatever defenses I had left.

"Coach, huh? It fits."

I tilted my head toward the hoop. "Keep playing like that, and I might start giving you drills."

Daisy's grin curved slow and wicked before she said, "Good thing I follow directions well, then."

The words landed low, soft but pointed. Immediately, my mind jumped to all the scenarios where I could test out that claim, and my dick gave a quick, traitorous twitch in my pants.

Fuck.

I reached up to fiddle with my hat, only now remembering *she* still wore it. My hand dropped uselessly to my side before I shoved it into my pocket, heat crawling up the back of my neck.

A low whistle sounded behind me right before Beckett's hand clapped down on my shoulder. "Well, this is a fun new development."

"Shut the fuck up," I said, but the words didn't have a bite to them.

Beckett laughed, then we walked inside my sister's house.

Daisy was in the kitchen hugging my sister, and I just stood there and stared. For one stupid second, I felt just as bashful and off-kilter as my team.

She looked right at home in my world, and for the first time, I had to face the truth: no matter how bad our timing was, I didn't just want to take care of her for the next six weeks.

I *wanted* her.

And maybe I always would.

11

Daisy

Emmy's kitchen was bright and wild—magenta cabinets, hand-painted mugs, mismatched dishes—but it was the island that stopped me short.

Three neat pyramids of subs sat on a massive platter: ham, turkey, and a third no one seemed interested in. A basket of chips, a tray of fruit, another of cookies, and a case of Gatorade rounded it out.

"That is a lot of sandwiches," I murmured to Junie.

Apparently, the teenagers disagreed.

Miles dove in first, stacking three ham sandwiches onto his plate.

Molly swooped in after him and yanked one away. "Yeah, no."

Delgado reached over them, grabbing two sandwiches. "Turkey's mine."

Jace nodded toward the untouched pile. "Veggie. Any takers?"

"No one wants that." Miles cringed.

Delgado went in for a third sandwich, one already shoved

in his mouth chipmunk-style, and Beckett narrowed his eyes. Delgado grinned, lifted his shirt, and flexed. "You don't get this body by holding back."

Molly smacked him in the stomach. "Good thing you've got brawn, Delgado. Brains were clearly out of stock."

The kid doubled over, and I couldn't help but smile.

Junie sat in the middle of the chaos, perched on a stool with her ham sandwich clutched in both hands. She beamed up at Jace, who split a cookie in half for them to share, looking content.

Across the room, Beckett leaned against the counter behind Emmy, arms wrapped around her waist, chin resting on her head as she talked to Ty about summer practice schedules.

I hovered at the edge of the room, acutely aware that I didn't fit here.

This wasn't what I'd pictured when I imagined Junie in Colorado. In my head, it had been quiet. Temporary. Just the two of us, keeping our heads down, surviving one day at a time.

But this was loud. Crowded. *Full.*

And my sister—

Not now.

As if sensing I needed rescuing, Emmy appeared beside me. "I hope you like Diet Coke. There might be some Topo Chico, or you're welcome to a Gatorade."

I took the can out of her hand and cracked it open. "I'll take a fridge cigarette any day."

"I knew I liked you." She touched the rim of her can to mine in a toast. "Are you doing okay after today?"

"Yes?" I said, the answer sounding as shaky as I felt. "No. I don't know."

Emmy nodded, then took a sip of her Diet Coke, not forcing the conversation. We stood together and watched the kids huddled around the table, doing anything to make Junie smile.

"Delgado almost got fired when he found out Junie was here today," she said after a minute. "Miles had to talk him out of bailing on his delivery shift."

I blinked, staring at the goofy kid who had pretended to faint on the floor. Junie sat there and grinned down at him, giggling around a cookie.

"He was going to ditch work?"

She glanced over at me. "He and Miles both. That niece of yours has half the team wrapped around her finger. It's a little terrifying, honestly."

I hummed, leaning back against the wall as I watched Jace help Junie steal a second cookie when no one was looking. That used to be my job—the fun, carefree aunt—but now I'd have to be the responsible one, wouldn't I?

"Did you know her?" I asked. "Violet, I mean."

Emmy shook her head. "Not well. By the time I moved here last fall, your sister didn't leave the house much. I met her a few times at the hospital."

At the word *hospital,* something sharp caught in my chest.

"She never told me," I whispered, letting loose the one thing I hadn't admitted yet. "I didn't even know she was sick until... until it was already over."

Emmy didn't answer right away. She just watched the group—Beckett ruffling Jace's hair, Miles teasing Junie, Ty doing that half-grin at something Delgado said.

"She talked about you," Emmy said finally. "That she knew you'd come. That you'd know how to make Junie happier than anyone. She also asked me to take good care of you. Said you might need a friend."

A tear slid down my cheek before I could stop it. I swiped it away fast and tugged the brim of Ty's hat lower.

Damn you, Violet. Still taking care of me.

Emmy's shoulder brushed mine. "For what it's worth," she said, "I like you. I would have befriended you no matter what."

The words shouldn't have made my throat tighten, but they did. "Yeah," I rasped, still half-hidden under the brim of Ty's hat. "I think I can handle that."

When I finally lifted my head, Ty's gaze was already on me from across the room.

He didn't come over. Didn't ask if I was okay. Just stayed where he was, watching me like he'd clocked the moment my shoulders tightened.

For a split second, I wished he was close enough to take my hand like he had earlier today—that steady, grounding touch that asked nothing of me.

But he didn't move. And somehow, that felt just as intentional.

I wasn't running from reality. I was getting through *today*.

The courthouse.

The paperwork.

Junie.

There would be a moment I couldn't outrun the fact that Violet was gone.

Just... not yet.

And Ty didn't seem to mind waiting.

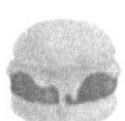

By the time the food was demolished, the kitchen quieted down. The teens drifted out one by one—Miles muttering something about an essay he needed to finish for summer school, Delgado promising Beckett he wouldn't skip work again, and Molly rolling her eyes like she'd heard that lie before.

Junie leaned against the counter, heavy-lidded and yawning, the crash from the long day catching up to her. Jace ruffled her hair before heading upstairs, and she smiled after him, slow and sleepy.

"She's toast," Ty said from behind me, and the warmth in his voice slid straight under my skin.

We said quick goodbyes, and then the three of us stepped out into the cool night. Ty opened the passenger door of the truck and helped Junie climb into the back, buckling her into her booster seat with a practiced ease that said he'd done this before.

Her stuffed rabbit waited for her, propped neatly in the corner. Junie sighed when she saw it, and she tucked it into the crook of her arm. Within seconds, she sank against the seat, already half asleep.

As Ty shut the door, I whispered, "You planned that."

He shrugged. "She's cranky when she's tired. I value my life."

I chuckled, the sound easing some of the tightness in my chest. We climbed into the cab, and as he pulled onto River Street, the lights from the shops reflected across the windshield. Linwood at sunset belonged on a postcard, pinks and oranges sinking over the mountains.

"So," I said, leaning back against the seat, "youth hockey, huh?"

Ty flicked his gaze toward me. "Beckett roped me in last fall. The team was going to fold."

"Of course." I smiled. "Injured puppies, one-eyed llamas, foster kids, homeless aunts, and now entire youth hockey organizations. So much to save. So little time."

His mustache twitched like he was fighting a grin. "You're hilarious."

I rested my elbow against the window, turning just enough that our knees brushed. "Yeah, well. That and my winning personality are all I've got going for me these days."

He glanced at me again, the corner of his mouth tipping up just enough to make my stomach flip. "Pretty sure you're underselling yourself."

"Oh, yeah?"

"Yeah." His jaw worked as if he was choosing his words carefully. "You're—"

He stopped.

I turned my head toward him. "I'm what?"

His grip on the wheel tightened a fraction before he seemed to notice and loosened it.

"...Not just funny," he said finally.

The odd compliment shouldn't have warmed me the way it did, but I liked that, for once, it wasn't me who was off-kilter.

"That's a very safe answer, Coach."

"Don't call me that."

I blinked. "Coach?"

"Yes." His jaw flexed. "Please."

"Why?"

A quick breath of laughter left him, and then he glanced at me again. His eyes traced my face, lingered at my mouth, then dipped lower before his gaze snapped back to the road.

"Because," he said, voice rough around the edges, "I can't be thinking of you when I hear that word."

The air in the cab went tight and charged all at once.

"Oh," I managed, the smile dropping off my face.

He cleared his throat, eyes fixed forward with exaggerated focus. "Yeah."

"Okay."

He nodded once. "It's Ty. Just Ty."

I nodded. Anything more might tip the moment into something neither of us was ready to touch.

"Okay," I said again, softer. "Ty."

He didn't look at me this time, but the corner of his mouth lifted just enough to tell me he heard me.

The road wound out of town, headlights slicing through the dark as the river ran low and steady beside us. Junie's breathing evened out in the backseat, her rabbit tucked snug beneath her chin.

Above us, the stars stretched wide and sharp, unfiltered by streetlights or city glow. I'd forgotten how big the sky felt here —how it demanded your attention whether you were ready for it or not. As a kid, Violet and I used to lie on our backs in the wildflowers and make up stories for the constellations, convinced they were maps to somewhere better. Somewhere happy. Somewhere safe.

Now, I focused straight ahead, trying not to look.

We slowed as Ty turned onto the gravel drive, tires crunching beneath us. The road split ahead—one curve leading toward his house, the other disappearing into shadow at the front of the property.

I knew what was there without looking.

Not now.

The truck rolled past, headlights sweeping the trees instead, and I closed my eyes to keep my emotions in check.

When Ty killed the engine, I finally opened them again. Junie didn't stir.

Rowdy waited for us on the front porch, his dark shape curled on the mat. He lifted his head and thumped his tail once, slow and satisfied we were home.

Without a word, Ty climbed out and opened the back door, unbuckling Junie with practiced care. She slumped against his chest, her rabbit dangling from one hand, and he carried her up the steps with ease.

Rowdy and I followed, feeling like I'd stepped into a routine I didn't know existed.

Inside, Ty didn't turn on any lights. He moved through the house as if he knew every creak, every shadow, straight down the hall and into Junie's room.

Last night, exhaustion had blurred the details of her bedroom. Tonight, I noticed.

The walls were a soft, pale blue—her favorite color. Black-and-white frames hung above her bed: Rowdy mid-leap, eyes crossed; Uno's tongue lolling to one side; Dolly caught mid-acrobatics, jumping down from the barn rafters.

This wasn't just a cute kid's room someone had thrown together in a hurry.

This was *hers*.

It was warm, intentional, and full of everything she loved.

Ty lowered her into bed and tucked the blankets around her in one smooth motion. She rolled onto her side, the rabbit clutched tight.

He leaned down and pressed a kiss to her forehead. "Goodnight, bug."

Her reply came thick with sleep. "Night, Ty."

He clicked on a small nightlight by the dresser, soft purples and blues spinning across the ceiling in a galaxy of soothing colors. Junie sighed once and gave in to sleep.

When he turned around, I still stood in the doorway, watching him.

"You love her," I said softly.

"I love her," he answered. No hesitation. No qualifiers.

My chest squeezed at the admission, and the truth settled heavy and undeniable.

Violet hadn't chosen Ty as Junie's guardian because he was convenient. Or close. Or safe on paper.

She'd chosen him because Junie deserved to be loved like this—without conditions, without uncertainty.

And standing in this room, it was impossible to argue with her.

Ty pulled the door mostly shut, but left it cracked. He jerked his chin toward the kitchen, and I followed on quiet feet.

Neither of us said anything while he filled the kettle, set it on the burner, and pulled down a jar of loose tea. I just watched him move, noticing the tense set of his shoulders, the tic of his jaw.

Steam curled between us as he poured the water, then slid a mug across the counter.

"Chamomile," he said. "Figured you could use it."

I wrapped my hands around the mug, grateful for the warmth. "Thank you."

He leaned against the counter across from me, not crowding, but not retreating either.

The kettle clicked, the sound small in the quiet kitchen. We both drank our tea in silence, but the set of Ty's shoulders told me he still had something he needed to discuss.

His gaze dropped to the floor, then lifted again. Finally, he looked at me.

"You're staying," he said. Not a question. Not quite a statement.

"The judge didn't give me much wiggle room," I said. "And if the renovations are as extensive as they said, I don't have the funds to find an apartment while I fix up the place. So, yes, if the offer still stands, I guess I'm staying here for the next six weeks."

His jaw tightened. "And after that?"

I stared down into the tea, watching the steam rise. "I don't know yet."

This time the silence didn't feel empty. It pressed in, weighted with everything neither of us said.

"I just want what's best for her," he whispered.

I nodded. "So do I."

Six weeks stretched between us, undefined and heavy.

Too long to pretend nothing would change.

Too short to pretend everything wouldn't.

He nodded once, then drained the rest of his tea and set the mug in the sink.

"Goodnight, Daisy."

I watched him disappear down the hall, Rowdy padding after him, and stood alone in the kitchen—Junie asleep, grief waiting in the dark, the stars still burning overhead.

Not now.

But soon.

12

TY

Junie was in meltdown mode, the kind reserved for mornings when you had somewhere to be.

I stood in her bedroom doorway, holding what I *thought* was the right turquoise shirt, but had her stomping around in her pajamas. She still wanted to go to the rink with Beckett, and to make that happen before I left for work, we needed to leave soon.

She scrunched her face up, cheeks blotchy, hair sticking out in twelve directions. "That's not the one," she wailed. "I wanted the turquoise shirt with the hearts on it. That one's plain!"

"They look the same," I said, then immediately regretted it.

She flopped backward on the bed with all the drama her eight-year-old body could muster. "They're *not* the same!"

Even without this morning's meltdown, I didn't need a reminder that grief could show up sideways. I'd read the books, sat through the counseling, learned how kids her age reached for control when everything else felt unstable. Some days routine helped. Other days, it gave her something to push against. Today was the latter.

And after yesterday, after hearing *six more weeks* spoken out loud in a courtroom, I wasn't about to rush her through a rough morning to make my life easier. Junie came first, even when it made everything else harder.

Daisy was in the hall bathroom with the shower running, taking her time, and that was okay. This morning, having Junie with me felt like the right call. If Daisy needed a moment alone to fall apart, she deserved that too.

I dragged a hand down my face. "Okay. Let's retrace our steps."

Junie sat up, sniffling. "I wore it last week."

"Right," I said. "Maybe it's in the laundry."

She gasped, then bolted down the hall, Rowdy thumping after her. "The laundry room!"

Before I could follow, the shower shut off and Daisy's voice called from behind the door. "Everything okay?"

"Wardrobe emergency," I said. "We're working on it."

A moment later, the bathroom door clicked open behind me.

I turned, expecting a quick check-in, maybe a tired smile.

Instead, Daisy stepped into the hall on bare feet, a towel twisted around her hair. She wore tiny pink pajama shorts and a thin matching tank top; her skin still flushed from the heat of the shower. The sight of her like this—soft, real, and unguarded—hit me square in the chest.

This was supposed to be practical. Temporary. It was my idea to co-parent for the next six weeks of shared space and shared coffee, but apparently, I hadn't thought through the logistics of sharing a house with a woman I was deeply, *stupidly* attracted to.

The house felt too small. Too intimate. Too easy to imagine this being my new normal.

"Morning chaos?" She tugged the towel off her head as she passed me. Her hair spilled down her back, still damp, and the smell of strawberry shampoo bloomed in the narrow hallway, sweet and impossible to ignore.

"Something like that," I managed. My voice sounded like I'd swallowed gravel. My hands flexed uselessly at my sides, itching to burn off the sudden heat crawling under my skin.

Daisy walked into the laundry room where Junie was half-buried in a pile of warm clothes. She asked what Junie was looking for, unfazed by the little girl's big emotions.

I stood in the doorway, watching her dig through the baskets of clean clothes I hadn't folded or put away yet.

She bent to reach deep into the dryer, and my brain betrayed me with the sudden, visceral awareness of pink shorts and bare legs and the fact that I was not supposed to be noticing any of it. But dammit, I couldn't look away. Couldn't stop myself from imagining what my big hands would look like on those hips.

Heat flooded my face and lower, sharp and unwelcome. I was thirty-seven—I should've had better control than this.

I looked away a beat too late, jaw clenched so tight my teeth ached.

"Found it!" she said, then pulled out the infamous turquoise shirt with the hearts. "Oh, it's super cute. I can see why this was your choice for today."

Junie wiped away her tears, then took the shirt from her aunt.

"You know what?" Daisy said, kneeling beside her. "I've got a shirt this same color in my bag. Want to be twins today?"

"Twins?" Junie's voice wobbled.

"I don't know how anyone will tell us apart," Daisy said. "You just need to grow about a foot and a half."

"That's impossible," Junie said, hiccuping a laugh. "The average growth spurt for an eight-year-old is two inches. Maybe two-and-a-half if I increased my iron intake."

"Okay." Daisy shrugged. "I'll just have to stay down here on my knees then. Kinda weird, but I *am* weird, right?"

Junie grinned, a full smile I was more than happy to see. "A little, yeah. But I like it."

"Me too." Daisy tugged Junie into her chest, and my girl wrapped her arms around her aunt's neck. Daisy gave her a quick squeeze, then kissed her forehead. "Now go get dressed. You don't want to be late for hockey, hm?"

Junie ran by me, then down the hall to her room. I leaned against the doorframe, relief loosening something in my chest.

"Need anything while I'm down here?" Daisy said.

I looked back at her, and any relief I'd felt flew right out the window.

She was still on her knees, pulling clothes out of the dryer and into a basket nearby.

The question was innocent. Practical. But the position— her looking up at me, damp hair on her shoulders, thin tank clinging in all the right places—sent a jolt straight through me. My stomach muscles locked. My breath snagged somewhere behind my ribs.

Dark eyelashes framed the brightest blue eyes before she seemed to realize what she'd said and the position we'd found ourselves in. Her pupils dilated and her cheeks flushed, her gaze drifting down my body as if she couldn't help it. And holy shit, I couldn't either.

My blood roared in my ears. I could feel the exact spot

where my pulse hammered at the base of my throat, could feel the inconvenient heat pooling low in my gut.

Bare legs.

Soft skin.

Nipples pebbled in the cool morning beneath that tiny little shirt.

"Do we have more pancakes?" Junie called from the other room, and I snapped my gaze up to the wall above Daisy's head, forcing oxygen back into my lungs. "I don't want yogurt."

When the tension finally snapped, Daisy scrambled to her feet and rushed down the hall, her shoulder grazing mine as she passed. The brief contact burned like a live wire. A second after she disappeared, I remembered to breathe again—shallow, but steady.

I pressed the heel of my hand against my sternum, trying to slow the frantic thudding.

This was *my* idea. My practical, temporary, torturous idea.

And I was already in way over my head.

"Ty?" Junie called again. "Pancakes?"

I scrubbed a hand over my face, then spun on my heel toward her. "Yeah, bug. They're in the oven."

By the time I got Junie situated with her purple plate, pink fork, and pancakes the way she liked them, the opening notes of *Safety Dance* drifted through the ceiling speakers.

Junie's head popped up just as Daisy slid into the kitchen in pink socks, cutoff denim shorts that weren't much better than her pajamas, and a shirt the same turquoise shade as Junie's. Her hair was up in a messy bun now, and she held a hairbrush like a microphone.

She didn't hesitate—she sang, loud and off-key and unself-conscious, like nothing in the world hurt.

Junie tried to hide her grin behind her fork, but Daisy caught it.

"Oh, come on," she said between verses, pointing the brush at her like a mic. "I know you know this one."

Junie shook her head, giggling.

Daisy kept going anyway, hips swaying, committing so hard it was impossible not to get swept up in it.

I leaned against the counter, arms crossed, unable to look away.

When Daisy broke into a terrible robot—arms stiff, knees jerking—Junie finally cracked, laughter spilling out of her like it had been trapped behind her ribs all morning.

Daisy clutched her chest. "Ladies and gentlemen, we have a smile. I've said it once and I'll say it again—almost anything can be solved with a dance party."

I adjusted my hat, not to grin. "Almost?"

She flashed me a look. "Almost." Then, grinning, she jabbed the brush toward me. "You're next."

"Hard pass."

"You don't dance?"

"Not like that."

"Then you're no friend of mine, Huddy."

Junie hopped down to join her, and the two of them started spinning in circles around the kitchen, laughter echoing off the walls. It was equal parts adorable and terrifying, and I couldn't look away.

Daisy shone so brightly that it took a second to notice the cracks. Her smile stretched a fraction too wide, her eyes flicking up toward the ceiling before she wiped at her cheek and looked back down at Junie, smile already back in place.

She was holding herself together with noise and movement

and sheer willpower, and it only made me want to protect her more.

By the time we made it to the front door, shoes on and Rowdy waiting, Daisy held her palm up.

"Good work, partner."

"Partner?"

"Yeah." She nodded. "You're the bedtime whisperer. I handle morning meltdowns. Teamwork makes the dream work."

I huffed out a laugh and smacked my hand against hers.

The warmth shot straight through me.

Junie darted out to my truck humming *Safety Dance*, and Rowdy hopped in the truck with her.

"Will you be okay today?" I asked from the porch steps. "I need to catch up on some paperwork at the hardware store, but..."

But I didn't want to leave.

Daisy's grin snapped into place like armor, but it didn't quite meet her eyes. "Let me guess—a tiny little mom-and-pop store that was going out of business before you saved it?"

When I didn't answer, her eyes widened.

"Wait, seriously?" she laughed. "You did."

I exhaled through my nose. "You probably shouldn't ask about the rink either."

She laughed, shaking her head. "You can't be this nice *and* have a mustache."

"Is that a rule?"

Her gaze dipped to my mouth and lingered there for a beat too long. "It should be."

My pulse jumped hard enough to be a problem, but she just smiled, not caring that she'd just set the air between us on fire.

"See you later, Huddy." She turned to go back inside, hair swinging, bare legs flashing with every step.

I should've let her go, but without Junie or music filling the space, the strain in her expression was impossible to miss.

"Daisy," I said before I could stop myself.

She paused in the doorway, glancing back. The brightness in her expression held, but barely.

"If you need help today," I said carefully, "with arrangements. With any of it. You don't have to do that alone."

For half a second, something real flickered across her face.

Not humor. Not deflection.

Just grief.

Then she blinked, quick as a shutter.

"I'm fine," she said, too fast, voice too light. "I'm basically the mayor of Doing Great."

Before I could say anything else, Junie yelled from the truck, "Come on, Ty!"

Daisy waved a hand at me, already stepping back like she needed the space. "Go be responsible, Mr. Fix It. We've got this. I'm good."

A single nod was safer than saying anything that might crack her open.

I walked off the porch and into the truck, helping Junie buckle in before pulling out of the driveway.

The plan was simple—drop Junie at the rink, head to the hardware store, keep moving.

But my chest stayed tight the whole way, my thoughts stuck on Daisy Winslow standing on that porch, smiling too hard, insisting she was fine.

And hating that I was leaving her alone with the day anyway.

"Knock knock," Emmy's voice said from the open door to my office.

Rowdy lifted his head from where he'd claimed the rug by my desk, tail thumping once when he saw her.

"Thought I'd come check on you," Emmy added, already stepping inside. "And I brought lunch."

"Those are the magic words."

Rowdy stood, did a slow, hopeful circle, then sat again when I nudged him back with my boot.

I shoved a stack of invoices aside while she unpacked a brown paper bag from Slice & Spice—the local Mexican-Italian hybrid that somehow made both tacos and pizza work. She set the food out with practiced ease, popped the lid on a bowl of salsa, then slid into the chair opposite me, tapping her Diet Coke with a peachy-pink fingernail.

The office at Hudson Hardware hadn't changed much. Two dented filing cabinets. A scarred wooden desk. A pegboard wall cluttered with outdated calendars and tools I didn't remember ever using. One narrow window looking out toward River Street.

Everything was how my dad had left it. Same smell of sawdust and oil. Same expectation that I'd sit here and just pick up where he stopped.

"How was my girl this morning?" Emmy asked, too casual to be casual.

I grabbed a barbacoa taco, more out of obligation than hunger, and leaned back in my chair. "Fine."

She didn't buy it for a second.

"You know I once had an eight-year-old, right?" Her

brows climbed. "That kid was exhausted last night, and that's before factoring in everything else in her life right now. I'd sooner believe the Earth was flat than this morning went smoothly."

I sighed, scrubbing a hand over my jaw. My gaze drifted back to the papers—numbers blurring together, dates I'd already checked twice and somehow still didn't trust. "There may have been a meltdown over a shirt."

She winced. "Bad?"

"I mean… it wasn't great. But she's clothed, fed, and at the rink. So I'm calling it a win."

A corner of her mouth lifted. "Did Daisy handle it?"

That made me pause.

Because, yeah—she had.

And I still wasn't over how fast she'd stepped in, how effortlessly she'd read Junie and flipped the whole morning on its head with a dance party and a hairbrush microphone. Five minutes, tops.

"She did," I admitted, unwrapping my taco. "She's good with her."

Emmy watched me for a beat longer than necessary, her gaze drifting from my face to the untouched paperwork, then down to where Rowdy had settled against my leg like an anchor. Like she could see the way my mind kept slipping sideways—back to the rink, back to the porch, back to a woman insisting she was fine when she clearly wasn't.

"And you?" she asked. "Are you okay?"

I nodded automatically, then stopped. The lie felt too easy. Too practiced. Just like sitting in this office, pretending the weight of it all didn't press in on my ribs.

"I'm here," I said instead. Which wasn't the same thing at all, and she knew it.

Emmy watched me for a long second, as if she was lining something up in her head. "Why haven't you sold it?"

I frowned. "Sold what?"

She gestured around the office. The desk. The filing cabinets. The whole damn building. "The store."

I leaned back in my chair, arms crossed. "Because it's our name on the building. It's our legacy."

She shook her head. "That's not a reason."

"Well, it's the only one I've got."

She nodded once, accepting that—but not letting it go. "Okay. Then why not hire a manager? Someone to run it so you're not buried in invoices and supply orders like this."

I glanced down at the paperwork again. "Because it's supposed to be me. The Hudson men. That's how it's always been."

Emmy's eyes softened, but her voice stayed steady. "Says who?"

I opened my mouth, then shut it again.

She leaned back in her chair. "You know this isn't your thing, right? This was never your thing."

I shrugged. "It's fine."

"Hockey was your thing," she went on. "Hockey *is* your thing. I didn't ask you to coach the Mayhem because I didn't want to put one more thing on your shoulders—but every single day, I'm glad Beckett volunteered you. Those kids? That team? They brought you back to life."

Her gaze swept across the office. "Here? You're just taking care of stuff no one else wanted to deal with. And that doesn't mean you're required to keep doing it forever."

I exhaled through my nose, staring past her at the window. River Street looked the same as it always had: quiet and predictable. Nothing in my life felt that way anymore.

"It feels like I'd be letting him down," I said.

"Dad?" she asked. "Maybe it serves him right to be let down. He can have a taste of his own medicine."

That landed harder than I liked.

She let the silence stretch. Rowdy sighed at my feet, as if he felt it too.

"My point is," Emmy added, "you don't owe him—or anyone—anything. You don't have to love this just because he did. You're allowed to want something different."

I didn't answer. Couldn't.

Emmy tilted her head, studying me again. "You're carrying a lot right now, Ty. And I get why you are. I really do. But doing everything doesn't make you more reliable—it just makes you tired."

I picked at the edge of the desk, jaw tight. "I can handle tired."

"I know you can," she said. "But you shouldn't have to."

"Are you done?" I asked.

Emmy studied me for a second, then nodded. "For now." She reached for a chip, then paused. "Yesterday—how did it go?"

There it was. The question she'd been circling since she walked in.

"We got joint temporary custody," I said. "They'll reevaluate in six weeks."

Her brows pulled together. "So Junie's staying?"

"For now."

"And Daisy?" she asked. "She's okay with that?"

"She agreed it was best for Junie," I said. "At least until she gets her feet under her."

Emmy nodded. "Which means?"

I adjusted the brim of my hat and gave her the short version

—the job situation, her sister's place, why Junie couldn't stay there. The logistics. The gaps that didn't leave Daisy with many options.

"She moved into my guest room," I finished. "It made the most sense."

Emmy's expression shifted as the pieces clicked into place, concern softening into something deeper. "Oh."

"She's trying," I added. "Hard."

"I didn't think otherwise," Emmy said. "That's a lot for her."

"And for you," she added after a beat.

I shrugged. "I can handle it."

"I know," she said. "You always do."

Silence settled between us, and I picked up another taco, taking a bite. Rowdy rested his chin on my knee, giving me those big eyes in hopes I'd let him have a bite.

Then her eyes sharpened again, curiosity slipping back in. "I didn't realize you knew her from Chicago."

I pointed my taco at her. "This is the problem with you being engaged to my best friend. You know too much."

She laughed. "I know just enough. Name, city, tragic circumstances, and that you opened your house to her."

"For Junie," I corrected.

"I know." She held up her hands. "I'm just saying—having a woman in your house is different than a kid."

I adjusted my hat again, and she grinned.

"Stop it, Emmy."

"I'm not doing anything, Ty. Just being a kind sister."

I grabbed my hat, this time setting it on my knee so I'd stop messing with it. "Please stay out of it, Em. Junie is the priority here, not whatever misguided attempt at match-making this is."

"I'm not saying anything. Except that maybe Junie's not the only one benefiting from her being here."

I didn't rise to the bait, shoving the last of my taco in my mouth instead.

The silence didn't last long, but it never did with Emmy. "So, what happens when the six weeks are up?"

I let out a low laugh that didn't have any humor in it. "I don't fucking know, Em. She's Daisy's niece. I'm just..." I gestured around the office, around town. "I'm convenient."

"You're more than that, Ty."

I shrugged. "Yeah, maybe. But that doesn't mean it matters."

I'd thought about it all night. If Daisy got on her feet—got a job, found stability—she'd get full custody. Even with me listed in the Will, CPS would override it for family, if they thought that was best. And I wouldn't stand in her way. Hell, I *wanted* her to get her feet under her. Junie deserved a stable future, and if Daisy could give her that, then she should. Even if it gutted me.

Emmy popped the tab on her Diet Coke, the fizzy sound drawing my eyes up. "Then we make her want to stay."

My head dropped back and I let out a low groan, staring at the ceiling. "No."

"Yes," she shot back. "This town is magic, Ty. Linwood brought me peace, and I think you found it here too. She used to come here as a kid, right? That's Maggie's younger niece?"

I looked back at her. "I forgot that, but yeah. Did you ever meet her?"

Emmy shook her head. "No, I don't think we ever crossed paths—she's what, eight years younger than me?"

"Something like that."

"Maggie bought the farmhouse from Dad the year you left

for Juniors, and I only vaguely remember seeing the girls there when I was home and pregnant that first summer. Safe to say, I wasn't paying much attention to random kids."

I hummed, trying to remember if I had ever noticed them before, but came up blank.

"But my point is, I think we can get her to stay. We just have to show her how great this place is."

"Em."

She held her hands up in surrender. "I won't meddle."

Before the words were out of her mouth, her phone on my desk lit up with a stream of text messages.

I pointed at it. "I don't even kind of believe that."

With a grin, Emmy shoved a taco in her mouth and grabbed her phone, thumbs flew across the screen as it dinged with incoming text messages.

"Jesus Christ."

She just grinned wider. "We've got six weeks. Operation Win Daisy Over is officially live."

I didn't bother arguing, knowing my bubbly little sister would just steamroll me. She'd always been this way, but finding Beckett and her own happiness had seemed to make her hellbent on ensuring everyone around her was just as happy as she was.

When we finished lunch, she grabbed a bag of peach sour candy from the front counter like she always did, kissed my cheek, and swept out the door with a singsong, "You're welcome!"

I stood in the doorway for a second, watching River Street hum outside. Same little town. Same bell on the front door. Same everything. But everything else in my life felt like it was shifting under my feet.

I'd kept this store running for the last three years since I retired from the NHL. Kept every shelf organized the way Dad liked it. I told myself it was about legacy, about honoring him. But Emmy was right.

The store wasn't my dream; hockey was. And so was Junie. But this... the store was a weight I didn't need to carry anymore.

"Hey, Steve," I called to the kid at the register. "Go grab lunch. I've got it."

Steve looked up, then grinned. "You sure?"

"Yeah," I said. "Take your time."

He grabbed his keys and headed out, giving Rowdy a quick pat on the way past.

I slid in behind the register, scratching Rowdy's head as I reached for the notepad and pen I kept tucked beneath the counter. My brain was already drafting a job listing—general manager, full-time, steady, capable. Someone who wasn't me.

Maybe it was time.

The bell over the door jingled. I looked up, pen still in my hand. A woman stood just inside the doorway, a blanket tucked in her arms, her smile soft and unsure.

"Welcome to Hudson Hardware," I said, setting the pen down. "How can I help?"

She shifted the bundle, and it moved.

"You're Ty Hudson, right?" she asked. "The one who rescues things?"

I huffed a quiet laugh. "Guess that's me."

She glanced down at the blanket, then back up. "Room for one more?"

13

Daisy

The mountains stood sharp and undeniable from Ty's front porch, sunlight catching on the snow still clinging to the highest peaks. I wrapped both hands around my coffee mug and let my gaze slide down the hill to the farmhouse I hadn't let myself look at last night.

In the dark, it had been easy to ignore. Just a shape swallowed by shadow as we drove past, something I could deal with later.

In the morning light, there was nowhere for it to disappear to.

The house sat where it always had, quiet and waiting. Summers here as kids had been a pause from real life—wide open space, too much freedom, imagination allowed to run wild, all of it shadowed by the knowledge that it wouldn't last. The farmhouse was a refuge from a father who never hid how much of a burden we were after our mom's accident.

Without fail, on the last day of school, Aunt Maggie waited on our front steps to take us with her. She loved us loudly.

Made us feel wanted. Held us accountable. Taught us how to rise above the things life threw at us.

I'd spent years wondering why she hadn't fought harder for full custody—why she'd sent us back when school started. Standing here now with a stack of CPS paperwork in my hand, I understood it probably wasn't that simple.

Her death had crept up on us. Not sudden like Mom's, but inevitable all the same. I'd been here briefly with Violet afterward, but everything had blurred together—boxes, grief, half-made decisions. Neither of us had been cataloging the state of the house. We'd just been trying to absorb yet another loss.

Once I moved to Chicago, the house didn't come up. Violet and I talked about Junie. About work. About the small, manageable details of life. The rest stayed untouched—something I realized now we'd both done on purpose, careful not to weigh the other down when life was already heavy enough.

I should have come back.

The thought landed hard and sudden—and just as fast, my reality followed.

Not now.

From a distance, the house didn't look so bad. Wildflowers bloomed around the yard, and the painted siding still held some of its color. If the caseworker hadn't called the inside *uninhabitable*, I might've believed this place was still as magical as I remembered.

"Now or never, Daisy," I muttered as I took another sip of my coffee.

With one last sigh, I stepped off the porch, papers tucked under my arm. I still needed to read through Violet's Will, review the rest of the CPS paperwork, and figure out if I was going to have a funeral, even though she'd been cremated.

Tears burned at my eyes, and I blinked rapidly, shoving the thought aside.

Today's goal was the house. I needed to solve something—or at least make a plan to solve it. I had six weeks to prove I was responsible enough to take care of Junie on my own, and that was my next priority.

The chickens clustered in the driveway like a feathery little barricade, pecking at the gravel as if I were the one trespassing.

"Hey, girls," I said, inching forward on cautious feet. "I just need to get by you. Big emotional day ahead. You get worms, I get existential dread. Everybody loses."

The hens didn't care.

I waved the papers in my hand like a sad little flag. "Shoo. Please. I've got trauma to process, and I'm not afraid to admit you scare me."

A few of the hens shuffled aside. The rooster, however—oh, he was locked in. Chest puffed. Feathers ruffled. Murder in his beady little eyes.

"Okay, buddy." I held up my coffee like we were in a hostage negotiation. "Let's make a deal. You let me pass, and I'll become a vegetarian. Pinky swear."

He took a step toward me.

"I mean it, Cluck Norris," I added, remembering his name. "Kale smoothies. Tofu. So many beans. We can be friends. I'm very nice, I promise."

Apparently, he called bullshit.

The rooster let out a crow so loud it startled me back a step, then charged.

I shrieked, spinning around, papers flapping like white flags as I bolted down the drive. "You're right! I'm a liar! I'd betray you for a twelve-piece and a crispy Diet Coke in a heartbeat!"

Coffee sloshed out of my mug as I ran, gravel crunching

under my sneakers. The rooster thundered after me on his tiny velociraptor legs, wings flapping like the world's angriest parade float. I threw what was left of my coffee behind me and sprinted faster.

Uno watched from the fence line, his expression deeply judgmental, like this was premium llama entertainment.

"Don't look at me like that, Cyclops!" I yelled as I flew past him. "I'm grieving!"

By the time I reached the bend in the drive, Cluck Norris gave one last triumphant crow before strutting off.

"What the fuck," I muttered, then bent forward, hands braced on my knees as laughter ripped out of me in sharp, breathless bursts. It wasn't even that funny. My heart was still hammering, and the sound that came out of me shook—unsteady, like if I let it go on too long, it might turn into something else entirely.

The papers were crumpled in my fist, their edges biting into my palm. Coffee dripped down my arm. I squeezed my eyes shut and let the cool air hit my flushed face, pulling myself back together.

When I finally straightened up, the farmhouse was right there. Silent. Waiting.

No matter how badly I wanted to put a hit out on that damn rooster, he'd done it.

He'd gotten me here.

I took a deep breath and forced myself to look at the house —not the way I remembered it, but the way it actually was. Now that I knew there was a laundry list of problems hiding behind those rainbow flowerpots, they were harder to ignore.

The porch didn't just lean in a charming, old farmhouse way anymore. It slouched, as if it was contemplating the benefits of giving up and sitting down on the lawn.

The siding looked like it had lost a fight with too many winters. A couple of boards looked warped, and a suspicious patch near the steps sagged in a way I was pretty sure wood wasn't supposed to. One section of gutter hung at a strange angle, dripping onto what might've once been a flowerbed but was now a weed jungle.

I pressed my lips together and blew out a shaky breath.

"I have no idea what I'm looking at," I told the porch. "But I'm pretty sure it's bad."

The house stayed quiet, just as judgy as the damn llama.

"Cool. Love this for me." I glanced at the sagging gutter again. "Definitely gonna need a miracle."

With a sigh, I climbed the porch steps, testing each one before trusting it with my full weight. They creaked in protest, but none of them gave way, which felt like a win.

I reached for the doorknob and twisted it. Nothing.

"Dammit," I muttered, resting my forehead against the cool wood. "The key is in my car, but that's on the other side of the chickens, and no fucking way am I going back through the gauntlet again."

I stepped back and scanned the porch. "Tell me you hid a spare key for me, Vi."

The doormat? Too obvious.

Under the frog? I crouched, tipped it forward, and found nothing but a spider the size of a dime. I yelped and dropped it.

"Nope. Nope. Absolutely not."

Standing again, I surveyed the yard, trying to channel my sister's brand of practical chaos. "Okay... where would you have hidden a key..."

My gaze landed on a faded metal mailbox still clinging to its post, the lid askew. "Old-school. I respect it." I opened it —junk mail and another spiderweb that had me batting at imaginary bugs I was sure were crawling up my arms. No key.

I kept moving along the porch, talking to no one and everyone. "Remember when you hid a spare key in a sock inside Dad's shed? You thought you were such a genius. 'Who's going to look for a key in a sock?' you said. Yeah—because a random sock in a shed wasn't suspicious at all."

My laugh came out watery, half a giggle and half a sniff. "Come on, Violet. Help me out here. I was the sneaky one, so your choice would've been pretty—"

Something cracked and familiar caught my eye near the porch—a ceramic planter with purple flowers painted all over it, half-buried in weeds and half-forgotten. I dropped to my knees and brushed away the dirt, revealing a glint of metal.

"Ha!" I held it up to the empty yard. "A flowerpot. What a rookie move."

The chickens clucked somewhere behind me, unimpressed.

"Don't start," I warned as I fitted the key into the lock. "You've already inflicted enough emotional damage for one morning."

The key turned with a solid click. I swallowed, hand trembling just a little, then pushed the door open—ready or not.

The hinges creaked, and the faint scent of sawdust hit me first.

The front room was... not what I remembered.

Paint cans sat stacked in the corner, lids splattered with evidence of good intentions and bad follow-through. One wall was missing drywall, exposing a mess of wires I was ninety percent sure wasn't supposed to look like that. Studs framed the space like the skeleton of my childhood memories, and it was obvious Violet had been in the middle of making this place something bigger.

Something hers.

The living room hovered between construction zone and cozy nest. Maggie's soft, overstuffed couch was draped with a blanket that matched nothing except Violet's chaos, sitting in front of an old TV. Fun throw pillows in every color imaginable were shoved into the corners.

On the coffee table sat the cheap CD player Maggie had given me for my twelfth birthday.

And on top of it—a letter, with a daisy drawn in thick black marker.

My throat tightened the instant I saw it.

Even in this half-finished house with its exposed bones, Violet was everywhere. In the colors. The mess. The stubborn joy bleeding out of every corner.

My chest constricted, sharp and hot. For a second, I just stood there in the middle of the room, surrounded by studs and sawdust, fighting back the wave that threatened to pull me under.

"Damn it, Vi," I whispered, not sure what else to say.

I crossed the room slowly, every creak of the old wood floor under my sneakers loud in the quiet, and stopped in front of the coffee table. With a deep breath, I sank to the floor and opened the letter.

Well, shit.

A laugh stuttered out of me, tears gathering in my eyes at the first words on the page. I could hear it in Violet's voice, as if she was sitting right there on the couch after a long day.

Messed this one up, didn't I?

I keep thinking there's a better way to start this, something softer or smarter, but you know me—I was never great at pretending things weren't what they were. And you've always been able to hear the truth in my voice anyway, even when I tried to hide it. You've always been my sunshine girl. No matter how awful life got, you were the one who believed tomorrow would be better. That there was a silver lining somewhere if we just kept moving. You were so sure we were almost out of the dark, even when we were standing knee-deep in it.

And I couldn't be the one to drag you back there again.

By the time I understood how bad the cancer was, there was nothing left to do. No plan. No miracle. Just time running out. I made a choice—a selfish one—and I didn't tell you.

I told myself I was protecting you. That I was being your big sister one last time, because that's what I've always tried to do, whether I was any good at it or not. I couldn't stand the thought of being your third. First Mom. Then Maggie. And if you're reading this, now me, too.

I couldn't watch that happen to you again.

So I stayed quiet. I carried it by myself.

And I'm sorry, Dais. I know that an apology fixes nothing, but it's still true.

I know what I've left behind. The house. The mess. Junie. None of it was supposed to land in your lap, and I hate that it did. But I also know how much my sweet girl loves you, and I trust you with her more than anyone in the world. That part was never a question for me.

You might have been surprised to see Ty's name beside yours in the paperwork, but know that wasn't an afterthought. I chose him carefully, and I need you to trust me on this.

I don't want this to be what breaks you. I want it to be what roots you. What reminds you who you are when everything feels like it's slipping sideways.

Even if you don't believe that yet, I do.

If I know you (and I really, really do), you're crying right now, and you hate crying.

So here's what we're going to do.

Today is not a Sad Day.

Today, you get one more day to pretend that I'm just gone a little longer than expected.

That you're here to watch Junie until I get back. You get one more day to be stubborn and in denial, because honestly, that's how you've survived everything else life has thrown at you.

Tomorrow can be heavy. Tomorrow can hurt like hell.

But not today.

Today, you're going to ignore the paperwork sitting somewhere nearby. (Yes, I know you haven't opened it yet. Don't make that face.) You're going to grab the gardening gloves in the bucket by the porch, pull some weeds, and breathe in the mountain air like we used to.

And you're going to press play on the little stereo.

I love you, Daisy Winslow. Always have. Always will. You're stronger than you think, and I tried my best to make sure you don't have to do this alone.

To the moon,

√

A sob hiccuped out of me, but I smiled through the tears as I wiped the back of my hand across my face. My fingers trembled when I reached for the little CD player and popped the lid. Inside was a burned CD I vaguely remembered, Violet's handwriting scrawled across the silver plastic.

The Anti-Frown.

Of course it was.

I let out a soft, broken laugh, remembering all the mix CDs she'd made over the years. Music had always been our escape hatch—something we could slip through together when everything else felt too heavy. I snapped the lid closed, and the player hummed as it whirred to life.

The opening notes of *Footloose* blasted through the room at full volume.

I ducked my head, grinning through watery eyes, and waited for the lyrics to kick in. My foot started tapping almost immediately, then my head followed, the beat tugging at me whether I wanted it to or not. I could see it so clearly—the summer Violet and I had memorized the dance, laughing our way through every wrong step.

When the chorus hit, something cracked open inside me just enough to let the pressure out.

I stood, the music thrumming through the studs and floorboards. The CD player was scuffed and ancient, but I scooped it up anyway and tucked it under my arm.

By the door sat a pair of Violet's heart-shaped sunglasses and, like any good little sister, I claimed them as mine. The world tinted pink—too bright, a little ridiculous, and exactly what I needed.

Outside, the mountain air rushed against my cheeks, cool and sharp. I set the stereo on the porch railing and cranked the volume, letting the music spill out across the yard.

I kicked off my shoes and hopped down into the grass, toes curling as I threw my arms up and sang at the top of my lungs. I twirled, stumbled, laughed—and kept going. Tears streaked hot down my cheeks, but I didn't stop. I just wiped them away with the heel of my hand and danced harder.

It wasn't graceful. It wasn't even good. But for the first time in days, I could breathe.

Nothing about this place made sense without her. Not the house. Not the sun warming my shoulders. But the music did. And for a little while, it felt like Violet was right there with me, laughing and dancing as she always had.

When the chorus rolled around again, I didn't slow down. I spun until I was dizzy, flinging my arms wide, singing with zero concern for pitch or dignity.

When the song ended, I sprinted back to the porch and smacked the CD player to start it again. This time, I went all in —every ridiculous, half-remembered move from that summer.

By the second chorus, my hair clung to my neck and my cheeks ached from smiling, and I didn't care. I spun once more, then collapsed backward into the grass, staring up at the endless Colorado sky as the music played on.

For one long, impossible heartbeat, there was nothing but the sun, the breeze, the beat, and Violet's ghost tangled up in all of it.

No court hearings.

No grief.

No next steps.

Just this.

The distant crunch of tires on gravel broke the spell some-time later. I propped myself up on my elbows, squinting toward the driveway as Emmy's SUV came into view.

She slowed when she spotted me splayed out in the grass, music still blaring through the valley. When she parked and stepped out, her ponytail swung as she took me in with an amused grin.

"You good?" she asked, hands braced on the top of the door like she might need to call for backup.

"What? You don't think a dance party is normal grief behavior?" I scrambled to my feet, brushing grass off my jeans, and hurried to turn down the volume.

As if mocking me, the next song that came on was *Stayin' Alive.*

The irony punched me right in the chest. Emmy's eyebrows shot up, her gaze bouncing between me and the little stereo, not sure if she should laugh or hug me.

A laugh ripped out of me first—sharp, unhinged, and way too loud—and then I doubled over, clutching my chest as I lost it to a fit of giggles. When I finally straightened, breathless and sniffling, Emmy leaned against the side of her car, her mouth curved in a barely contained grin.

"I mean," she said, "you seem good."

"Sure," I said, sliding my heart-shaped sunglasses up onto my head. "Hell of an impression I've made."

Emmy waved me off. "Please. I know everything I need to know about you already."

My eyebrows rose. "Oh yeah? And what's that?"

Her gaze flicked toward Ty's house, then back to me. "You're still here. And that means you're holding it together in the absolute shitstorm life handed you. Or... okay, maybe not *together*"—she nodded toward the stereo—"but I'll give you points for flair."

I smiled. "Joke's on you. I have no idea what I'm doing. I love Junie more than anything, but I don't know how to take care of a kid."

"Yes, well, welcome to the club."

I blinked at her. "What?"

She shrugged. "I've got a teenager. Half the time parenting's just making shit up and hoping you don't scar them for life. Or at least only in new and exciting ways. You'll figure it out. We all do."

She pushed off the car and came a few steps closer. "Besides, you've got a cheat code."

I huffed a laugh. "And what's that?"

"Ty." She pointed up at his house. "My brother is freakishly good at this. He adores Junie, and your niece worships him. Which is still baffling to me, because this is the same man who once told me licking a frozen pole wouldn't make my tongue stick. And let's not even talk about when he swapped out my shampoo for maple syrup."

I snorted. "Ah, to be the younger sibling."

"A true survival test." Emmy grinned. "But my point is, Ty will hold down the fort while you get your feet under you. That's just who he is, and your sister knew that about him. You've got a whole crew who's got your back. You don't have to be perfect, Daisy. You just have to be present."

I stared at her for a long moment, something raw and grateful working its way through me.

"Yeah," I finally said, turning toward Violet's house. "I'm trying."

Cluck Norris crowed from behind us, and Emmy went back to her car. "Need anything while I'm running errands in Glenwood Springs? Groceries? Target run? Rooster defense system?"

I laughed, the sound a little shaky but real. "Maybe some chicken nuggets I can eat in front of Cluck Norris so he knows we aren't on speaking terms."

Emmy tossed her head back and cackled. "I knew I liked you."

My smile lingered even as my chest ached. But just behind

the lightness, the weight settled back in. Chicago. My things. The note I'd left behind. The mess I wasn't ready to face.

Not now.

Before she backed out of the driveway, Emmy rolled down her window and tossed something out. A business card fluttered through the air and landed in the grass.

"My number," she said. "Also, I own the Pilates studio in town. There's a private class on Tuesday nights with a few friends. You should come sometime."

I picked it up, tapping the Elevation Pilates logo against my palm as I looked back at her.

She was staring at the house now, two faint lines between her brows. "Are you sure you're okay alone?"

I followed her gaze, taking in the visual representation of the wreckage my life was.

"Yeah," I said. "Today, I think I am."

Violet had given me permission for one more day of denial, sunshine, and bad dancing.

And today, I was going to take it.

14

TY

I stared down into brown, beady little eyes, wondering how the hell my life had turned into this.

A tiny piglet stood in the middle of Hudson Hardware, pink snout snuffling at a stray screw left on the floor. Black-and-white patches covered her round little body, one eye smudged in black like a pirate's patch. Her hooves made the faintest tapping sounds against the old wooden floor, curious about everything. She looked like a football with legs.

A warm, squeaky, living football.

"This is not how my Tuesday was supposed to go," I muttered, leaning against the counter.

Rowdy huffed from his usual spot near the register, resting his chin on his paws. His whole expression said, *you've officially lost it.*

I rubbed a hand over my face, still reeling from the fact that a volunteer from the county animal rescue had dropped off a piglet twenty minutes ago, handed me a half-empty bottle of formula and a bag of feed, then hurried back to her truck with a promise to call later.

She's not keeping weight on, she'd said. *We were hoping you might help. Just for now.*

Just for now. Famous last words.

"Well," I said to the empty store. "Now what?"

The piglet answered by snuffling closer and chewing on the toe of my boot. She was warm against my calf, and when I bent to scoop her up, she fit in the crook of my arm. Her round little belly rose and fell fast against my palm.

"You're kinda cute. I'm not sure this is what the grief counselors meant by stability and routine, though."

I grabbed my phone, thumb flying as I searched how to take care of a mini potbelly piglet. A dozen links popped up at once.

Warm bedding.

Socialization.

Heat lamps.

Vaccines.

Bottle feeding.

Enclosures.

I exhaled slowly. I had most of that—straw in the barn, heat lamps left over from chick season, and an old dog kennel I could scrub down and set up inside.

The rescue had sent her with a bottle and formula to get through the night, but not much more than that.

"So," I muttered, eyeing her round belly before setting her down on the counter, "we're improvising."

The piglet made a soft grunt, curled into a little loaf on top of a stack of lumber receipts, and closed her eyes. Rowdy stared up at me, his dark eyes carrying more than a little judgment— even as his tail gave a soft thump against the floor.

"Don't look at me like that." I shook my head. "This one's not on me."

As if my day hadn't already gone off the rails, my phone lit up with a call from Beckett. My pulse kicked immediately.

"Is she okay?" I asked, already regretting dropping Junie off at the rink with him this morning after her meltdown. She'd said she wanted to go, but I should've known she wasn't ready. "Tell me she's okay."

"She's fine," Beckett said, and I sagged against the counter. "Junie asked if she could take a nap in Tate's office instead of sitting on the bench with me. She's not upset, but I think she hit her limit today."

Relief loosened something tight in my chest, even as guilt crept in behind it. "I'm on my way."

I grabbed my keys and waved to Steve as he came back in from lunch. He took one look at my phone, then the pig on the counter, and gave me a slow thumbs-up.

Rowdy's ears perked the second I moved, and he was halfway to the door before I hung up.

I looked down at the sleeping pig, then back at Steve. "Well, I can't leave you here."

She cracked one dark, sleepy eye open, then closed it.

With a sigh, I scooped her up.

Minutes later, I had a pig tucked against my chest, a dog in the passenger seat, and the distinct feeling my life had spiraled into a very weird place.

The piglet made squeaky grunts whenever the truck jostled, then burrowed deeper into my shirt. Rowdy leaned as far away as possible, pressed flat against the passenger door.

"Yeah, yeah," I told him. "I wasn't expecting to give you a little sister today either."

He sighed. The pig snorted. I shook my head and hit the gas. Every scenario I'd rehearsed in therapy lined up in my head, neat and useless.

Junie wasn't upset.

She was just tired.

Tired was normal. Expected, even.

She'd been holding up so well after everything. The grief counselor I'd been seeing for months drilled the same thing into me every time we talked: *Meet her where she is. Safety first. Routine second. Love always.*

"She's been through hell," I told the pig, because somebody had to listen. "Kid gets a free pass for at least a decade, don't you think?"

She snuffled against my ribs. I took it as an agreement.

The Linwood Rink still looked like hell from the outside— dirty brick siding, a flickering sign—the kind of place you drove past unless you knew better. Inside, though, it was home. Cold air, old concrete, and the sound of blades cutting ice.

I pulled into the first available parking spot and climbed out, pig still in my arms, Rowdy right on my heels.

Tate's red eyebrows nearly disappeared into her hairline the second she spotted us. I'd known her my whole life—before the rink was hers, before it was partly mine too—and she knew better than anyone when to stop asking questions.

"You know," she said, "I'm lenient with Rowdy because he's awesome, but that's—"

"A service pig," I deadpanned, shifting the pig in my arms. "In training."

The piglet squealed on cue, sticking her happy little face out toward Tate.

A smile cracked her serious façade.

I didn't wait long enough to be denied, barreling through the lobby and up the stairs to her office. Blueprints littered the tables—early plans for the expansion Beckett had been pushing since he, his brother Mason, and I invested. Everything was still up in the air, but the Conway brothers did nothing halfway.

Junie lay curled in the old recliner, rain boots kicked off, hair mussed from sleep.

Her eyes flicked open when I knelt beside her.

"Hey, bug."

That tired little smile just about wrecked me. "You're here."

"Of course I am," I said. "I told you I was just a phone call away."

Her gaze dropped to the bundle in my arms, and her whole face lit up. "Is that a pig?"

"Indeed, it is."

Her hands flew to her mouth. "Can we keep her?"

I sighed, already defeated, but loving the look of pure adoration taking over my girl's face. "Yeah. Probably."

She reached out and brushed her hand over the piglet's back, reverent. "She's so warm."

The pig snorted. Rowdy leaned in, resigned to the chaos. Junie giggled—a sound I'd do just about anything to keep around.

"How'd you get her?" Junie asked once I had her buckled into her booster seat in the back of my truck, the pig settled in her lap. One small palm rested protectively against the piglet's back. Rowdy rode shotgun with a long-suffering expression, judging me with every breath.

Sunlight flashed through the trees on the side of the road, and I wondered if I was about to make this better or worse.

"A woman dropped her off at the hardware store earlier today."

Junie's brow furrowed. I caught her expression in the

rearview mirror and hesitated, already questioning the wisdom of continuing.

"She didn't want her?" Her voice cracked, tears filling those bright blue eyes. "How could she not want her?"

"This piglet's mom died," I said, choosing each word with care. "She's too little to survive on her own, so they brought her to me."

Junie nodded as tears spilled over her cheeks. She squeezed the piglet, holding on. "You'll be okay, Piggie," she whispered. "Ty's good at taking care of us."

I blinked fast, throat tight, because fuck. Seven words and she'd destroyed me.

Junie moved right past the moment, still murmuring to the pig. I stared out at the road, forcing myself to breathe, to keep it together.

Be steady.

Be safe.

Be what she needs.

I didn't know what I'd done to deserve her, but Junie was the best thing to ever happen to me. I couldn't screw this up for her.

"Do you want to live in my room, Piggie?" Junie said. "Ty painted it blue, and it's really cute. We can put a picture of you on the wall. You just have to make a funny face first."

I glanced at her in the mirror. "Piggie, huh?"

"Yeah. Isn't that the rapper you listen to in the barn? Piggie Smalls?"

I laughed, the sound surprising even me. "Yeah, bug. That's a great name."

Junie grinned wider, pleased with herself.

Piggie Smalls sniffed at Junie's face, her wet nose burrowing into the crease of her neck until Junie let out a soft giggle. I still didn't know what the hell I was doing, but with Junie humming softly, Rowdy's head heavy in my lap, and Piggie snoring against Junie's stomach, it almost felt like maybe we were going to be okay.

The gravel crunched under the tires as we turned down the long driveway. Daisy wore pink heart-shaped sunglasses that covered half her face as she knelt in the garden by Violet's house, wielding a trowel like she was determined to wrestle the weeds into submission.

All day I'd been worried about her, not sure how to help a grieving woman. Was it the same as a child? Offer her stability and just meet her where she was at? Maybe I should ask at my next therapy appointment.

Music blared out of a little stereo on her sister's porch, so it took her a minute to realize I had parked there. But the second she spotted Junie in the back seat, she frowned.

I pointed at my house, and Daisy followed me up the drive to the top of the hill. The moment I had the truck in park, Junie flung the door open and tumbled out with Piggie clutched to her chest.

"Dizzy!" she yelled, hair flying everywhere as she ran toward Daisy.

Daisy straightened, brushing her palms on her shorts. "Hey, cutie. Why are you—" She caught sight of the pig, then looked at me. "What the hell is that?"

"A pig," I said.

"A pig," she repeated.

"Yep."

By the time I rounded the front of the truck, Junie was halfway up the porch steps, piglet in her arms. Daisy met me at the base of the steps, eyes narrowed, half amused and half overwhelmed.

"There is a lot to unpack here."

"I didn't have a pig when I left this morning." I didn't know why I clarified that, but today had been weird on all fronts.

Her eyes crinkled. "I noticed that."

"She came from a rescue," I added. "Long story."

That earned a soft chuckle, and fuck, I loved that sound from the Winslow girls. "Of course she did."

Junie didn't even look up when we stepped into the house, already spreading a blanket on the living room floor. Her hockey mascot stuffed animals sat in a nearby pile while Piggie Smalls waddled through the middle.

"Okay, you go here because you're in the same division," Junie said, dropping a plush mascot into a neat line. "And you can't stand by him because you're rivals after the 1999 Stanley Cup."

Piggie sniffed one, then another.

Daisy stopped short beside me, watching the scene unfold. "Wow," she whispered. "So... hockey is a thing."

"You should hear her when she gets going on stats," I said. "That kid is the smartest person I know."

Junie glanced up, eyes bright. "If pigs could play hockey, do you think she'd be a goalie?"

As if demonstrating her skills, Piggie flopped down in the middle of the blanket, legs splayed, snout tucked against a stuffed animal's side.

Junie giggled and immediately launched into a detailed explanation of which mascots were nice, which ones were villains, and why Piggie couldn't trust the orange one with the weird eyes.

I leaned against the doorframe and let the noise wash over me—Junie's steady stream of hockey facts, Piggie's snorts,

Daisy's quiet laugh beside me. For a second, I stayed there, hands braced on the wood, grounding myself in the normalcy of it.

"Was she okay today?" Daisy asked after a few minutes.

Rowdy sat heavy at my feet, eyeing the living room chaos. "Yeah," I said. "Beckett called. Junie hit her limit."

"After this morning, I'm surprised she made it this long. I say we call it a win."

I nodded, glad we were on the same page.

Daisy took a tentative step into the living room, then sank down on the floor beside Junie. My girl beamed, showing her how to hold Piggie just right, like she'd been doing this for years instead of an afternoon.

"Are you good?" I asked.

Daisy lifted a thumb without looking back, already absorbed. "We're good."

I lingered another second, watching Junie curl closer to her, then turned away before my chest could tighten too much.

I stepped back outside, already making a mental list of everything we'd need for tonight.

15

TY

The evening settled around us, surprising for such an odd turn of events.

When Junie insisted again that the pig could sleep in her room, I shut that down gently but firmly. Daisy backed me up, and the pig ended up in a dog kennel with a soft blanket and a heat lamp from the barn.

Junie sat on the floor to feed Piggie from the bottle, the piglet's snout making wet snuffling sounds as she drank.

Daisy sat beside her, hair falling over her shoulder, a soft smile tugging at her lips. She played with Junie's hair absently, looking like the most natural thing in the world.

"You know, my mom died," Junie said as she brushed a hand over Piggie's face. "And Dizzy's mom died when she was little too."

Daisy's hand stilled, but she didn't interrupt.

Junie tipped the bottle a little higher. "That doesn't mean you don't have a family." She glanced up at Daisy, then down at the piglet. "We can be your family."

The words hit me low and hard.

Daisy leaned down and kissed the top of Junie's head, tears glistening in her eyes.

I leaned back against the doorframe, arms crossed over my chest. Between helping my sister rebuild her life and stepping into caring for Junie, I'd spent the last year holding everyone together with sheer stubbornness.

I wasn't the flashy forward. Never had been. I was the defenseman—the one who held the line, took the hit, and made sure everyone else stayed standing.

Protecting my sister. Junie. Daisy. Hell, this whole chaotic little world.

That part I understood.

But how did I protect people from the pain that didn't come with an opponent I could see?

Their grief wasn't something you blocked or absorbed—it was something you lived with. I couldn't take it from them or carry it for them, no matter how badly I wanted to. And that hurt me, too.

Together, the three of us got Piggie settled for the night, then it was Junie's turn for bed. Daisy helped her through bath time, then lay in her bed next to her, making up stories better than any children's book I'd ever read. Their soft laughter drifted down the hall to where I sat in the living room. I soaked it in, already dreading the day the house would be silent once more.

The living room was quiet, bathed in the soft glow from the TV. Rowdy was curled up in front of it, chin resting on his front paws, eyes half-lidded.

Daisy tiptoed down the hall after changing for bed, barefoot and sleepy, her hair tousled from lying beside Junie. The cushions dipped when she sank onto the couch, and for the first time all day, everything felt still.

"Baseball, huh?" She gestured toward the TV, where I had the volume turned down on the game. "I played softball as a kid."

I glanced her way, surprised. She'd never said much about her childhood aside from her brief mention in court. "Shortstop?"

"Yeah." She nodded, then looked over at me. "How'd you guess?"

"Impulsive. Optimistic to a fault. A little reckless, right?"

Her lips curved. "That's right. Guess you were listening, hm?"

If she only knew how many times I'd replayed that night in my head—her nervous chatter, the way her laugh hit me harder than a slapshot. I'd told myself it was nothing, timing gone sideways. But I'd never stopped hearing her laughter in the back of my mind.

Daisy tucked her legs under her, turning toward me. Even in the dim light, her eyes caught the flicker from the TV, crystalline and curious.

"I don't get you, Ty Hudson. Are you this nice all the time?"

My mustache twitched as I tried not to smile. "You say that like it's a bad thing."

"No," she said, shaking her head. A loose wave of hair slid forward, brushing her cheek. "It's just a lot. You're the animal rescue, hockey coach, foster dad superhero. Doesn't it get exhausting being that *good*?"

I shifted toward her, one arm resting along the back of the couch. The movement drew her in too—close enough that her knee brushed against my thigh. The touch was nothing, but it still sent a low hum through my chest.

When her hair fell forward again, I reached up and brushed

it back. My fingers grazed her skin, warm and soft, and she inhaled—barely audible, but enough to wreck my focus.

"I like those things," I said, forcing the words out. My hand lingered, thumb tracing a faint arc against her temple before I dropped it. "I like taking care of the people I love."

She held my gaze, the dim light catching in her eyes. "But who takes care of you, Ty?"

There was a double edge to it—like she was talking about more than responsibility, like maybe she saw the cracks I kept hidden from everyone else. She didn't move away, and I didn't want her to.

I managed a rough exhale, leaning back just enough to keep from reaching for her again. "I'm okay."

"So, I see you have yet to stop saying it's okay when it's not."

A rough chuckle left me. "This is the reason we said *questions you'd never ask on a first date*. You're not supposed to know these things."

"You better believe I'm not drinking that chocolate milk in the fridge either, now that I know it's full of backwash."

My chin dropped to my chest, shaking with silent laughter.

The TV lit up, and the announcer called out Ethan Stone's name.

"Oh, he's my favorite," Daisy said, pointing to the screen. "Every time he's at the plate, it's like forearm porn."

I tugged my hat off my head, holding it in my hands instead, because, *fuck*, I did not like the sound of that. "We had the same agent. I know Ethan."

She chuckled, then tugged her sleeves down over her hands. "Of course you do."

"Stone's been on fire this season," the announcer said, voice rising with excitement. "If he keeps this up, he's headed for Hall of Fame status and a household name up there with the greats."

As if he'd heard them, Stone hit the ball hard down the line, the crack of the bat sharp even through the low volume.

I should've been watching it. Instead, I was watching Daisy.

The way her eyes lit up when she leaned forward. How her sleeve hung over her knuckles as she curled her hands together. The quiet little sound she made under her breath.

I'd seen a thousand games like this, but sitting here with her, sharing this small, ordinary slice of my life felt different.

"Get out, get out, get out," Daisy said, perched on the edge of the couch now, locked in.

The ball clipped the very top of the wall and dropped back into play. She fell back with a groan.

"Damn." She gestured toward the TV as the announcers confirmed Ethan stopped at second. "That was so close."

I nodded, still a half-beat behind, my attention slow to catch up.

"Yeah," I said, finally looking away.

We watched the game together, her quizzing me about which players I knew—a lot of them—and asking for gossip about each one. Unfortunately for her, three years out of the city meant everything I knew was old news, and not as juicy as she hoped.

"So, no one is secretly dating the manager's daughter?" she asked. "Or maybe a player's sister? No rivals hooking up in their hotel rooms?"

I turned my hat in my hands and gave her a lopsided grin. "Not that I'm aware of, no."

"Well, that's kind of a bummer."

I laughed, then stood to get myself a drink. "Want anything while I'm up?"

She waved me off, then turned around to watch me go. The longer she stared, the wider her grin spread. I looked away to reach into the fridge, pulling out a Gatorade. When I cracked the lid, she let out a little huff.

"I thought I was about to witness your little act of rebellion."

"Well, I can't now that you're watching me."

She shook her head, then went back to watching the game. "How was your day?"

"Had a pig dropped in my lap," I said between sips. "So, weird."

Her laugh was small but real. "I'm thinking that's just a regular Tuesday for you," she said, tilting her head back toward me, eyes glinting.

"Maybe."

"At this rate, you should start building an ark or something."

"Junie would be thrilled," I said, lips twitching. "Two of every kind."

She grinned, quick and bright. "Right. You, me, a couple of chickens—boom, we could restart the population."

I choked on my drink, orange liquid drenching my shirt.

"I did *not*—" she stammered, clapping a hand over her mouth. "That came out so wrong."

As I lost it to a coughing fit, her face turned scarlet.

"I meant animals! Obviously, the animals, not—"

"Procreation as an emergency survival plan?" I smirked, then grabbed a towel to wipe up the mess I'd made.

"Ty!"

I bit the inside of my cheek to keep from laughing. "What? You're the one planning on repopulating the world."

She groaned, hiding her face behind both hands. "I hate you."

"Pretty sure you started it."

"I did *not* start anything!"

But when she dropped her hands, still pink and smiling, something unspoken lingered between us. An image neither of us had asked for, and now I was trying very hard not to think about.

I stared at the TV, but the game was just background noise now. Every cell in my body was aware of her—her warmth lingering in the air, the scent of her shampoo wafting through the dim room, the way her hoodie had slipped to the right just enough to expose the curve of her collarbone.

She sighed, the sound catching halfway between tired and honest, and I looked back at her.

"I went inside Violet's house today."

That pulled me straight out of my head. "Yeah?"

She nodded. "I didn't stay long. I thought I could handle it —just clean something up, maybe sort through boxes—but the second I walked in, it all hit me." She swallowed. "So I turned around and walked right back out."

"That's okay," I said without hesitation.

"I know. I just..." She sighed, rubbing at her palm like she could scrub the feeling away. "I hate I couldn't do it. Every time something gets hard, I bail. I make jokes, I make plans, I move on to the next thing instead of—" Her voice wobbled, then steadied. "It's like my brain sees pain coming and goes, *Nope. Next adventure. Distraction, aisle five.*"

I shook my head. "That's not weakness."

"Maybe not. But it makes me feel like I'm always running." Her shoulders sagged. "And I'm so tired of running."

I leaned forward, forearms resting on my thighs, keeping my voice low and even. "You don't run because you're broken, Daisy. You run because you know how to survive."

Her eyes lifted to mine.

"You're good at finding light," I continued. "Movement. Motion. Action. That's not something you need to fix. It just means sometimes you forget you're allowed to stop, too."

She huffed a shaky laugh. "I don't do still very well."

"I know," I said. "So don't force it. You don't have to face everything tonight. You don't have to be brave or productive or strong." My gaze held hers. "You're allowed to come back later. Or tomorrow. Or not at all yet."

Her breath caught, eyes glassy now. She didn't respond. Just sat there breathing shallowly, fingers worrying the cuff of her sweatshirt like it was the only thing tethering her to the moment.

I stayed right where I was—close enough to steady her, far enough not to crowd—letting her be who she was, without asking her to change a thing.

The room went quiet, thick with unspoken words, so I checked on the piglet one more time, then refilled Rowdy's water bowl. I settled back down next to her, acutely aware of the space that felt both too close and too far.

She had the neck of her hoodie pulled over her chin, her brow furrowed in thought. I reached over, my fingers brushing down the small creases on her forehead before I even realized what I'd done.

Her blue eyes met mine, wide and shimmering, a spark igniting between us at the simple touch.

"Sorry," I murmured, wishing I hadn't removed my hat,

craving something to occupy my hands. "I shouldn't have done that. You just looked—"

"Why didn't you ask for my number?" she interrupted, eyes searching mine.

This time it was my turn to stare at her, wide-eyed and surprised.

"I came back downstairs, you know." Her voice cracked, vulnerability creeping in. "The second the elevator doors closed, I knew I'd made a huge mistake letting you go."

Her admission hung in the air, and it took me a moment to register the weight of her words, my heart thundering in my chest.

A laugh escaped her, but it was a fragile sound. Those bright blue eyes glistened, threatening to spill over. "I've thought about that night so many times. Wondered if I'd just imagined how close I felt to you. I made it up, right? That wasn't real."

"Daisy."

She shook her head. "No, it's okay. I shouldn't have said anything. I'm a sappy mess, and you always say the right things, and I just—never mind."

She stood before I could respond, then grabbed the hem of her sweatshirt. My breath caught as I watched her lift it over her head, revealing the delicate pajama set beneath. The thin material hugged her curves, illuminated by the soft glow of the TV, each contour accentuated in a way that left me breathless.

I froze, torn between the desire to reach out and the fear of shattering this fragile moment.

Once free of the fabric, she held the sweatshirt out to me. "I should give this back."

I stared at the hoodie, my heart racing as I processed the

familiar fabric, the faded Storm logo, realizing only now how deeply intertwined our past and present had become.

Three years ago, I admitted how deeply I feared not being chosen back. But here she was, standing in front of me, telling me she *had* chosen me. And still, I'd walked away.

"You didn't imagine it," I whispered, my heart racing with the admission.

Her gaze lifted to mine, glassy and uncertain.

"I've thought about you every day for the last three years. Wondering how your life had turned out. If you'd found your happiness. But never did I imagine we'd be here, standing in my living room together, given a second chance."

I stood, closing the distance just enough to take the sweatshirt. But instead of pulling it from her hands, I folded her fingers back around it.

"Keep it," I whispered, meaning it more than she knew.

My shirt.

My heart.

My home.

She blinked. "Ty—"

"It's yours. It always was."

Her throat bobbed as she swallowed, and for a second she looked as if she might argue. But she didn't. Instead, she tugged the sweatshirt back on, pulling it close.

We stood there for a beat longer, the space between us humming with everything we weren't ready to touch yet.

"I should check on Junie," she whispered.

"Yeah," I replied, though the word cost me more than it should have. "Good idea."

She turned toward the hallway, glancing back at me. Then she was gone, her bare feet padding down the hall.

I stayed where I was, my chest tight in a way that felt unfamiliar and right all at once.

I'd spent most of my life thinking love meant *doing*—fixing, carrying, stepping in before anyone else could fall. But Daisy didn't need me to rescue her.

What she needed was someone steady.

Someone who wouldn't disappear the moment things got hard.

Someone who could weather the storm.

And, maybe most importantly, someone to help her find the light again once it had passed.

I was that someone, and this time—no matter how messy or ill-timed or complicated it got—I wasn't walking away.

16

Daisy

I didn't sleep much that night. Every time I closed my eyes, I saw the flicker of the TV on Ty's face, the quiet steadiness in his eyes when I didn't know what to say.

He never rushed to fill the silence or tell me it would all be okay.

He just *listened*.

No fixing. No escape hatch. No plan.

For someone like me who'd built her entire life on outrunning the hard things or fixing them as fast as possible, that kind of steadiness felt terrifying. Nothing he said had been earth-shattering, but all of it together? It made me feel seen. Maybe even wanted. And that confused my brain.

When I finally drifted off, it was to the faint scent of pine clinging to his sweatshirt and the echo of his voice still threading through my head.

I've thought about you every day for the last three years.

By morning, I had convinced myself I was fine, or close enough to fake it. Sure, I stayed in denial longer than Violet gave me permission for, but each day it got easier to come up with another reason I couldn't stop to grieve *today.*

I had to keep moving, to stay busy, running from the invisible monster biting at my heels.

Luckily, the next week in Linwood went by faster than I expected. The days fell into a rhythm—early morning coffee on Ty's porch, the mountains pink and hazy in the sunrise, followed by the sound of Junie's voice drifting in from the barn.

Ty had her helping with the animals, which meant she followed him around asking endless questions about feed schedules and how many chickens was too many chickens. I didn't know the answer, but one rooster seemed like one too many.

Piggie Smalls was an eight-week-old menace with hooves and had declared herself queen of the barnyard. The little black-and-white mischief-maker followed Rowdy everywhere, who then followed Junie, making them a chaotic train of cuteness as they paraded around the property.

Meanwhile, I stayed busy outside Violet's house. The flower beds were free of weeds and full of bright colors that screamed Colorado summer. I also swept the porch and removed the rotted boards—the front steps no longer looked like a lawsuit waiting to happen.

Every time Ty asked if he could help, I politely told him no. He was already doing plenty to save my ass; the last thing I wanted was to take anything else from him.

And yet, Thursday morning when I walked down to her house ready to work, the exact supplies I needed were in a neat pile on the driveway. I looked over at the truck where he was buckling Junie in, heading to the rink. He was staring right back.

Moments later, they rolled down the drive, stopping in front of me. Rowdy hung out of the open window, tongue lolling off to the side, and Piggie was in Junie's arms. Ty was busy typing on his phone, then dropped it into the cup holder.

My phone buzzed in my pocket, and I pulled it out.

TY

I'm not helping.

Below it was a link to a YouTube video showing how to repair a porch almost identical to mine.

The longer I stared at it, the easier it was to grin.

"Thank you."

Ty just nodded, then rolled down the driveway.

"BYE DIZZY! LOVE YOU!" Junie called out the window.

"TO THE MOON!" I yelled back, blowing her a kiss.

As soon as the words left my mouth, my phone fell from my hands, landing on the grass.

Such simple words, and yet saying Violet's and my phrase without her felt like I'd taken a blow to the chest.

Not now.

Not now.

Not now.

My hands shook as I looked at my phone, focusing on it instead.

Eventually, I breathed again, and I threw myself into fixing the porch. That was something tangible, and that was easier than unpacking my emotions.

The mismatched boards didn't line up perfectly, and the stain I picked was a shade too bright. I didn't realize until it was too late that I should have power washed the rest down and re-stained it all to match, but that was a later-me problem.

I couldn't go back inside, though.

Not today.

Every time I got close to the door, my chest went tight, feeling every inch of Violet's loss all over again.

Luckily for me, there wasn't much time to dwell on it. For such a little town, Linwood stayed busy. Between Emmy stopping by with every single one of Junie's favorite foods she just happened to "buy too much of," Beckett showing up to talk hockey and somehow ending up grilling in the backyard, and the entire Mayhem crew making frequent appearances to see Piggie Smalls, the house was rarely quiet.

I kept avoiding the paperwork I needed to fill out and ignoring the emails from the funeral home. Junie was safe, and that was all that mattered. I could keep breathing, keep living, even though it felt like the hole in my chest was growing with each shallow inhale.

As long as I kept moving, I was okay.

Which was how I found myself standing in front of Emmy's Pilates studio the following Tuesday night, heart pounding harder than it should have over something as simple as *Girl's Night*.

"Holy shit, you're here!" a woman I hadn't met yet shrieked as I walked through the glass doors into the studio. Her dark blonde hair was in a high ponytail, and she wore bike shorts and an oversized tee that said *World's Okayest Mom*. She bounced on her socked feet, clapping her hands in front of her chest in excitement, then shoved her hand forward to shake. "I'm Stevie, and I have been waiting patiently to meet you."

"Patient?" another woman said from behind the front desk, her black hair covering most of her pale features. "You got here two hours early and have mentioned Daisy twenty-seven times." She pointed a long, black fingernail at a tally on a piece of paper, then slid it across the desk.

Stevie's shoulders dropped, and she rolled her eyes. "You're so dramatic, Shannon."

"Facts don't care about your feelings," Shannon said dryly, the corners of her dark-painted mouth twitching. She wore ripped black jeans, a Slipknot tee, and enough gold jewelry to set off every airport scanner in the state.

"Wait," I said, looking at her more closely. "Did you grow up here? You look so familiar."

Shannon stared at me for a beat, her grey eyes focused on me. "I did. Did you?"

"Only in the summer."

She slapped the desk, then gave me a crooked grin. "Yes. Holy shit, Daisy. Why didn't I put that together?"

"Wait," Stevie said, "You know each other?"

"Summer between my junior and senior year of high school, we worked at—"

"Slice N Spice," we said together.

"The year it opened."

"That's right." I grinned. "We ate at least three za-cos a day that year."

"I still can't look at them without gagging," Shannon said. "Pizza, sure. Tacos, okay. I do not need both at one time, ever again."

I couldn't help but laugh, remembering how much fun I'd had that summer. It was the only summer I came to stay with Aunt Maggie without Violet, and the entire drive from Missouri to Colorado I'd been dreading a long, boring summer alone. Instead, I got a job and chopped more tomatoes than any one human should ever touch.

"This is so fun!" Stevie's hands were clasped under her chin as she smiled at me, then at Shannon. "Who knew Shannon had friends?"

Shannon snorted. "I have friends. You're just not one of them."

Stevie leaned down and squeezed Shannon in a bone-crushing hug, all while Shannon swatted at her arms. A little girl with bouncy blonde curls appeared from behind them, clinging to Stevie's thigh like a barnacle.

"And this is Harper," Stevie said when she let go of a now-rumpled Shannon. "She's two, and has decided Shannon is her emotional support goth."

Shannon's mouth quirked. "That's right, little bestie. *We're* friends, aren't we?"

Before I could respond, another voice joined the chaos. "If you're not careful, Stevie will rope you into making friendship bracelets."

I turned to see a tall redhead with the calmest energy of the bunch. She was stretching on a mat just beyond the front desk, her long hair braided down her back.

"That's Tate," Emmy said from the far side of the studio, where she was setting up a reformer. She looked put-together in green leggings and a matching cropped tank, her short brown hair tucked behind her ears. "She owns the hockey rink, and she pretends not to like us, but don't let her fool you. Tate is just as invested in this weird little bunch."

Tate smiled, then straightened her grey and green Mayhem Hockey Club tee. "I'm easily bribed with snacks and sarcasm."

"Here, here," Shannon said.

I glanced around at the group. "So, are you all moms?"

Stevie lit up. "The Moms of Mayhem."

Shannon and Tate groaned in unison.

"We are not moms," Shannon said, pointing back and forth between Tate and herself.

"And I still don't know how I got roped into a group chat titled *Puckin' Exhausted*," Tate added.

Emmy grinned from her mat. "Because you love us."

Tate stretched her legs out in front of her. "I said I tolerate you. There's a difference."

The four of them broke into overlapping chatter and laughter, speaking of familiarity and deep-rooted friendship. I watched them, amused and a little in awe. They didn't make sense together—Stevie with her toddler mom chaos, Shannon looking like she'd fit better in a mosh pit than a Pilates studio, Tate giving off calm mountain-yoga energy, and Emmy glowing like the sun—and yet somehow, it worked.

I had no idea how this mismatched group of women had become friends, but as I stepped farther into the room, I wanted to be a part of it.

Following the sound of laughter, I walked past the front desk and around the half-wall that divided the lobby from the studio.

The room stretched long and narrow, softly lit by purple LEDs that glowed along the mirrors. A dozen sleek contraptions filled the space in two perfect rows—all wood and metal, each one topped with a padded carriage that slid back and forth on rails. The reformers looked like something between a high-end workout machine and a medieval torture rack.

Next to each one was a mat and a basket of rings, straps, hand weights, and other items I didn't recognize. There wasn't a treadmill or dumbbell in sight, and I suddenly regretted every time I'd ever thought of Pilates as "fancy stretching."

It was quiet, organized, and terrifying.

I stepped onto the mat Emmy pointed out for me, trying not to look like the rookie who didn't know which end was up.

"Have you ever taken a reformer Pilates class before?" Emmy asked, and I shook my head.

"Me neither," Stevie said, her hand in front of her mouth. She sat on another reformer across from mine, legs crossed with a bag of potato chips between them.

My brow furrowed, and Tate must have sensed my confusion from where she lay on her back on the machine next to me. "She comes every Tuesday and has never so much as laid down on the shuttle."

"Well," Shannon said from the back of the room where she sat inside a little playpen full of toys, Harper in her lap. "One time she did."

Stevie launched a chip in her direction, then looked back at me with an exaggerated sigh. "I fell asleep once and they never let me forget it."

"It was your first time here," Emmy said, barely containing her laugh. "I've never seen someone doze off so fast."

"Puckin' exhausted isn't just some cute little pun I made up," Stevie shot back. "It's a way of life."

Tate just shook her head, then put her feet on the bar and pushed away in a smooth movement. "Workout, or don't, Daisy. Your call. It's just me, sometimes Emmy. Never Shannon or Stevie."

At the mention of their names, the two polar-opposite women each held up a hand and air high-fived from where they sat.

Emmy grinned, then came to stand in front of me. "Do you want to try it? No pressure."

I looked around the room, unsure what I'd gotten myself into, then lay back on the padded reformer, mirroring Tate's pose. Emmy helped me get into position, and I followed her instructions through a series of stretches that felt more than a little weird.

"Okay." Stevie wiped her hands on a wet wipe, then put the bag of chips on the floor next to her. "Let's talk about the rink now. What's the plan, Tate?"

I stood with one foot on the reformer, one on the floor in a lunge deeper than I'd ever attempted before. Sweat beaded between my boobs, but I did my best to listen to the women and not tip over.

Emmy laid a hand on my back, then nudged my foot on the ground a half-inch to the right, and suddenly the stretch felt glorious.

"I signed the papers to bring Beckett, Mason, and Ty on as investors in the rink a few weeks ago," Tate said, and I looked up at the mention of Ty. "I'm the majority stakeholder, but those three goons are pushy as hell."

The women hummed in agreement, and I chuckled at their take. Ty hadn't been pushy with me, but he was protective. Of course, he was saving the rink too.

"I don't know how Mason made it happen and I'm beyond asking questions of his methods"—Tate let out a laugh that sounded somewhere between frustrated and amused—"but blueprints for an expansion project arrived at the rink the next morning. A second rink, a roof that's angled and won't collapse under the weight of another Colorado winter, a huge commercial kitchen upstairs where the observation deck is for both rinks. He thought of everything, except for the fact I'm not taking millions of dollars from them when I don't have funds to contribute too."

"What if we all contribute?" Stevie asked. "How much is it going to cost?"

"Do you have $20 million lying around that I'm unaware of?"

Shannon let out a long whistle. "I'm out."

"Yeah, I don't have that," Stevie said. "Holy shit."

Tate let out a long sigh, then Emmy guided us both to sit on our reformers. I gave up trying to mirror Tate's movements, turning to sit criss-cross on the reformer like Stevie instead, invested in this conversation.

"What about a fundraiser?" I asked, thinking of the many community events I'd organized in Chicago. "You need the down payment for the construction loan, right? And the rink's a big deal in town."

"Yeah," Emmy said, hands on her hips as she stared at me. "What are you thinking?"

I shrugged. "I don't know. The town I grew up in had a huge street carnival every year to raise money. That would probably work great here."

Tate sat upright, staring at Emmy and having some sort of silent conversation. Stevie's knees bounced where she sat with her hands in front of her mouth, as if she could barely contain her excitement.

"Would Beckett go for it?" Tate asked, her brow creased.

"Are you kidding?" Emmy waved her off. "He's ready to sink his retirement account into getting the Mayhem back on top. Yes, I promise he'll do it, and if not, I'll just bribe him with favors of the sexual variety."

Shannon made a retching sound. "Let's not go back to discussing your sex life. You're engaged and in love, we get it."

Stevie squealed, practically exploding off the reformer she'd never once used, then ran to the front desk to grab a pad of paper and a pen. "I love this idea. What are we thinking? I bet I can get Luke to round up some of the local builders to sponsor it. And if we advertise in the ski towns, the summer tourists will come in droves."

Tate laughed, sounding more disbelieving than amused. "You guys realize this would have to happen fast, right? Like, within the next few weeks if we want to hit summer traffic around the Fourth of July. That's not much time to plan something this size."

"Good thing chaos is our love language," Emmy said, already pulling her phone from her pocket. "We'll do it the Linwood way—volunteers, donated booths, every business pitching in. We can set up in the community park across from River Street."

Stevie scribbled. "We'll need food trucks, a dunk tank, games, live music, raffles—oh! Maybe a bake-off?"

Tate groaned. "You just want to win a ribbon for your snickerdoodles."

"Maybe I do," Stevie said. "Don't be jealous because my cookies are spiritual experiences."

Shannon looked up from her phone. "I bet I can get the Lantern to set up a beer garden. As much as I hate it, everyone is more likely to come if there's alcohol."

Emmy grinned. "Perfect. A carnival for the whole town—family fun, live music, food, drinks, maybe a few classic booths for nostalgia's sake." Her eyes flicked toward me, and her smile grew wider.

Within minutes, we'd somehow formed an unofficial committee. Stevie was gathering vendors, Tate was calling the town board for permits, Shannon was designing flyers, and Emmy had already texted Beckett that she'd volunteered him to help "with the heavy stuff." And I was in charge of it all.

By the time I stood to leave, my head spun with half-baked

plans and the sound of Stevie singing *Best Friend* under her breath.

Emmy pulled me into a quick hug before I could make it out the door. "Welcome to the mayhem," she said with a grin. "And for the record, you're stuck with us now. Pilates, carnivals, all of it."

I hugged her back, soaking in the warmth that radiated from her. "That doesn't sound so bad."

"Glad you agree." She released me and nudged me toward the door. "Go kick my boys out and give that little girl a kiss goodnight for me."

Outside, the evening air was cool and sweet with pine. I climbed into my car, the seat still warm from the sun, and started the drive home.

The road wound through town, past River Street and up toward the ridge. By the time my headlights cut across Copper Ridge, they caught the pale siding of Violet's farmhouse at the bottom of the hill.

For the first time all week, my chest didn't ache when I looked at it.

Not as much, anyway.

Tomorrow, I promised myself, I'd try again.

And maybe this time I'd go inside.

17

TY

"You got any princess kittens?" Beckett asked from across my kitchen table on Tuesday evening. "I can't tell if that's a crown or a tiara, so maybe it's a queen kitten."

I stared at him. "Do you hear yourself?"

My best friend grinned, unbothered by neither the girly deck of cards in our hands nor the tiny pastel teacup painted with flowers pinched between two fingers. He took a sip, the slurping sound ringing out through my quiet house. "A man's gotta adapt after retirement. Some guys golf. You, apparently, traded your skates for tea parties. Should we braid each other's hair next?"

I slid him a card. "Fuck you."

He took another sip from his tiny cup, pinky still out, tattooed forearms flexing with the little movement. "I'm flattered, but I'll have to pass. Your sister, though? She—."

"I could bury your body anywhere on this ranch, and no one would ever find you. So, think hard before you finish that sentence."

A squeal coming from the laundry room that was half-

Junie, half-Piggie drowned Beckett's deep laugh out. My mustache twitched as I held back a smile at the delighted sound.

Raising a bottle-fed potbelly pig wasn't on my bingo card, but Junie had thrown herself into learning and caring for Piggie over the last week. I knew it was her way of avoiding grief, but I couldn't stop myself from doing anything that brought her an ounce of happiness.

"So." Beckett laid down a set of sparkly princess kittens holding a donut. "How is playing house with Daisy going? Emmy was so excited she showed up to girls' night tonight."

"We're not playing house."

One dark eyebrow lifted to just below his backward hat. "You live together, you parent together, and you adopted a potbellied pig. That sounds pretty domestic to me."

"I'm helping her," I said, maybe a little too fast. "We both love Junie. That's it."

His chair creaked when he leaned back. "Uh-huh. Not awkward at all? No tension? No late-night *'oops, our hands touched reaching for the milk'* moments?"

A deep sigh escaped me, and I tapped my cards on the table. As ridiculous as Beckett's question was, I couldn't help but replay Daisy's and my conversation from a few nights ago.

Maybe I shouldn't have admitted I've thought about her every day for the last three years, but damn, it was true.

Since then, she'd been polite. Careful. Always busy with Junie or Piggie or something that needed doing—never alone with me as we had been that night.

Maybe this was just what parenting looked like—everyone too tired to poke at feelings, too focused on surviving the day.

Or maybe I'd said too much, and she was already pulling away.

That thought pissed me off. "Do you want to play cards, or do you want to get punched?"

Beckett chuckled. "Buddy, I've been punched by you before. You don't scare me."

I grabbed my hat, readjusting it on my head. "I hate you."

"No, you don't." He grinned. "But thanks for confirming I'm right. Something's going on here."

I flipped through my cards—unicorns, mermaids, and a dolphin wearing sunglasses—and decided I was too damn tired for this conversation.

Over the last several months, I'd thought about becoming Junie's guardian logically, preparing my house and my life for a child. But nothing had prepared me for the emotional toll of being responsible for a little person.

Sure, I'd dealt with physical exhaustion as part of my job for years, but this was a different tired that sank all the way to my bones.

My brain was tired from overthinking every smile, every sigh, every shrug of indifference Junie had tossed out lately.

My heart was tired from worrying about her non-stop.

And my soul was tired from imagining a day she wouldn't be mine to worry about.

But the laughter drifting through the house tonight was genuine, and I relaxed a fraction at the sound. We weren't out of the woods, but I wasn't failing yet either.

"Do you have any mermaids?" I muttered, and Beckett's laugh filled the kitchen as he tossed a glittering mermaid my way.

"I like that Daisy girl," Lori said from where she sat in the living room. "She was always a nice child, too. Maggie adored her."

I looked at Beckett's mom as I slapped the two mermaids

on the table. "Nope. You're not allowed to chip in to this conversation, Mrs. Conway."

"It's *Lori.*" She shook her head. "We've discussed this. I'm old. You're old. We're all on a first-name basis."

Beckett brushed a hand over his beard. "Got any flamingos, Boomer?"

"Shut the fuck up," I muttered. "Go fish."

Lori came to join us at the table, her cane tapping on the wooden floor as she walked. Beckett hopped up to pull back the seat next to him and helped her into the chair. Her chin-length white-blonde hair framed a face still sharp with humor and command, even if her hands trembled when she brushed it from her face. It was hard to see the untouchable, unshakable Lori Conway battle Parkinson's disease, but she was still the same tough-as-nails woman I remembered.

"I swear, you boys and your dirty mouths," Lori said once she sat down. "Like I didn't teach you better."

"Yeah, Ty," Beckett said with a smug grin, right before his mom slapped him upside the back of the head. "Ow! What was that for?"

"Please, I heard you two at the grill earlier talking about the rink expansion. I just couldn't get out there fast enough to slap you then."

I looked down at my cards, glad the brim of my hat was hiding the amusement I was having difficulty holding in. "Have any unicorns?"

"Which color?" Beckett asked, staring at his cards. "There seems to be a lot of f—un unicorns in this deck."

"Ask him for the purple one." Lori stole a handful of chips from the bag still sitting on the end of the table, the last remnants from our burger night. "He has that one."

"Mom." Beckett sounded more than a little exasperated as he passed it over.

I didn't have a purple unicorn in my hand—mine was teal—but I hated losing, no matter the game.

A soft thump and a squeal from the hallway had Beckett glancing up, and I followed his gaze.

"About time," he said as Jace stepped out of the laundry room. His shaggy hair stuck out from under his hoodie, and the bored expression he usually wore had more than a few cracks in it.

Right behind him was Junie in purple unicorn pajamas, Piggie Smalls in her arms. She held out the pig like a proud show-and-tell exhibit. "She needed goodnight kisses."

"Well, how could anyone sleep without that?" Lori asked. She leaned forward to scratch Piggie's ear as the piglet snorted happily. "Goodnight, cutie patootie."

Jace rolled his eyes in full teenage fashion, though the smile tugging at the corner of his mouth betrayed him. "Did you know Mom *wallpapered* her kennel in the laundry room? It might be nicer than mine."

Beckett grinned. "Yes, well, your room looks more like a pigsty than Piggie's, so that makes sense."

Junie dissolved into giggles, then put Piggie down on the floor. The piglet's wet nose sniffed along Lori's ankles, and she let a delighted laugh loose. Even my grumpy nephew chuckled as he shoved his hands into his hoodie pocket.

I leaned back in my chair, taking in the mess of it all—laughter, noise, Piggie's squeals, Junie's wild hair, Beckett's shit-eating grin—and wondered how I ever thought I preferred quiet nights alone to this.

"Speaking of bedtime"—I stood and stretched—"it's your turn, kiddo."

Junie groaned, but she scooped up Piggie and headed down the hall. Beckett and Jace helped Lori up, their voices soft and familiar as they gathered her things and said goodbye. I started clearing the table—cards, chip crumbs, half-empty glasses—while the house quieted around me.

When the door closed behind them and only the hum of the fridge and faint giggles from the laundry room remained, I glanced at my hands resting on the sink full of dishes and smiled to myself.

"Okay," Junie said as she skipped down the hall toward her bedroom. "I'm ready for bed!"

"Brush your teeth, kid," I said loud enough she stopped and looked over her shoulder at me with enough sass to tell me her teen years would be a trip.

She rolled her eyes, then went into the bathroom first. I went into my room to change from my usual jeans into a pair of gym shorts and an old Storm tee, then followed her to her bedroom.

Junie's room had a faint purple glow, the star projector she loved painting constellations across the ceiling. Tiny galaxies spun above the bed she'd filled with stuffed animals, books, and one very smug pig-shaped pillow Stevie found for her.

"Alright, kiddo." I leaned against the doorway. "Did you brush your teeth?"

She nodded, glasses on her nightstand now, then pointed to the farm animal encyclopedia we'd gotten from the library. "Did you know pigs dream when they feel safe? All day today, I watched Piggie nap to see if I could tell. She's very twitchy, so I think it's true."

I smiled, crossing the room to sit on the edge of her bed. "Sounds like you're doing a great job then. She must be happy here."

Junie climbed under the blankets, her shoulders slumped more than before. "Maybe. I think she misses her mom sometimes, though."

My throat worked as I tried to find the right words. "Yeah," I said. "I bet she does. Maybe she always will, and that's okay."

She was quiet for a long time, tracing a little pattern on her blanket. "What happens to people when they die?"

That one hit square in the chest.

I rubbed the back of my neck, watching the stars crawl across her ceiling. "I don't know for sure," I said. "Some people think they go to heaven. Some people think they're still around us in ways we can't see. But"—I pointed to the bright scatter of lights above us—"I like to imagine they turn into stars. That way, when we look up, we can still find them."

Junie tilted her head back, eyes reflecting the twinkling starlight. "Do you think my mom's up there?"

"Yeah," I said, the word coming out rougher than I meant. "Yeah, kiddo. I think she's shining pretty bright."

She scooted over and patted the pillow beside her. "Will you look with me?"

I hesitated for a moment, then lay down on top of the covers, careful not to jostle the mountain of mascots Junie had neatly arranged. Rowdy curled up on the rug, and for a while, we just breathed—two heartbeats syncing under a galaxy of blinking stars.

Junie pointed at one of the moving constellations projected on the ceiling. "That one looks like Piggie."

"Yeah? Where?"

"Right there." She drew her hand through the air. "See her funny nose?"

I chuckled. "Yeah, bug. I see it."

She turned her head toward me as her little hand wove its way into mine. "I love you, Ty."

My chest squeezed so hard it hurt, and I reached over to kiss the top of her head. "I love you too, bug."

She nodded once, then her eyelids fluttered closed, hand still in mine. I rolled onto my side to face her, watching her for a long time—this little girl who'd lost everything and still managed to find wonder in pigs and stars—and felt something twist deep inside me.

Loving Junie was the easiest thing I'd ever done. What wasn't easy was admitting that somewhere along the way, I'd started needing her just as much as she needed me.

And Daisy... that was worse.

Wanting her wasn't simple. It was complicated and messy and maybe even a little selfish.

It wasn't just that my body was craving her—though that was getting hard to ignore.

But I liked who I was with Daisy.

She didn't make me feel reckless. She made me feel *alive*.

But how the hell did I ask for anything from them?

They were doing their best to put one foot in front of the other, surviving the shitty hand life had dealt them. So what right did I have to say, *don't forget about me*?

Lying there in the dim light, Junie's small hand in mine, I had to face the truth.

I didn't just want to keep them safe.

I wanted a place in their world.

And wanting that felt dangerous.

Because if I ever lost it, it wouldn't just hurt. It would break me.

Daisy

The house was quiet when I let myself in; the door clicking shut behind me. I kicked off my shoes, still buzzing from a head full of plans for the rink fundraiser.

"Ty?" I said, looking in the kitchen for him. I was quickly discovering he was a man who thrived on routine. Each night after Junie went to bed, he cleaned the kitchen, started the laundry, then sat on the couch to watch sports. Some nights it was baseball, others tennis, or soccer, or golf. From what I could tell, he liked anything with a scorecard.

He didn't answer, and the kitchen was empty, save for a note stuck to the air-fryer on the counter.

THOUGHT YOU MIGHT WANT THIS.

Curiosity got me, and I opened the small appliance to find a cheeseburger waiting inside. It was still warm, cheese melted over the sides, and I couldn't help but grin. As if this weren't thoughtful enough, when I grabbed the plate he'd left nearby, there was a small packet of mayo on top.

My heart felt lighter than it had any reason to, given the circumstances, the longer I looked at the stupid little burger.

But this seemed to encapsulate everything I liked about Ty.

He wasn't loud with his affections. He wasn't flashy or demanding. He was *constant.*

And with each passing day, I was coming to realize just how special that was.

I put the burger on the plate, then spread the mayo over the top, thinking about that first night.

Rowdy's head poked out of Junie's bedroom door as I crept down the hall. "Hey, handsome." I crouched to ruffle the fur around his neck. "Where's everybody hiding?"

He huffed, then limped back into the bedroom.

I followed him, my steps soft on the wooden floor and a smile already tugging up at the corners before I saw them.

Ty lay stretched across the top of Junie's bed, one arm thrown protectively over her small frame. Junie was out cold, her constellation light throwing slow-moving stars across the ceiling.

Like this, he looked peaceful. The hard edges I expected were gone, softened by sleep. He shifted just enough that I saw his hand wrapped around Junie's, and the sight undid me.

Not the mustache.

Not the messy hair.

Not the body.

But *that.*

The tenderness of it. The way this man—who didn't owe her a damn thing—had become her anchor in a storm I could barely stand in myself. He looked so solid, so heartbreakingly gentle, holding my niece as if she were his own.

Needing to preserve this moment, I pulled out my phone

and snapped a picture. It was just a quick shot—the stars, Junie's little hand, the curve of Ty's arm around her.

Before I thought about what I was doing, I opened my messages.

DAISY

BRB just died of cuteness overload

The second I hit send, the truth hit like a gut punch.

I'd sent it to Violet.

My chest tightened. My vision blurred.

I locked my phone and pressed it to my chest, swallowing the lump in my throat. Rowdy nosed my hand, sensing the shift.

"Yeah," I whispered. "I know."

I turned off the hallway light and backed out, closing Junie's door with care. My phone buzzed in my palm, but I knew it wasn't Violet, and that was the only person I wanted to talk to tonight.

In my room, I sank down on the edge of the bed and let the silence hit me. The laughter from girls' night. The fundraiser plans. The way I'd smiled and pretended the world wasn't falling apart.

But it was.

And it had.

Everything I'd been avoiding for a week all pressed down at once, heavy and unrelenting.

Violet wasn't coming back.

Junie needed me.

Ty was... I didn't even know anymore.

And tonight, I couldn't ignore any of it.

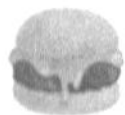

The doorbell woke me up the next morning after a terrible night's sleep.

Rowdy barked from down the hall, and I groaned, shoving tangled hair out of my face. The house was otherwise quiet, and I blinked against the harsh morning light streaming through my blinds.

When the doorbell rang again, I dropped my feet to the floor.

"Okay okay, I'm coming," I sighed, already tugging on Ty's sweatshirt as I padded toward the entryway.

A delivery driver waited on the porch, holding a clipboard and looking like he'd rather be anywhere else. "Delivery for Daisy Winslow?"

I signed, rubbing a sleeve over my face after a night of the worst sleep I'd had in weeks. "That's me."

With too much pep in his step for this early in the morning, the driver jogged back to his truck, then wheeled two boxes up the walk. They were taped tight and stacked like the world's least sentimental monument.

When the truck drove off, I stood there, the sound of the engine fading down the gravel drive while chilly air rushed around my bare legs.

Two boxes. That was it.

Two boxes to hold everything from the apartment I'd shared with Lauren.

"You've got to be fucking kidding me," I muttered to myself as I inspected the boxes. Each one had *D. Winslow* scrawled in black ink, handwriting I didn't recognize.

I hadn't heard from my horrible ex-roommate since I'd left

Chicago a little over a week ago, which was now hitting me in full force. Sure, I'd trusted her to get me my things like any decent human, but maybe I'd given her too much credit.

Even if whoever had packed these boxes was a Tetris master, there was no way my closet, let alone my bookshelves, would fit in *two boxes*. The furniture had come with the room, so I wasn't worried about that, but where was the rest of it?

With a deep sigh that hinted at the rage bubbling up in my chest, I stormed back down the hall into my room to grab my phone.

My hands shook as I stabbed Lauren's name, then stomped back to the foyer, slid on my shoes, and closed the front door behind me. It went to voicemail, so I hung up and dialed again. She didn't wake until well after noon most days, but I was beyond caring if I disrupted her beauty sleep.

"Daisy?" Lauren answered after the fourth phone call. "What the fuck?"

"What the fuck?" I nearly screamed into the phone. "Are you fucking kidding me with this shit? Where's the rest of my stuff?"

"Did you not get your boxes?"

"I got *two* boxes, yes. But where's the rest of it, Lauren?"

I ripped the tape off the first box only to find a picture frame lying on top, the glass cracked over a picture of Violet, Junie, and me.

A bitter laugh tore through me, my skin buzzing with energy.

"Your clothes were all so ratty, I told the maid to take them. It was time for a new wardrobe, Daisy. You're welcome."

My hands tightened on my phone, my teeth near cracking I held my jaw so tight. "You—you donated *all of it?*"

"No one should wear clothes that old. I did you a favor."

My pulse hammered in my veins as I ripped open the second box, glancing inside at the throw pillows from my bed... and nothing else.

"Where are my books?"

"Daisy, calm down—"

"Don't you dare tell me to calm down! You had Daddy get me fired because you were too much of a coward to see me at any of your little events! To be reminded that you are an awful human."

"You think *I'm* awful?" Lauren squawked. "You didn't even try to pack your stuff! You just left an address and skipped town. I had to hire someone to come do it for you—which I'll be charging you for, by the way—and had to postpone my party!"

"Because my *sister died!*" I screamed, sharp and broken. It was the first time I'd said those words aloud, and they ripped the last of my denial straight out of me. "She's dead, and I can't bring myself to go pick up her ashes, let alone *breathe*. But yes, tell me about how much I've inconvenienced you."

"I didn't know—"

I paced across the porch as Rowdy barked at my tone. "Excuse me for ever expecting you'd be nice just because. I don't know why I expected anything more. You are, quite literally, the worst person I've ever met."

"Jesus, Daisy. You don't have to be so rude."

A clatter from the driveway made me glance over—a hen had escaped the coop again, flapping and squawking like she was cheering me on. Cluck Norris strutted out behind her, chest puffed and ready for a fight.

"Don't test me," I hissed, pointing at him. "Not today, Satan."

"Who the hell are you talking to?" Lauren asked.

"The devil incarnate!" I shouted. "You'd get along *great.*"

"Daisy—"

I hung up. Hard.

My pulse throbbed in my ears. I stood in the middle of the porch, paralyzed by the anger bubbling up in me, struggling to pull oxygen in and out of my lungs.

Ty's old truck turned into the driveway, driving toward me. Dust flew up behind his tires until he stopped by the porch and walked toward me.

"What?" I barked as he studied me a beat too long.

With a shake of his head, he walked by. Before anger for his callous judgment could even surface in me, he came out again with a pair of work gloves, a mask, and safety glasses.

I blinked at him, more than a little confused.

He held them out to me. "Maybe it's time to break some shit."

I stared. "You're serious?"

"You look like you're about to explode."

Cluck Norris crowed again, probably loving the sound of chaos and destruction.

Ty jerked his head toward Violet's house. "Junie's with Stevie and the kids at the library this morning. We have a few hours."

I exhaled shakily. "Oh."

"Ready?"

No.

Not even kind of.

But this energy bubbling inside me needed somewhere to go. I was too wired, too angry, too tired of trying to hold everything inside.

The walk down to Violet's house felt longer than usual. My breath came out in short bursts, my chest feeling like it was about to crack. By the time we reached the refinished porch, I trembled with more than a morning chill.

Ty stopped beside me. "Do you want me to come inside with you?"

"No," I said, but that was a lie. "Yes."

The key turned with a familiar click. I hesitated, then shoved the door open, the hinges groaning in protest.

The house looked the same as it had the last time I'd been here—half-finished, half-forgotten. Violet's death lingered in every corner, daring me to face it.

Ty followed me inside, silent but steady.

I tugged on the gloves, then put on the glasses and mask.

The kitchen was a wreck.

Cabinet doors sagged, warped and split where water had soaked in. The tile backsplash bowed, almost falling off the wall. But the biggest problem was the mildew smell clinging to the back of my throat.

Nothing in this room could be saved. Too damaged. Too far gone.

Was I the first person to empathize with a cabinet? Maybe.

Ty disappeared down the hall and came back a moment later with a hammer. He tipped his chin toward a cabinet hanging crooked on the wall. "Start there."

Something in my chest snapped.

I took the hammer and glared at the cabinet as if it had offended me. When I swung, a scream ripped out of my throat, but the hammer barely left a dent, bouncing off with a dull, useless thunk.

I swung again. Harder.

Still standing.

"Of course," I growled, bringing it down a third time.

Wood finally cracked, a splinter flying loose across the floor. "Of course I'd fuck this up, too."

The cabinet groaned but didn't fall.

I laughed, sharp and bitter. "Doesn't that just figure."

Ty's voice came from behind me, low and maddeningly calm. "You're pulling up when you hit."

"I don't need you," I muttered through gritted teeth, drawing the hammer back again.

"Well aware, sweetheart."

Before I could tell him where to shove his *sweetheart*, he stepped in behind me—close enough that his heat brushed my back.

"Here," he said, his voice rougher now.

His hand slid over mine, guiding my grip on the handle. "Keep your wrist straight. Let your shoulder do the work."

My breath hitched. He wasn't gentle, but he wasn't condescending either. He met my fury head-on—steady, grounded, and unafraid of it.

"Now," he said, pulling my hair away from my face, "swing through."

I did.

The cabinet split with a sharp crack, wood splintering clean down the middle.

"Good," he murmured, stepping back just enough to give me space. "Again."

So I swung harder this time. Then again. Each hit landed deeper, shaking something loose in my chest—grief, rage, all of it tearing free in jagged pieces.

When the cabinet gave way, my gaze snapped to the backsplash. Rows of chipped tile glinted under the light, crooked and smug, and I hated them.

Without thinking, I brought the hammer down.

Ceramic shattered. Sharp fragments flew, clattering across the counter and skidding over the floor. The sound rang through the house, violent and echoing.

I didn't stop.

The crash of tile against plaster filled the room, rhythm and chaos blurring together until it didn't matter what I hit anymore. Only that I kept swinging.

By the time I slowed, my arms trembled with effort. Sweat dampened my hairline. My heartbeat thundered in my ears, then gradually gave way to music.

I frowned, turning toward the sound.

A stereo sat on the rickety table near the door, some angry rock song blasting loud enough to make the surface vibrate.

Ty leaned against the wall next to it, arms crossed. There was no pity on his face, no attempt to soften the moment— just quiet approval in his hazel eyes, like he saw every ugly piece of me and hadn't flinched.

That did more for me than any comforting words ever could.

I straightened, chest still heaving. "That felt good."

"I bet," he said. "You needed it."

As the last of the anger drained out of me, I took in the damage. Cabinets demolished. Tiles shattered across the counter. Wood crunching under my boots.

The kitchen was a disaster, and so was I. My hoodie was dusted white, hanging low over my hips. Only then did I realize I was wearing... not much else.

Heat crawled up the back of my neck when I remembered I'd thrown it on over a sports bra and boy shorts to answer the door. In the middle of my rage, I'd stopped being a person and become pure motion.

Now I was very much a person again.

I lifted my gaze to Ty, realizing how close he'd been and how exposed I was.

But he looked almost as undone as me.

Gone were his typical jeans and work boots. Instead, he wore black athletic shorts, running shoes, and a backward cap. His faded gray Mayhem Hockey Club tee had the sleeves ripped off, showcasing broad shoulders and corded muscle I didn't have language for.

And then—

The tattoos.

Holy hell.

Black ink wrapped his right shoulder in bold geometric lines, curving down his bicep before disappearing beneath the cotton. Another snaked along his thigh—a compass surrounded by mountain peaks and what looked like Norse runes, stark against sun-warmed skin.

I swallowed. "You have tattoos."

He lifted a brow, his mustache doing a terrible job of hiding his smile. "Sharp observation."

"I just—wow. Okay. That's new information."

He tilted his head. "Didn't fit the flannel-and-boots version of me you had in your head?"

"No," I admitted, heat blooming higher on my face. "Not even a little."

His chuckle was low and warm.

Before I could find something resembling composure, the song changed, and I looked over at the stereo. It sat on one of Aunt Maggie's old side tables, rocking with the bass. With each vibration, a sliver of white edged farther out until a piece of paper slipped free and fluttered to the floor.

My chest tightened.

I set the hammer down and crossed the room on unsteady legs.

Just like last time, the envelope had a simple daisy drawn on the front.

Tears blurred my vision as I bent to pick it up, my hands shaking so badly I almost dropped it again.

Oh, good. You stopped avoiding me.

My knees gave out. I sank to the floor, the letter clutched against my chest.

"Dammit, Vi," I said through a watery laugh, surprised yet again by my sister's antics, even now.

I can't cash in on bets anymore, but I'm going to say it's been at least a week, and my ashes are sitting in some facility waiting for you to call and pick them up. That's fine. I deserve to wait, because fuck me, right?

I laughed again, swiping at my cheeks with my sleeve.

Today my doctor told me I'm dying. Not in a might-die kind of way. It's inevitable. And I'm angry.

I'm outraged at my body for betraying me. Furious at how much I'm leaving behind. Livid that I'll never see Junie's awkward teenage years or teach her how to drive or watch her fall in love with the wrong person and have to sit there silently while she makes her own mistakes.

But most of all, I'm angry that she doesn't have a parent who was supposed to love her. Her dad couldn't be bothered to stay. And now I'm about to check out too.

The only reason I can breathe through that is you.

You, Daisy Winslow, my human hurricane, are the one thing that makes this whole thing feel not so unbearable. You've always been the fighter. The one who keeps everyone else afloat even when you're drowning.

You're probably reading this with your jaw set and your fists clenched, pretending you're fine. But you're not fine. I'm not fine. And that's okay.

So let's be mad. We <u>should</u> be.

Yell at the sky. Scream at me. Curse the universe. Let it out.

But let's not let it change us, okay? I need my Daisy girl, now more than ever. Not the fake version you've been clinging to in Chicago, but my precious, obnoxious baby sister who can find good in any situation, for better or worse.

Tears slipped free, hitting the paper in fat droplets, but I kept reading, not wanting to let go yet.

But do you know what I'm not mad about?
I'm not mad that you're in Linwood, back where we were always happiest.
And I'm not mad that the cute neighbor with the dog and the savior complex thinks Junie hung the moon.
When I look for the good in this fucking terrible story, I hope maybe this—coming home, cleaning up my chaos, loving my kid—helps you find yourself again.
You're probably crying right now and pretending it's just dust. Maybe you're mad this letter isn't full of some profound acceptance garbage.
That will come later.
Today, we'll be angry. Messy. Break things.
And when we're done breaking... build.
Build me a new home, a new life. Fill in the gaps and make it yours. Knowing you, it'll be better than I ever could've imagined.
Now go take care of my girl.
And yourself.

And maybe let the hot neighbor help with both.

To the moon,

V

P.S. If you find the wallpaper I bought for the hallway—burn it. It looks like an old-lady couch. I was on pain meds, and I deeply regret it.

19

TY

The kitchen looked like a storm had come through and changed its mind halfway.

Cabinets lay splintered on the floor. Tile shards glittered across every surface. A fine haze of dust hung in the air, softening the edges of the destruction. And right in the middle of it sat Daisy, cross-legged on the floor, a letter trembling in her hands.

I'd let her wreck the place.

Every instinct I had screamed to step in, to fix it—but she didn't need fixing. She needed the chaos. The swing. The noise. The motion. She'd needed something she could hit that wouldn't hit back. After the hand she'd been dealt—losing her sister, losing her job, losing the life she thought she'd built—it was a miracle she was still upright at all.

Now, watching her read the letter, I could see the anger draining out of her one word at a time.

By the time she reached the end, her shoulders shook with tears she'd been holding back since the moment she arrived. She folded the paper, pressed it to her chest, and closed her eyes like she could keep the world from falling apart if she held tight enough.

Something in me split open.

The radio changed songs, rock music faded into something slower, steadier—piano first, then a familiar ache that settled deep in my ribs. I nudged the volume up on *Love Will Keep Us Alive*, letting the song fill the wrecked kitchen, the dust, the quiet grief sitting on the floor.

When I stepped closer, Daisy blinked up at me through tears and drywall dust. "What are you doing?"

"Testing a theory," I said, holding out my hand.

Her voice was rough as she wiped at her cheeks with the sleeve of her hoodie, smearing dust instead of clearing it away. "And what's that?"

I wiggled my fingers. "We dance."

A breathy huff escaped her—half laugh, half disbelief—as she slid her hand into mine. "Ty, I can't dance right now."

"That's fine." I gave a gentle tug. "Just stand."

I pulled her close until her chest brushed mine. With our hands clasped, we weren't quite hugging, but her presence anchored me and I hoped mine did too.

"This is dumb," she whispered, voice fraying as her free hand settled against my chest.

"Maybe." I wrapped my arm around her waist and tugged her nearer. "But maybe dumb is what we need."

I felt her laugh more than I heard it, a soft tremor against my ribs. Little by little, she began to move with me. The stiffness eased from her shoulders as I guided us in a slow two-step, broken tile crunching under our shoes like a metronome.

Her fingers brushed my neck. "You're covered in dust," she murmured.

"Then we're a matched pair."

With a long exhale, she deflated, her forehead falling against my chest.

Holding her felt natural. Like I'd been built for it. Like if she leaned hard enough, I'd find a way to hold it all.

"You asked me last week why I didn't ask for your number that night."

Her breath caught, but she didn't lift her head.

"I wanted to." My throat tightened around the truth. "Fuck, I wanted to. But I didn't have anything to give you."

Her fingers curled in my shirt.

"My life was empty back then," I went on. "I'd just retired. I didn't know who the hell I was without hockey. No plan. No home that felt like mine. And you were this bright, impossible thing. All light and laughter. Like a dream I didn't deserve to touch twice."

She squeezed my hand, still silent.

"I told myself it was better that way," I admitted. "That you'd go live your big, messy, beautiful life, and I'd get my shit together. But I never stopped wondering where you ended up. Or if you found someone who made you laugh like I did."

Without thinking, I brushed stray hair from her face and pressed a kiss to the top of her head. Barely there. Pure instinct. But the second I did it, my pulse kicked hard.

What the hell was I doing?

I wasn't supposed to cross that line. I wasn't supposed to want to.

But her weight against me felt too easy. Too good.

She didn't move. Neither did I. I rested my chin on her head, breathing her in like oxygen.

"I thought you couldn't dance," she said, sidestepping everything I'd just laid at her feet.

"*Didn't*, not couldn't." I tightened my arm around her.

"But someone once told me almost anything can be solved with a dance party."

She tipped her head back, and the sight of her smile—small, exhausted, and real—nearly took my knees out.

"Is it working?" I asked, thumb brushing her cheek.

Her gaze flicked over my face like she couldn't find a safe place to land. Then she nodded once and folded back into me.

"Yeah," she whispered. "I think so."

The music wrapped around us. For a long moment, nothing existed beyond the quiet rasp of our breathing and the slow sway of her body softening against mine.

Then her voice came, barely there. "You keep thinking you have to earn it somehow—love, worth, a place to belong. But you don't, Ty," she whispered. "You're enough. You always were."

The words hit like a punch to the gut.

"Daisy," I warned, but there was no warning left in it. Only surrender. My hand slid up her back to the base of her neck, turning her face toward me. She came easily, eyes wrecked and open.

"Tell me not to kiss you," I said, voice gone to gravel. "Tell me this is too complicated."

For a heartbeat, the world narrowed to the inches between us. My thumb traced her jaw. Her eyes dropped to my mouth, then lifted again.

"I've waited for three years, Ty."

My name in her voice undid me completely.

Fuck it.

The space between us vanished.

In an instant, I caught her mouth with mine.

The moment our mouths met, the noise in my head went quiet. Like some restless part of me had finally found where it was supposed to land. And the rest of me followed without hesitation.

The kiss started soft, almost careful. But the restraint didn't last.

Three years of wanting broke loose all at once, rushing through me like a storm surge. My hands slid to her waist, pulling her closer, deeper into it.

Her fingers dug into the back of my neck, dragging me in as if she couldn't bear even an inch between us. I groaned against her mouth, and she answered by arching into my touch.

I lifted her without thinking. She wrapped her legs around my waist and I backed us to the kitchen table and set her down, my body pressing between her knees.

Everything was heat and breath and disbelief that this was happening.

When her tongue brushed my lips, I opened for her. When her hands tugged at my shirt, I peeled it off and tossed it somewhere into the wreckage. When she shifted against me, desperate and searching, I felt it everywhere.

Anything she wanted from me, it was hers.

"I've wanted you for so long," I muttered against her mouth, the words spilling out like a confession. "You have no idea how bad."

Her cheeks were flushed, her eyes blown wide. "Then show me."

I didn't hesitate. My hands slipped beneath her hoodie, lifting it over her head.

Underneath, she was barely dressed—sports bra, tiny shorts, all warm skin and vulnerability that I'd gotten peaks of in her adrenaline-fueled rage. But seeing her like this, spread out before me?

My breath punched out of me.

"Daisy..." My voice went rough. "Do you have any idea what you do to me?"

"Off," she whispered, lifting her hips. "Take them off."

I flattened my palm over her instead, feeling the heat of her through the fabric, the way she moved against me.

It damn near tore me apart.

But something in me held. Not because I didn't want it, but because I wanted it *all*.

"Not today," I murmured, kissing her again, slower this time. "Not like this."

Her breath shuddered. "Then when?"

She trembled when I pulled her closer, when my forehead pressed to hers.

"Haven't I waited long enough?"

"Daisy," I groaned, kissing her like I could pour everything into it—every missed chance, every night I'd wondered what would have happened if I hadn't walked away.

Her fingers slid into my hair. "What are you waiting for?"

The words lit something fierce inside me.

"I want you so fucking bad," I rasped. "But I want to take my time. I want to do this when it isn't grief and adrenaline holding the wheel."

Her eyes flickered, softening even through the want. I kissed down her throat, then over the thin fabric of her bralette, testing every inch of my restraint with each little moan she let go.

"Please, Ty. Make me forget," she begged, her core grinding down on me in search of friction. "Get me out of my head."

The tremble in her voice almost did me in, confused by what the right thing to do here was.

She dragged my face back up to hers, pupils blown out and full of need.

She was fucking stunning, so beautiful I couldn't look away. Couldn't remember why this was—

A car horn blared outside the window, echoing off the kitchen walls.

We both jolted.

Daisy blinked, dazed, like she'd been dropped back into her body too fast. Her hand slid from my chest, leaving heat in its wake. "What was that?"

I swallowed hard, trying to find my voice. "Delivery truck, maybe."

Another honk, followed by the sound of car doors.

Her cheeks flushed pink, her gaze darting to the window before landing on the disaster around us—the splintered cabinets, the shards of tile, our clothes scattered on the floor.

And just like that, the spell broke.

"I, uh…" She cleared her throat, looking at anything but me. "I should go see if that's Junie."

"Yeah." My voice came out low as I rested my forehead on her shoulder. "Okay."

She slid out from under me, then bent to grab her clothes. Through the open window, the breeze carried the sound of the car door slamming and voices outside—Stevie's laugh, Junie's chatter.

I turned toward the wrecked kitchen, dragging a hand over my face. My pulse still thundered, my body aching with everything that had almost happened.

"Hell of a time to be early for once, Stevie," I muttered.

With a sigh, I forced myself to pick up the mess.

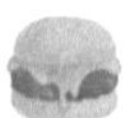

By the time I had the remnants of the demolished cabinets discarded in the garage and the floors swept, Stevie had left, and Junie and Daisy were back at my house. I toed off my shoes, then lifted the hem of my tee to wipe the sweat off my forehead as I walked into the kitchen.

When I looked up, Daisy's eyes were zeroed in on my abs before realizing I was staring right back. She jerked upright, but not before I saw the flash of heat in her eyes.

"Sandwich?" she asked, her voice sounding a little odd. "We're making grilled cheese."

I couldn't help but smirk, glad she was just as flustered as me. "I want anything you'll give me."

Daisy choked on the sip of water she'd just taken, coughing into her hand.

"Wrong pipe?" Junie said, her little feet kicking back and forth where she sat at the island, oblivious to the tension simmering between us.

Stoking the fire was just too easy, though, and I couldn't seem to stop. "Sorry. I should have warned you I can be a choking hazard."

"Oh my God." Daisy fanned her face, her cheeks still bright red. "Stop."

"That's true," Junie chimed in, chin resting on the counter as she waited for her food. "One time he made me laugh so hard, milk came out my nose."

"I don't doubt it," Daisy said, then scooped a grilled cheese onto Junie's favorite plate and slid it across the counter to her. "He's a pretty talented guy."

It was my turn to choke on air. Sensing her eyes on me, I snapped my gaze to Daisy's, catching the glittering mischief in those blue eyes right before she held out her glass of water.

"Thirsty?"

"Did you run this morning, Ty?" Junie asked, her mouth full of grilled cheese. "I was reading an article in the library this morning about altitude and electrolytes. You should be drinking 24-48 ounces per hour that's a mix of water and electrolyte supplements. Otherwise, you're at risk for hyponatremia. Or, at least, I think that's what it was called."

"You're so smart."

Daisy's hand trailed across my low back as she walked behind me, Piggie following a step behind. And holy shit, that one touch had no business setting me on fire again.

"What other fun facts did you learn today?"

Junie launched into an enthusiastic explanation involving protein and stretching and something about bananas, while Piggie sniffed every corner of the kitchen.

The girls ate their grilled cheese at the island, chatting like the world hadn't almost tilted off its axis ten minutes ago. Meanwhile, I spent an unreasonable amount of time in the laundry room, standing in front of the spare freezer with the door open, pretending I was looking for something.

Rowdy stood beside me, his little black face tipped up in question.

"Didn't see that coming, did we, boy?"

He chuffed, then nudged the stash of bones I kept in the freezer. I grabbed one and handed it over, and he trotted off toward the fireplace.

"Ready for your sandwich?" Daisy said when I wandered back into the kitchen, only to be cut off by the doorbell.

"Knock, knock!" a woman's voice called through the open windows. "It's Sandra Diaz with CPS."

Daisy and I froze, staring at each other. Panic flashed across her face before she mouthed, *Oh, shit.*

"Anyone home?" Sandra called again.

Junie hopped down from her stool and headed for the door.

I moved fast, blocking her with a gentle hand. "Hey, bug. You know the rule. No opening the door."

She peeked around me toward the porch, fingers clutching the back of my shirt.

I crouched to her level. "What's wrong?"

Her lower lip trembled, blue eyes rimmed with tears. "Is she here to take me away? I don't want to leave."

The ache in my chest was immediate. I brushed my thumb over her cheek, waiting until she looked up at me.

"No," I said. "She's just checking in. And if anyone tries to take you, I played defense for fifteen years. I like our odds."

Junie sniffed, then smirked. "You can't fight her. That's against the law."

"Shoot, I forgot about that." I pressed a kiss to her temple. "Come on. Let's go show her how good you're doing instead."

When I opened the door, Sandra smiled. "Sorry for the surprise visit. We keep these check-ins unannounced."

"No problem," I said, stepping aside. "Don't judge the kitchen—we just made lunch and have been out all morning."

She chuckled, taking in the open space—rain boots by the door, a half-finished puzzle on the coffee table, a bright pink throw draped over the couch like it belonged.

"This house looks wonderful, Mr. Hudson," she said. "You've made it feel like a home."

Her gaze shifted out the window toward Violet's place down the drive. The porch was cleared, the weeds gone, but, even from here, you could see it had a long way to go.

"Progress on your sister's house?" she asked Daisy.

Daisy passed Piggie into my arms and shook Sandra's hand. "Slow, but steady. We were working on kitchen demo this morning, so we can mitigate some mold we found. Once that's taken care of, I need to hire someone for wiring and drywall."

Sandra nodded, jotting something down. "And work?"

Daisy stiffened, her panicked gaze flicking to mine. With everything going on over the last week, I wasn't sure she'd done anything about the job hunt yet, and who could blame her?

"I—"

"She's starting this week," I said. "Working for the Linwood Rink."

Daisy blinked. Piggie squealed like she'd caught me in a lie.

I held Daisy's gaze, hoping she understood the unspoken *trust me*.

Sandra's face lit up. "Oh, that's wonderful! I heard the rink was expanding."

"Yes," Daisy said, finding her footing. "I'm organizing the summer carnival fundraiser."

My brows lifted, because damn. That was good.

"Community engagement, stable employment, ongoing renovations," Sandra said, flipping her page. "These are all positives, Daisy."

She crouched in front of Junie. "And how are you liking it here, Juniper?"

Junie shrugged, still half-hidden behind me. "Good."

"What's your favorite part?"

"The animals," she said. "Piggie Smalls is cute."

Sandra laughed, eyeing the squirming pig in my arms. "Can you show me where she lives?"

Out back, Junie gave a full tour of the pig pen we'd begun building her, her nerves melting away as she explained feeding schedules and the importance of enrichment toys.

Once we made it back to the front of the house, Sandra straightened, clipping her pen to her clipboard. "Juniper's thriving here. Placement will stay as is for now. Once Daisy's house passes inspection, we'll reassess."

"Thank you," Daisy said, voice unsteady.

Sandra smiled. "These cases are never easy, and I was worried about two strangers sharing custody. But I'm happy to see you're both doing a wonderful job."

When her car disappeared down the gravel drive, Daisy turned to me, eyes wide.

"Working for the rink?"

I shrugged. "You're the one who suggested a carnival. I like it. Let's make it real."

"I didn't mean—well, I kind of did. Tate doesn't like the idea of not contributing to the down payment for an expansion, so we were thinking something like this would help. But Emmy was going to mention it to Beckett first, then—"

I put a finger under her chin, forcing her to look up at me. When our eyes met, her words trailed off. "I love this plan," I said. "And I am also a partner in the rink. You ask me, not Beckett."

Her lips curved into a small grin. "So, you're offering me a job you just invented?"

"I would offer you the whole damn world if you'd let me."

The words hung between us, heavier than I'd meant them to be.

Daisy's gaze dropped back down to my mouth, her breaths coming uneven. "Let's start with a job, then go from there."

I nodded, hope taking root in my chest. "Deal."

20

Daisy

Shannon Wilder added Daisy Winslow to the group chat
Puckin' Exhausted

SHANNON

Be cool, girls.

STEVIE

Who meeeeeeeee? I'm cool.

TATE

I think I'd go with enthusiastic over cool,
but to each their own.

STEVIE

Oh, I like enthusiastic. That fits. I'll take it.

EMMY

GIRLS. FOCUS.

Hi Daisy

DAISY

Hi friends

STEVIE

SHE CALLED US FRIENDS OMG I
MIGHT CRY

SHANNON

And this is why we're not friends

TATE

What's up, Emmy?

STEVIE

Right. Sorry. I'll shut up.

EMMY

We need to chat about the date auction.
Are we doing this? I'm sure Beckett can
get some of his buddies to agree to it.

SHANNON

I'd rather oversee the port-a-potties than
have anything to do with that.

TATE

If you put me in that date auction, I'm never
speaking to you again.

EMMY

K, so I'll put you two at the top of the list.

STEVIE

What about you, Daisy?

Or are you and Ty a thing now?

SHANNON

As subtle as a brick through a window.

TATE

Good lord, Stevie.

STEVIE

What?

EMMY

Okay, focus. Daisy, zero pressure. We can make the auction players-only and be done with it.

STEVIE

UNLESSSSSS

DAISY

There's nothing to tell.

STEVIE

Dammit, I swore I saw sex hair when you scampered out of the house.

EMMY

Quick reminder: Ty is my brother. Please don't make me leave the chat.

SHANNON

For the record, when we got coffee last week, he lingered.

DAISY

Have you met Ty? He's polite.

SHANNON

And you live with him. Tell me why that man would need to linger when he sees you every day.

TATE

He does it around the rink, too.

EMMY

Not you too…

STEVIE

SEE!!!!

Does he wait for her after meetings? Sit next to her?

WAIT NO! Across from her, so he can stare longingly into her eyes the whole time?!

TATE

Both

EMMY

I regret starting this conversation.

TATE

He hovers, Emmy.

SHANNON

Men who hover are either in love or about to mansplain the shit out of you.

EMMY

You realize Daisy will never speak to us again, right? This is so intrusive.

I am very sorry, Daisy.

STEVIE

As Shannon says, she's a bitch, not a liar.

SHANNON

Glad you remember.

EMMY

You know what, Daisy? I'll do you a favor and remove you from the chat. Feel free to block us.

SHANNON

Please don't. This is fun.

DAISY

Let me think about the auction and get back to you.

STEVIE

GASP! THAT IS NOT A NO!

TATE

Well, I can guarantee the only one you'd be
going on a date with is Ty because he will
lose his freaking mind.

EMMY

I can't even argue with that.

SHANNON

And here I was thinking I didn't want
to go...

Two weeks slipped by faster than I expected. Between the smell
of sawdust and the hum of construction at Violet's place, the
days blurred together. With a new job on my plate, I hired a
contractor to wrestle the wiring and drywall into submission.
It swallowed what little money I had left in my savings account,
but Stevie's husband worked in construction and called in
some favors to help me out.

With their help, the house was looking like a home instead
of a disaster zone.

At the rink, I'd thrown myself into the marketing role like
my sanity depended on it—which, maybe, it did. Tate was
thrilled to have me on board, claiming this was the first decision the guys had ever forced on her she agreed with. Each day I
spent with her, a little more of her personality showed itself.
She was sarcastic, whip-smart, and unbothered by anyone with
an inflated ego.

I hadn't met the infamous Mason Conway in person yet,
but judging by the way Tate's jaw tightened every time his voice
chimed in on a conference call, there was history there.

Junie had settled into a rhythm too—either at the rink with
me, at the ranch with Ty, or with Stevie and her crew. If Ty or I
got stuck working late, Emmy swooped in or one of the

Mayhem players lined up to babysit. For the first time, the perks of small-town life were easy to see.

Grief didn't hit all at once anymore—it hung around the edges, just waiting for me to stop moving.

So, I didn't.

I kept my hands busy and my mind busier—anything to make the silence a little less sharp.

Pulling off a summer carnival in two weeks was ridiculous on paper, but Linwood had its own brand of magic. Or, maybe more accurately, the Conway brothers refused to take no for an answer.

Between their name recognition, their contacts, and the way they tossed around money, the whole town seemed to fall in line. Permits that should've taken months cleared overnight, sponsors crawled out of the woodwork to have their names on everything, and famous friends showed up in droves.

And Ty... God help me. Nothing else had happened between us; the moments we were alone were few and far between. I could tell he was waiting me out, but I was tired of feeling fragile.

By the time carnival day rolled around, I was running on Diet Coke, adrenaline, and the stubborn belief that sheer grit could pull a carnival together.

Luckily, it was working.

River Street had transformed overnight—tents, food trucks, game booths, and a makeshift stage sprouting up as if someone had waved a magic wand.

I'd barely finished tying down the last corner of a banner when a breeze lifted it back up, slapping me in the face. Somewhere behind me, a deep laugh rumbled, and instantly I warmed at the sound.

"Need a hand?"

Ty stood there in a ball cap and a green T-shirt, arms crossed and wearing a smug grin.

I rolled my eyes, trying to hide the smile tugging at my lips. "Always coming in with the savior complex."

"For you?" he said, those hazel eyes alight with mischief. "Yes."

I climbed down from the ladder, letting Ty take my place. "What's Junie up to this morning?"

"She's at Emmy's, working on a secret project with Jace," Ty said, reaching up to retie the banner for me. His biceps flexed with every pull, the cotton of his shirt stretching in all the right ways. But my attention caught on those damn shorts.

"Are you intentionally doing this to me?"

Ty glanced down, all fake innocence. "Doing what?"

"That." I pointed to his shorts and the black ink peeking from beneath them. "Hoochie daddy shorts. I swear, every pair you wear is shorter than the last ones. Are you trying to catch a hockey mom today?"

He laughed, the sound deep and easy, then hopped down off the ladder to stand over me. "Don't worry, Daisy. I don't care about their attention."

My belly swooped, heat washing over me. "No?"

His lips tugged into a mischievous grin. "Just yours."

The world tilted, a dizzying mix of heat and nerves and something I wasn't ready to name.

Ty turned back to the banner and left me standing there, completely undone by a man in too-short shorts and a grin that said he knew it.

I was still trying to remember how to breathe when a voice broke through the haze.

"Found you!"

Stevie strode up the street, clipboard in hand. She was

decked out head-to-toe in Mayhem Hockey Club gear—logo tee knotted at the waist, denim shorts, and green sneakers to match.

"We've officially sold out of advance tickets," she beamed. "Over fifteen hundred sold online, and people are still lining up at the gate. Between sponsors, bake-off entries, and vendor fees, we're sitting right around fifty thousand dollars raised, and the day's just getting started."

"Fifty thousand?" I blinked. "You're kidding."

"Nope. Turns out your marketing campaign hit the Vail Valley crowd just right. Half these people drove in from the resorts looking for that 'small-town charm,'" she said, using air quotes. "Which apparently means bounce houses, corn dogs, and questionable parking. The gates open in five minutes."

"And you." Stevie pointed at Ty, who turned around to look at us. "I don't know what favors you called in, but there is a large donation from the Chicago Storm Youth Foundation, so thank you for that."

I beamed up at him. "We'll take it."

"Hell yeah, we will," she said. "This is great."

Before I could respond, Ty adjusted the brim of his cap. "So where do you need us?"

"Good question." Stevie scanned her notes. "You're scheduled to get the Mayhem kids started at the street hockey shootout, then head to the hardware store."

He groaned. "For that petting-zoo nonsense?"

"Yup," she said, all cheer. "Uno and Piggie Smalls are the main attraction. Plus, someone dropped off a few goats this morning. I'm not quite clear if this was a donation *to you,* or if someone is coming to claim them at the end of the night? So that will be a fun little surprise for us all."

Ty muttered something under his breath, and I bit back a laugh.

He looked at me. "Where are you headed?"

Stevie flipped her clipboard, scanning. "I've got you as a floater, until 3 p.m. when you're headed over to the—" Her smile turned devious. "You know what? We'll chat later."

"That sounds ominous," Ty said. "Should she be worried?"

"I've never been so excited in my life," she sang, already walking away to talk to someone else.

I chuckled, staring after my new friend. "Is she always like this?"

"From what I can tell, yes." He tipped his chin toward the street. "I'm gonna check on the kids before they riot."

As he spoke, the sound of cheers erupted from the direction of the ticket counter, and I noticed a wave of people spilling through the open gates, laughter and excitement filling the air. In minutes, the street was alive with families and friends, moving toward the booths and games.

Across the way, Beckett stood in the middle of a makeshift street hockey setup—orange cones, fold-up nets, taped lines— with a group of teens in Mayhem jerseys. Beside him towered a broad-shouldered man I didn't recognize.

Ty crossed to them, his stride steady. Beckett said something that made the teenagers groan. Ty didn't laugh, not really; he just shook his head, lips twitching. He wasn't a man who laughed often, except with me.

I shouldn't have liked that distinction, but I did.

A cluster of hockey moms gathered nearby, chatting with the guys, tossing their hair, and laughing too loudly. I told myself it was none of my business, but jealousy had a way of slipping through cracks you didn't know you had. Ty said something to one of them, and she touched his arm. My stomach gave an absurd little twist—until he glanced up.

Straight at me.

For half a heartbeat, that quiet, unreadable man was focused on me. His lips twitched—barely there, but enough to undo me.

Shannon appeared beside me, sipping an iced coffee the color of midnight. Despite the heat, she was dressed head-to-toe in black—distressed jeans, combat boots, chipped dark polish, and a faded Megadeth tee knotted at the hip.

"So, you're doing the auction," she said.

I chuckled. "I am?"

She rolled her eyes. "The way he looks at you is so nauseatingly sweet, I might throw up, but"—she took another long sip of coffee—"damn if it isn't kind of adorable."

Before I could respond, Stevie rejoined us, looking between me and Ty. "Have you decided?"

Emmy crossed the street toward us then, her *Moms of Mayhem* T-shirt tucked into a pair of cutoff shorts, a green baseball cap pulled low with her brown ponytail sticking out the back.

"Look at my boys," she said. "I love seeing Ty and Beckett happy."

"They're wrangling teenage hockey players next to a goat pen."

Emmy laughed. "Trust me. That's paradise."

I nodded toward the blond man standing beside Beckett. "Who's the Viking?"

"That's Mikko Laaksonen," Stevie said. "Beckett's old teammate."

"Oh," I said, curiosity pricking. "Do we like him?"

Shannon scoffed, the sound sharp enough to cut. "We tolerate him."

Emmy didn't miss a beat. "Someone's protesting a little too much."

"Please." Shannon flicked her sunglasses higher on her nose, voice bone-dry. "If I were protesting, you'd need riot gear."

Stevie leaned over to whisper, "Translation: she likes him."

"I don't like any hockey players," Shannon said, but the quick glance she shot across the street betrayed her.

The three of them exchanged a look that passed so fast I almost missed it—part amusement, part secret, all confirmation that I'd just stepped into something above my current level of Linwood gossip clearance.

Before I could ask more, Tate emerged from behind the main stage, her red hair piled into a bun, sunglasses on top of her head.

"Has anyone heard from Mason?" she asked, glancing over at the hockey team. "He was supposed to be here an hour ago."

Stevie shrugged. "Maybe he's late."

"He's never late," Tate said, frowning. "Not when there's an audience."

"Maybe he's planning another one of his big gestures," Shannon said dryly. "You know, something subtle."

"That's what I'm afraid of," Tate warned.

Before anyone could comment, two uniformed officers started walking down the street, waving people to the sidewalks.

"Make way! Clear the road! The parade starts in ten minutes!"

Stevie turned to me, eyes wide. "Wait, you planned a parade?"

I frowned. "Absolutely not. I barely survived getting insurance for the bounce houses."

And then came the distant sound of drums.

"You've got to be kidding me," Tate muttered as the crowd gathered in excited rows on either side of the street.

Minutes later, the Linwood High marching band rounded the corner, uniforms gleaming, trumpets blaring. The drum line hit a cadence so loud it rattled the vendor tents. The crowd erupted in cheers, clapping along.

"Holy shit," Stevie whispered, delighted.

Behind the band came a line of classic cars—sports cars, vintage trucks, even a hot-pink Cadillac with *Linwood Loves Mayhem* painted across the side. But my favorite was the bike parade, carrying a swarm of kids pedaling with streamers and flags, honking little horns.

Right in the middle of it all was Junie, smiling bright. Jace rode along next to her like a protective big brother.

Her little blue bike sparkled with tinsel, and Rowdy sat in a basket on the back of Jace's bike wearing a sign that said *Mayhem's Smallest Mascot*. She waved and smiled like this was the best day of her life, and the lump in my throat hit fast and hard.

"Okay," I whispered. "That's adorable."

Emmy nudged my shoulder with hers. "She's really something else, Daisy. Look at her thriving. You're doing a great job."

Just as tears welled in my eyes at her kind words, the cheers grew louder and a fire truck turned onto River Street, lights flashing. People whooped and clapped until someone shouted, "Is that Mason Conway?"

And sure enough, there he was.

Mason Conway walked behind the firetruck and was

impossible to miss—scruffy dark beard, snapback hat turned backward, dark hair sticking out just enough to look like he hadn't tried too hard. His blue eyes sparkled with that now familiar Conway confidence, but told me he'd never met a spotlight he didn't like. A vintage black-and-green Mayhem jersey clung to his broad shoulders, sleeves shoved up to his elbows, paired with athletic shorts and the easy swagger of a man who lived for game day, on or off the ice.

Still on the active roster for the Dallas Outlaws, Mason carried himself like someone used to being watched. He lifted the microphone, voice rich and playful as he started singing *My Girl*. Every step down River Street felt deliberate, a wink to the crowd, a twirl for his mom Lori filming from the curb with the knitting club.

But when his gaze finally locked on Tate, everything else seemed to fade. His grin widened, mischievous and just a little too confident the closer he came.

"Don't you dare," Tate muttered, already shaking her head.

"Oh, he's daring," Shannon said, practically gleeful, the first hint of a smile tugging at her dark-painted lips.

Mason crossed the last few steps to her, dropped smoothly to one knee, and extended his free hand. "Tate. My sweet yam. My little spud muffin. Marry me?"

21

TY

By late afternoon the sun sat low, baking the asphalt until it shimmered. The smell of funnel cake, sunscreen, and melted snow cones hung in the air. The crowd hadn't thinned once all day—steady from the minute the gates opened—and damn if I wasn't impressed.

Daisy had pulled it off.

A booth showcasing the expansion plans for the rink sat near the beer garden the Lantern had set up, and it seemed to be the heart of the chaos. Poster boards with renderings of the second rink and upstairs viewing deck lined the space, a donation box on the table stuffed to the brim with cash and checks.

Beckett, Mason, and Mikko stood nearby, each holding a bottle of water. I crossed the street toward them, wiping sweat from the back of my neck.

"Hell of a turnout," Beckett said, scanning the crowd. "I'm shocked how many vendors showed up with this little notice, but this is impressive."

"That's what happens when you put three NHL players on

a flyer," Mason said. He cupped his hands and yelled, "You're welcome, Mayhem!"

"Shut the fuck up." Beckett punched his brother in the stomach, and Mason doubled over.

I scanned the street. "Where's Junie?"

Beckett nodded toward the booths farther down. "Jace took her to walk around. They were determined to win a bigger teddy bear than the one still sitting in my old room."

"Good luck. That thing's the size of a couch."

Mikko tapped one of the poster boards. "This is impressive," he said, his Finnish accent barely noticeable after a decade playing hockey in the U.S. "Are these expansion drawings real?"

"Yeah," Beckett said. "Final schematics. Once financing closes and the permits clear, we're green-lit."

"When do you break ground?" Mikko asked.

"Late August," I answered. "Two new locker rooms, a second rink, upstairs viewing windows, and a kitchen big enough to feed half the county."

Mikko nodded. "Good. The kids here deserve it."

"Tate deserves it all," Mason said.

Beckett groaned. "You're lucky she didn't murder you in front of children."

"But she didn't," Mason said, more than a little smug. "Progress."

Mikko laughed. "Never change."

Mason nudged him in the ribs. "Speaking of not changing, you big brute. Aren't you supposed to age? How am I gonna beat you to the puck next season if you keep getting *bigger?*"

"And faster," Beckett added.

"When are you heading back to Finland, Mikko?" Mason asked.

"In a few days," Mikko answered. "I'll see my parents. Spend time at the lake. Speaking of, how's Lori doing?"

Beckett's grin softened at the mention of his mom. "Good. Not much change with her Parkinson's, but I'm glad to be back in town."

Mikko nodded. "That's great. Is Shannon still with her?"

"Yeah," Beckett said. "But her school schedule is changing soon as she starts her clinical fellowship year in speech pathology. She's been looking for remote placements she can earn her credits and stay in town, but we'll see what that looks like."

"And her dad? No more trouble?"

The three of us turned to look at him.

Mason's grin spread. "Well, well, well. That sounds a lot like concern."

Beckett raised a brow. "Sure does, brother. You've got a lot of questions about a woman you met once."

Mikko's jaw tightened. "She's a nice person."

Mason barked out a laugh. "Nice? Shannon Wilder? Buddy, she's as nice as a grizzly in lip gloss."

Beckett grinned. "She made a grown man cry at the bake sale an hour ago."

Mikko shrugged. "He deserved it."

"How the hell do you know that, man? You were chasing a damn pig for the last hour."

Beckett elbowed me. "Are you hearing this? I haven't heard him mention a girl in years. Not after what's-her-face left him high and dry in Finland a couple of summers ago."

Mikko's ears pinked. "Shannon has had a tough life. I want better for her. That's all."

"Right," Mason said, dragging the word out. "You think a game of hide the Finnish sausage would make her feel better, Mikko?"

Beckett shook with laughter, and I shoved Mason in the chest, nearly knocking over a display. "Leave him alone. The man's been here a day."

"Exactly," Mason said. "Chop, chop, buddy. Are you going to make a move?"

"Should I propose?" Mikko asked him. "How bad does it hurt to be rejected, since you're so good at it?"

Beckett barked a laugh so loud that several people around us turned to stare. I ducked my head, laughing quietly under the brim of my hat.

We talked rink logistics for a while, then drifted down River Street beneath twinkle lights strung through the trees. The air smelled like lemonade and cotton candy, music thumping from the stage. People were everywhere—sticky-fingered, smiling, and happy.

Every vendor had a line, but a crowd formed halfway down the street by a red-and-white striped tent.

Beckett squinted. "What the hell is that?"

Delgado stood at the back, bouncing on his heels. "The date auction! Bidding restarts in five minutes. This is my shot."

"Date auction?" Beckett echoed. "I forgot Emmy mentioned that. How long has this been happening?"

"Oh, all day, but it's been guys. Can't say I blame the ladies for not wanting to participate. I'd choose the bear too."

"So who are you bidding on?" I asked, jaw already tightening.

We walked closer, and the chatter in my head died off.

Daisy stood right in the middle of the tent with a donation box that read *Kiss the Old Rink Goodbye* in swirling green marker.

Mason let out a low whistle, his arms crossed over his chest. "Oh, she's a ten."

Mikko's mouth curved, staring at Daisy, and then at me. "Isn't that—"

"Yep," Beckett answered, staring right at me. "Sure is."

My stomach dropped.

Bob, the owner of the Linwood Grocer, tapped the mic, feedback squealing loud enough to make half the crowd wince. "Alright, Mayhem, who's ready for the next date auction?"

The cheer that followed made something hot twist in my chest.

"This is a wholesome date with our very own Daisy," Bob continued. "She's 27, new to town, and ready to be shown what Linwood is all about. Like the other auctions, this date is cashed in today at the carnival. Food, games, maybe the Ferris wheel. No funny business, no pressure, and all proceeds go to the rink expansion project."

Daisy leaned into the mic. "I was told this would be low-stress," she said. "So, I expect to win at Skee-Ball and get my own funnel cake."

The crowd roared.

I stood utterly still, watching the woman I hadn't touched in two weeks get introduced like a prize.

Bob lifted the mic again. "Bidding starts at fifty dollars!"

"Fifty!" Delgado shouted, jutting his hand into the air.

I turned. "Smash."

He grinned. "Hell yeah, fuck yeah, Coach."

Daisy's gaze flicked to me, her smile spreading wide.

"Do I hear one hundred?"

"Hundred!" Luka's voice cut in from the side of the crowd, smug as hell. That punk had worked at the coffee shop for a decade and would flirt with a damn wall.

"One-fifty," Mikko said, hands still tucked in his jacket pockets.

That did it.

Something snapped in my chest, all the patience I'd clung to evaporating in an instant. I'd kept my distance because she was grieving. Because timing mattered. But watching these assholes bid on her like she was a goddamn raffle basket?

I stepped forward. "Five hundred."

The crowd went silent, all eyes on me.

Daisy's head whipped toward me. "Ty—"

"Five hundred!" Bob repeated, eyes wide. "Wow, okay! Do I hear six?"

Delgado blinked. "Coach, come on—"

"Seven hundred," Luka laughed.

"Two thousand."

The silence this time was absolute.

Beckett swore. Mason choked.

Bob stared at me. "Oh, wow. Okay. Two thousand dollars. Do I hear $2,100?"

Mikko's brows lifted. "For charity, right?"

"Careful, buddy," Beckett answered.

"Twenty-five hundred," Mikko said after a beat. He stared right at Shannon standing off to the side when he said it, her grey eyes mere slits in her face as she stared right back.

I didn't hesitate. "Five thousand."

A ripple went through the crowd. Someone laughed nervously.

Bob cleared his throat. "Five thousand dollars! Do I hear—"

"Ten thousand," I said, knowing this wasn't how an auction worked, and not caring at all.

"Sold!" Bob shouted, slamming his gavel down on the podium. "To Ty Hudson for ten thousand dollars!"

Applause exploded around us, but I was already moving.

I rounded the table, caught Daisy's wrist—firm but careful —and pulled her behind the tent.

"Ty, what the hell are you doing?"

"Winning," I said, jaw tight.

We disappeared behind the tent, the noise of the carnival muffled but still buzzing in my ears. I released her wrist only to plant my hands on either side of her, caging her against a nearby booth without touching her.

Her chest rose and fell fast. Mine matched it.

"You don't get to do that," she said, voice shaking a little. "You don't get to throw money at me because you're jealous."

I leaned in, stopping just short of her mouth. "You don't get to let half the town bid on you and expect me to be fine with it. This is what Stevie was talking about this morning, wasn't it? You knew you were signing up for this?"

Her eyes flashed. "You've been the one keeping distance."

"I was trying not to make this harder on you," I shot back. "But watching someone else take you on a date? That was never going to happen."

She swallowed. "Truth or dare, Ty."

My pulse pounded under my skin, heart racing as I inched in closer. "Dare."

I should have seen it coming, but nothing prepared me for the moment Daisy rose on her toes and dragged my face down to hers. Our lips collided, and every rational thought I'd been holding onto shattered.

My hands tightened in her hair, pulling her closer, her fingers curling into my shirt as if she was afraid I'd stop. Not a chance in hell.

Weeks of restraint burned away in seconds. There was only her, soft and wild and finally mine to touch.

She kissed as if she'd been wanting this just as bad. Her

nails grazed the back of my neck, and my breath caught. The way she sighed my name, half warning, half surrender, ruined me.

"Daisy..." I murmured against her mouth, and she swallowed it, pulling me back in.

It wasn't careful anymore. It wasn't patient. It was weeks of holding back turned to wildfire—her back against the booth, my body pressed to hers, her hips rolling against my palm when I rested it there.

A shrill buzzer blared beside us, and both of us jumped, heads whipping toward the sound.

A ring toss game a few feet away erupted in cheers, the triumphant ding of a winning bell echoing right next to the tent. The laughter rolled like a wave, snapping the spell we'd been drowning in.

I froze, still breathing hard, forehead resting against hers. Her lips were swollen, her eyes wide, like she wasn't sure if she wanted to kiss me again or kill me for starting this when, once again, I couldn't finish it.

"Ty," she whispered, voice unsteady. "Don't back out on me again."

"Okay, sweetheart," I said, stepping back just enough to see her face. "I'm yours."

A new sound rose over the crowd—Mason's voice, smug and far too loud.

"Auction's still closed," he yelled, "but I'm taking bets on how long you two make out back there."

Daisy groaned, pressing both hands to her face. "Please tell me that wasn't Mason."

"Can't do that."

She peeked through her fingers, eyes sparkling with mortified laughter. "You just spent ten grand to play Skee-Ball with me, and I think this might be more embarrassing."

"Maybe," I said, still catching my breath. "But that sounds like money well spent."

She looked up at me, something soft flickering across her face. "You're insane."

For a second, it felt like we might start again right there. Her fingers brushed mine, that same damn spark shooting straight through me.

But then another cheer went up, the microphone squealing to life as someone announced the next auction, and reality shoved its way back in.

I sighed. "We should probably get back out there before Mason turns this into an underground gambling ring."

She bit her lip, eyes back to that fiery blue. "Good thing we live in the same house," she breathed. "Less crowd control to worry about later."

My pulse kicked hard. "You planning on testing that theory?"

Her grin turned wicked. "Guess you'll have to wait and see, Huddy."

Then she brushed past me, straightening her hair and her shirt before stepping back out into the sunlight. I stayed behind the tent, wrecked, breathless, and certain that self-control was a thing of the past.

I followed her back out to the main strip and nearly collided with her when she stopped short. My hands landed on her hips before I could catch myself, steadying her against me. When she didn't move, I looked up and saw why—half the town had apparently witnessed our walk of shame.

Beckett and Emmy stood nearby, sharing that conspiratorial look couples did. Shannon lingered off to the side with

Mikko, both of them trying—and failing—to hide their amusement. A few yards away, Tate and Mason were mid-argument, her pale face flushed while he grinned like the sun.

Front and center stood Stevie, waving a hand in front of her face, tears streaking her cheeks. "I just love love," she sniffed.

She came barreling toward us, arms open. Daisy gave a nervous little laugh as Stevie wrapped us both in a hug. "You're so freaking cute together I could sob for days. And Junie? Oh, God. A family."

"Okay," Stevie's husband, Luke, said as he gently pried her loose. "That's enough for one day."

"You love me for it!" she called over her shoulder while Luke led her away, still chuckling.

"You were played," Beckett said, glancing at Emmy.

"Like a fiddle," Mikko added, and Shannon turned away, hiding a grin.

Emmy crossed her arms, entirely too pleased with herself. "My brother's always needed a good shove in the back to go after what he wants."

"Emmy," I said, low in warning.

She only grinned wider. "You're welcome."

Beside me, Daisy exhaled, her shoulders folding in, eyes flicking between them all. The longer the teasing went on, the smaller she seemed to make herself.

Before she could retreat, I slid my hands to her waist and gently turned her around. She ended up facing me, her back to the crowd, her palms instinctively finding my chest.

"Hey," I murmured, low enough that only she could hear. "Eyes on me."

Her breath hitched. I tilted my head, keeping my voice

steady and quiet. "You're fine, Daisy. Let 'em talk. They'll move on."

For a beat, she just breathed, her forehead resting against my collarbone. Then she nodded, the tension easing out of her shoulders. My hands stayed where they were, grounding her while I looked up at the others.

"Alright," I said, raising my voice. "Show's over, folks. I appreciate the enthusiasm, but maybe go grab a funnel cake or something. And the rest of you"—I looked straight at my family gathered around us—"can fuck off."

Laughter broke through the crowd, and just like that, the spell snapped.

Before anyone could throw something back, the loud-speaker crackled overhead.

"Attention, everyone!" a voice boomed. "Please find a good spot to settle in. Fireworks will begin at sundown!"

Every head turned toward the end of River Street, where volunteers were ushering people toward rows of chairs that had somehow appeared.

Tate threw her hands up. "Fireworks? Who authorized that?"

Mason lit up like a kid who'd just won the Cup. "That'd be me, Red. You're welcome."

Tate groaned, dragging a hand down her face. "You can't just *order fireworks*, Mason!"

"Actually, you very much can," he said.

The groans were unanimous.

A soft, shaky laugh escaped Daisy, and I felt it against me.

"See?" My hands smoothed once down her back, unable to stop myself. "We took too much attention, so Mason had to one-up us."

She looked up, eyes still bright, but the nerves gone. "Are you all this nuts?"

"Yes, unfortunately." I grinned down at her. "But I will say, it's never boring here."

She laughed, then stepped away, but not before her hand slid down my arm, her fingers entwined with mine. I gave her a gentle squeeze, knowing in my gut that whether they'd shoved me into this or not, I was already too far gone.

22

TY

As the sky darkened and the crowd began shifting toward the park, Mason led the way toward the spot he'd picked for us. Sure enough, he'd reserved an entire "VIP section" at the edge of the lawn—blankets spread in a wide semicircle, camp chairs arranged around a portable propane fire pit flickering steady and warm in the middle.

The air had turned crisp, the easy heat of the afternoon traded for the sharp mountain chill that always came after sunset.

Emmy arrived carrying a box from the booster table. "Mayhem hoodies for everyone!" she called as she tossed them to us.

I snagged one midair and handed it to Daisy. "Here. You're cold."

She smiled, that small, secret smile, and slid her arms into the oversized green sweatshirt. It was so big on her—just like that day we'd ripped out the kitchen—that I had to look away before thinking too much about it.

"Thanks, Coach."

"Nope," I whispered, loud enough for only her to hear. "We talked about this."

Daisy chuckled, the sound mischievous and soft.

Just then, my Mayhem players came striding across the grass, each one with one of Stevie and Luke's three kids in tow. Miles walked hand in hand with Wyatt, both sticky with cotton candy. Delgado and Reid were locked in a plastic-sword duel, their footwork carrying them closer to the group. Molly had Harper on her shoulders; the kid slapped a slightly deflated balloon animal against the top of her head.

Jace brought up the rear beside Junie, who was hauling a stuffed cow almost as big as she was. Her hair was windblown, cheeks pink from the cold, eyes bright as if she'd just conquered the world.

She broke into a run when she saw me.

"Dad! Look what I won!"

The word hit like a body check to the ribs, sudden and impossible to brace for.

The group froze for half a second. Even Mason stopped talking.

Junie didn't notice. She stumbled to a stop in front of me, the cow tipping forward to thump into my shins as she wrapped her arms around my waist.

"It's a cow! I won it with Jace at the ring toss! We had to use all our tickets, but I got the last ring myself!"

I crouched to meet her eyes. "That's a serious trophy, bug."

"Holy cow," Mason muttered behind me. "Am I right?"

Tate smacked his stomach. "You're so dumb."

Laughter rippled through the group, breaking the moment.

Junie grinned, holding up one floppy ear. "Jace said it's bigger than Beckett's bear, so I win!"

Emmy appeared beside us, fishing another hoodie from the box. "Here, honey. This one's yours."

Junie lifted her arms, and I tugged it over her head. The hem grazed her shins and the sleeves swallowed her hands. She giggled as I rolled them up so her fingers reappeared.

"There," I said, straightening the hood. "Perfect fit."

Her nose scrunched. "I called you Dad."

"Yeah," I said quietly. "You did."

She searched my face. "Is that okay?"

"That's up to you, kiddo. But I liked it."

She smiled then—small, shy. "Me too."

I tugged the hood strings so the fabric bunched around her chin.

"Come on, cowgirl. Let's get you warm."

She slipped her hand into mine, dragging the stuffed cow behind her as we walked toward the fire pit. Chairs and blankets glowed in the firelight as everyone settled in.

I sank into a chair beside Daisy, and Junie curled into her lap, the cow wedged between them. Daisy wrapped an arm around her, rubbing slow circles into her back as Junie launched into a breathless recap of the day. When Daisy shivered, I snagged a nearby blanket and draped it across them, covering all three of us.

Across the fire, Beckett kicked the back leg out of Mason's chair just enough that it folded halfway. Mason yelped, catching himself before he hit the grass.

"Real mature," he snapped, straightening it.

Beckett grinned. "I thought you loved surprises."

From a few feet over, Lori let out a dry laugh. "You'd think nearly forty years on this earth would've taught you two how to share."

Beside her, Shannon smirked. "They'll still be fighting over shit in the nursing home."

"Probably," Lori said. "Heaven help whoever has to judge the wheelchair races."

That set everyone off again.

Junie snuggled deeper into her hoodie, face tucked under her aunt's chin. Daisy leaned into my shoulder, unguarded and easy.

"Hey," Mason said, glancing around. "Where's our Finnish giant?"

Beckett frowned. "Mikko was right behind us."

Shannon didn't look up from the firelight reflecting off the gold rings on her hands. "His mom called twice, so he went to call her back."

"From Helsinki?" Beckett asked. "What's the time difference again?"

"Nine hours!" Junie said, lifting her head. "I looked it up after he told me where he's from. Did you know Helsinki has more public libraries per person than almost any city in the world? They decided a long time ago that everyone should have free access to knowledge, no matter where they live. I think that's cool."

The group stared at her.

"Well, dang, kid," Mason said. "You're cuter and smarter than all of us combined."

Junie beamed and burrowed back into Daisy's lap. Daisy laughed, one arm tightening around her.

Then the first firework cracked open above the mountains.

A low whistle rippled through the crowd, followed by a collective *ooh* as red and gold sparks bloomed against the sky.

Junie twisted in Daisy's arms, pointing. "Dad! Look!"

"I see it, bug," I said as she waved at the next burst.

The fire pit flickered, reflecting in Daisy's eyes as she leaned closer, her shoulder pressed to mine. Around us, kids squealed, Mason made exaggerated sound effects, and Tate muttered something about never trusting him again.

A streak of green and white flared in the shape of a heart, and the cheering swelled.

"Yeah, yeah," Tate muttered, trying not to smile.

Stevie popped up a few blankets over, phone held high. "Okay, okay! Before Mason sets something else on fire, I have news!"

"Is this the part where you tell them you married well?" Luke called, juggling a juice pouch and one overtired toddler.

Stevie grinned. "Correct. And also the part where I say my husband is very handsome and very good with his hands. I mean that in all the ways."

Luke laughed. "I feel seen."

She cleared her throat, scrolling.

"We have preliminary numbers in from ticket sales, raffles, booth donations, and sponsorships."

Tate raised a brow. "You already added that up?"

"Of course I did," Stevie said. "I'm me."

"Ladies, gentlemen, hockey players, and assorted small children... as of an hour ago, the Linwood Summer Carnival has raised"—she paused as Mason started a drumroll—"one hundred and forty-two thousand dollars!"

The group erupted.

Beckett whistled. Mason whooped. Tate just stared.

"You're kidding," she said.

"Not even a little," Stevie said. "Every penny goes straight into the rink expansion fund—and thanks to these guys, the sponsorships are still rolling in."

"Holy—" Tate cut herself off, glancing at the kids. "That's unreal."

Stevie's grin softened as she looked across the circle.

"And none of this would've been possible without the woman who made it happen—our very own marketing director, and the newest member of the Moms of Mayhem."

Applause broke out. Daisy laughed, hands pressed to her face. Junie hugged her tighter.

I leaned in and kissed Daisy's temple. "I'm so damn proud of you."

Another firework burst overhead, gold light flashing across Daisy's face. Her grin was the same as three years ago—the kind that hid nothing.

Eventually, the fireworks faded into smoke and stars. Chairs folded. Kids yawned. The fire pit dimmed as the flame was turned down.

Junie was half asleep in Daisy's arms, her head lolling against her chest, the stuffed cow drooping beside them.

Mason and Beckett argued about hauling the fire pit back to the truck. Tate and Emmy rolled their eyes. Stevie corralled her kids while Lori and Shannon chuckled on their blanket.

It was perfect. Quiet. Enough.

Until Mikko walked back across the field.

Even in the dark, he looked off—shoulders tight, jaw locked, firelight carving harsh lines across his face.

"About time," Mason called. "You missed the show."

Mikko didn't answer. His gaze swept the group, landing on Shannon. Her smirk faded as she sat straighter.

Beckett lowered the fire pit he was holding. "Everything alright, buddy?"

Mikko swallowed. "I—" He looked down, then up again. "I have a daughter."

He dropped into a chair we hadn't folded up yet, elbows on his knees, hands in his hair. Beckett crossed the distance and crouched in front of him.

"What's happening?" Daisy whispered.

Emmy didn't look away. "If you'd asked me five minutes ago whether Mikko had a kid, I'd have said no. He hasn't even been in a relationship for years. Which means nothing—but this is new."

Shannon helped Lori into her wheelchair, the walk to the cars too much for her Parkinson's disease. Her eyes never left Mikko.

"So... like a baby?" Jace asked.

"You know as much as I do," Emmy said, smoothing a hand over Junie's back. "And yes, I heard that."

"Yeah, Dad," Jace said. "Thanks for the cousin... I guess."

I watched as Beckett pulled Mikko into a hug. The big man folded into it, then lifted his phone, speaking rapidly in Finnish.

Mason and Tate headed toward the parking lot with Lori and Shannon. Stevie and Luke ushered their kids away with help from the team, leaving just us.

"Go," Emmy said gently. "I'll keep you posted."

"Don't let your mom carry the fire pit," I called to Jace.

He scoffed, then grabbed the handle Mason had carried earlier.

"Goodnight, you three," Beckett said, mischief back in his voice. "Go home."

I flicked him off over my shoulder. Daisy laughed.

When my hand dropped back down, she slid her fingers into mine, and I couldn't help but think this was what home was supposed to feel like.

23

Daisy

The house was quiet after a long, perfect day.

Junie was in bed, her hand resting against the stuffed cow she'd insisted on dragging into her room. I brushed a hand through her hair, smiling at how quickly she was falling asleep again after we got her inside.

"Big day, huh, cutie?" I whispered.

Her eyelids fluttered, but she didn't answer. I leaned forward and kissed her forehead, letting my lips linger before straightening again.

All of this—today, the carnival, the laughter, the people—was more fulfilling than I could've imagined. I'd been so afraid of stepping back into this place, of being the outsider, the new girl in a town where everyone had known each other since kindergarten. Where every time someone looked at me it was with pity in their eyes and sadness in their tones, knowing what I was going through.

But that wasn't what happened. No one skirted around Violet's name or tiptoed in conversations. They were just friendly, supportive, and understanding when I occasionally needed a moment to myself.

Still, nothing had prepared me for Junie shouting *Dad!* across the park.

It kept replaying in my head—the way her face lit up, how natural it sounded, as if she hadn't even realized she'd said it.

And the look on Ty's face... Shock, sure. But also this quiet, stunned joy I'd remember forever. Like she'd handed him the most precious gift of all.

I wasn't sure how it made me feel.

It didn't hurt. It didn't feel wrong. If anything, I was sure Violet would've loved it. She'd always said she wanted Junie to grow up surrounded by love, that family wasn't just who you were born with, but who you chose.

It was impossible to look at Ty Hudson and not see how much he loved that little girl. It was written in every gesture, every word. The way he carried her when she was tired. How he always remembered to wash her purple plate, so it was ready for the next meal. He'd even let her paint his toenails last week, sporting bright pink nails for all to see.

It was simple, really. Junie loved him. He loved her. And if my chest ached at that, maybe it was because I knew exactly how she felt.

Because I loved the way he was with her. And I loved the way he was with me.

It was too easy to say I only liked him because he was good with Junie. That it was gratitude, or admiration, or some grief-shaped hole he'd filled. But that wasn't true.

I liked him three years ago, back when he was just some stranger on the street. He had that same dry sense of humor, that calm, quiet steadiness that always seemed to cut through my chaos.

And now? Now he was all of that, multiplied.

He was thoughtful without trying to be. He was patient in ways I couldn't understand, never rushing, never demanding. He didn't step in and take control; he just stood by, waiting to help when you needed it most.

Sometime in the last few weeks together, I'd fallen for him.

I traced my fingers through Junie's hair again, the soft rhythm of it soothing and steady.

I didn't a little bit want this.

I very much wanted this.

That was the problem.

Because if this moved forward with Ty—and I really, *really* wanted it to—what happened if it went sideways? How could I ever leave? How could I break something that made Junie this happy?

The thought hollowed out my chest. I leaned down and pressed one more kiss to her forehead before standing, tugging the blanket higher around her shoulders.

"Night, cutie," I whispered. "I love you."

I shut her door quietly, easing out into the hall. The rest of the house was dark. Only one light was still on, a soft golden pool spilling from the kitchen at the end of the hall.

I hesitated for half a second, tugging at the hem of the Mayhem hoodie I still wore. It was big enough to hit mid-thigh, hiding the fact that my shorts and T-shirt underneath were long gone to comfort after a day in the sun. But right now, I didn't want comfort.

The air smelled faintly of wood smoke and pine, a scent that seemed to linger in every crevice of this house. I padded down the hall, quiet enough not to wake Junie, my heart thudding a steady rhythm.

When I rounded the corner, I found him exactly where I knew he'd be—sitting on the end of the sofa, waiting for me.

One arm was stretched along the back cushion, a drink loose in his other hand. His hat was on the coffee table, his dark hair sticking up in messy tufts after a long day. The lamplight from the kitchen spilled over him, catching on the edge of his mustache and the hard line of his jaw. His shorts rode up enough to show the tattoos on his thighs—bold black ink against tan skin, teasing at the hem every time he shifted.

And those eyes. Hazel, warm, and focused on me.

I couldn't look away if I tried.

Ty Hudson was gorgeous. Not in a polished, magazine-cover way—but in the real kind. The kind that crept up on you, steady and unassuming, until suddenly you realized your heart was in your throat.

His eyes flicked over my bare legs before meeting my gaze, then pointed his beer at me.

"Are you done avoiding me?" he asked, voice low, that little grin tugging at the corner of his mouth.

I crossed my arms, leaning against the wall. "Who says I was avoiding you?"

He lifted his can to take a sip, and the label caught the light. Daisy Cutter.

The same one I'd ordered in a dingy little bar in Chicago, on a night I'd remember forever. It felt like a lifetime ago, and yet here he was, always remembering every little thing about me.

Any hesitation I had about what came next vanished.

I crossed the room in a few steps, the wood floor cool beneath my bare feet, and stopped in front of him. His hand loosened around the can as I reached out, setting it down on the end table beside us.

"You're always so patient," I murmured.

His brow furrowed, lips parting to say something, but I didn't give him the chance.

I slid into his lap, straddling him, the hem of the hoodie slipping higher up my thighs. His breath hitched, and his hands came up to my hips in a steadying grip.

My fingers found the edge of his jaw, the faint stubble rough under my touch. His eyes searched mine, heat and disbelief warring there. With him looking at me like this, I wasn't scared of the future. I was scared I'd hate myself forever if I let this man walk away from me twice.

"You think I'm patient?"

I trailed my thumb along his cheek, then smiled. "You're the most patient man I've ever met."

He huffed a quiet laugh, the sound vibrating through both of us. "Not anymore."

The space between us disappeared.

His mouth met mine with that same careful heat that had been simmering between us for weeks—steady at first, then hungry. All the restraint we'd both been clinging to fell away.

The day, the carnival, the crowd—it all blurred until it was just this. Him. Me. The quiet hum of the house and the soft sounds of the night around us filtering in through the open windows.

When I pulled back, his forehead rested against mine, his breathing uneven.

"Now what?" he said.

"Now"—I kissed along his jaw, waiting until he tipped his head back. When my teeth grazed over his skin, he let out a low groan—"Now, you take me to bed."

His hands slid beneath me, strong and certain, and I was in

the air. My arms flew around his neck with a startled laugh that turned into a soft gasp when he adjusted his grip.

"Ty," I squeaked, half protesting, half dizzy. "You can't just—"

"Yes, I can," he said, the grin in his voice impossible to miss.

He started down the hall, his steps steady even with me clinging to him. I was short, curvy, and expecting him to set me down any second, but he didn't. Not once.

Ty nudged open the door to his room with my ass, the faint light from the hallway spilling across us. He kicked it shut behind him, the soft click of the lock echoing in the quiet.

His mouth found mine again as he set me on the edge of the bed, then shifted his weight forward until I was forced to lie back. My fingers tangled in his hair as his hands slid under the green hoodie, pushing it up.

"*Fuck*," Ty said, his stubble scraping against my neck when he pushed it over my hips, revealing how little I wore underneath. "Every time I see you in one of these big hoodies, I can't stop picturing you in just these little panties underneath."

His hands slid over the fabric covering my center, pushing just hard enough that I gasped, my back arching against the mattress.

"Look at you, so wet already," Ty said, still rubbing me over the fabric. "Have you been like this for hours, sweetheart?"

I nodded, words lost to me as he dropped to his knees on the floor and trailed open-mouthed kisses along my upper thighs.

"Tell me I can taste you," he said, his breath hot against my skin. "Tell me I can have these pretty legs over my shoulders and lick up every drop like I wanted to weeks ago. I want to feel you come apart under me like I've been imagining for years."

"Do it," I managed, my voice breathless with even these little teasing touches. "Please."

"What a good fucking girl you are, Daisy." His fingers hooked under the fabric of my panties, pulling them down my thighs before tossing them aside.

I expected him to lift my legs up over his shoulders, staying on his knees to fulfill these dirty promises, but Ty was never quite what I expected.

Instead, he stood, stripping off his shirt with that one-hand overhead grab men did. Next came those short-shorts, leaving him in nothing but black boxer briefs stretched tight. His hand slid over his hard cock under the fabric, giving it a squeeze.

Moonlight cut through the window, painting him in a glowy haze that only amplified how chiseled every inch of this man was.

I leaned on my elbows, raising a brow in challenge. "Chickening out?"

"Not a chance," Ty said, the side of his mustache lifting with that crooked grin that was more than a little wicked. "Not a fucking chance, Daisy."

With one more stroke over his thick cock, he climbed over me until I laid back once more. His hands slid under the hoodie, pushing it up and off, while his mouth trailed over every inch of exposed skin. By the time he threw it to the side, leaving me bare beneath him. I could hardly breathe, I wanted him so bad.

My fingers dug into the skin on his back, urging him to drop his weight down on me, but he didn't. No, his mouth found mine, pulling me in for a kiss so hot I couldn't contain the little moan that slipped free. My knees bent, making room for him to drop his hips down, but he still didn't move; those thick biceps holding him in a hover just out of reach.

Just as I was about to beg, his hands slid around my hips and pulled. We flipped, and suddenly, Ty was beneath me, my knees on either side of his chest. I gasped at the warmth of his skin on my most intimate parts, but he didn't give me a moment to adjust.

His hands gripped my hips and pulled me until his face was right between my legs. With that first drag of his tongue through my center, my whole body sagged forward. I grabbed his headboard, holding myself upright as Ty's fingers gripped my ass, moving me against his mouth just how he wanted me.

It felt so good, so right, but fear pricked the back of my mind, that I was too big, too heavy for him. When I lifted my hips, he pulled me down harder, fingers digging into my thighs.

"Ride my face, Daisy," he growled, and my mouth dropped open at the sound.

Before all of this, I'd thought Ty was just about the hottest man I'd ever seen, but this... this was unexpected.

When I didn't immediately comply, his hand smacked down on my ass, jerking me forward and right into his waiting embrace. "What did I say, sweetheart?"

This time, when he pulled down on my hips, I didn't fight it.

"Fuck, yes," Ty said, right before his mouth closed over my clit and sucked. My whole body buzzed, my breaths coming uneven with each pass of his tongue. When his hand slid beneath me, circling my entrance, I was almost hyperventilating.

"You want me here too?" Ty said, pressing just the tip of his finger inside me.

I nodded, breathing through the sensations overwhelming my body. "Yes."

His mouth returned to my clit, tongue circling just right, as he pushed a thick finger in. I couldn't think about anything but how he worked me, each slow drag of his hand drawing me higher and higher until sweat dripped down between my breasts.

"Another?" Ty said, dragging his finger out, then pushing it back in. "You're so fucking tight, pretty girl. How much can you take?"

"More," I panted, staring down at him working so diligently between my legs. It was so fucking hot, I could have come right then. "I can take more."

"Yeah, you can," he said, pushing two fingers inside this time and crooking them just right. His mouth came back to my clit, and the world faded out around me, narrowing to just how good it was.

I needed to feel him, to know he was as desperate as me, so I reached behind me, my hand finding the thick bulge still beneath his boxers. His hips lifted into my touch, as greedy as I was for the connection, and I tugged his boxers down, pulling him free. The thick head bobbed up against his stomach, and for the first time, I felt how big his cock was.

"Fuck, that feels good," Ty said, his words muffled against the inside of my thighs. "Keep touching me and I'm gonna come all over that pretty little hand while you ride my face."

"The mouth on you," I managed, the words coming out between pants and a little laugh. "Holy shit."

As if encouraged by my words, his tongue circled my clit, and any restraint I had left evaporated. It all felt too good, too right. My entire world focused in on the feel of his fingers inside me, his mouth devouring me, my hand barely able to wrap around his thick girth.

Stars exploded behind my eyelids, my whole body shaking

as I tightened around his fingers. He kept moving, shoving his hips up into my grip while he worked me through my orgasm, until he pulled his mouth off me and groaned against my thigh. Warmth coated my hand, and I let out a little laugh, stunned by what had just happened.

Once the world came into focus around me, I grabbed his discarded shirt and wiped my hand on it. Ty lay sprawled on the bed beneath me, a small smile on his face. His eyes were closed and his mustache and stubble glistened with moisture.

I shimmied down, then off him, but his arm wrapped around me, holding me against his body. "And where are you going?" he asked with his eyes still closed.

"Bathroom, then bed?" The words were more a question than a statement, not sure how to navigate whatever this was between us.

He cracked an eye open, then turned his face to look at me. "Bathroom, sure. But then you're coming back to *my* bed, Daisy. Right where you belong."

When I opened my mouth to protest, he rolled over me, pinning me in place. "If you think I'm letting you run scared right now, you're dead fucking wrong. Unless you tell me you don't want this, I'm not letting you leave. Understood?"

I couldn't quite figure out where to focus; my breaths coming rapidly until he dropped his hips down on mine. He was well on his way to hard again, and he rolled his hips, just enough that I felt every unbelievable inch of him against my thigh.

His hand settled on my chin, holding my face still until I opened my eyes once more. I expected heat, the same bossy tone he'd had the moment that door locked, but I found the same steady man I knew from these last few weeks staring back.

"Tell me you want this," Ty said, his voice hitching, showing just a little insecurity when I didn't answer. "Tell me you want me."

My hands came up, grasping either side of Ty's face until he met my gaze. "Fuck me, Ty. Make me yours."

24

TY

"Fuck me, Ty. Make me yours."

Her words slammed into me like a full-speed check into the boards, stealing my breath. My hands still framed her face, thumbs brushing the heat blooming across her cheeks. I stared, trying to etch every detail into my memory—Daisy, naked and sprawled across my sheets, blonde hair a wild halo, chest flushed pink with want, lips swollen from my kisses.

Mine.

Not a question. Not a maybe. A demand that lit me up from the inside.

I dropped my weight, letting her feel every inch of how hard she'd made me again. She gasped, hips rolling up, slick heat gliding along my cock. And fuck, I was already teetering on the edge.

"Careful what you ask for, sweetheart," I growled against her ear, nipping the lobe. "I've been dreaming about this for three damn years. I might not be gentle."

Her laugh came out shaky, fingers digging into my shoulders. "I don't need gentle. I just want you."

That was it—restraint gone. I reached between us, gripped myself, and dragged the head through her wetness just to watch her squirm. She was soaked, thighs trembling, arching like she couldn't wait another second. I notched at her entrance, but my last thread of sanity stopped me.

I pressed my forehead to her shoulder, breath ragged. "Daisy... condom. We should—"

She shook her head, eyes locked on mine, dark and certain. "I'm on the pill. And Ty, it's been years since I've been with anyone. You've been right there in my head since the moment I met you, making sure no man ever stood a chance." Her fingers curled into my hair, tugging lightly. "I want to feel you. All of you. Just us."

My pulse roared in my ears. The thought of nothing between us, of spilling inside her, claiming her in the most primal way—it hit me so hard I had to clench my jaw to keep from losing it right there.

"Are you sure?" I rasped. "I'm clean."

She nodded, a small, wicked smile curving her lips. "I'm sure. I want you bare, Ty. Want you to ruin me for anyone else."

A groan tore out of me. The image flashed unbidden—her belly rounded with my kid, Junie's little sibling kicking under her skin someday. A family. The thought lodged deep in my chest, warm and fierce.

I kissed her hard, pouring every ounce of that want into it. "You're gonna kill me, woman."

"*La petite mort*," she whispered against my mouth. "Die happy, Ty."

I pushed in inch by torturous inch, watching her eyes flutter, her mouth fall open on a silent gasp.

Tight.

So fucking tight, hot and wet and perfect.

She clenched around me, and I had to stop halfway just to breathe, forehead pressed to hers, sweat beading on my back.

"Ty—" she whimpered, nails raking down my spine.

"I know, sweetheart. I know." I slid the rest of the way home, buried to the hilt, and we both groaned. The fit was unreal—nothing between us, just skin on skin, her heat gripping me like a promise. I pulled back, then thrust in again, deeper, harder, setting a rhythm that had the headboard tapping the wall in a steady beat.

Her legs wrapped around my waist, heels digging into my ass, urging me faster. I gave it to her, the room filling with the sounds of us: skin slapping, breath hitching, the wet slide of her taking me. Her tits bounced with every thrust, and I couldn't resist dropping my mouth to one nipple, sucking hard until she cried out.

"Quiet," I warned, grinning against her skin. "Junie's down the hall."

She bit her lip, nodding, but when I angled my hips and hit that spot inside her, her head fell back, a muffled moan slipping free. I swallowed it with a kiss, tongue stroking hers in time with my cock. She was close—I could feel it in the way she fluttered around me, the way her thighs shook.

I slid a hand between us, thumb finding her clit, circling fast. "Come on, Daisy. Let me feel it. Fall apart for me."

That did it.

She shattered—back bowing off the bed, pussy clamping down so hard I saw stars. I fucked her through it, drawing it out until she gasped my name, her body trembling beneath me. Only then did I let go, burying my face in her neck, thrusting deep as I came with a guttural groan, spilling inside her in hot, endless pulses.

We stayed locked together, breathing hard, hearts hammering against each other. I didn't want to move—didn't want to lose the feel of her around me, under me, *mine*.

Eventually, I rolled to the side, pulling her with me so she draped across my chest. Her hair tickled my jaw, and I smoothed it back, pressing a kiss to her temple.

"Are you okay?" I murmured, voice rough.

She laughed, soft and sleepy. "I'm... wow. Yeah. More than okay. Might have some beard burn in awkward places later, but that's what you get from a mustache ride, I guess."

I grinned into the dark, tracing lazy circles on her back. "You only have yourself to blame for this facial hair, sweetheart."

Her head lifted, eyes wide and playful. "No regrets."

"Whipped from day one," I confessed, running a hand through the thick mustache.

She buried her face in my neck, body shaking with a soft chuckle, melting into me as if she'd always belonged there.

"Hearing you say you want me bare..." I groaned, replaying her voice in my head. "You have no idea what that does to me."

Her eyes opened, looking up at me as that smile turned wicked. "Oh, yeah?"

I rolled us until she was partially under me again, staring right now into those pretty blue eyes. "It makes me think about someday."

Her eyes softened, glassy with emotion. "Ty..."

"I know," I said, resting my forehead against hers and hoping I wasn't blowing this, but desperate for her to know how serious I was. "It's too soon."

She pulled me down, kissing me as if she was sealing the promise. "I get it," she whispered. "I like the idea of someday."

I held her close, the weight of it settling in my chest.

Someday.

I could wait for someday if every night ended like this—with her in my arms, bare and mine, dreaming of the life we'd build together.

The room went quiet, just the hum of the night outside and the steady beat of her heart against mine. I traced lazy patterns on her back, feeling her tense beneath my touch.

"Talk to me," I murmured into her hair. "Did I make you nervous?"

She was quiet for a long second. "I'm scared."

My arms tightened. "Of what?"

"This. How much I want it all. Junie called you Dad today. That child does nothing without thinking about it first, so I know she meant it. I can see you *both* mean it. So now I keep thinking, what if I mess this up? What if I let myself need you, and then—"

"Stop." I pulled back enough to make her look at me. "You're not going to mess this up. *We're* not. This isn't some fling, Daisy. Not for me."

Her eyes searched mine, a little glassy. "It isn't for me either. But I come with big, heavy baggage. A niece I'm raising. Grief. A whole life I didn't plan—"

"I want the baggage," I said, voice rough. "I want the kid. I want the mornings when Junie demands pancakes on her purple plate and critiques them like she's Gordon Ramsay. I want the nights when you fall asleep on my chest, naked and spent. An obnoxious little pig running around, a rooster that bullies everyone, and a weird llama you can't make eye contact with. I want all of it."

A tear slipped down her cheek, and I wiped it away with my thumb.

"I've been alone a long time," I said. "Not lonely, just waiting. But you, Daisy... you were plucked straight from my dreams and brought to life. You're bright, and fun, and loving, and so fucking gorgeous it's hard for me to look away. And have you seen these tits?" I grabbed a handful, then dropped my mouth to kiss along them, dragging it out until she let out a small laugh, her hips already moving again. "Delicious."

She pushed my shoulder until I lay back down beside her, but her face tipped my way. The smile melted off her face in slow motion, turning emotional once more, and I let it.

"She never told me," Daisy whispered, ducking her chin to stare at the sheet twisted between us. "I didn't even know she was sick."

I went still, the lazy circles I'd been tracing on her skin freezing mid-stroke. Sure, I'd known Daisy wasn't here those last months before Violet passed, but this—this was a gut punch.

"Jesus, Daisy." I cupped her jaw, tilting her face up. "Before I realized it was you, I thought the worst. That you knew and stayed away anyway."

Her eyes flashed, hurt and understanding all at once. "You know I would've been here. If I'd known, I would've dropped everything. I would've held her hand through the headaches, learned how to make those stupid green smoothies she loved that tasted like grass, hugged Junie when she asked why Mommy wouldn't wake up."

"I know that," I said, voice rough. "I know *you*. And Daisy, you got here as soon as you could. That you've been dealing with this on your own and still showing up for Junie every day... I'm in awe."

She shook her head. "Violet's first letter said she didn't want me to watch her die. Called it her 'last selfish act'— protecting me from the countdown."

I got that reflex. I was an older sibling too, and I fought like hell my whole life to protect Emmy from the same emotional neglect I felt at the hands of our parents. But this was different. This hurt her.

"She was wrong." Tears slid down Daisy's face, and I wiped them away with my thumb. "But I get why. And that makes me furious. I'm grateful for the months I didn't lie awake picturing her last breath... and I hate her for stealing the choice. I missed everything."

"Grief's not a straight line," I said, echoing the counselor I'd sat with every Thursday for weeks before Violet died. "It's a damn scribble. You can love her, miss her, and want to scream at her all at once."

She hiccuped. "Well, that was wise. You're not just a dumb jock, huh?"

"I hope not after those grief counseling classes I took, so I'd know what to say when Junie asked why her mom's in the ground but the sun still rises." I kissed her again, hoping she felt that I understood. "Anger's part of it. The situation sucks. Violet took something huge from you, even if she wrapped it in love. But that doesn't make missing her any easier."

Daisy's fingers curled into my chest. "I keep thinking—if I'd known, maybe I could've done something. Or, at least, helped Junie more."

"You're helping her now," I said. "You dance, and smile, and cry, and tell stories, and keep on living even when it feels impossible, showing Junie she can too. That's what matters."

She looked up, eyes softer. "Grief counseling, huh? Is that like sitting in a circle with strangers for eight weeks?"

"Every Thursday. We learned about grief bursts and memory boxes. Junie's got hers under the bed. We pressed some wildflowers last week and added them."

Daisy's smile wobbled. "You're a good man, Ty Hudson."

"I'm a man stupid in love with that kid," I said. I almost slipped *and you* in there, but was terrified that would scare Daisy off even more than implying I wanted her to have my kids someday.

So instead, I said, "I'm not going anywhere. Not when the nights are good, and not when the grief rips you open all at once. We'll scribble through it together."

She pressed her face into my neck, arms tight. "Okay."

I held her until her breathing evened, until the moon slid lower and the room went dark. Then I whispered, "Sleep, sweetheart. I've got you."

25

Daisy

The sun had already burned off the morning chill by the time Junie and I spread the picnic blanket under a tree in Violet's front yard. Mid-July in Linwood meant wildflowers every-where—columbine, paintbrush, lupine—and the air smelled like warm grass and river water and the strawberry jam I'd slathered on Junie's sandwich.

Rowdy eased down beside the blanket with a sigh, settling into the shade, while Piggie Smalls snorted through the grass nearby.

Junie sat cross-legged, purple plate balanced on her knees, inspecting her sandwich. "Did you know the average straw-berry has two hundred seeds?" she asked. "Ty has this seed catalog in the store I was reading a few days ago."

I grinned and handed her a lemonade with a curly straw. "That's crazy. Do you think we could grow a whole patch from a single strawberry?"

Junie nodded, straw already in her mouth. "Maybe if we did it right."

We ate in comfortable quiet; the mountains providing the

perfect soundtrack for this lazy day. Up close, the siding on Violet's house still looked like a before picture: peeling paint, a few boards warped from decades of sun and snow. But from the blanket it looked almost cheerful, the new porch rail gleaming white against the old farmhouse bones.

Ty had left after breakfast for the rink, ready for an off-season practice with the Mayhem and an investor's meeting to discuss the expansion project. He'd kissed Junie's forehead, squeezed my hand, and whispered, "Have a good day, girls."

Today, though, today was about me and Junie.

I pulled a fistful of clover and dandelions from the grass. "Want to learn something useless and pretty?"

Junie's eyes lit up behind her black glasses. "I like learning."

I laughed and started splitting stems with my thumbnail. "Flower crowns. My Aunt Maggie taught your mom and me when we were kids."

Junie scooted closer, sandwich forgotten. I showed her how to thread the stems, how to tuck the blooms so they wouldn't flop. Her tongue poked out in concentration, the same way Violet's used to.

Ten minutes later Junie had a lopsided halo of yellow and white; mine looked only marginally better.

"This is cool," she declared, plopping hers on my head. "Did you know dandelions are one of the first things to grow back after a fire?"

The soft chuckle that left me felt real, and so, so good. I set my crown on Junie's head, and she grinned back at me. "I didn't."

After we finished our sandwiches, I dusted off my overalls and grabbed the two terracotta pots I'd picked up from the hardware store last week. "Next project. Each summer, Aunt

Maggie insisted we paint her a new flower pot, so let's keep the tradition alive."

Junie tilted her head. "We have paints inside that would work. Mom let me pick the colors when we painted pots last summer. I can go get them."

I hesitated. Junie hadn't stepped foot inside Violet's house since I arrived. Every time we'd been outside, she seemed to ignore Violet's house altogether. I'd respected the boundary—because boy, did I understand—tiptoeing around it the way you'd skirt a sleeping bear.

But she was already standing, brushing crumbs from her shorts. "They're in the art cabinet in the living room."

I scooped up Piggie Smalls and followed, pulse thudding in my ears. The front door creaked the same as always, but inside, the house had changed. It all still smelled like sawdust, but the water-damaged drywall had been replaced, the ancient wiring was fixed, and the remnants of the demolished kitchen cabinets were nowhere to be seen. It didn't look like Violet's house anymore; it looked like a house in the middle of becoming something else.

Junie paused in the doorway, one hand on the frame. Her gaze swept the space, careful and quick—everywhere except the closed bedroom door to her right. Rowdy hovered right beside her, her constant companion.

"It looks good," she said. Then she marched to the corner cabinet, yanked it open, and pulled out a plastic bin of paints. "The mildew smell is gone."

I let out a slow breath.

We hauled the supplies back outside, then returned to our picnic blanket where Piggie sprawled out to bake in the sun. Junie unscrewed caps with surgical precision, lining brushes by size. I watched her squeeze paint onto a paper plate, the blue bright as the river.

"Mom and I painted the birdhouse this color," she said, not looking up. "She said it matched the sky."

I swallowed the lump in my throat. "Tell me about the birdhouse."

Junie's brush moved in careful strokes. "It was three years ago, right after you moved to Chicago. We got up every morning to watch out the window, waiting for someone to move in. A chickadee showed up the next week, and Mom bought me a nature journal so I could mark which days we saw it." She paused, then added softer, "Mom said chickadees are brave because they stay all winter. She stayed all winter too, even when the chemo made her throw up in the snow."

My eyes stung. I focused on a wavy line of whatever color gold she said mine was, settling for perfectly imperfect.

Junie kept talking, words spilling easy as the river. "Last winter we made glow-in-the-dark slime, and when the house was too cold, she put it in the microwave. It exploded, and the microwave glowed for days."

I snorted, picturing my sister in that chaos. Junie's mouth curved—almost a smile.

"She snorted when she laughed too, just like you do."

"Yes, she did."

She tilted her head, studying me. "Does it make you sad when I talk about her?"

The question was clinical, the way she always sought facts, but the words themselves felt like a slap to the chest.

"No, cutie. I love it. I missed too many stories." My voice wobbled, but I didn't hide it. "Sometimes I get emotional because I'm happy you had her, and because I wish I'd been here for the slime explosion. Was it gross?"

Junie nodded. "It was *everywhere.* We didn't make slime again after that."

I chuckled, drawing another little wavy line in a pattern on my pot. "I can't say I blame you."

"Your mom died when you were my age too, right?"

I blinked back tears, then let them fall instead, showing Junie that sadness was okay too. "Yeah. I was really sad, but I had my sister to make it better."

"Just like I have you."

She said it like a simple truth, then leaned forward and wrapped her arms around my middle, cheek pressed against my overalls. I folded myself around her and held on.

"Mom said emotions are like weather. Sometimes sunny, sometimes stormy. Both can happen at the same time and change just as fast."

"She was a smart woman."

We went back to painting, the only sounds the river and the scratch of bristles. Then I told her about the summer Violet and I built a fort in the backyard here. How we'd draped sheets over lawn chairs, pretending it was a castle, and Violet had declared herself queen, demanding tribute in popsicles.

Junie giggled, the sound so real, I couldn't help but laugh too. She then launched into the time Violet taught her to whistle with an acorn cap, which ended with a mouth full of bark. I countered with the road trip we took when I was sixteen, Violet navigating with a paper map she refused to fold correctly, getting us lost somewhere outside Denver but finding the best cheeseburgers along the way.

The sun shifted west, shadows stretching long across the porch. Our pots gleamed—Junie's a precise galaxy of blues and golds, mine a chaotic riot of every color in the bin. We set them in a row on the railing to dry.

Junie stood back, hands on hips. "Mom would approve."

I slung an arm around her shoulders. "She really would."

For the first time in weeks, the house didn't feel like a museum of ghosts. It felt like a place where new stories could still bloom alongside our memories—on the porch steps, in the paint under our fingernails, in the flower crowns in our hair.

Junie slipped her hand into mine. "Can we plant strawberries next spring? The seed catalog says they like full sun and well-drained soil."

"Deal," I said. "We'll start a whole patch. Two hundred seeds per berry, right?"

She squeezed my fingers. "At least."

We left the pots to cure in the sun and walked back to the blanket; the mountains glowing pink in the afternoon light. The day had healed nothing, but it had stitched something bright and living into the holes grief had left behind.

Junie plopped onto the blanket and reached for her lemonade again. Before she took a sip, Rowdy barked, alerting us just before we heard the crunch of gravel under tires.

A white county SUV rounded the bend, dust rising behind it.

Junie's shoulders tightened. Mine did too.

Sandra Diaz stepped out, smoothing her blouse against the July heat, her tablet tucked under one tan arm. She gave us a gentle wave as she crossed the yard, careful not to trample the flowers.

"Afternoon, ladies," she said, her voice warm but threaded with that official calm she always carried. "I was in the area finishing another home visit and thought I'd stop by for a quick check-in, if that's alright."

Junie leaned into my side, Rowdy between her legs, and I

squeezed her hand. "Of course," I said. "We were just painting."

Sandra's eyes flicked to the porch railing, the pots lined up like a mismatched art show. She smiled, then crouched to Junie's eye level. "They're gorgeous! Which one is yours?"

"The one with the stars," Junie said.

Sandra missed the importance of stars, but I didn't. She and Ty talked about them every night, pointing out which one she thought her mom was.

"Did you have fun at the carnival this weekend, Juniper?"

Junie shrugged. "Yeah."

"Good," Sandra said gently. She rose, tapping something into her tablet. "Since we're here, I'd love to see the progress on the house. Would you like to come inside with us? Only if you want to."

To my surprise, Junie nodded and took the lead, ushering Sandra through the front door and narrating each improvement like a tiny professor while Rowdy and Piggie trailed her every step. When we stepped back out onto the porch, Sandra wore a warm, approving smile.

"Everything looks great," she said. "I can't wait to see what color you paint the living room."

Then she turned to me. "Do you mind if we talk for a moment?"

Junie stiffened. "Are you taking me away?"

The question landed hard and fast, like she'd been holding it for weeks.

My heart dropped. "Not in a million years. She just needs to ask me something."

Junie sank back onto the blanket with her animal entourage, and I refilled her lemonade, then followed Sandra just far enough away to give us a sliver of privacy.

"She's doing so well," Sandra murmured. "I can see it."

"She's trying," I said quietly. "We all are."

Sandra nodded toward the house, then looked back at me. "Have you given any more thought to whether you plan to stay in Linwood? Or if you're returning to Chicago at the end of the six weeks?"

My breath caught, having avoided this thought for weeks. "I... I don't know yet."

Sandra nodded. "If you decide to return to Chicago, the courts would support full guardianship in your favor once probate clears. You're her next of kin, and the will names you. It wouldn't be a fight to get you primary custody."

My chest tightened at the idea of taking her from Ty. Of leaving this place.

"But they'll also consider her adjustment here," she added. "How she's healing. How bonded she is to Ty. Stability matters as much as biology."

I looked back at Junie, at the house behind her, at the lopsided flower crowns sitting in the grass.

"I don't want to uproot her again," I whispered.

Sandra's eyes softened. "Then you're thinking about the right things."

She gave my arm a gentle squeeze and walked back toward her SUV. Junie scrambled up the moment the driver door shut.

"Is everything okay?" she asked, worry wrinkling her forehead.

I knelt and pulled her in for a hug. "Everything's okay, cutie. Promise."

Sandra backed down the drive, giving us one last wave through the window. When the dust settled again, Junie tugged my hand.

"Should we paint the front door too?"

"Yeah," I said, my throat thick. "Let's do it."

She grabbed a can of purple paint from inside, and we settled on the porch. The sun was warm on our backs, the river humming next to us, the pots gleaming bright on the porch—a little imperfect, a little new, just like everything else still trying to find a place in this new reality.

I watched Junie drag the brush in careful, perfect stripes, and I knew that this valley, this ranch, this life was where Junie belonged.

I also knew we were standing in the calm, and that the day grief pulled us both under was still waiting its turn.

26

TY

The chill in the Linwood Rink had that sharp, clean bite that woke a man up better than coffee. I leaned on the boards, whistle dangling from my neck, and watched the Mayhem fly through a two-on-two breakout drill. Skates carved the fresh sheet, pucks clacking off sticks, the echo bouncing off the rafters like gunfire. Off-season, sure, but these kids were hungry for another state championship, and it showed.

Beckett dropped next to me, elbows on knees. "Watch Molly go against Smash here. She's unreal."

On the ice, Molly's dark braid whipped like a battle flag as she spun past Delgado, who was yelling something about respecting her elders. She flipped him the bird without looking back.

Jace accepted a pass from Molly, then flicked a wrist shot at the goal. Miles snagged it with a glove save that there was no chance he would have made this time last year.

"Nice save, Pickles." I clapped my hands together, then let out a whistle. "That's what I like to see."

Beckett nudged me. "You're chipper today. What's with you?"

"Just watching my back-to-back state champs."

"Bullshit." He took a swig of water. "You were humming earlier. And don't think the whole town missed you sucking face with Daisy last night."

I busied myself with the clipboard. "Focus on the drills, not my love life."

Beckett wasn't letting it go. "So how are you going to juggle it all this fall? Store opens at 7, school drop-off at 8, practice at 3, and now you've got a girlfriend. You're one man, Huddy."

I exhaled, watching Jace and Delgado set up for another rush. "I promoted Steve to general manager last week. He's going to handle the day-to-day, and I can just be oversight."

Beckett raised a brow. "You sure? Will your dad have anything to say about that?"

"Don't know. Don't care."

"Amen, brother."

On the ice, Molly stole the puck from Delgado again, cackling as she roofed it top shelf. Pickles flopped dramatically, and stayed down. "What the heck was that?"

"Skill!" Molly shouted back. "You should try it!"

Jace skated over, leaning on his stick. "Coach, tell Smash he can't check me just 'cause I'm prettier."

Delgado grinned. "Pretty doesn't stop pucks, Juice."

"No cap," Beckett said, and they all groaned in unison.

"I hate it when he does that," Molly said. "Stop trying so hard."

I blew the whistle for a water break. The kids coasted to the bench, sweaty and grinning. They all chattered about everything and nothing, but movement in my periphery caught my eye.

Junie marched down the ramp to the rink in an oversized Mayhem hoodie, leggings, and rain boots. Daisy followed, sunglasses pushed up into her hair, her paint-splattered overalls doing a terrible job of hiding the curves I memorized last night.

"Hi Dad!" Junie waved. "We brought snacks!"

My heart lurched at the word again, a wide grin spreading across my face as she ran toward me. Her arms wrapped around my legs, squeezing tight, and I hugged her back.

"What's up, Rookie!" Molly knocked her on the shoulder, and Junie grinned up at her. "You're late!"

"This isn't an official practice," Junie corrected, already climbing onto the bench. "So I can't be late."

Daisy gave a little wave, then busied herself setting the basket on the bench. I tried not to stare, but Beckett elbowed me hard enough to bruise.

"Subtle," he muttered.

"Shut up."

Junie was already in third-coach mode, pointing at the whiteboard. "Have they run the Carolina breakout yet? I watched replays with my dad last week, and the second forward needs to curl higher or the D will pinch."

Delgado blinked. "Okay, pint-sized Gretzky."

Junie looked right at him. "You should work on your gap control before the season starts."

The kids howled. Even Pickles cracked a grin, his goalie mask perched atop his head.

Daisy slid onto the bench beside Beckett, leaving a careful foot of space between us. "Hope we're not interrupting."

"Never." I pulled her in for a kiss on the temple, hand on her back. "Junie's got notes."

Beckett leaned forward. "Hey, Daisy. Nice basket."

She narrowed her eyes. "Thanks, Beckett. Nice whistle."

He smirked. "So, how was the rest of your night? Restful? Sleep well?"

Daisy's face went scarlet, and she busied herself unpacking lemonade and cookies. "Slept great, thanks for asking."

"Good, good," Beckett said, grinning right at me. "Love to hear it."

I kicked his skate. "Focus."

Junie tugged my sleeve, and I looked down at her. "Can I blow the whistle?"

"Yeah, bug," I said, handing her the clipboard and whistle. "Call the next drill."

She scrambled up, standing on the bench. "Triangle regroup! Molly, you're F1. Juice, F2. Smash, trail but don't lag —your edges are lazy!"

Delgado saluted. "Yes, Coach Rook."

They hit the ice, Junie barking orders with the confidence of a kid who'd spent too much time with me at practice over the last few months. Daisy watched, a soft smile tugging at her mouth.

Beckett pointed at Junie. "She's good for them."

"She's good for everyone," I said.

My best friend leaned against the boards, his focus on Daisy, not the kids on the ice.

Even though I knew I shouldn't, I couldn't help staring at her too. Last night was still burned into my skin—Daisy's hands in my hair, her voice breaking on my name, the way she'd fallen asleep curled against me like she'd always belonged there.

Daisy caught us staring. "What?"

"Nothing," Beckett and I said at the same time.

She rolled her eyes, but her blush deepened.

Practice rolled on, Junie's voice echoing over the ice. She corrected Pickles' stance and praised Molly's one-timer like a seasoned analyst. The kids ate it up, skating harder and laughing louder.

When the Zamboni rolled out, the team circled up, sweaty and buzzing. Junie stood between Molly and Jace, clipboard clutched to her chest.

"Great work," I said. "Hydrate, stretch, and—"

"Slice and Spice!" Delgado yelled. "Coach is buying!"

Junie bounced. "I love their garlic knots! And, oh! We can play the trivia machine!"

"I haven't been there in ages," Daisy said, arms wrapped around Junie's shoulders. "Will you share some of your knots with me?"

"Pickles, do you need a ride?" Beckett asked, and the goalie gave him a thumbs-up, heading to the locker room.

Molly nudged Junie's shoulder. "You owe me a rematch on the hockey trivia."

Junie grinned bigger than she had in weeks. "Prepare to lose."

She rushed toward the parking lot while the players went to undress in the locker room. In record time, the kids piled into trucks, sticks clattering, voices loud enough to scare the magpies from the pines. Daisy's hand found mine as we walked to my truck, fingers lacing as if they'd done it a thousand times.

Junie climbed into the back seat, already quizzing Molly through the open window about power-play statistics.

I started the engine, glancing at Daisy through the open window as she climbed into her car. "Are you sure you're ready for this mayhem?"

She smiled, soft and certain. "Absolutely."

Slice and Spice sat on River Street across from Hudson Hardware. The building was painted the shade of a ripe jalapeño, its hand-painted sign swinging crooked above a red door strung with chili-pepper lights. Inside, the air was a glorious clash of oregano and cumin, red-checkered tablecloths bumping up against papel picado banners, and the chalkboard menu boasted "za-cos"—flour tortillas folded over pepperoni and a three-cheese blend with a whisper of salsa, griddled until the cheese bubbled out like molten lava and the edges curled crisp.

"They haven't changed a thing," Daisy said, staring up at the mismatched decor, including the life-size statue of a waiter wearing a sombrero.

"It's weird," Emmy said as she came in the front door. "We know it."

Beckett stood and kissed her, then helped her slide into the booth across from Daisy and me.

"How was the studio?" he asked, twirling a stray lock of dark hair that had escaped Emmy's ponytail. "Good day?"

She nodded. "Yeah. We had your mom and the knitting ladies in this afternoon. They told me to tell you they miss you."

Beckett laughed. "Next week, I'm there. Tell Ruth she's going down."

"Is Pilates a competition?" Daisy asked.

Emmy shook her head.

"Anything's a competition if you try hard enough," Beckett said.

Their voices overlapped easily after that. I watched Daisy

slot into it without effort, laughing with Emmy, trading looks with Beckett like she'd been doing it for years. Something in my chest ached in the best and worst way.

This was what it could look like.

And I wanted it so badly it scared me.

As if she sensed my gaze lingering, Daisy glanced my way and winked.

I dropped my eyes to my hands, doing my best to hide my grin.

The bell over the door jingled, and Shannon walked in, dropping into the last open chair at our table. "Same table-cloths. Same food. Same jukebox that only plays Dean Martin or Vicente Fernández."

"Where's Mom?" Beckett asked.

"The knitting club headed to Vail today to ride the gondola," Shannon said. "Mason took her. I'm on my own until tonight."

Emmy tapped a finger against her lips. "Interesting. Because Tate bailed on our plans tonight to go ride the gondola too."

"Well, shit, little brother," Beckett said with a laugh. "Maybe this isn't such an uphill battle anymore. Think they'll end up together someday?"

I raised a brow. "Oh, so we're just playing matchmaker with everyone now? Is Shannon next?"

"Don't you dare." Shannon pushed back from the table, already halfway to standing.

Beckett caught her arm, grinning. "Relax. You're safe for now. These two, though." He pointed between Daisy and me. "I'm invested."

"Leave them alone," Emmy said, elbowing him. "You'll scare her off."

"Don't do that," Shannon added. "I like her better than you."

Daisy grinned. "I like you too, Shannon."

I draped an arm over the back of the booth, and Beckett's grin turned devious—but for once, he kept his commentary to himself.

Our server dropped off two pitchers of soda and a stack of red plastic cups. The kids abandoned pinball the second the garlic knots and cheese sticks hit the table. Junie climbed into the booth between Molly and Jace, already lecturing them on the physics of a cheese pull.

"The mozzarella has to hit two hundred and thirty degrees to stretch like that," she said, demonstrating with a cheese stick. "My mom and I tested it last year."

Molly pointed a garlic knot at her. "This is the information I like. Keep it coming, Rook."

Daisy laughed, low and warm, sounding genuine even though it touched on a memory of her sister. My hand drifted to her back, settling on her hip as I pulled her closer. She leaned into me without hesitation.

The first round of za-cos hit the table—golden, sizzling, leaking cheese and salsa onto wax paper. Delgado took one bite and groaned loud enough to earn a glare from the old couple in the corner.

"Smash," I said. "Inside voice."

"Can't," he mumbled. "This is religious."

Pickles adjusted his glasses, studying his food. "On paper, this should not work. Tortilla. Pepperoni. Salsa. It's chaos."

Daisy tore off a corner and popped it into her mouth. "It tastes exactly how I remember it."

The bell over the door jingled again, and we all looked up.

Two men walked in, broad and rough-edged in a way

Linwood didn't see often. Dirty blond hair, leather vests, heavy boots.

It took me half a second to recognize Cash and Colton Wilder, Shannon's older brothers. I hadn't seen them in over a decade—not since we were kids sharing ice time. They'd been mean back then. Cheap shots. Cruel mouths. Not caring that their decisions cost us the game.

They looked meaner now.

Shannon went rigid. "Nope."

Cash sauntered over, kicking the leg of her chair until she sat facing him. Colton hung back, eyes sweeping the room.

"Shan," Cash said. "I thought that was you who walked in here."

"I'm kind of shocked that brain of yours was capable of that much," she said, then turned back to the table. "Leave."

"We just need a little help," he said. "Dad's not doing great. You know how he gets."

"She asked you to leave," Beckett said, standing from the booth.

Cash backed up a step, and a wicked smile carving his face. "Relax, Conway. This is a family matter."

"You're not getting money from me, especially not for him," Shannon said, staring hard at the table. "Not now. Not ever."

"You always were selfish," Colton said from behind his brother, and I stood to join Beckett.

Cash smirked. "Still playing the hero, Hudson?"

I stepped between him and Shannon, voice calm and cold. "Door's behind you."

Cash walked backward toward the door, Colton turning to leave. "Don't think I've forgotten all we've done for you, baby sis. We'll see you around."

They left, the door slamming hard enough to rattle.

Beckett stayed standing, eyes still on the door. "Are they a problem?" he asked quietly.

"No," Shannon said.

"Because if they are—"

"You don't get to fix everything for me, Beckett."

Beckett nodded once. "Okay."

"I've got it," she said, looking away.

I wasn't so sure she did—but I kept that to myself.

When Beckett and I sat back down, his phone lit up on the table. He reached for it, then said, "Oh, good. Mikko landed in Helsinki."

"And what's this about a daughter?" I asked.

He shook his head. "Someone dropped off a toddler with his mom, claiming she's his."

Shannon sat up straight, looking more bothered by this than she had been by her brothers moments ago. "Define *dropped off*."

"You know as much as I do."

Her gaze flicked to the kids crowded at the end of the booth, Junie safe and laughing, then she stood and walked out.

"Fuck," Beckett said. "I should have thought about that before I said it. I'm sure that hit a nerve with her, considering her own mom walked out when she was a kid."

Emmy chewed her lip, staring at the door. "We should let her cool off right? Swing by the house to check on her later?"

"Yeah, peach." Beckett kissed Emmy's temple, looking at her with open adoration. "I like that idea."

Maybe some guys would've bristled at their best friend falling for their sister, but I approved of anyone who looked at her like that.

Junie hopped down from the kids' table and padded over, climbing onto the bench between Daisy and me.

"So, is Mikko going to be a dad?" she asked. "I bet he'll be a good one. Like mine."

The table went quiet. My throat tightened, love hitting me so hard it almost knocked the air from my lungs.

Daisy's hand found mine under the table and squeezed. "I bet you're right," she said softly.

I cleared my throat. "Trivia machine's free. Who's brave?"

Junie shot up. "Me!"

The kids scrambled, laughter echoing as they rushed the machine.

Outside, the sun dipped behind the mountains. Inside Slice and Spice, the lights glowed. Daisy leaned into my side, Junie laughing somewhere nearby, and that wasn't just enough.

It was everything.

27

Daisy

I sat cross-legged on my bed, the letter balanced on my knee like a loaded gun.

The last four days had been a blur of sawdust and sweat as Ty and I installed the new kitchen cabinets in Violet's house. Between that, working at the rink, farm chores, taking care of Junie, and sneaking in every second of alone time I could with him, the days went by fast.

But it all came to a screeching halt when I'd opened Violet's bedroom door for the first time yesterday. The air inside was thick with dust from the construction work we'd done, but the lavender sachets still tucked in the dresser drawers clung to the air like a ghost that refused to leave.

I stood there until my legs shook, knees threatening to buckle under the weight of her absence, ready to close the door and come back another day—another week, another lifetime— when I saw it.

This paper was different, smaller, like a notepad you'd swipe from a roadside motel. But it had the same little daisy drawn on the front in her careful pen. Folded in half, it sat propped up on her nightstand.

I pocketed it, then closed the door, unable to handle crashing out right then. By the time I got back to Ty's house, Emmy, Beckett, Mason, Jace, Lori, and Shannon were in the backyard around the fire pit and staying for dinner. Talk had turned to a camping trip, and Junie bounced around excitedly when they'd asked her to join them.

So I stashed the letter in my room, too nervous to face whatever Violet had to say when everything finally felt good.

Now, it glared at me.

Tears burned my cheeks, but the sound of Junie's pounding feet down the hall had me tucking the letter beneath my leg and wiping away the tears as fast as I could.

"I'm ready!" Junie called as she spun around the corner and into my room. "How do I look?"

She posed with her hands on her hips, wearing a pair of cargo pants tucked into her rain boots, and a pink button-down fishing shirt. Her blonde ponytail stuck out the back of a Hudson Hardware hat, and she looked adorable.

"Like a professional camper." I slid off the bed and down to my knees in front of her. "I like these pants."

"There are *seven* pockets. I've never had that many pockets."

I chuckled, tugging on her hat until it sat straight on her face over her glasses. "Perfect for collecting flowers."

"That's what I said!" Junie wrapped her arms around my neck, squeezing me tight. I soaked in her warmth, holding onto this last piece of my sister. "I'll miss you tonight. I've never slept in a tent before, but Ty let me read about them last night on his phone. And Jace promised we can make s'mores. Will you be here when I get home tomorrow?"

Tears sprung to my eyes again, and I squeezed her a little tighter. "Always, cutie. I'll always be here waiting for you."

"Ready, bug?" Ty said from behind her.

He leaned against the doorway, looking better than he had any right to. His shorts were somehow even shorter than any I'd seen before, and the black tee stretched across his broad biceps I'd become very familiar with the last few days. The Mayhem hat he often wore was turned around backward, and he'd shaved his face clean, only emphasizing that mustache I loved so much.

A car horn beeped outside, and Junie squeezed me one more time, then let go, running back out the door as fast as she'd come in. I stayed there on the floor and blew out a deep breath, noticing Ty hadn't walked away yet.

We had one more day of work to finish the kitchen, but I could hardly stand the idea of getting up off the floor, let alone stepping foot inside her house again.

As if reading my thoughts, Ty asked, "Wanna get out of here today?"

I looked up at him through my lashes, studying the man who was learning to read me far too well.

"What do you have in mind?"

He walked toward me, then squatted down to lay a kiss on my lips. "I say we play hooky. Have a good day, just you and me. Maybe get naked at some point."

I grinned, letting a small chuckle slip free. "Last night wasn't enough for you?"

His nose rubbed against mine, then he dropped one more kiss on my lips. "Never."

"Ty?" Emmy called from the front door, and he stood up, walking back out of the room. I got to my feet and turned toward the bed, seeing the letter again.

My hands shook as I reached for it, then cracked it open.

I miss you so much.
This was a terrible idea.
I'd do anything to hug you one more time.

I flipped the paper over, craving more from her, but that was it.

I crumpled the note in my palm, then let the tears fall hot. No matter how fast I wiped at my cheeks, I couldn't seem to stop them.

At some point, the letters would stop, and that would be it. I'd never see her handwriting scrawled across a paper with new words of encouragement. Never laugh at one more of her jokes. Never feel like she was right there, talking me through grieving her.

And then what would I do?

Unfortunately, the tragic circumstances in my life meant I was all too familiar with grief and the grip it held on you for the rest of your days. Sometimes it felt okay, and then sometimes it would hit you like a freight train that appeared out of thin air.

But every time I'd grieved before, I'd done it with Violet at my side.

I'd turned to her when it felt too hard to breathe, too difficult to get out of bed.

With each letter, I understood her a little more.

She knew how hard this would be for me to do alone. Knew I wouldn't tell anyone how bad it hurt. Knew I needed her, even after she was gone.

But the letters couldn't go on forever.

Ty's heavy footsteps returned before I could pull myself

together. He stopped in the doorway, took one look at me, and crossed the room in three strides. Strong arms wrapped around me from behind, pulling me back against his chest. I sank into him, the note still clenched in my fist, tears soaking the collar of my shirt.

"I've got you," he murmured into my hair, one hand splayed over my stomach, the other stroking my arm. "Cry it out, sweetheart. I'm not going anywhere."

I turned in his hold, burying my face in his neck, breathing in cedar and sawdust and him. His heartbeat thumped steady under my cheek, grounding me. He didn't ask what the note said; he just held me until the sobs eased into shaky breaths.

When I finally pulled back, he wiped my tears with his thumbs, mustache brushing my forehead in a soft kiss. "Better?"

I nodded, managing a watery smile. "Get me out of here, please."

"Absolutely." He scooped the crumpled note from my hand and set it on my dresser. "That stays here. Today's ours."

He laced his fingers through mine and tugged me toward the door. I grabbed my heart-shaped sunglasses off the dresser, slipping them on to hide any lingering redness. Outside, the late morning sun glinted off his truck, Rowdy's tail thumping on the porch as he watched us walk by. Ty opened the passenger door, boosted me in with a quick squeeze to my ass, then rounded to the driver's side.

Engine rumbling, he reached over, palm open on the bench between us. I slid my hand into his. "Where to first, Huddy?"

"Oh, I've got a plan." He squeezed once. "Just you and me."

I leaned my head against the door, my hand out the window as I watched Linwood roll by, the weight in my chest lighter with every mile away from her house. Ty eased the truck down River Street, then pulled into a space in front of Hudson Hardware.

"Are we going to work?" I asked, eyeing the storefront.

"Nope." He killed the engine and nodded across the street. "Just parking. We're headed there."

Across the street, The Lantern looked nothing like the rowdy place Ty and Emmy had described in passing. The last time I'd lived in town, it was just a honky-tonk, only open at night. A little dingy, a little country, and exactly what you'd expect from an old mining town's saloon.

Now, the copper lettering above the door gleamed in the mountain sun. The big front windows were thrown open, letting out the scent of grilled onions and something smoky and fried. It was less "country bar" and more cozy mountain tavern, warm and lived in, waiting for the evening crowds that would turn it loud and wild.

Ty nodded toward it. "Ready?"

"For what?" I asked.

His grin was wicked and soft all at once when he opened my car door. "A redo."

I hopped out of the truck, and his hand slid right into mine.

Ty pushed open the door to the Lantern, and instead of honky-tonk chaos, a soft hum of afternoon quiet met us. Sunlight streamed through the open windows, casting long beams across the scuffed wooden floor. The faint clatter of dishes came from the kitchen, and somewhere overhead—

"What the—," I breathed, stopping in my tracks.

Every TV in the place was playing *Magnum P.I.* Tom Selleck stared down at me from every angle, that little dimple popping on his cheek when he smiled.

Ty tried to keep a straight face. "Weird coincidence."

I turned slowly, arms crossed. "You called ahead."

He didn't even pretend to deny it. "Come on," he said softly, leading me to a small wooden booth along the windows. Not cracked vinyl, not Chicago—but close enough to feel like an echo.

Afternoon light washed over the table as we slid in, and the server dropped off two drinks and a basket of steaming fries.

I blinked. "You ordered these already?"

"I know your priorities," he said, utterly unapologetic.

My lips twitched. "You make it very hard to pretend this isn't serious."

"Good." His voice dipped low, warm. "I'm not here to pretend."

The server came back to take our order, but Ty barely looked at the menu. "Two cheeseburgers. Grilled onions on both. Mayo on hers."

"*Extra* mayo, please," I added sweetly.

When the server left, Ty leaned in, forearms braced on the table. "Truth or dare, Daisy."

I huffed out a breath, forcing a smile like this was nothing. Like my insides weren't a carefully stacked house of cards. Like I didn't understand why he was doing this. But I couldn't do vulnerable—not today.

"Dare."

Something in his expression eased—not relief, exactly. More like recognition.

"Okay," he said, glancing around the table. "Easy one."

He nudged the basket of fries toward me. "I dare you to eat three fries. No distractions. No talking."

I blinked. "That's it?"

"I don't think you've eaten today," he said mildly. "Let's fix that."

I scoffed, but my mind came up blank for any rebuttal. "Do you have to notice *everything*?"

I picked up the first fry. Ate it. The second. The third.

I sat back, crossing my arms. "Better?"

Ty smiled, and it was disarming to see him so happy when I felt like my heart was about to explode. "You did great."

The softness and sincerity in his words made my chest feel weird, so I jumped in before he could say anything else.

"My turn." I leaned forward. "Truth or dare?"

His answer came without hesitation. "Truth."

Of course, he chose truth.

I stared at him for half a second, every real question backing away from the edge of my tongue.

Why does it feel like you see straight through me?

When does all of this become too much, and you'll decide I'm not worth the trouble?

How do I stay when every part of me wants to run from this pain creeping in?

Nope. Not today.

I waved a fry at him instead. "Why won't you try mayo on your cheeseburger?"

He blinked, then barked out a laugh. "That's your truth?"

"Absolutely," I said. "I need to understand the psychology."

He shook his head, smiling, but there was affection in it now. "Because it's unnecessary. The burger is already perfect."

I gasped. "Have you even tried it before? How do you know it doesn't make your burger that much better?"

"See, that's the part you're missing. I don't need the burger to be better. I love the burger just as it is."

I swallowed, staring down at my hands. I was pretty sure we were still talking about burgers, but the softness in his voice said this was something more.

"My turn," he said quietly. "Truth or dare, Daisy?"

"Dare," I said quickly. Too quickly.

Ty didn't smile this time. Not right away. He watched me like he was choosing his words carefully.

"I dare you," he said slowly, "to sit over here."

My brows knit together. "That's it?"

"That's it."

The booth wasn't big. We already sat close enough that our knees brushed under the table. But his side of the booth was different. His space. His warmth.

I hesitated just long enough to be obvious.

Then I rolled my eyes and grabbed my Diet Coke. "We're going to be *those people* now? The ones who sit on the same side of the booth, even when they're alone?"

"Yes," he said, completely unapologetic.

I slid out of my seat and into his side of the booth, the wood cool beneath my legs. The moment I settled, his thigh pressed solid and warm against mine. Not crowding. Just... there.

"Comfortable?" he asked.

I shrugged, staring at the table. "Kinda weird, but yes."

A beat passed.

Then he shifted—just enough that our shoulders brushed. His arm rested along the back of the booth, not around me, but close enough that I could feel the heat of him through the thin fabric of my shirt.

My breath hitched.

"Still good?" he asked softly.

I nodded, because speaking felt dangerous.

"Okay," he said. "Your turn."

I latched onto the game like a lifeline. "Truth or dare?"

His answer came easy. "Truth."

Why does this feel like standing on the edge of something?

Why are you so patient with me?

Why does letting you this close feel harder than being alone?

Nope.

"Do you secretly hate Cluck Norris as much as I do?"

His lips twitched. "No. I'm not afraid to be patient, waiting until he's ready to love me as much as I love him. Eventually, he'll realize his big personality doesn't scare me, and I'm not going anywhere even on his bad days."

Fuck. Now I definitely thought we weren't just talking about a rooster.

I reached for my Diet Coke, needing something to do with my hands while my mind spun out.

"My turn," he said quietly. "Truth or dare?"

"Dare."

"I dare you," he said, voice low and steady, "to let me hold your hand."

My heart slammed.

It was nothing.

It was *everything*.

I looked down at the space between us—at his big, open palm resting on the table like an offering. Always patient. Never demanding.

I slipped my hand into his.

Ty's fingers closed around mine, warm and sure, like this was the most natural thing in the world. And just like that, the room faded. The TVs. The chatter. The clink of glasses. All I could feel was his thumb brushing slow circles over the back of my hand, grounding and gentle and devastatingly kind.

He didn't say anything. He didn't need to.

This was his silent, *I see you. I've got you,* right when I needed it most.

The server appeared beside the table, balancing two plates. "Two cheeseburgers. Grilled onions on both. Mayo on the side."

Ty thanked the server, never letting go of my hand. I stared over at him as he picked up his cheeseburger with his left hand and took a bite.

"Really?" I chuckled. "We're turning this into a three-legged race, but with cheeseburgers?"

"Daisy," Ty said, then waited until I looked up at him. "I am never going to be the first one to let go. But if you need to, I understand."

My eyes stung with unshed tears I absolutely would not let fall right now. But I picked up my burger in my right hand and took a bite.

Should I have let go? Probably.

But I couldn't.

I didn't want to.

"Okay," I said, forcing a brightness I didn't entirely feel. "New rule."

His thumb paused mid-circle, but his hand stayed steady beneath mine. "Of course there is."

I nodded, grateful he didn't argue. "No truths. Only dares."

He nodded, then took another bite.

I slid the little dish of mayo toward him, and blinked up with a smile.

"Go on. I dare you."

Ty gave me the most deadpan expression I'd ever seen on him, then dipped the corner of his burger in the condiment. "This is cruel and unusual punishment, sweetheart."

I grinned. "Go on. Even Junie takes try-bites, right?"

He sighed, then took a bite. His jaw moved slowly, his expression never softening. "If you're expecting to change my mind, don't."

A laugh bubbled out of me, feeling a little manic. I grabbed my phone from across the table and snapped a picture of his grumpy face, then put it back down. "Just in case I ever forget this moment."

Ty shook his head. "I dare you to eat the rest of your cheeseburger, so we can get out of here."

I leaned my head on his shoulder, and he dropped a kiss to the top of my head like we'd been doing this for years.

We ate in silence, but this time, the laughter and comfort didn't ease the tightness in my chest.

28

TY

Daisy buckled in next to me, her fingers brushing mine on the bench seat as I pulled out of the parking spot. Her smile had faded, showing the cracks beneath it.

So I started talking—anything to keep her afloat after the weight of this morning.

"Beckett used to get grounded more than any kid I knew," I said, turning left at the light. "One time he tried to impress a girl by riding his mountain bike off the roof of the hardware store."

She blinked. "Off the roof?"

"Yep. Used a mattress in the dumpster as a landing pad." I shook my head, grinning. "Missed by about three feet and had a broken wrist and a black eye to show for it."

She smiled, so I kept going.

"Naturally, Mason saw that and decided he could do it better. Except he picked the grocery store roof—which is twice as high—and Bob came out screaming bloody murder when he spotted him climbing the drainpipe."

"Oh no."

"Oh yes. Emmy and I pretended we didn't know them while they were getting lectured by the sheriff and their mom in turns."

Daisy laughed again, but this time it didn't reach her eyes.

I drummed my fingers on the wheel, then made a decision.

Instead of heading toward home, I swung right down a narrow road that cut behind town and toward the ridge. I reached into the back seat, snagging the stack of blankets I'd tossed in earlier and dropped them onto the bench seat between us.

After a few seconds, she angled toward me. "Where are we going?"

"You'll see."

Her eyebrows lifted. "That's vague."

"Mmhmm."

The pavement ended, gravel crunching under the tires as we wound up the hillside. Tall pines crowded the road, sunlight dripping between them in gold streaks. The higher we climbed, the thinner the air felt, clean and sharp.

"Huddy," she said slowly, "are you kidnapping me?"

I smirked. "Relax. I promise you'll like it."

She shook her head, but I didn't miss the way her shoulders loosened a little, just like I hoped they would.

At the last bend, the trees opened up, revealing a flat pull-off overlooking the whole valley. The Gore Range stretched out in jagged blue layers on every side, and down below, Linwood looked small enough to fit in the palm of my hand.

"This," I said, putting the truck in park, "is Elkhorn Point."

"Is this where you brought girls to make out?" she asked, one eyebrow arched high.

"Absolutely," I said without shame. "Some of my best work happened up here."

She rolled her eyes, but she was smiling now, and this one was genuine.

I hopped out, grabbed the blankets, and rounded the truck. "Come on."

Her door shut behind us as we stepped into the thick quiet of the trees. A narrow path cut between the aspens, worn down by hikers. The air was cooler up here, crisp enough to sting my lungs a little. Daisy kept up though, her hand still in mine.

The sound of distant, rushing water came first, then the trees parted to reveal a pond tucked into the bowl of the mountain. It was still and perfect except for the shimmer of a waterfall feeding into it on the far side.

A rope swing hung from a thick branch overhead, swaying gently above the clear water.

Daisy stopped beside me, eyes widening. "Ty..."

Before she could say anything, I laid out my blankets on the little pebbly beach, then toed off my shoes, and dropped them on the edge of the blanket.

"What are you doing?" she asked, half laughing, half alarmed.

"Dares only, right Daisy?"

With a wink, I pulled my shirt off, then hooked my thumbs in the waistband of my shorts and let them fall, leaving me in nothing but my black boxer briefs. Cool air hit my thighs, tattoos on full display.

Daisy made a small noise—something between a gasp and a laugh—then upped the ante.

She peeled off her top and shorts, letting it pool at her feet. Next went her bra and underwear.

Naked. Gloriously, unapologetically naked.

The cool mountain air pebbled her nipples instantly, goosebumps racing across her skin, but she didn't flinch. She lifted her chin, eyes locked on mine.

"If we're doing this," she said, voice low and daring, "we do it *right*."

My mouth went dry. I shoved my boxers down, kicked them aside, and stepped toward her. I cupped her face, kissed her quick and hard, then hurried up the slope to grab the rope.

"Watch this."

The air was chilly as I swung over the water, but it was nothing compared to what waited for me. I let go, plummeting into the icy depths, the shock stealing my breath. I surfaced with a gasp, treading water, grinning through chattering teeth.

"Your turn, sweetheart!"

My brave, strong Daisy didn't hesitate. She grabbed the rope the same way I had, ran, and *launched*—a delighted shriek ripping from her throat as she flew. She hit the water with a splash, disappeared, then shot up sputtering.

"TY HUDSON, THIS IS *FREEZING!*" she yelled, hair plastered to her face, blue eyes wide with betrayal.

I laughed and swam over to her. "I forgot to mention that only teenagers are stupid enough to swim up here."

She splashed me. "No fucking shit! I think my nipples just froze off."

I grabbed her by the arm, pulling her chest to mine. "Well, we can't have that. I guess I should warm you up, then."

Her legs wrapped around my waist, arms looping my neck. She was shivering, but her mouth found mine, hot and demanding, and suddenly the cold didn't matter.

We kissed like it could keep the rest of the world at bay— grief, fear, the weight of tomorrow. Her tongue slid against mine, teeth nipping, hands fisting in my hair. I groaned into her mouth, hands gripping her ass, holding her tight against me.

"Ty," she gasped, pulling back just enough to breathe. "Shore. Now."

I didn't argue. I dragged her through the water, legs still locked around my waist, her slick skin sliding against my chest with every kick. The cold bit at my shoulders, but her heat—fuck, her heat—kept me grounded. My feet finally scraped the pebbled bottom, rocks shifting under my weight, and I hauled us both out of the water. Goosebumps raced across her arms, her thighs, but her eyes burned into mine, fierce and alive.

I carried her the last few steps to the shore, arms tight under her ass, and lowered her onto the blankets. The wool had soaked up the sun so it was a warm, soft cradle against her back. She sank into it with a shuddering sigh, hair fanning out in wet gold strands, nipples tight from the chill and want. I followed her down, covering her body with mine, skin on skin, my chest to her breasts, my thighs bracketing hers. The contrast was electric—her cool, wet curves against my furnace-hot skin, chasing every last shiver away.

She arched up, nails raking down my back in sharp, stinging lines that made me hiss. Her cold little hand found my hard cock, sliding down over the smooth skin until I could hardly breathe.

"Need you," she breathed, voice raw, urgent, like the words were torn from her throat.

I didn't make her wait. I slid into her slow—her heat gripping me like a lifeline, velvet and fire and *home*. She moaned, low and broken, legs wrapping around my waist, heels digging into the small of my back, urging me deeper. Every roll of my hips drew another sound from her, soft gasps that echoed off the water and sank into my bones.

"Faster," she whispered, hips rising to meet me, desperate.

I gave it to her—hips snapping, the slap of wet skin on skin ringing out sharp and rhythmic, mingling with the rush of the waterfall. The blankets bunched beneath us, wool rough against my knees, but I didn't care. She was everywhere—her scent, her taste, the clutch of her around me.

But still, I could tell she needed more. With a quick twist, I rolled us so she was on top, water dripping from her hair onto my chest as she straddled me. Her hands braced on my pecs, nails digging in, and she rode me hard and fast—head thrown back, breasts bouncing, thighs flexing.

She moved like she could outrun every shadow chasing her, every ghost whispering in her ear. I let her take what she needed —pleasure, distraction, *me*.

My hands gripped her hips, fingers bruising, guiding but never stopping. I slid a thumb between us, finding her clit, circling tight and fast. She shattered—back bowing like a drawn bowstring, a cry tearing from her throat, raw and unrestrained. Her walls clamped down, pulsing around me, and I followed her over the edge, spilling inside her with a guttural groan, hips jerking up to meet her one last time.

I pulled her down to my chest, arms locking around her, our hearts hammering in sync. We stayed like that—tangled, breathless, slick with water and sweat and us. The sun warmed our skin, drying our bodies, the water lapping gently at the shore.

She pressed her face into my neck, lips brushing my pulse, voice muffled and small. "Don't let go."

I tightened my hold, one hand splayed across her back, the other tangled in her hair. "Never," I said, the word a vow against her skin. "Not ever."

When she shivered, I reached across and grabbed the other blanket, then threw it over us, pulling it tight around her.

The sun slipped lower, gilding the water in molten copper, and the world around us started to speak again. The waterfall hissed steady on the far side of the pond, a low white-noise heartbeat. Wind combed through the needles, shushing them like a lullaby. My own pulse slowed to match the rhythm of the mountain, Daisy's weight a warm, steady anchor on my chest.

I thought she'd drifted off. Her breathing had evened out, lashes dark against her cheeks, one hand curled loosely over my heart. I traced idle circles on her shoulder blade, content to stay right here until the stars came out.

"Ty," she said, voice small and cracked. "Dare me to go pick up her ashes from the funeral home."

The words hit as hard as the cold water had earlier. I blinked, the lazy haze snapping.

Today.

After four weeks of dancing around it—mailing the death certificate, signing papers, letting the funeral home hold the urn like it was just another package—she wanted to do it *now*.

I swallowed, throat suddenly dry. "I can't do that, sweetheart."

She nodded against my skin, but her fingers tightening on my chest. "I'm scared. If I pick them up... it's real. I can't pretend she's coming back. I can't keep running."

Her voice cracked on the last word, and something in my chest splintered. I pressed my lips to her hair, smoothing it from her face. "I'll go with you. Or I can go alone—pick them up, bring them home, whatever you need."

"No." She pushed up so her chin rested on my chest, eyes glassy but steady. "I have to do it. I'm just really fucking terrified."

I cupped her cheek, thumb brushing a tear she hadn't let fall. "Then we do it together."

We dressed in silence, skin prickling in the cooling air. The walk back to the truck felt longer, every step heavier, the pine needles crunching like brittle bones underfoot. I tossed the wet blankets in the bed, started the engine, and the cab filled with the low rumble that usually felt like home. Today it sounded like a countdown.

The drive down the ridge was quiet. Linwood unfolded below us, tiny and oblivious to the weight of this moment. Daisy stared out the window, arms wrapped around herself, knuckles white. I wanted to reach over, pull her into my lap, absorb every ounce of this hurt, but grief didn't work that way. This was hers to carry.

The funeral home sat on the edge of town, a low brick building with petunias out front like it could out-pretty the ugly tears that happened here. I parked under a nearby pine and killed the engine. The silence rushed in, thick and suffocating.

I didn't get out to open her door. Gave her one last out.

She stared out the windshield for a long beat, then drew a shaky breath, popped the handle, and stepped out. She crossed the lot, shoulders squared like she was walking into battle, and I followed a step behind.

Heart in my throat.

Ready to catch whatever pieces fell when the weight finally broke her.

29

The automatic doors to the funeral home sighed open and I stepped through, the air-conditioning slapping my damp skin like a reprimand for taking so long to get here. My pulse thundered in my ears so loud I couldn't hear my own footsteps, couldn't hear the receptionist's greeting, couldn't hear anything except the frantic drum line in my skull.

Ty's hand settled warm between my shoulder blades, steady and grounding, but the rest of me floated somewhere above my body, untethered. I caught the receptionist's eyes flick to him, then back to me.

She knew him.

Of course she did.

She didn't ask my name; she just nodded, murmured something I couldn't parse, and disappeared through a side door.

I stood rooted to the tile, staring at a scuff mark shaped like a comma. Time expanded, seconds stretching into years, all while my lungs forgot how to work.

Then she was back.

In her hands was a ceramic urn no bigger than a loaf of

bread, hand-painted with daisies and violets tangled with juniper sprigs. A tiny envelope taped to the side had that same little daisy drawn, and that was the last straw.

The floor rushed up to meet me.

My knees buckled. The urn, the letter, the room—everything tilted sideways. I heard a distant clatter, felt the cold tile smack my palms, but the sound was muffled, like I'd plunged underwater once more.

Strong arms scooped me up, and Ty's voice rumbled against my ear. It was low and urgent, but the words dissolved into static.

I couldn't hear.

Couldn't feel.

Couldn't see.

The world narrowed to the steady *thump* of his heart under my cheek and the white-noise roar in my own head.

Car door.

Seat belt.

Engine.

Motion.

None of it registered.

Then he scooped me up again, and the faint smell of pine and woodsmoke told me we were home.

His hard body gave way to the soft mattress beneath me.

I was horizontal, staring at the ceiling fan spinning lazy circles, the blades a hypnotic blur.

Only then did the dam break.

The first sob tore out of me like shrapnel—raw, ugly, and unstoppable. Tears flooded hot and endless, soaking the pillow, my hair, the collar of Ty's T-shirt when he lay beside me and pulled me into his chest.

I couldn't breathe around the grief; it clawed up my throat, choking me.

My fingers fisted in his shirt, knuckles white, anchoring to the only solid thing left in the universe.

He didn't shush me.

Didn't tell me it would be okay.

He just held on, one hand stroking my back in slow, steady passes, the other cradling my head like I might shatter.

And hell, maybe I would.

I cried for the mornings Violet would never make Junie's favorite pancakes. For the mix CDs she'd never burn for me again. For the inside jokes and memories that lived only in my head now. For Junie's questions I'd never have perfect answers to. For the bedroom door I'd opened and the life that had spilled out in dust and lavender sachets.

I cried until my ribs ached, until my throat was raw, until the tears slowed to a trickle and my body felt wrung dry.

Ty never moved.

His shirt was soaked, his heartbeat a metronome under my ear. When I finally hiccuped into silence, he pressed his lips to my temple, lingering there.

"I've got you," he whispered, voice rough. "I've got you, sweetheart."

The urn sat on the nightstand behind him, daisies and violets glowing softly in the lamplight. The envelope leaned against it, unopened. I stared at it until my eyes burned again, but I didn't reach for it.

Not yet.

Ty shifted, tugging the quilt up over us both. Outside, crickets started their evening chorus.

Inside, there was only the sound of two people breathing— one steady, one shattered.

I curled tighter into him, fingers still twisted in his shirt. The tears stopped, but the ache didn't.

It sat heavy in my chest, a stone I'd carry forever.

But Ty's arms were a harbor, and for the first time since the funeral home doors sighed open, the roar in my head quieted to a whisper.

I wasn't okay. I might never be okay again.

But I was here. And so was he.

30

TY

I stared at the curtains fluttering in the breeze, trying to hold myself together when Daisy couldn't. All summer I'd watched her hold Junie up with one hand and herself with the other. She laughed, she danced, she planned the carnival, she hammered boards into Violet's porch, moving through each day like if she just kept busy enough, grief couldn't catch her.

But yesterday it tackled her from behind.

The moment she saw the urn, her legs gave out, and I'd never felt so useless. I caught her before she hit the tile, but I couldn't catch the sound she made—like something inside her ribs snapped clean in two.

I carried her out past the hushed sympathy and too-sweet florals, her whole body shaking so hard I felt it in my teeth.

With each ragged breath, my heart broke.

The night swallowed her afterward. Hours of sobs that sounded like pain clawing its way out. I held her through it, arms locked around her, whispering useless things into her hair until she finally sagged against me.

By dawn, the shadows under her eyes looked bruised. Blonde hair fanned wild over my pillow, pieces stuck to her cheek. She looked like grief had scraped her clean and left a shell of her behind.

I wanted to keep her right there forever. Pull the quilt over both of us, lock the door, tell the world to go to hell. Instead Cluck Norris screamed bloody murder outside the window like a feathered alarm clock, reminding me the animals needed feeding, the day needed living, and the world kept moving, even when it shouldn't.

I pulled her tighter against my chest anyway, breathed her in, and let myself drift into an uneasy half-sleep for as long as I could.

Gravel crunched a while later, and I cracked one eye open to see Beckett's truck through the blinds.

Junie's voice floated in through the open windows, bright and unstoppable. "DAD! You'll never guess what Jace did!"

I eased my arm out from under Daisy's neck. She made a small, lost sound—half protest, half dream—and I froze, heart in my throat. When she didn't wake, I stood there like an idiot, just staring.

This was the part no one warned you about—how loving someone meant their pain hit you harder than your own, how it split you open and left you broken right beside them.

But I couldn't break, not when they needed me.

I tiptoed across the dark room, Rowdy's eyes following me as I moved to the dresser and pulled out a clean tee, replacing my tear-stained one. The urn still sat on the nightstand like a grenade with the pin pulled, and I looked back at Daisy still asleep in my bed.

Boots stomped on the front porch, so I grabbed the urn and put it on the dresser across the room instead. Still there, but not the first thing Daisy would see when she woke up either.

"Stay," I said to Rowdy, whose dark tail thumped twice on the bed, understanding the assignment.

I quietly pulled the door closed, then went down the hall.

Junie exploded through the front door, cheeks sun-pink, cargo pants covered in marsh mud, rain boots halfway kicked off already.

"Oh my gosh, Dad, camping was so fun. We rented canoes and Jace got us stuck on the wrong side of the lake for an hour."

"I didn't get stuck," Jace hollered from the porch. "You said you wanted to be an explorer, so we were checking out uncharted shores. There's a difference."

Beckett snorted, ruffling Junie's tangled ponytail as he stepped inside with a duffel over one shoulder. "Took me and a rope to tow Captain Explorer back."

Emmy followed, sunglasses pushed up into her dark hair, iced coffee in each hand as she stood in the open front doorway. "Don't worry. I got it on video."

Junie spun toward the hallway. "Where's Dizzy? Is she up? I have to tell her about the chipmunk that stole my marshmallow!"

I crouched down to her level, brushing dirt off her cargo pants in the foyer. "She's here, but she had a rough night. Let her rest a little more, okay? You can tell her all about camping when she wakes up."

Junie's face fell just enough to twist something in my chest, but she nodded. "Pancakes?"

"You go get the ingredients ready and I'll be right there."

She wrapped her arms around my shoulders, squeezing tight. "Okay, Dad."

Emmy's eyes flicked to mine over Junie's head, sharp as ever. Once Junie darted toward the kitchen, she asked quietly, "Is she okay?"

I stood back up and glanced down the hall toward my closed door, jaw working. "No," I said, voice rough. "We went to the funeral home to get Violet's ashes, and it finally hit her last night."

"Shit," Beckett murmured.

Emmy's mouth pressed into a sad line, tears brimming in her eyes. "Anything we can do?"

I was ready to tell her no—that this was one of those storms we just had to weather—when a contractor's truck pulled up in front of Violet's house. Fresh cedar siding stacked in the bed, four guys in tool belts hopping out like this was just another day. Luke hopped out of his truck next to them, already getting his crew into motion.

Something sharp twisted low in my gut.

I looked at my sister, then Beckett and Jace.

"Yeah," I said. "Round up everybody. Neighbors, teammates, the whole damn town if they'll come. We're finishing Vi's house this week. All hands on deck, Linwood style."

I couldn't fix Daisy's heart.

Couldn't bring her sister back.

Couldn't carry this grief for her.

But I could finish the one thing Violet left undone.

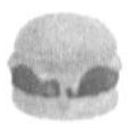

Two hours later Violet's house looked like a home-improvement flash mob had invaded.

Shannon stood in the middle of the living room in paint-splattered jeans, hair in a messy knot, wielding a paint roller like a sword.

"Listen up, idiots!" she bellowed. "We are turning this house into a home today, so follow my color-coded system or I swear on my signed Metallica shirt I will end you."

Beckett nudged Jace. "Eyes down, kid. She can smell fear."

Jace gulped. "I'm not—oh shit, she's looking right at me."

"Mop Top and Has-Been"—Shannon pointed at Beckett and Jace—"you're painting the living room walls. If I see a drip I will make you start over."

Jace lifted the lid off the can, then frowned. "This is pink."

"It's coral. Happiness in pigment form," Shannon snapped, then made a face like she was disgusted by the idea. "Roll it or perish."

Luke was already on a ladder in the kitchen, swapping out the ugly boob lights for matte-black pendants. "Hey, Ty! Can you send a runner to the store for me? We need new lightbulbs pretty much everywhere."

I grabbed my phone to text Delgado who was already on his way to the hardware store for more rollers. "On it."

Stevie swept in with an armload of shopping bags. "You said decor, and I said de-MORE! Throw pillows, linens, dishes, and three different duvet vibes because we need choices."

Emmy stared. "Stevie. Why are there fourteen pillows?"

"Fifteen," Stevie corrected. "Pillows make me happy, and this house needs happy."

Mason wandered in holding a paintbrush like it might bite him. "Shan, you sure I can't help Tate with the wallpaper? Seems like it might be a two-person—"

"Nope," Tate and Shannon said in unison.

Shannon pointed her roller at the baseboards. "Tape it off

for your brother, or I'll make you clean grout with a tooth-brush instead."

Mason sighed, then sat on the floor with a roll of blue tape.

I stood near the front door, overseeing everything that was happening all at once, and keeping an eye on the kids outside. Miles and Molly were already racing toward the barn with Stevie's kids, but Junie lingered on the porch, not quite focused on anything.

I crouched beside her, tucking a stray hair behind her ear. "Hey, bug. You okay?"

She twisted her fingers together. "Mom wanted everything to be floral, like our names. All the upstairs rooms are supposed to be like a hotel so she could rent them and we'd never have to move again." Her chin wobbled. "But I... Can I stay outside?"

I pulled her into my chest, hating her sadness just as much as Daisy's. "Of course you can stay outside. You don't have to do anything that hurts today. And hey—thank you for telling me about the florals. We'll make it sunshine, exactly like she wanted."

She nodded, eyes glassy, then ran after the others.

Molly looked up as Junie joined them, eyes on me. Luckily, she seemed to understand the hard set of my jaw and scooped up Junie into a piggy back ride, insisting they go check on Uno.

Once I heard her peal of laughter, I went back inside.

Everything was a flurry of motion and color, the whole house transforming before my eyes.

I handed Luke another fixture, smiled when Beckett painted a coral stripe down Jace's back "by accident," even helped Shannon carry new headboards upstairs.

But every stroke of paint on the walls, every floral pillow fluffed, every new light that flicked on and made the place glow warmer—every single thing sharpened the knife in my gut.

This house was becoming perfect.

Exactly what Violet dreamed.

Exactly the kind of place that would sell in a heartbeat for stupid money.

Enough for Daisy to pack Junie into whatever car she wanted, point it toward Chicago or Portland or any city big enough to swallow the memories, and never have to look back.

Enough for her to outrun the grief.

Enough for her to outrun me.

Beckett bumped my shoulder as we unloaded a new porch swing from his truck. "You're brooding so loud I can hear it over the chatter, buddy."

I shook my head. "Just thinking about how we're going to anchor this into the ceiling."

"Bullshit." He set his end down and wiped sweat off his forehead. "Talk to me."

I glanced around at the people around me, each one essential to my life in a way I hadn't quite named before, but none moreso than the little girl climbing a tree in the yard and the woman asleep in my bed.

I swallowed, but my voice still sounded like gravel as I said, "She could list this place tomorrow. One signature and they're gone."

Beckett put his hands on his hips and let out a deep sigh. "I've thought of that too."

I stared through the open front door at the fresh white trim, the coral walls, the wildflower curtains Stevie was hanging. It was beautiful, and one-of-a-kind, just like Daisy.

"What if she sees this finished and it hurts too much? What if this is her sign to leave?"

Beckett clapped a hand on my shoulder and squeezed. "Or

she looks at the guy who made it happen and decides it's her sign to stay."

I didn't answer.

Couldn't.

Because all I could see was the most beautiful exit ramp imaginable.

And if she took it, she'd would take my whole damn heart with her.

31

Daisy

The door creaked open, light spilling into the room and dragging me up from a sleep that felt thick and endless. I blinked awake, cotton-mouthed and disoriented, the world swimming before the familiar scent of pine and woodsmoke grounded me again.

Junie stood in the doorway wearing one of Ty's old Hudson Hardware T-shirts, the faded navy fabric hanging past her knees like a dress. Her blonde hair was damp, curling in little ringlets around her ears the way Violet's used to. She looked so much like her mom, it stole my breath.

"Hi," Junie said with a smile that looked as fragile as I felt. She carried a wooden tray balanced in both small hands.

Ty stood behind her, broad shoulders filling the doorframe. He hesitated, just long enough to scan the room like he was taking inventory of what grief had rearranged, then nodded once. "Can we come in?"

I pushed myself up, the sheet sliding to my waist. At some point, I'd changed out of my clothes and into Ty's old hoodie, but I didn't remember doing it. My eyes felt swollen, my cheeks tight with salt, but I scooted over and patted the mattress. "Yeah, cutie. Come here."

Junie set the tray down on my lap with exaggerated care, then climbed up like a little mountain goat—knees and elbows everywhere. She settled cross-legged in the middle of the bed, the hem of the hardware shirt pooling around her like a security blanket.

"I made you mac and cheese," she announced proudly. "Well, Ty helped with the stove part because I'm not allowed yet. But I stirred the sauce."

Behind her, Ty shrugged. "She's a pro at the cheese-to-noodle ratio."

"Thank you, Junie." My voice cracked on her name. I leaned over and kissed her forehead, breathing in the smell of my strawberry shampoo she liked to use. "That was so nice of you."

Junie studied me over the rims of her glasses, waiting for me to take a bite. When I didn't move fast enough, she asked in a small, careful voice, "Are you sick?"

The words landed like a fist to the sternum.

How many times had Junie been the only one there when Violet couldn't get out of bed?

How many times had she carried trays just like this one?

"No, sweet girl." I set the tray to the side and pulled her into my lap. She came willingly, all long limbs and warm skin, curling into me like she was still the baby I remembered. "I'm not sick. I'm just sad. I miss your mom a lot today."

Junie nodded against my shoulder, small fist twisting in my hoodie. "I miss her too," she whispered into my collarbone. "Sometimes I forget for a little while and then I remember and it hurts again. Do you think it will ever stop?"

This kid.

My body had wrung itself dry hours ago but my face burned with unshed tears anyway. I pressed my lips to her hair. "I don't know, cutie. I hope it gets quieter. I think it will." I pulled back just enough to look at her. "And on the days it's loud again? That doesn't mean you're doing anything wrong."

Ty still hovered near the doorway, watching us with that steady presence he had. Knowing he'd be better at this than me, I patted the empty side of the bed.

He crossed the room and climbed up on Junie's other side. The mattress dipped under his weight. He lay on his side propped on one elbow, leaving a careful few inches of space between us, like he still wasn't sure he was invited into this moment.

But Junie had no such reservations. She wriggled until she was the filling in our sandwich—head on my chest, feet kicking lazily against Ty's shins, one small hand reaching across to rest on his forearm like she needed to touch both of us to be comfortable.

None of us said anything for a moment, and the silence felt heavy.

I cleared my throat. "You know what Vi would hate most in the universe?" I said, surprised at how almost-steady I sounded. "Us sitting around being sad and quiet. She always said sad was okay, but quiet was a waste of perfectly good air."

Junie tilted her head up, glasses slipping down her nose. "So what do we do instead?"

"We tell happy stories," I decided. "Silly stories. We keep her alive in the parts that made us love her the most. Every time we tell one, she gets a little more real instead of less."

"Like what?"

"Well," I said, thinking back on a lifetime of memories with my favorite person, "the summer Violet was ten and I was seven, we moved into a new house. Our garage was full of empty boxes, and your mom saw so much possibility. We spent a whole day taping them together, turning it into a tour bus."

Ty chuckled, but Junie looked up at me. "Why did you make a tour bus?"

"Obviously we were going to be famous pop stars named The Sparkle Sisters." I held my palms up in little jazz-hands, and Junie giggled. "We spent three straight days decorating it— flowers, stars, our fake signatures—until there wasn't an inch of brown cardboard left. Every night after dinner we dragged our boom box into the garage, draped ourselves in feather boas, and practiced our choreography."

I picked up Junie's hand, pretending to dance with it. "Your mom loved to dance, didn't she?"

"She did. We danced a lot."

"One night we even dragged our sleeping bags inside the biggest box, zipped ourselves in, and slept there, pretending we were on the road to Hollywood. Violet woke me up at three a.m. screaming because a spider had walked across her face. We laughed so hard we almost wet ourselves, then fell back asleep holding hands through the spider trauma."

Junie giggled so hard she had to push her glasses back up her nose. "Did you really sleep in a box?"

"We absolutely did," I said, smiling at the memory. "Your mom insisted we needed the authentic experience. Grammy winners don't sleep in beds, they sleep in luxury tour buses made of refrigerator boxes."

Junie's went next, launching into the Easter Violet let her mix the egg dye by herself that ended in disaster when she dyed her arms blue from the elbow down.

Ty idly traced circles on the back of Junie's hand where it rested on his chest. "The day I met your mom," he said, "I was convinced my life was over. Hockey career done, body broken, came home to this quiet street to lick my wounds and scare children with my grumpy face."

Junie poked him in the ribs. "You're not grumpy."

"Back then, I was doing my best impression. But she came over with a tray of cookies that looked better than they tasted."

I snorted.

Junie grinned. "She burned a lot of cookies, but sometimes they were okay."

"You're right, bug." Ty kissed her head. "But do you know what I remember most about that day?"

"What?" Junie asked.

"Behind your mom was this tiny kindergartener with a sand bucket full of wildflowers." His eyes went soft, the gold flecks catching the last of the hallway light as he brushed her blonde hair off her forehead. "She looked up at me, squinted real serious, and said, 'Why do you have a barn if you don't have any animals?'"

He huffed a quiet laugh. "No hello. No fear. Just immediate disappointment in my life choices. And I remember thinking—well, hell. Guess I better fix that."

He glanced at me over Junie's head. Something heavy and unspoken passed between us, landing warm in my chest like a small stone dropped into still water.

Junie yawned, huge and dramatic, and within minutes her breathing evened out—glasses crooked, mouth open, one small hand fisted in my shirt, her legs thrown over Ty's like he was the world's largest body pillow.

I reached over and gently slid her glasses off, folding the earpieces and setting them next to the bowl of mac and cheese. The room was dark now, just the silver of moonlight sliding in through the blinds.

Across from us, Violet's urn caught the light, the floral-painted ceramic seeming far too happy for the reality contained within.

Ty's hand stilled for half a second at my hip, like he felt it too.

I stared at the urn until my eyes watered again, but no tears came. I was hollowed out, nothing left but ache.

Still, the sight didn't knife me the way it had last night.

Maybe because Junie's warm weight anchored me to the mattress, or because Ty's arm rested across Junie's back so his big, calloused hand lay on my hip.

Everything still hurt, raw and exposed. Maybe it always would.

But the three of us, together, felt better.

The night kept breathing outside—bullfrogs croaking down by the river, crickets chirring, aspens rustling like they were whispering secrets to the moon.

Ty's voice came out of the dark, barely louder than the crickets. "That was good, Daisy. She'd be proud of you. Proud of both of you."

My throat tightened until breathing felt optional. "It didn't feel good. It felt like ripping open a wound just to stare at it."

"Sometimes that's the only way it heals," he murmured.

I let out a shaky breath that sounded too loud in the quiet. "I don't feel like I'm healing, Ty. I feel... broken."

His thumb brushed a slow circle at my hip, steady and grounding. "You're not broken," he said, voice fierce and quiet at once. "You're grieving. There's a difference."

That pulled something raw and ugly out of me. "I don't want to be more weight you have to carry, Ty. You've already—"

"Stop." The single word cracked like a whip, soft as it was. "You are not weight, Daisy. You and this little girl—you're the reason I get up in the morning. You're what I dream about when I close my eyes. You're all I've ever wanted, no matter the circumstances this all came to be."

My eyes prickled again, tears I didn't think I had left gathering hot and sudden. "What if I fall apart again tomorrow? Next week? Next month?"

"Then I'll be right here," he said, no hesitation, no pretty lie. "I'm not going anywhere."

He paused, forehead lowering closer to mine. "I'm not going anywhere," he repeated, like he was saying it to himself as much as to me.

Junie stirred, murmuring something about cows in her sleep, and burrowed deeper into both of us, small hands clinging like we were the only solid things in her dreams.

It split me open and stitched me shut in the same breath.

"Ty..." I whispered, not sure what came next.

Thank you.

I'm terrified.

Everything hurts.

You're too good.

I don't deserve this.

His hand slid from my hip to the small of my back, palm spread wide and warm, grounding. "It's okay to crack," he said again, like a vow. "I'll hold the pieces until you're ready to put them back together. However long that takes."

A long silence settled, soft and full as a down comforter. I closed my eyes and let my forehead rest against his, just above Junie's curls. The warmth of him, the steady rise and fall of Junie's breathing between us—it felt like the only place the world wasn't spinning faster than I could bear.

32

TY

I leaned against the corral fence, watching the afternoon turn gold over the river. Everything was peaceful, the steady quiet I loved out here, and yet my pulse thumped loud enough to drown it all out.

The house was finished.

Over the last three days, everyone I knew had shown up to help, and Violet's house was completely transformed from a few weeks ago. Part of me was excited to see Daisy's reaction to it all, but the dread...

Fuck, the dread was heavy.

What if seeing it finished didn't make Daisy happy?

What if every time she looked at it, it was another painful reminder that her sister was gone?

But this was a house, not an urn. And it was right there, at the end of my driveway.

There was no hiding this reminder. No avoiding it.

Uno stood beside me, his judgy one-eyed stare only emphasizing the feeling that this might have been a mistake. Just as I was about to go check on the girls, the screaming started—

pure, delighted terror.

Junie had Daisy by the wrist and hauled her toward Violet's house at top speed. Daisy's blonde hair was still in the same messy knot she'd worn for three days straight, strands escaping like pale ribbons. But she was upright, wearing paint-splattered overalls and a cropped white tee. And she was laughing in a way I hadn't heard in weeks—breathless, startled, *real*.

"Run, Dizzy!"

Cluck Norris sprinted after them at the head of his posse, neck feathers flared like a red cape, eyes murderous. The hens streamed behind him in a clucking avalanche, wings half-spread for balance. Rowdy darted between the girls and the angry rooster like the tiny superhero he believed himself to be, yapping for all he was worth. Piggie squealed and bolted after them, tiny black hooves skittering across the gravel.

I couldn't contain the chuckle that rumbled out of me, even on the brink of a panic attack.

The girls hit the porch in a heap of limbs and laughter. Junie recovered first, scrambled up the steps, threw open the purple front door, and hauled Daisy inside before either of them had a chance to second-guess this decision.

I stayed put a minute longer, heart thumping harder than it had any right to.

The house looked nothing like the sagging, sad thing Daisy had walked into at the beginning of summer. New cedar shakes glowed honey-warm in the late sun. Pink petunias spilled from the window boxes I'd hung yesterday, their scent drifting down sweet and dizzying. The new porch swing—wide enough for three, with thick cushions in Violet's favorite floral—moved gently in the breeze like it had always belonged there.

From inside came Junie's voice, bright and bossy and

impossible to resist. "Close your eyes—no peeking—okay, okay, NOW!"

I pushed off the fence and walked down to join them. By the time I reached the porch, Junie had Daisy by both hands and was towing her through every room like an over-caffeinated tour guide.

"This is the living room," Junie announced, spinning in place. "Do you love the pink? Emmy said it's the exact coral Mom pinned on her Pinterest board. And the beams—we left all the old knots but stained them dark so it still feels like a real mountain house but also kind of like a fairy cottage."

She dragged Daisy toward the kitchen, not waiting for a reply. I trailed behind, hands shoved deep in my pockets, trying to look casual while my pulse hammered in my chest.

Daisy stopped in the middle of the kitchen, turning in a small circle. The farmhouse sink gleamed white against the butcher-block counters Luke had planed smooth. Copper pots hung from a rack above the island like wind chimes. Down the hall you could see the refurbished claw-foot tub that waited behind a barn-door slider we'd salvaged.

"Ty," Daisy whispered, reaching out to touch the cool lip of the sink. I studied her face, trying to read her expression, but I didn't trust myself to interpret it right now. Was the little frown that pulled at her lips shock, or was it panic?

"Come see the upstairs!" Junie called, racing toward the steps. "There's five bedrooms now—three upstairs and two downstairs—and two-and-a-half bathrooms, just like she wanted. The big bathroom downstairs has penny tile that looks like fish scales and one upstairs has a shower so big, it's like standing under a cloud."

Her feet stomped on the stairs. Daisy followed slower, fingertips trailing the banister I'd sanded until it felt like silk. I brought up the rear, every step creaking under my feet, bile rising in my throat the longer Daisy stayed silent.

Junie flung open doors like a game-show hostess. "This one's the Lupine Room—see the purple quilt? The big one at the end is Poppy with lots of red. It has its own balcony and looks straight at Castle Peak on clear days. And this one is the Wild Rose Suite because roses climb right up the trellis outside the window. I like this one the best."

They came back downstairs to look at the last bedroom—the one that was supposed to be Junie's—that Stevie had turned into a kids' bunk room. Toys sat in neat arrangements, everything rainbow bright, and it all felt like a hug.

Junie skipped the last doorway entirely. Didn't slow, didn't glance at the closed door at the end of the hall that no one had opened since we boxed up Violet's things. Just breezed past it like it was painted with invisibility.

Daisy stopped in the middle of the hallway, her eyes wide and shining.

"You did all this?" she asked, voice small and cracked right down the middle.

"I had help," I managed. I ruffled Junie's hair and she beamed up at me. "Shannon was the one in charge. Luke knows every tradesman in the Valley. Emmy and Stevie handled decor. The boys and I just showed up and tried not to get in the way."

When she didn't say anything, I asked, "Did I overstep?"

Daisy laughed once—wet and startled—and pressed her fingers under her eyes like she could hold the tears back by force. "No. Not at all." She looked around again, slower this time. "Thank you, Ty. Thank you for this. Violet would have loved it."

Junie bounced over and grabbed Daisy's hand again. "Now

we can rent the rooms like Mom wanted! Since we're going to live at Ty's forever, there's even more room, and maybe we can make enough to buy mini cows. I want fluffy ones with bangs, like those videos. And I read they don't like to be alone, so we'll need at least two."

My stomach dropped straight through the refinished floorboards and kept falling. Junie had just put bright, confident words to the conversation Daisy and I hadn't touched yet.

Daisy's smile flickered. She crouched, tucked a curl behind Junie's ear with trembling fingers. "You're full of ideas, aren't you, cutie?"

That was when the white county SUV crunched up the drive, tires spitting gravel.

Sandra stepped out in her sensible flats, clipboard in hand, stopped on the path and gasped when she saw the house. She did the full walk-through, checking off every needed improvement and asking Junie if she was excited for third grade. Junie answered with clipped words, but she didn't hide behind me this time.

After Daisy turned off all the lights inside, Sandra pulled us onto the porch, leaving the door open as Junie ran back in to grab one more cookie from the new jar in the kitchen.

"Everything is beautiful," she said. "Junie's thriving. I spoke with the school district and they're more than prepared to take Junie back this fall, ready for any impending needs should they arise for counseling." She flipped a page. "I also spoke with Tate at the rink and she's thrilled with your progress so far, so you've got stable employment. Really, Daisy, I'm very impressed with the progress you've made this summer."

"Thank you," Daisy said. "So what happens next?"

"I wish every case was this simple," Sandra smiled. "With the house finished, you've now met every requirement. The judge has already signed off that he's ready to give you full physical and legal custody, Daisy, keeping Juniper with family as we always wanted. You can decide what role Ty keeps in her life, but this case is closed. Congratulations."

I stared at the floor, heart hammering in my chest, hearing the words I'd dreaded all summer. No matter how much I loved Junie, no matter what Violet had put in her will, she wasn't mine.

Not anymore.

Unaware she'd just wrecked my world, Sandra turned the page again. "And Daisy, once the order's signed, you're free to relocate to Chicago. Just file interstate transfer paperwork and notify the court with the new address for the yearly wellness checks. Routine stuff."

Chicago.

The word hit me like a hip check I never saw coming—fast, low, and right to the ribs. All the air left my lungs in one silent whoosh.

Daisy nodded, small and careful, arms wrapped tight around her middle.

"And Ty," Sandra said, her small hand on my shoulder. "Well done. This is always the hardest part, letting your foster kids go. But I think we both can feel good about the fact that this little girl will live a happy life with a loving family, hm?"

I nodded, because that's what she expected, even though each word out of her mouth hit like a blow.

Sandra left. The dust from her tires settled slow, like it didn't belong here anymore.

"Chicago?" I asked. My voice sounded far away, my head was spinning so fast. "You're still thinking about going back?"

Daisy leaned against the new siding and stared out at the

river catching the last of the sun. "I haven't decided," she said quietly.

I haven't decided.

Not *No.*

Not *We're staying.*

Not even *I love you more than it hurts to stay here.*

Just *I haven't decided.*

I swallowed hard, searching for anything that wouldn't sound like begging. My mouth opened and closed twice.

Before I could find words, a small voice floated through the font door, tiny and trembling.

"We're moving to Chicago?"

We both spun.

Junie stood halfway out the door, clutching the wall with one hand and her forgotten cookie with the other. Her eyes were huge behind the lenses, flicking from Daisy to me and back again, filling fast.

Daisy took a half-step forward, hands out. "Cutie—"

"I don't want to go," Junie continued, voice cracking on every word. She looked straight at me, eyes glassy. "Then I'll lose my dad too."

The porch went so quiet I could hear the wildflowers closing for the night, petals folding like secrets. I could hear the river a quarter-mile away, steady and ancient. I could hear my own heart trying to punch its way out of my chest and run straight to that little girl I loved so damn much.

Junie had heard everything.

And she didn't want to leave.

33

Daisy

The door shut behind us with a click that settled heavy in my chest. Junie's hand slipped out of mine the second we stepped off Violet's porch, and she took off up the gravel road toward Ty's house without looking back. Her rain boots kicked up dust that hung thick in the last slant of sunlight, and then the clouds swallowed the sun whole. Piggie chased behind her, hooves moving faster than I'd thought possible for such a little pig.

I followed slower, dragging my feet. An hour ago, the valley had looked drunk on summer, all bright colors and hazy sunlight. Full of life, of possibility, of a future.

Now, it was like the weather mirrored my emotions. Storm clouds piled black against the peaks, moving fast and out of control. The temperature dropped ten degrees in the space of a heartbeat, and the wind carried the sharp smell of rain.

Ty walked at my side, hands shoved deep in his pockets, shoulders curved inward. Neither of us spoke, not sure what to say. Sandra's voice still echoed in my skull, light and bureaucratic and kind: you're free to relocate to Chicago.

Free.

Like I could just walk away from it all. From the pain of losing my sister. From the house she loved so much. From the life she'd built here. From the new friends who'd shown up for me even though I had nothing to give. From the father Junie had chosen for herself. From the man who saw me better than anyone ever had.

No matter how much it hurt to see Violet everywhere around me, I couldn't do that to any of them. I just had to survive this bone-deep pain, too.

Junie reached Ty's porch first, climbed the steps two at a time, and disappeared inside without a word. She left the front door open, and I hesitated for a second, already feeling the depression pull me under once more. Inside, a bedroom door slammed shut, and I looked down to Rowdy standing at my feet.

Ty paused at the bottom step, looked up at the sky, then at me. "I'll get the animals in," he said, voice flat. "Storm's coming fast."

I nodded, throat too tight for words. Too tired to do anything but let them hate me.

He headed for the barn. I stood there for another useless second, wind whipping my hair across my face, then forced my feet up the steps and into the house.

Rowdy stood at my side, the only one who wasn't mad at me.

I kicked off my shoes, then padded down the hallway toward Junie's room. I raised my hand to knock on the closed door, then let it fall.

What was I supposed to say?

I'm trying so hard, and it still isn't enough.

I want to fix everything, but I don't know how to fix myself.

Every choice I make feels like the wrong one, and I'm terrified I'll be the reason we all fall apart.

I couldn't say any of it. Not without making things worse.

I went back to Ty's room instead, sank onto the bed, and pulled my knees to my chest. Rowdy climbed up beside me and laid his head across my feet. I scratched behind his ears without thinking, staring at the tray where Junie's half-finished friendship bracelet still lay, purple and pink threads tangled like everything else.

She'd dumped the beads out earlier, sorting them by letter, but I couldn't look away from the numbers.

One. Violet's death.

Two. Junie's sorrow.

Three. Ty's pain.

Three bad things, then one good thing, right?

But everywhere I looked lay chaos and sadness.

Maybe the good thing wasn't coming this time.

Maybe I didn't deserve it.

Thunder rumbled, followed by a crack of lightning, drawing my attention to the open window. The curtains snapped in the wind, carrying the smell of the summer storm. I got up to shut it, leaning into the frame when the sound of something fluttering drew my eye to the dresser.

The corner of a folded letter peeled away from the tape on Violet's urn, hesitating for a beat before the wind caught it. It drifted off the dresser, carried across the room in an uneven arc, brushing the air just long enough for me to realize what it was before the latch clicked shut and the storm was locked outside again.

The letter wavered, then settled on the floor at my feet.

Rowdy's head came up, ears pricked. I stayed still, heart thudding so loudly I could hardly hear the storm outside.

When I bent to pick it up, I already knew what I'd see.

That same little daisy stared back at me.

The last thread of my strength snapped. I sank down onto the floor and opened the letter with shaking fingers, suddenly desperate to hear what she had to say.

I've been trying to figure out how to write this without sounding like one of those "live laugh love" signs, but they might be on to something.

This is it. Our last goodbye. But before I go, I owe you an explanation.

Three years ago, you were brand new in Chicago, scared shitless even though you didn't want me to know. But at five in the morning, I got a text from you asking if I believed in soulmates.

I do, but not the way you meant it.

You, my sweet sister, have always been my soulmate. My better half. My shining star.

I was sick to my stomach the entire time you drove from Linwood to Chicago, desperate to tell you to come back, and terrified you would if I asked. But then you texted me about this mystery man, and I knew I'd made the right choice. Knew I'd set you free to go find your own path.

Everything that came after was a whirlwind of sadness for all of us, and damn, I wish we weren't so familiar with that feeling. Junie was sad you were gone. I missed you more than I could ever tell you. And you were heartbroken that Huddy had walked away.

So, imagine my surprise when our reward for surviving all that stood in my driveway.

Each day, Ty showed up and proved he was exactly who you told me he was after that first night together. Just as caring and protective and good. And each day, I tried to figure out how to tell you he was right here waiting for you to find him.

I even had a whole rom-com meet-cute planned for the first time you'd visit, where I'd send you up to his house to borrow a cup of sugar. You'd gasp. He'd gasp. Fireworks would go off behind you, and we'd all live happily ever after as neighbors in this little perfect town.

But then I got sick, and Ty showed me his true colors.

As much as I love the idea of you and Ty

riding off into the sunset together, I didn't nominate him in my will because of you.

I did it for Junie.

Daisy, you are everything my too-serious little girl needs.

You make life brighter just by walking into a room. You make boring things fun and hard things bearable. You show kids that joy isn't frivolous—it's survival. You're spontaneous and brave and full of magic, even when you feel broken.

Junie needs someone who can pull her back into her childhood, and that someone is you.

And Ty... Daisy, Ty is everything my grieving girls deserve.

He is steady. He is gentle. He is dependable in a way most people only pretend to be. He loves with his actions, not his words, and that's the kind of love that lasts.

I love the idea of the three of you, happy and loved. But it's not my life to live anymore. And it's not my decision to make.

You have always had better instincts than you give yourself credit for. You feel things deeply. You know when something is real. We've just had a lifetime to prove it's never quite that simple.

But trust your gut.
About him.
About Junie.
About the future.
I don't need you to step into my shoes and live the life I left behind. I just need you to choose love instead of fear.
Maybe you aren't ready for acceptance yet, but I am.
I accept my life ended sooner than I wanted.
I accept I didn't get all the years I dreamed of with my daughter.
But I also accept that she is safe with you. That you are exactly who she needs.
Like the dandelions in the field outside, we've always been the girls who grow back even after the fire. Stronger. Brighter. Stubborn as hell.
The Winslow girls always rise.

To the moon,
V

I stared down at Violet's letter, her words humming through my chest like one last hug. The storm pressed hard against the windows, rain lashing sideways, thunder crawling across the mountains like a warning.

Before I could breathe, the bedroom door flew open.

"Is she in here?" Ty yelled.

I jolted, clutching the letter to my chest. "Who?"

"Junie," he said, breath sharp, eyes wild. His shirt was soaked, rain dripping down his hair, his jaw tight in a way I'd never seen. "She's not in her room."

My stomach plummeted. "What do you mean she's not in her room? She went in there when we got back. I thought she—"

"She's not there now." His voice broke on the last word. "The window—Daisy, the window's still open and she—she's not—"

I jumped to my feet, Violet's letter falling to the floor.

"Okay." I grabbed his forearms with shaking hands. "Okay, breathe. We'll find her."

But Ty was beyond listening. He tore through the hallway, yanking open doors, calling her name with a panic so raw it rattled the walls. "Junie! Juniper. June bug —Junie!"

He was unraveling. And for the first time since I'd stepped foot on this mountain, I wasn't.

I followed him into the living room. "Ty, listen to me."

But he didn't. He was already halfway down the hall toward the mudroom.

"Did you check the barns?" I asked, louder this time. "She likes the cats. Ty, did you check?"

"Yes!" he yelled back, voice ragged. "I was just there—she wasn't—Jesus, where is she?"

He threw open the pantry door. The linen closet. The bathroom.

"Junie!" His voice was hoarse. Desperate.

Rowdy barked, pacing circles around us.

"Okay," I whispered, forcing myself to think like Junie would.

Ty darted into the backyard, disappearing into sheets of rain, screaming her name into the trees.

I moved toward the front door instead.

Rowdy followed me to the porch, the rain hitting my face like a slap. Thunder boomed overhead. I scanned the gravel road, the dark curve of the river, the silhouette of the barn—

And then I saw it.

A pale glow.

A single light burned in the window of Violet's house down the drive.

The house I had turned dark earlier.

The room Junie hadn't dared set foot in all summer.

The walls that held everything she'd lost.

My breath hitched, and I ran.

Feet slipping on wet gravel, rain needling my skin, wind whipping my hair into my eyes. Rowdy bounded beside me, barking, as the light grew brighter, closer, realer.

I slammed through Violet's front door, breathless.

The living room was empty, quiet except for the storm battering the windows. But a soft line of yellow light glowed under the door to the bedroom Violet and Junie used to share.

My heart squeezed.

I pushed it open.

Junie lay on the bed with her eyes closed, clutching a picture of her mom against her chest. Her cheeks were streaked with dried tears, her glasses crooked. Piggie was curled at her side, snout tucked against her arm.

She looked so small.

So young.

So tired of being brave.

I climbed onto the bed beside her, and the mattress dipped just enough to stir her awake.

Her eyes blinked open, glassy and swollen. "Dizzy?"

"I'm here, cutie." My voice broke. "I'm right here."

"I miss her," she whispered, lip trembling. "I don't want to move. What if I can't feel her anymore?"

I pulled her into my arms, pressing my cheek to her damp hair. "Oh, sweet girl," I breathed. "You'll always feel her. She's always with us. In your heart. In your memories. In everything she loved." I kissed the top of her head. "She's not going anywhere."

Junie nodded against me, a small, shuddering sound escaping her.

"And listen to me..." My voice steadied, somehow. "We're not moving. We're not leaving. We're staying right here."

A floorboard creaked in the hallway.

I looked up just as Ty stepped into the doorway, hair plastered to his forehead, rain dripping onto the floor. His chest rose and fell as if he'd run the whole valley. Fear and relief warred across his face.

"So, we're not going to Chicago?" she asked, arms looped around me in a vice grip.

"No," I whispered, then turned to look at Ty, making sure he heard me too.

The truth didn't hit me all at once. It clicked into place like a puzzle piece I'd been holding upside down.

Ty's love wasn't loud. It wasn't dramatic or overwhelming. It didn't burn hot and bright like the lightning outside.

But he was my lighthouse in the storm, the beacon calling me home.

He didn't flare or vanish, drifting in and out depending on

the weather. He just stayed, no matter how much I threw at him, ready to pull me back in, time and time again.

And I was in love with him. I didn't ever want to let him go.

I brushed Junie's hair off her forehead, kissing her one more time. "Why would we need to leave when we're already home?"

34

TY

Junie was asleep before I even lifted her out of Daisy's arms, her cheek pressed to my shoulder, fingers tangled in my shirt like she'd fused herself there. Piggie trotted behind us, snorting as if she knew to stay close, and by the time we crossed the porch, the storm had blown itself out.

I carried Junie back to the house, then down the hall, and tucked her into her bed. She didn't stir. Not when I smoothed the hair from her forehead, not when I checked and double-checked that the window was locked, not when I stood there in the doorway long enough for my eyes to sting.

She was home. Safe. Breathing.

The moment Daisy stepped into the room behind me, everything inside me unraveled.

I backed into the hallway to give her space. She leaned over Junie, kissed her cheek, and whispered something soft only she and the sleeping girl would ever know. And when she stepped out and pulled the door closed to leave just a crack how Junie liked—

My legs gave out.

I slid down the wall before I even realized I was falling. My hands shook so hard I had to brace them on my knees, and my breathing came in sharp, uneven gasps.

I'd been strong all summer. Strong when Junie cried for her mom at the hospital. Strong when the judge said I might lose Junie in six weeks. Strong when the house fell apart and when Daisy did too.

But the sight of Junie's empty bed—the open window, the rain, the fear—

It broke me clean in half.

My shoulders shook, silent and raw. Tears hit my knees before I even realized I was crying. I pressed the heels of my hands to my eyes as if I could stop the shaking by force.

Then Daisy was there.

She said nothing at first. Didn't ask. She just slid down the wall beside me, her hip brushing mine, her warmth seeping into my shoulder. Then she put an arm around my shoulder and pulled my head into her lap.

I didn't fight it.

Couldn't.

Her fingers threaded through my wet hair, slow and steady. I let my forehead rest against her thigh, letting myself be small for the first time in years.

"It's okay," she whispered, voice cracking with its own exhaustion. "Ty, it's okay."

It wasn't—not in my head. Not in my chest. Not in whatever part of me was still trapped back in that bedroom, staring at an open window and an empty bed.

But she kept going, voice soft but sure.

"Junie's okay."

Her hand slid down to the back of my neck.

"We're not leaving."

She brushed the hair from my temple.

"I love you."

Everything in me went still.

I lifted my head and turned to look at her. Her eyes were red. Her face was blotchy from crying. Her hair was damp from the storm. And she was the most beautiful thing I'd ever seen.

"What did you just say?" I asked, voice hardly more than a breath.

She cupped my cheek with her palm, thumb brushing the tears I didn't realize were still falling.

"It's okay," she whispered. "Junie's okay. We're not leaving. And I love you."

"You're not leaving."

She nodded. "That's right."

"And you love me."

"I really, really do."

The world narrowed to her. Just her.

I leaned in and kissed her—soft at first, then not soft at all. A summer's worth of fear and longing and almost breaking poured into it. She kissed me back with every piece of herself, every shattered part, every brave part.

When we pulled back, her forehead rested against mine. My hands slid around her waist, helping her up.

"Say it again," I breathed, then lifted her off the ground until our faces were level, her legs wrapped around my waist.

She nodded, fingers curling at the base of my neck. "As many times as you need. I love you, Ty."

"Good." I carried her down the hall toward my room, her face buried in my shoulder, her breath warm against my skin. "That's very good."

The storm was gone.

Junie was safe.

And Daisy was staying.

She wiggled out of my hold once we were in my bedroom, then pulled me into the bathroom. "You're freezing."

The door clicked shut behind us, and she turned on the shower, steam curling into the air as the pipes groaned to life. I helped her peel off our damp clothes, the sound of fabric hitting tile mixing with the rush of water.

We stepped beneath the spray together, heat cascading over us, washing away the sharp edges of the night. The steam wrapped around us like a cocoon, quieting the last of the chaos in my head. For the first time since I saw Junie's open window, my chest didn't feel like it might cave in.

Daisy's hands were gentle as they moved over me, like she was mapping every place the fear had carved into my skin.

She pulled back just enough to meet my eyes. "Turn around."

I did.

The spray pounded against my back, but it was Daisy's warm, soapy hands I felt. She started at my neck, thumbs pressing into the knot that lived there permanently, working slow circles until my head dropped forward with a rough breath. Her lips followed, kissing away the tension.

When I sagged into her touch, she moved to my shoulders, down my arms, lacing our fingers together for a heartbeat before continuing lower. When she stepped closer, her body brushed my back, warm and soft, grounding me in a way words never could.

"You carry so much," she whispered against my skin. "But I've got you."

I closed my eyes and let myself believe her.

She turned me back toward her, and our eyes locked. No

words. Just the steady rhythm of water and the certainty in her gaze.

I see you. All of you. And I'm still here.

My hands found her waist. Hers slid over my chest, slow and reverent, like she could feel my heart trying to climb out and hand itself to her. The kiss that followed was deep and unhurried, full of relief and gratitude and promises we hadn't said out loud yet.

She washed my chest next, palms gliding over my heart like she could feel it trying to climb out and hand itself to her. Lower, over my stomach, the line where muscle met hip. When her soapy fingers curled around my cock, I sucked in a breath so sharp it echoed off the tiles.

"Daisy—"

"Shhh." She rose on her toes and kissed the corner of my mouth. "I've got you."

She stroked me with the same unhurried rhythm she'd used everywhere else. Long, slick pulls from base to tip, thumb circling the head on every upstroke until my hips rocked forward on instinct. My hands found her waist, gripping hard enough that I was afraid I'd leave marks, but she only leaned into it, encouraging.

When it all felt too good, I slid my hand between her thighs and found her pussy already swollen, slick beyond what the shower could claim. Two fingers slid inside her easily; she gasped against my jaw, hips rocking forward to meet me, clit throbbing against my palm when I pressed it there.

We moved like that—hands and mouths and ragged breathing—until the tension coiled too tight. She came first, quiet but fierce, inner walls fluttering around my fingers as she trembled against me, biting her lip to muffle the sound. I groaned at the feel of her pulsing, at the way her hand tightened on my cock in rhythm with her orgasm.

But she didn't let me finish like that.

She pulled my hand free, kissed me hard, then turned so her back was against my chest. With one palm on the tile, she arched just enough and reached back to guide me.

"Inside me," she breathed. "Please, Ty. I want to feel you come inside me."

And fuck, that sounded good.

I notched myself at her entrance, pushing in slow until I was buried to the hilt. She moaned, head dropping forward, water streaming down her back. Fuck, she was perfect.

I wrapped one arm around her waist, the other hand finding her clit again, rubbing firm circles while I moved with deep thrusts that had us both gasping. The angle let me hit that spot inside her that made her whimper my name. Her hips rolled back to meet every stroke, chasing it, taking what she needed while giving me everything.

"Say it again," I rasped against her ear.

"I love you," she panted, pushing back harder. "Forever, if you'll have me."

The words snapped something in me. I drove in deeper, faster, fingers working her clit in tight, relentless circles. She came again—harder this time—her pussy clenching around my cock like a fist. I followed right after, burying myself as deep as I could and spilling inside her with a broken groan, pulse after pulse until I was shaking, empty, and hers.

For a long minute we just stood there under the spray, hearts hammering in tandem, my arms wrapped around her like I'd never let go.

She was the first to speak, voice wrecked and tender. "I meant it, you know."

I kissed the wet curve of her shoulder.

"I'm not just staying for Junie." Her eyes found mine when she turned in my arms. "I'm staying for you. For us. This—whatever messy, beautiful forever looks like—I want it. All of it."

My throat closed so hard that it hurt. I kissed her instead of trying to answer with words, slow and deep and certain.

By the time the water cooled, we stepped out, warm and sated and calmer than before. I pulled on clean boxers and shorts, waiting for Daisy to finish wringing out her hair.

But with each passing minute, my heartbeat raced again, the panic returning as I imagined Junie's bed empty once more.

I padded down the hall and pushed open her door, only to find her right where I'd left her. Sound asleep. Rowdy curled at her feet like a sentry.

My chest loosened and tightened all at once. I rubbed at it as if I could smooth the fear out by force.

Daisy's lips touched my shoulder, warm and certain, then she brushed past me and slipped into Junie's room wearing my oversized hoodie.

Without hesitation, she climbed into the bed beside her.

Junie stirred at the shift in the mattress, then turned into her aunt's chest, tucking her face beneath Daisy's chin with a sleepy sigh. Daisy pressed a kiss to her hair, brushing it back from her forehead before lifting her gaze to me.

"Get in the bed, Ty. Squeeze in here. Let's hold our girl."

The stars spun across the ceiling above me, soft bursts of color from her little nightlight. I stared at them for a second, grounding myself in the ordinary magic of it. Then I crossed the room and climbed in on Junie's other side.

I slid an arm over Junie's back, my hand finding Daisy's at

the same time she reached for me. She laced our fingers together across Junie's small body, sealing us around her.

"Sleep, Ty," she murmured, eyes already closing. "We're all here."

Junie's breathing evened out between us.

Daisy's thumb brushed once over my knuckles.

And for the first time in months, I believed it.

Finally, I slept.

35

Daisy

The courthouse smelled the same as it had six weeks ago: lemon oil, old paper, and the faint metallic tang of nerves. But everything else had changed.

I stepped through the heavy oak doors in a pale blue dress, the color of perfect afternoon skies. The fabric skimmed my hips and stopped just above the knee, far more respectable than the jeans and dirty tee I'd worn the last time I was here.

Ty walked half a step behind me, close enough that the sleeve of his suit jacket brushed my arm. He looked like a man who had his shit together, not the same man who'd sat on the hallway floor, elbows on his knees, crying into my lap because he was terrified of losing her.

Junie sat in the very back row with Emmy, legs swinging above the floor, wearing the navy-blue dress with tiny white flowers we'd picked out together last weekend. She'd thought about wearing the shoes we bought to match, but the pink rain boots were still on her feet, and that was fine by me. Every time our eyes met, she gave me a small, brave smile that cracked my heart clean open.

We took our seats in the front. Ty's knee bounced twice before he caught it, pressed his palm flat against his thigh like he could still the tremor that lived under his skin now. I reached over without looking and covered his hand with mine.

A lot had happened since our last hearing. Not fixed. Not healed. But we were here, together.

Sandra stood. "Your Honor, CPS has completed its review. Home visits were successful; Ms. Winslow has refurbished her sister's house and secured a steady job. For all intents and purposes, Juniper's care has remained stable. With these findings, we recommend granting Ms. Winslow full physical and legal custody of her niece, Juniper Winslow."

Ty's hand tightened around mine until I felt the bones grind. He stared straight ahead, jaw locked, waiting for the blow he was certain was coming.

The judge turned his attention to me. "Ms. Winslow, before I rule, do you have questions?"

I stood, then smoothed my dress down over my legs.

"Yes, Your Honor," I said. "I have a question."

Ty went still beside me.

I turned to face him as I spoke, wanting him to see my eyes when I did what Violet told me to and followed my gut. "Can we honor my sister's wishes and make Mr. Hudson's and my temporary joint arrangement permanent?"

The judge blinked. "Ms. Winslow... are you requesting an adoption?"

Ty's head snapped toward me so fast I was surprised his neck didn't crack. His eyes were wide and glassy and absolutely wrecked. His lips parted, but no sound came out.

I nodded, not looking away from him. "I'm asking if Ty would like to adopt her with me."

From the back, Junie scrambled to her feet on the bench,

clutching Emmy's sleeve like it was a lifeline. "YES!" she shrieked, loud enough to echo off the vaulted ceiling. "I mean, yes, please!"

The judge's eyebrows climbed toward his hairline. He cleared his throat but didn't hide his smile. "Young lady, we try to maintain some decorum."

Ty twisted in his seat, looking at her like she'd just handed him the moon.

The judge cleared his throat and looked down at the documents in front of him. "Well," he said, adjusting his glasses, "it appears Mr. Hudson already has a completed background check, home study, and foster certification on file with this county."

Ty's breath stuttered, and I reached across to lace my fingers with his.

The judge continued, "These were conducted when he was approved as Juniper's kinship foster parent. All requirements for adoptive placement are therefore already satisfied."

Sandra nodded behind the table. "CPS has no objections."

The judge looked back at Ty. "Mr. Hudson, do you understand that adoption is permanent? You would be Juniper's legal father. This is not temporary or easily undone."

My fingers tightened in his grip, doing my best to ease the tremor gripping him.

"Yes," he said, voice raw. "I understand."

"And your answer?"

He looked at me. Then at Junie.

"Yes," he said, stronger. "If she wants me, I would love to be her dad."

Junie nodded so hard her glasses nearly fell off.

The judge's grin widened. "Well then, this is a fun surprise.

Given that all legal criteria are met and CPS recommends permanency, I see no reason to delay."

He gestured for Junie to come forward. She vaulted over the bench in front of her, rubber boots squeaking against the wooden floors as she sprinted into Ty's arms. He caught her and lifted her up, holding her as if she was the most precious thing in the world.

I stepped beside them, smoothing her hair, feeling the three of us form a tight circle at the front of the courtroom.

The judge leaned forward over his bench until he was eye level with Junie. "Juniper, is it your wish to be adopted by Mr. Hudson as your legal father?"

"Yes," she breathed, then squeezed her arms around Ty's neck tighter. "He already is."

Ty made a broken sound, forehead pressed to hers.

The judge turned to me. "And Ms. Winslow, do you wish to continue as Juniper's legal guardian—her aunt, her family—with Mr. Hudson?"

Junie reached back and threw an arm around my neck, pulling me into their little group hug. "Yes," I said, rubbing a hand up and down her back. "Always."

The judge picked up his pen.

"Then, by the authority of the State of Colorado, I grant the adoption of Juniper Winslow to Ty Hudson, with joint legal guardianship retained by Daisy Winslow."

The gavel came down, making it official.

Junie wrapped her arms around both our necks, shaking with relief and joy. "We're a family," she whispered. "My family."

Ty kissed her forehead. I kissed her cheek. And for the first time since Violet died, the world didn't feel sharp.

It felt different, changed, made anew.

36

TY

The gavel was still echoing when my knees went weak.

Adoption.

Father.

Permanent.

Words I'd never dared to imagine for myself.

But then Junie threw her arms around my neck and whispered, "My family," and something inside me cracked open so wide I wasn't sure it would ever close again.

The judge said a few more things, but it all sounded like a radio underwater. I just kept holding Junie, breathing her in, feeling Daisy's hand on my back like an anchor keeping me upright.

When we stepped into the hallway, the air had changed. The door clicked shut behind us, muting the courtroom and all the noise inside my chest.

Emmy bounced up and down, eyes glassy as she held her hands out for a hug. I went right to her, letting my sister wrap me in her arms. Together we shook with silent tears, her hand stroking up and down my back. "I am so proud of you, Ty. You are one of the best men I know, and no one will love that little girl more than you."

I didn't answer. I couldn't.

Junie launched herself at our legs, wrapping her arms around us. "Should I call you Aunt Emmy now?"

"You can call me whatever you want, sweet girl," Emmy said, then leaned down to hug Junie. "But I'm thrilled to call you mine."

Junie beamed, then looked up at Daisy. "This is cool. Now I have two aunts."

Daisy stood a little to the side, arms wrapped around herself, but smiled. "That's right, cutie. The cream of the crop, too, if you ask me."

Emmy stood and hugged Daisy next, squeezing her tightly. Daisy's eyes never left mine, even when she hugged my sister back. "I know I could never replace Violet, and I never want to, but I'm so happy to call you family, too."

Daisy's smile slipped off her face, tears brimming in her eyes as she hugged Emmy tighter. "I may be too selfish to deny that offer."

I leaned back against the wall, unsteady. The adrenaline from the hearing, the relief, the shock—all of it hit me at once.

Emmy backed away, wiping tears from her face, heading toward the exit. Her phone lit up in her hand, and she glanced at it before smiling up at me. "I have to go, but dinner tonight. We need to celebrate."

"Emmy..." I warned, but my sister grinned wider, then spun and walked out of the courthouse.

Daisy turned toward me, Junie's hand in hers, and smiled. Not a bright, masking smile. Not a polite smile. This one was soft, sure, and meant only for me. Like she knew what she'd done for me.

My breath left my body in a slow, shaking rush.

She'd chosen this.

She'd chosen me.

Not by default.

Not by convenience.

Not because she had to.

But because she wanted me in Junie's life forever.

My throat locked up. My eyes burned. I pressed the heel of my hand against my brow and tried to hold it together, but emotion rolled through me too fast to catch.

Daisy stepped closer, her voice low enough that only I could hear. "Hey," she whispered. "You okay?"

I let out a shaky breath. "I don't... I don't know what to do with any of this."

She smiled again, small and gentle, and reached up to cup the side of my face.

"You don't have to do anything," she said. "You already did it. You loved Junie in all the ways that mattered long before today made it official."

My eyes closed, holding back the wave of emotion pulling me under.

She stepped a little closer, her thumb brushing across my jaw. "Ty, look at me."

The moment I opened my eyes was my undoing. Daisy was looking at me like she'd never look away again. Like she meant it when she said she wasn't going anywhere. Like it wasn't Junie in my life forever, it was her too.

"I love you. We love you."

Junie tugged on my jacket until I picked her up, sandwiching her between us in one more hug.

This was my family.

My little girl.

The woman I loved.

The life I never thought I'd have.

"I love you both, too."

The drive back to the ranch felt unreal, my hands positioned at ten-and-two knowing I carried the most precious cargo. My girls, forever.

Junie sat in the backseat, clutching the embossed folder the clerk had handed us, rereading the formal-sounding words that declared her Juniper Mae Winslow-Hudson.

Daisy rode almost the entire way home twisted backward in her seat, as if she too was having a hard time believing that this had really happened.

Every time Junie whispered her new name, it sounded a little more reverent, a little more in awe, and my eyes burned anew.

By the time we turned into the driveway, the sun had dipped low enough to paint the valley gold. I slowed, but then stopped dead at the sight in front of me.

On my porch stood everyone I loved, there to welcome us home.

Beckett stood front and center, holding a gigantic bouquet of pink balloons that said IT'S A GIRL!

Next to my best friend were Emmy and Jace, both grinning. Behind them stood my entire mismatched family:

Lori sat in a chair someone had pulled out, her hands folded, face soft with emotion.

Shannon, in all black with a lopsided smile, clutched a bakery box.

Stevie, already wiping tears with the sleeve of her shirt.

Luke, one arm around her and the other holding a wiggly toddler, smiling so wide his dimples might crack.

Tate, arms crossed over her chest as she leaned against a post, her entire face glowing with pride.

And Mason, standing at her side with his hands cupped around his mouth, yelled, "And for tonight's starting lineup, the newest Little Huddy!"

Daisy climbed out of the truck first to help Junie down, and the minute her feet hit the ground, the cheering started. Loud and messy, and totally unnecessary.

Shannon shoved her cupcakes into Daisy's hands. "Congrats," she said. "Glad you're staying."

Stevie hugged all three of us at once, sobbing, "I'm so happy I can't even see!"

Beckett slapped my back and shoved a bouquet of balloons into my hand. "A girl dad, huh? It fits."

Mason joined our trio, a finger flicking the pink balloon hovering over my head. "Aren't these for a baby shower?"

Beckett waggled his eyebrows at me, then at Daisy. "Well, with these lovebirds? Give it time."

Daisy turned bright crimson while I choked on my own saliva, but I reached for her hand, pulling her into the chaos.

Junie piped up, delighted, "Well, I am a girl!"

Mason cackled, then pulled Junie into his arms, hugging her tight. "Incredible. Zero notes. Perfect comedic timing, Little Huddy."

Jace stepped up next. "Thanks for the cousin," he said. "I think I'll keep her."

Junie threw herself into his arms, hugging the surly teenager tight. "I've never had a cousin before."

Then Lori reached for my hand, her fingers trembling, but

her grip was warm and sure. "I'm proud of you," she said. "So very proud."

Her gaze slid to Daisy. "And you, sweetheart... welcome to the family."

Daisy blinked. "I... thank you," she said, voice thick.

With Lori's words, the line of hugs started all over again, this time for Daisy.

Stevie sniffed, hugging Daisy so tight her back arched. "You're stuck with us now."

Luke grinned, giving her a quick handshake. "No take-backs."

Shannon crossed her arms. "You wear a lot of pastels for me to consider you a friend, but I guess the term fits."

Tate nodded once. "Seconded."

And Mason threw his arms open like a game-show host. "Congratulations, Aunt Daisy! Welcome to the mayhem!"

Daisy stared at me over Emmy's shoulder in yet another bone-cracking hug. Her smile was small and real, and so full of emotion it nearly put me on my knees.

This was the family neither of us had grown up with, but we were making it together.

37

Daisy

Acceptance didn't come all at once. I didn't wake up one morning and think, today's the day I can say goodbye to Violet. I certainly didn't wake up and think, it doesn't hurt as bad.

It hurt every time I looked at her house down the road.

It hurt when one of her favorite songs came on the radio.

It hurt on Junie's first day of third grade when once again I forgot I couldn't just send her a picture.

But by the end of September, when the leaves were changing on the aspens and the entire valley was painted gold, I knew it was time to let her go.

We stood in the field that stretched between Violet's house and ours, where the wildflowers had lasted the longest. Little bursts of purple and pink and white swayed in the tall late-summer grass, giving one last stubborn show before winter took them under.

"Are you sure about this?" Ty asked, voice low and careful. He stood just behind us, giving me space, but always there when I needed him.

Junie stood at my side, Violet's urn in her hands. I ran a

hand through her blonde hair, soothing both of us with the little motion.

"What do you think?" I asked, my words meant just for her.

Junie nodded, then looked up at me. "Mom always loved the fall here."

The wind kicked up, lifting the grass in waves, carrying the scent of pine and cold air and the faint musk of dying wildflowers. I gazed out at the picturesque mountains around me, white coating the tips with the promise of winter coming soon. Everything was green and gold and beautiful, even as dead leaves fluttered to the ground.

Fall was an ending, but not the harsh, dramatic kind. It was softer, holding hope for tomorrow, and clearing the world for life to begin again.

Not today.

Not tomorrow.

But someday.

Together, Junie and I twisted the lid, my breath catching when it loosened. Ty stepped closer, placing a hand between my shoulder blades, just enough to remind me I wasn't doing this alone.

Junie looked up at me. "Now?"

"Yeah," I said, guiding her small hands. "I think so."

Together, we tilted the urn.

The ashes lifted on a gust of wind, soft and pale and weightless, drifting out over the field, caught in the breeze. They blew toward Violet's house, over the wildflowers, and up into the mountains she loved.

Junie pressed into my side, a tremor running through her. "Did it work?"

I wrapped my arms around her shoulders. "Yeah, cutie. It worked."

Ty pulled us both into his chest to ward off the chill. "She's everywhere she loved," he said. "Right where she wanted to be."

The three of us stayed like that—a small circle against the wide, golden valley—until the last of the ashes sparkling in the sunlight disappeared in the wind.

Junie wiped her cheek with the back of her hand. "Do you think she's happy?"

My throat tightened. "Are you kidding me?" I whispered, stroking my fingers through her hair. "This was where she wanted to be, with you forever."

Ty squeezed my hand. "All of us together."

Junie nodded, then smiled up at us. "Family."

None of us moved, still huddled together in the field, until the sun sat just above the mountains and the temperature dropped fast. The chickens clucked from the driveway, and Junie took that as her cue.

"I'll go get them inside," she said, walking toward the hens waiting for her.

Ty brushed a stray blonde curl from my face and tucked it behind my ear. He leaned forward and kissed me softly, then pulled back. "Okay?"

"Yeah," I answered, giving him a soft nod. "I think I'm—"

The sound of a phone vibrating cut through my words, and Ty frowned. He pulled it from his pocket, staring at the screen where Sandra Diaz—CPS scrolled across the top.

"Hello?" he answered on speakerphone, staring right at me.

My breaths came in quick gasps, but before my mind had time to conjure up a million scenarios of why she might call, Sandra spoke.

"Oh, I'm so glad you answered," Sandra said, her voice more than a little frazzled. In the background, I heard a baby cry, and Ty and I stared at each other. "I know you have a lot going on with the hockey season starting back up and Juniper back in school this fall, but I just had an emergency placement dropped in my lap, and I have nowhere for him to go."

"A placement," Ty said, staring down at the phone. "Foster care."

"Yes," Sandra said, then let out a deep sigh. "It's a complicated story, and I can tell you more if you say yes. I don't think it will be a permanent placement, but I have a one-year-old little boy in need of a safe home tonight."

I looked up at Ty, feeling a whole new wave of emotions. We'd talked a lot about his decision to foster Junie in the last few weeks, and how important that had been to him. After everything he'd done for our little girl, I couldn't help but see how much it meant to him.

On the off chance something like this would happen, I'd completed the required foster training and paperwork, not wanting my presence in his life to be the reason he couldn't help more children.

"Ty, are you still there?" Sandra asked, and Ty looked away from the phone, right at me.

"Yeah," he said, eyes searching my face. "Sorry, I'm just surprised you'd pick me."

"Please," Sandra said, and I reached forward to grab Ty's hand, holding it in mine. "With the way you took care of that sweet girl of yours? Any child would be lucky to be loved by you, whether it's just for tonight or for a lifetime."

"Daisy?" Ty asked. "What do you think?"

I grinned up at him. "I think I agree with Sandra."

"Should I ask Junie?"

"Ask me what?" Junie said as she came back toward us, Piggie and Rowdy trotting at her side.

Ty squatted down in front of Junie, taking her hands in his, leaving his phone on the gravel at his feet. "Sandra has a baby boy who needs somewhere safe to sleep tonight. She wants to know what we'd think about having him here?"

"Like a brother?"

"I can't promise that," Ty said gently.

"But we can show him what it means to be part of a family, can't we?" I said, laying a hand on Ty's shoulder. "For however long he needs us."

Junie nodded, then reached down to pick up the phone Piggie was busy pushing around with her snout. "Does he like pigs?"

Sandra chuckled, and I grinned at my most favorite little girl in the universe. "I'm not sure if he's ever met one."

"Okay," Junie said, then handed the phone back. "I'll tell Piggie to be extra nice."

"Is that a yes?" Sandra asked, and I squeezed Ty's shoulder, giving him my approval.

"Yes," Ty said, reaching up to take my hand in his. "Yes, it is."

Sandra exhaled a shaky breath of relief. "Thank you. We'll be there in an hour."

Ty ended the call, still crouched in front of Junie, still holding her little hands. For a long moment, none of us moved. The wind whispered through the tall grass, brushing past us like Violet herself was slipping between our shoulders, nudging us toward whatever came next.

Junie pushed her glasses up and looked between us. "We should get ready, right? Babies need bottles and blankets and those squishy fruit pouches, and a crib. Maybe Stevie has one."

Ty smiled, small and a little undone. "Yeah, bug. We should get ready."

She took off toward the house with Piggie snorting behind her, shouting, "I'll clean my room! And make a sign! And find some toys he won't choke on!"

Her voice faded as she ran, swallowed up by the golden field and the fading sun. Ty rose slowly, brushing off his jeans, and turned toward me.

He wasn't grieving the way Junie and I were—not with the same sharpness, not with the hollow ache that had shaped our entire summer. But he'd carried us through it. Loved us through it. And the tenderness in his eyes held the weight of all of it.

"Are you sure?" he asked, searching my face. "This is a big change."

I stepped into him, sliding my hand into his, the wild-flowers brushing against our legs as the wind swept through the valley again.

"Of course I'm sure," I said. "The hardest part of losing someone is realizing life keeps going anyway. But maybe that's the point—we keep going too."

His breath hitched, as if he took that right into his bloodstream.

Behind us, the last of Violet's ashes drifted along the field, settling into the earth. I looked up into Ty's hazel eyes and felt the truth of it settle deep inside me.

We weren't replacing Violet.

We weren't erasing the loss.

We were growing around it, making a life that honored her.

Ty squeezed my hand. "Okay," he whispered, more to himself than to me. "Okay."

We stood there for another moment—just long enough to

watch the sky shift from gold to rose to violet—and then he nodded toward the house.

"Come on," he said, a soft smile tugging at the corner of his mouth. "We've got a room to set up."

I leaned into his side as we walked, our steps matching without effort.

Behind us, the wildflowers bent in the wind. Ahead of us, the porch light flickered on.

Together, Ty and I walked toward the house, toward our little girl, toward the tiny boy who needed a place to land.

Toward a future that was ours to build.

Daisy

Five Years Later

"In order for this wall calendar to work, you have to fill it out," Junie said from the kitchen, decked out in Mayhem black-and-green and ready to go. Her dark blonde hair was braided with the precision of a girl who thrived on routine, and glasses replaced with contacts I was still getting used to. Gone was the baby-face, and she looked more like Violet by the day. "This was supposed to be a way to get the things out of your head, because your head is"—she circled her hand near her temple, all teenage sass—"a very unreliable filing cabinet."

I, on the other hand, was nowhere near ready. "Now is not the time for a new system, June." I hopped on one foot, trying to wedge my boot on, but that was easier said than done when you couldn't see your own toes. "But thank you. Can you show me how to use it again tomorrow?"

She nodded, then pushed the button on the screen to make the fancy digital wall calendar go dark.

"Have you seen your brother's jersey?"

"I have it," a deep voice said from the stairwell that led to the new second story of our home. "Ty laid it out for me before he left for the rink this morning."

"Of course he did," I muttered under my breath. "What time is your game again?"

"Puck drop is at 6:30," June said in the tone of a girl who had decided she was running the show until I was no longer pregnant or breathing—whichever came first. She was thirteen now, and insisted on being called June. Not Juniper. Not Junie. Not cutie. Bug was still allowed, but only from Ty. But Little Huddy was the nickname I heard most often these days. "We need to leave in three minutes if we're going to make it to the rink on time."

Right on cue, the baby monitor crackled to life; Zara waking up from her late afternoon nap.

"Can one of you—" I groaned, pressing a hand to my belly as I finally got the boot on. Seven months pregnant was not the time for snow boots, but it was December in Linwood, and the world outside looked like a snow globe.

"I'll get her," Micah said as he walked by.

I smiled up at my teenage son—broad-shouldered, impossibly tall these days, dark curls brushing his forehead. When he first came to us three years ago—quiet, guarded, and clutching a duffel bag with everything he owned—he was supposed to stay for a weekend. He didn't unpack. He didn't ask for anything. He kept his things lined on the dresser like he was waiting to be moved again.

But that weekend passed, and he helped June with her farm chores. Skated with Ty. Ate dinner beside me as if he'd always belonged. And little by little, he let us in.

There wasn't one moment he became ours. Just a hundred small ones that added up before we even noticed.

A weekend turned into forever, and the day we signed his adoption papers was just as celebratory as the day we'd signed June's.

Micah disappeared down the hall, and a minute later returned with Zara—our newest placement—propped on his hip. Three months in, and we all adored our little toddler, and she us. Her little hand fisted in the collar of his hoodie, dark braids squished against his chest, blinking sleepily as if she wasn't sure which universe she'd woken up in.

Being a foster family was beautiful and brutal in equal measure. You opened your door knowing you might have to say goodbye, and you loved them anyway. But knowing you were choosing to show up when they needed you most? That made it worthwhile.

"Hey, cutie," I said, taking her from him and settling her on my hip. "Long nap?"

She yawned so big that her whole body trembled. Answer enough.

The front door opened, cold air sweeping in as Ty stepped inside, cheeks pink from the wind. Rowdy trotted in behind him—older now, grayer in the face, but still determined to greet every member of this household as if they were the best part of his day.

"Are you ready?" Ty asked, leaning down to kiss me, then Zara's cheek, then my belly, warm and full under his palm. He held out his fist, and June and Micah each bumped it—June's accompanied with an eye-roll—but she knew he wouldn't leave her alone until everyone felt his attention.

"Define ready." I tugged at Ty's Mayhem hoodie that barely stretched over my growing belly. "For a cheeseburger? Yes. For hockey season? Debatable."

He smirked. "Fair." Then he nodded at Micah. "First varsity game. Big night. Are you nervous?"

Micah shrugged, but June snorted. "He's got the highest defensive zone recovery rate on the team, but only when he doesn't panic."

"Shut up," Micah muttered. "I don't panic."

"Oh, you definitely panic," June corrected, doing an excellent job of taking on the role of little sister these last three years. "Let's just hope Skylar isn't there to see, because then you'll really panic."

"You're one to talk." Micah knocked June on the back of the head, just enough to mess up her braid. "What time is Roman's game this weekend?"

June blushed, and I chuckled at the mention of June's first crush. Roman played on the middle school hockey team, and June's interest in the sport had taken on a whole new meaning.

It hurt that Violet wasn't here to witness her daughter in the sassy, awkward teenage years, but I felt her in every reluctant hug. Saw her in every eye-roll. Heard her in June's quick comebacks.

Ty gave them both the Dad Look. "Enough."

They quieted, muttering identical "sorry"s under their breath. As much as it didn't sound sincere, Micah and June loved each other just as much as any siblings I'd ever known. And God, I loved them so much it made my ribs feel too small.

"You on the bench with me tonight?" Ty asked June, who grinned back at him.

"Yeah, Dad."

He looped an arm around her, kissing the top of her head before she ducked out of his hold, and I leaned my head down on Zara's. "Someday you won't want to hug us anymore either, and I'll be sad, but it'll be okay. I'll know it's not because you don't love me anymore."

Zara snuggled closer, like the idea was as absurd as watching my snuggly little niece transform into a teenager before my eyes.

June came over to us, kissing Zara's chubby cheek, then wrapped her arms around us both for the fastest hug in existence. "Love you."

"I love you too, cutie," I said, my eyes watering like they did so often lately. Damn pregnancy hormones.

We herded ourselves out the door—Rowdy included—and piled into the SUV. As we rolled down the long driveway, the headlights washed across the house at the end of the road. Warm lights glowed through the windows of Violet's house, making it feel like home.

"Did you get everyone settled?" I asked, watching Ty's eyes soften as we passed it.

"Yeah," he said. "Layton starts his job at the hardware store tomorrow. I checked Nora's paperwork, and she's good for next semester at the community college. And the twins are picking up extra holiday shifts at the outfitters with plans to move out in the spring. They're doing great, Daisy."

I looked at the house again—no longer quiet, no longer heavy. The Floral Farmhouse, as it had been dubbed, was filled with teens aging out of foster care who needed somewhere safe to land. Somewhere gentle to start over. Somewhere Violet would have been thrilled to call her own.

"She would've loved this," I whispered.

Ty reached across the console, found my hand, and spun my wedding band around my finger until the diamond caught the moonlight. "I couldn't agree more."

I nodded, blinking up at the sky dusted in stars as the SUV

hummed down the road, all five of us tucked close inside—messy, mismatched, and yet somehow made for each other.

Made for this.

Made for mayhem.

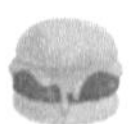

UP NEXT! Mikko Laaksonen

He's the NHL's best defenseman—
and a brand-new single dad.

She's the speech therapist who understands
his daughter better than anyone.

When a desperate lie turns into a fake marriage,
he gets the stability he needs... But falling for his wife?
That was never supposed to happen.

Preorder Mayhem Hockey Club Book 3 here!

TY

I woke up to lips on my jaw and a warm, familiar weight draped over my chest.

For one blissful second, I didn't open my eyes. I just let myself exist there—sunlight slipping through the curtains, Daisy's hair tickling my shoulder, her breath warm against my skin.

"Happy birthday," she murmured.

I cracked one eye open. "Is this how you're planning to celebrate?"

She smiled, slow and wicked, and shifted her knee higher along my thigh. "I had a few ideas."

I rolled her beneath me before she could say anything else, pinning her wrists to the mattress. "I like ideas."

She laughed—soft, bright, still half asleep—and it hit me the way it always did.

Nothing made me feel more alive than her.

"I was going to let you sleep in"—she brushed her nose against mine—"but I decided that was wildly overrated."

"I agree," I said, lowering my mouth toward hers.

A loud thump in the hallway had us both jerking our heads toward the door.

"Wakey wakey, eggs and bakey!" Junie called from the hallway. "Happy birthday, Dad!"

I closed my eyes and exhaled, dropping my head onto Daisy's shoulder. "Thank you, bug."

Two knocks. "I got out the stuff for pancakes," Junie announced. "And also, you need to come outside."

Daisy buried her face in my shoulder to hide her laughter. "We'll be out in a minute," she called.

Junie's footsteps raced down the hall and I loosened my grip on Daisy's wrists. "So much for my good morning present."

I rolled onto my back, pulling her with me. She rested her chin on my chest, studying me.

"Just so you know," she said, tracing the scar along my chest. "You are the hardest man in the world to shop for."

"That feels dramatic."

"It's not," she insisted. "Your hobbies include hockey. And farm."

I huffed a laugh. "Farm isn't a hobby."

"I'm sorry, do you not randomly show up with new animals or equipment?"

My mustache twitched, barely containing my smile. "I guess that's fair."

She propped herself up on her elbows. "I know nothing about hockey equipment that you don't already own or could just buy yourself. And every time I ask about farm stuff, you get suspicious."

"Because you and my sister have a weird habit of decorating things like chicken coops and pigpens that have no reason to be decorated."

She waved that off. "Irrelevant."

I narrowed my eyes. "Daisy."

"So," she rushed on, "I outsourced."

"You outsourced."

"I trusted an expert."

My stomach dropped in a way that had nothing to do with fear and everything to do with my daughter. "You let Junie plan my birthday?"

"She knows you better than anyone," Daisy said. "And she was very passionate about this."

I scrubbed a hand down my face. "That's concerning."

Daisy grinned. "You're going to love it."

I believed her, not because I had any confidence in whatever chaos was waiting outside, but because she was here. In my bed. In my house. And nobody knew me better than my girls.

What she didn't know—what neither of them knew yet—was that this birthday wasn't about gifts.

Today was the day I asked Daisy to be mine forever, to be a Winslow-Hudson too.

I'd also channeled a little of Daisy's energy and impulsively bought her something ridiculous.

It was time she had an animal of her own.

"What are you thinking about?" she whispered.

I brushed my thumb along her jaw and leaned down to kiss her. "That I already have everything I want."

Her expression shifted—tender, open, as if she was about to say something equally dangerous.

Then the knocking started again. Not subtle. Not patient.

"You're taking too long!" Junie yelled. "It's a surprise, and they're both being very good, but I don't know how long that's going to last!"

Daisy went still.

I blinked. "*Both*?"

Silence on the other side of the door.

"...I didn't say that."

Daisy slowly turned to look at me.

I slowly turned to look at her.

"You bought an animal," we said at the same time.

Her eyes widened. "Wait. *You* bought an animal?"

"What do you mean, *I* bought an animal? Of course, I bought an animal. Junie said you'd love it, and I couldn't say no. But *you* bought an animal?"

From the hallway: "Can we please move this along? They're licking things!"

Daisy slapped a hand over her mouth.

My whole chest shook with laughter.

"Have we been master manipulated?" she whispered.

"I think that's exactly what happened."

Junie groaned. "I cannot be the only responsible one in this family! Hurry! Up!"

I pushed off the bed, grabbed my jeans, and looked at Daisy —hair wild, cheeks flushed, grinning like the chaos of our lives was her natural habitat. And damn, I loved her.

"Okay, so what did you get me?" she asked suspiciously.

"A cow," I said. "A mini Highland cow."

Her mouth fell open, and a laugh ripped out. "You've got to be kidding me."

From outside our window came a faint but unmistakable little moo.

Followed by a second one.

Junie clapped in the hallway. "BEST. DAY. EVER."

I laughed under my breath.

Two cows, a daughter who knew about both of them and hadn't said a word, and a ring burning a hole in my future.

What more could I want for my birthday than this?

I reached for Daisy's hand and squeezed.

"Come on," I said. "I need you to meet Heifer Sutherland."

She laced her fingers through mine, eyes shining with laughter. "And Moozie Q."

And I decided that if the day was already this unhinged, it was the perfect day to ask her to stay forever.

THE END

Love Bites

Call of the Norns

A Viking Time Travel Fantasy Trilogy

Fates Illuminated

Fates Promised

Fates Defied

ACKNOWLEDGMENTS

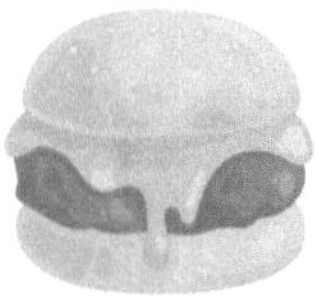

Excuse me while I exhale the biggest exhale to ever be exhaled.

Writing this book was a little like going through the stages of grief:

1. Denial. "It won't be that sad! Sure, it's a book about grief, but it's really about healing together, and the bond that forms when you come out the other side. I'll be fine." — my famous last words to my editor, Brit

2. Anger. "Why did I do this? I can't even blame anyone else for these poor decisions, because I MADE IT UP." — me, to me, and anyone who would listen

3. Bargaining. "Help me come up with anything other than making these characters miserable. PLEASE." — again, me, to random strangers on the street

4. Depression. "I guess this is it. It's a sad book. I just need to be sad." — me, over and over and over again while I wrote and rewrote (and rewrote more than I ever have before)

5. Acceptance. "Okay, I reread it, and maybe I was wrong. Maybe this book is really special." — me, two days before my deadline, where everyone just rolled their eyes at me

To anyone who has been through grief before, you understand. It's not a one and done cycle. I described it in this book as an invisible monster biting at your heels, and I can't get that imagery out of my head.

Loss doesn't go away. It doesn't even really lessen. It just becomes the new normal, no matter how much it sucks. And losing a sibling... It really, really sucked.

To the readers—thank you for picking up this book, for telling me repeatedly how excited you were for Ty and Daisy (and Junie). You are the reason these stories exist, and I'm endlessly grateful for every message and review. You make the mayhem worth it.

To my editor, Brit—I knew from the beginning that asking you to come on this journey with me would be harder than before, and yet you showed up for me the way you always do. I love you times infinity.

To Britt, my assistant and chaos wrangler—the fact that you churn out graphics and content and materials for me while subtly pointing out you haven't read the book yet—you're truly the best (and I'm sending it to you right now, oops).

To Sarah—I know I tell you this all the time, but what would I do without you? Thank you for coming to my rescue, alpha reading, then reading it again (and again). You're always honest with me, always patient when I'm slow to believe it's not all garbage, and always willing to hear me out on every random pivot I come across. You've earned the title of Hype Queen Supreme, and I adore you.

To B and Vanessa—thank you for every bit of encouragement, every giggle, every "Okay, when do I get the next part?" You make it easier to keep going, even when it feels hard.

To Chelsea—you know, I said last time this was my favorite cover, and then you one-upped yourself. This is my favorite cover.

To my brother, Eric—my very own Ty, for always having my back and encouraging my dreams. Buddies forever.

To my girls—I had so much fun borrowing your smart, inquisitive, and giggly energy for sweet Junie. But so we're clear, I'll never be okay with the fact that bananas are actually berries, even if it's true. It's just wrong.

And last but never least, to Chris, Mr. Aimee Vance Books, the Bookmark Guy—walking side by side with you through grief wasn't something I imagined when we said I do, but nothing has ever made me love you more.

We love you, Josh. Always and forever.

ABOUT AIMEE VANCE

Aimee Vance writes heartfelt and hilarious romance featuring sassy heroines, grumpy heroes, and small-town happily-ever-afters—preferably with a Diet Coke nearby. Her romcoms blend humor and heart with sharp banter, big feelings, and love stories designed to make readers laugh, swoon, and feel right at home.

A lifelong fantasy and romance reader, Aimee studied public relations at Texas Christian University. She lives in Texas with her husband, two young daughters, and a Labrador Retriever. When she's not writing, she's usually rereading her favorite romances or cheering from the sidelines of her kids' sporting events—occasionally at the same time.

facebook.com/aimeevancebooks

instagram.com/aimeevancebooks

goodreads.com/aimeevancebooks

amazon.com/author/aimeevancebooks

bookbub.com/authors/aimee-vance